The Tower

Anya's Story

Robert E. Christopher

To Kate and D

Towering Publications

Cover Artwork by Steve Skinley & Chris Harris

ISBN: 978-1-7398683-0-7

Dedication

To my children, who I hope live in a world that is magical and supportive. To Simon, who created the universe and to my wife who has to live with it, and for the joy of reading, which I hope this book supports.

Prologue

With a great effort he closed the hatch, plunging himself into welcome darkness.

He would die and worse, he knew, but there was still some small good he could achieve to atone for his foolish arrogance. The dark held no terrors, and he moved slowly but assuredly through the pitch black, knowing the way from many years of worship, his worsening limp the only hindrance to his progress. His shuffling footsteps echoed around him, strangely amplified by the tunnel, until their reverberations fell away into open space.

The man stopped. He fumbled in his pockets for flint and steel, striking it in the darkness. Using the meagre spark-light, he located the recess beside him and lit the waiting tinder. He reached for a torch and brought it close to the small fire. As it lit, he watched the flame spread. Entranced, for long moments the man stared at the fire, his expression peculiarly vacant. The moments stretched, and still he looked, unnaturally devoid of purpose, his existence reduced to the conflict between guttering light and flickering dark.

He jerked, eyes widened with fear, and he cursed the creeping frailties afflicting both his mind and body, seeking to thwart his final revenge on Mordenar. Breathing heavily, his chest tight beneath clothes slick with sweat, he shook his head to clear it, and saw the book lying where he had left it. He made to move towards it, but his feet laboured to obey his commands and he fell, tripping over an unseen obstacle on the floor.

It was a body.

Her throat was cut. A deep wound, deeper than was necessary. Religious fervour, he supposed. His lip curled in disdain. They had been like children, naive and stupid. His eyes moved down, uninterested, across her naked chest to her abdomen, which had been ripped open, spilling her entrails onto the dusty stone. He frowned. That had not been part of the ritual.

Irrelevant, he told himself, and tried to stand. His legs would not move. He tugged at them, willing them to serve once more, but they were cold and unfeeling. Desperately, he looked up at the alcove containing the book - his only hope - and dragged himself across the intervening space, scrabbling for purchase against the dusty stone with every grasp of his hands, pushing the torch before him. At last, he reached his target, and used all his remaining strength to haul his failing body up into the carved seat.

For a time, all he could do was catch his breath, wondering with each if it might be his last. The thought jolted him out of his reverie and he gathered up the quill and ink.

Shaking, he began to write.

Myths and Legends

"And in the darkness wrought by man, hidden by our ambition and our greed, the world we had neglected, the world we had violated made to form from the power of earth and rocks, the power of the fire that burns within, the power of the wind and sky, our gods!" The speaker paused, his arms held high, illuminated from beneath by the communal fire. He watched the gathered clan as they listened with rapt attention.

"Made manifest in the totems of our clans, they stalked the mighty warlocks and all who saw them were afraid. And though none spoke, all present heard them cry, 'Enough! Look at the use to which you bend this power, the anguish you wreak upon the land you loved, forgotten in the madness of your lust for dominion! From this day and henceforth, power shall be denied to you and your descendants. No brook or stream, no meadow, no mountain will give of itself to fuel your spells for you have shown yourselves unworthy of their gifts.'

"And the people looked around them and were ashamed and abased themselves and cried for mercy, but the warlocks stood proud and hard and laughed, 'Do you think we need your permission?' And they unleashed their magic, casting chains around our Gods, around our Elk and around our Bear, seeking to bind to themselves the very power of our divine guides. Though the people begged for them to cease their madness, they caused the chains to tighten, and it seemed that all was lost.

"Then 'Listen to me, my brothers, my sisters, my children, my kin,' came the cry from the Elk. 'Today we must sacrifice ourselves, our lives, but not our souls to deny from those who would oppress us, all our gifts. Let our sacrifice show for all time in the scorched ground on which we struggle, and let no man, from this day forward be granted our magic willingly. Our power dies to them this day, as do we!' And with a sound of thunder, of rolling earth, the ground shook, cried out, and was silent. The creatures, the trees, the rivers and the land, the very Gods that were ensnared had died, the land blackened and covered in ash, and with their death, so the power wielded by the warlocks died, never to be reborn. The clans left that desolated place, to roam p—"

"Why?" The question burst from Anya.

A fleeting scowl crossed Ujesh's face, but the story-teller rallied. "They had to move on, the land was devastated. Nothing grows there to this day, no animals roam, nor will they until—"

"No. Um, that is to say, I meant, why was it a sacrifice for the Gods to die? Because we still have the Gods, don't we? If we still have them, was it really a sacrifice at all?" Her voice trailed off as she heard the words issuing from her mouth.

"Anya!" Her mother's rebuke was not unexpected. "Always these questions, return to our yurt this minute, and stay there until you learn some respect."

Anya rose. Her cheeks flushed, visible even in the dancing half-light of the fire, and she appealed to her mother with a glance, but the look she returned brooked no argument. She fled. As she ran through the crowds, she forced herself to avoid the gaze of them, and so did not see the boy, Hiranjan, reach out and grab her ankle. As she sprawled, he laughed, and the boys around him joined in, mocking her.

"Why can't you just keep your tongue still?" Hiranjan scowled, as Anya scrambled back to her feet.

"My child," Ujesh called after her, "it is a good thing to be curious. But the mysteries of the divine may not be understood by mortal man or," he winked at the rest of the clan, "by mortal girl."

The laughter of the clan followed her as she retreated to her family's tent. She angrily threw aside the entrance flap and flounced inside. Anya cast herself down on her sleeping mat and fought to contain the sobs that threatened to humiliate her further. I will not cry, she thought. I am stronger than that. Why is it a bad thing to question the stories? If those boys had raised the question, would they have been dismissed so readily? So what if I am a girl, I'm as good as any boy. Let them laugh, I'll show them. Finally, the tears came. Anya cried herself to sleep.

She could not breathe. She could not move. She could not see. *A question lingered out of reach in the back of her mind.* She opened her mouth to call out, but it filled with earth. Panicking, she struggled, fear lending strength to her muscles. She jerked about, thrashing her limbs until at last she burst forth, breaking free of her grave.

Mist enclosed her, leaving her unable to see the object of her desire. *The question wanted something from her.* The ground sloped, and she began to walk up the incline, seeking to escape the fog, but the way ahead became no clearer. A sound startled her, a throaty growl, resonant with threat, and she spun, desperately seeking to locate the danger, but the cloud scattered the noise. Menace surrounded her. She must run, but to where?

She wanted to fly, but she could not. *Not demanding - an inquiry.* She stumbled and found a door, but she could not open it. Why was there a door? Why wouldn't it open? Aware of the creature stalking her, she whirled around, backing up to the door, to safety. *Permission?* Something tugged at her garments, seeking to drag her away, tearing her clothes as she resisted. Hot breath moistened her throat and a chittering behind her sent icy chills down her spine. At last she cried out for help, a hopeless, forlorn shriek. She braced herself for the feel of teeth ripping at her flesh.

A shadow coalesced in the haze around her. *What was her answer?* Multiple slanted red eyes began to emerge from the fog. She screamed once more, seeking a saviour. *Puzzlement.* The shadow appeared to glance around. *Understanding. "Wake up, Anya."*

Anya gasped as she sat bolt upright on her bed-mat, cold sweat poured down her chest and back and she quickly found her feet. She stumbled in the dark, narrowly avoiding stepping on her family as they slept. Her upturned nose wrinkled at the musky stink of her father's hookah pipe on his breath as he slept, and she frowned, imagining her mother's disapproval. At last she located the tent-flap, and staggered out, drawing in great lungfuls of the fresh night air.

Her heart still hammered behind her ribs so loud she was faintly surprised it had not woken the whole clan. She breathed deeply. Wide awake, Anya began to walk, not with any destination in mind, for the pleasure of movement alone, letting it calm her body, as it always did. She moved purposefully, her feet taking her where they would.

Much like the communal fire, the activity of the clan had dwindled. Nearing the edge of the camp, Anya spotted some animal-tenders beyond, watching the wild herd of elk and the semi-domesticated goats and knew that, out of sight, scouts surrounded the camp, looking out for any threats. Looking out for Rahksharu. Protecting them all from the monsters.

She studied the outline of one of the animal-tenders in the light of the stars, recognising Amman. Knowing his attention was elsewhere, Anya stilled her footfalls and stalked his position atop a small rise in the grassland of the valley. Fighting hard to contain her laughter, she placed one gentle footstep ahead of another until she lurked scant feet from where he sat. She crouched, imagining herself a mountain leopard, ready to devour her prey, and leaped at Amman. He shouted in a frenzy of incoherent alarm as she grabbed him across the shoulders, wrestling him prone, until he heard her mirth burst forth. Anya laughed as tears rolled down her cheeks, not letting go, containing his efforts to escape her grasp.

"Well done Anya," Amman said. "You got me."

Anya loosened her grip and sat back, still unable to stifle her amusement. Amman looked at her through the corner of his eye, his reddened face lowered slightly. "You really frightened me," he said.

"Oh, come on," Anya said. "You've got your back to the camp. What could possibly creep up on you from behind when you're sitting here, watching your precious animals?"

"Well, I don't know," replied Amman. "Some crazy wild girl or something."

They lapsed into silence, Anya wanted to talk, but was unsure of what to say. At last she sighed, reclining to gaze up at the stars. Amman remained sitting, his arms holding his knees close to his chest, but he watched Anya, waiting for her to speak.

"I'd be a terrible animal handler," Anya said. "I wouldn't spend any of my time watching the herd. Instead, I would just look up at the stars all night." Anya hesitated, and said, "What do you think their purpose is?"

"Ujesh says they are the fireflies of the Gods, provided to us to help us find our way in the dark."

"Then, aside from Derus and the other Wanderers[1], why do they all move together as one, and not swarm all over each other, like they do here on Sansara?"

---

[1] The 'Wanderers' is the name given to Sansara's fellow planets by the Tharom tribe, so called because unlike the stars, which are apparently part

Amman did not answer for a time. "Anya, you know as well as I do what Ujesh teaches. You're the smartest person I know. I bet you could have told the story of the Gods' sacrifice word for word, just as Ghandarva Ujesh did earlier."

Anya scowled, reminded of her humiliation in front of the assembled clan.

"What I mean is, you're not really asking me what I think. Why shouldn't our tribal stories be true?"

"I think if they were fireflies, they would move in glorious patterns all the time. Wouldn't that be wonderful?" Anya thought for a moment, and said, "I think they must be fixed to the globe of the heavens, but the sun and moons move differently, so what are they fixed to? I know Ujesh says they are travelling souls providing us with warmth and light but they don't look like much else than... than a ball!"

Anya was excited now. She sat up and her words came faster. "Maybe they are balls? Rolling around the globe, and, and ..." She stopped, thinking furiously. "That's why the moons aren't always round! Think about it, if you picked up a gaganwa fruit in the light of the fire at night, and walked around it, the light from the flames would shine only on the half of the fruit that's closest to the sun."

"Fire," said Amman.

"Yes, but I'm using the fire as a kind of substitute for the sun." Anya's eyes were aglow. "The sun shines its light on the moons in just the same way as the fire lights the gaganwa[2] fruit."

---

of a vast sphere of the heavens, they move unpredictably across the night sky. Of these, red Derus is the closest and brightest. "Mysteries of the Sansaran Sky".

[2] The fruit of the gaganwa tree is remarkably spherical in appearance, with a thick, smooth outer skin the colour of red sky at night, and noticeably spicy, juicy flesh. Many clans shred and soak the skin of the

"Hmm," responded Amman. "I don't know about that. How far away do you think the globe of the heavens is? Wouldn't that mean these balls of yours would have to be huge? Wouldn't they crush the fireflies as they rolled?"

Anya looked at Amman as though only just reminded of his presence.

He said, "Your ideas always seem to generate more questions than answers, Anya. I think I'll stick with the tribal stories that we learn from Ujesh."

He raised his eyes to meet hers as a gentle breeze ruffled her raven black hair. He opened his mouth, before closing it again and dropping his gaze. "How do you do it?" he said. "Interrupt Ghandarva Ujesh, I mean?"

"Just because he's our clan storyteller, it doesn't make him so different."

"It makes him an elder." Amman sighed. "I could never do it, I'd be too scared."

"What's so bad about it?" She frowned. "Besides getting told off by your mother." Anya kicked at some earth. "You'd interrupt me."

"Yes, but you're my friend. You can't tell me what to do."

"I bet I could."

There was silence for a time. The night insects produced their background sounds, a soft accompaniment to the scene as Anya stared into the middle-distance, not taking anything in of the peaks of the Yanuba mountain range around her. Amman's eyes were focussed on Anya.

---

gaganwa fruit, adding it to broth or stews as a flavour enhancer and thickener, but more often, the skins of the larger fruits are cured and stuffed with animal hair for use in ball games by the men and children of tribe. They are found exclusively in the Yanuba mountains, where they line the routes of the nomads who live there. "Flora and Fauna of Sansara, volume 1".

Amman sighed and lay back, transferring his gaze to the heavens. “I love the night sky. The way it’s framed by the mountains.” He smiled, and pointed up at a constellation. “Sometimes, when I’m watching the herd, I will see The Scout’s head appear over the Yanubas, as though he too is checking on the animals. Or on us. Then, gradually the rest of him appears and it’s like he’s clambering over the high passes, about to walk down the other side to join us.”

“My mother talked again about my marriage.” Anya cut across Amman’s musing. “She says I have no choice, that if I reject any more suitors, I’ll end up like Aunt Matreyi and bring further shame to our family.”

Amman again looked at Anya, a concerned expression on his thin face. He looked away and lifted his bony arms up, linking his hands to rest his head upon.

“Why should we be ashamed of Aunt Matreyi anyway, just because she chose not to wed? Perhaps she didn’t think she could love the men her family selected for her. Maybe she didn’t want to give up her independence and be subject to the decisions of a man?”

“Anya, I like your Aunt well enough, you know that,” Amman said. “But she is a bit odd, and besides, what is this independence you think she has? She is still subject to the decisions of a man, only instead of a husband, it’s your father, or the elders. She’s isn’t some girl who can run around doing as she pleases.”

Anya looked at him fiercely. “You’re as bad as all the others,” she exclaimed. “You don’t see that women could make their own decisions, be hunters... elders even.” Anya rose with her temper and looked down at Amman. “We can be just as good as men, just as good as you.” Her anger flared in her eyes. “I’m better than you,” she said. Anya turned on her heel and marched away, not looking back to see the mortified expression on Amman’s face.

Amman watched her leave. “I know,” he said, softly.

Survival

Anya sat on the woven rug, scowling at her bleeding thumb. All around her, the womenfolk of her clan chatted contentedly while repairing torn clothes and fabrics. She sucked the blood, finding some satisfaction in its familiar tang, and let the gossip wash over her.

"But he thinks so much of himself," one girl near her said.

"You say that like it's a bad thing," countered another. "Who wants a man who isn't proud, who doesn't take control?"

They giggled, whether at the vague innuendo or something else, Anya was not sure.

"Hiranjan will be a fine defender of the tribe, he's so fast and strong," said the second girl.

"And handsome too, though I'm sure you've not noticed that." They laughed again, and many other girls joined in, some blushed or exchanged knowing smiles with their friends. Already irritated, Anya attacked the two girls. "But he's so stupid! It took him a whole year to learn how to recognise the nine poisonous berries of our mountains. If it wasn't for Ghandarva [3] Ujesh, or me, he'd probably be carrion for the vultures by now."

---

[3] Each Tharom clan has a Ghandarva who keeps the lore of the tribe. They are traditional storytellers who teach the people about their history and culture, often via whole clan gatherings. In older times, most Ghandarva would be found roaming from clan to clan, often telling their

"Why is that important for a man, when his wife will prepare his meals for him?" the second girl replied. "He can concentrate on protecting the clan."

"Protecting the clan?" Anya gave her an incredulous look. "He'd likely spend too much time attending to the feathers on his hood, and forget to do his duty. Have you seen him pass by the Reflector, that artefact from before The Fall? It's like he's bewitched by his own reflection."

"What is it to you anyway?" The girl rounded on her. "Why can't you just admit he'd make a good husband?"

"Maybe that's it," said the first girl. "She does think he'd be a good husband… for her!"

Her friend shrieked. "Of course. That's why she keeps rejecting her suitors. That's why she always criticises him, she's just hiding her true feelings. She wants Hiranjan for herself."

"He could be the last man on Sansara and I'd spit on him before taking him for my husband," Anya said, fuming.

"You're so weird. If you turn down any more matches, suitors will stop coming and then where will you be? Alone with your Aunt Matreyi. You can't be so blind, that you would turn down Hiranjan—"

"When Anya marries, it will be to a man, not a boy like Hiranjan." Anya's Mother, Neeta, interrupted them. "Besides, like you, Elenara," Neeta nodded her head to the second girl, "Anya is not a first daughter and will therefore marry outside of our clan."

Anya returned her attention to the torn tent fabric in her lap and tried to force her needle to work the way she had been shown so often. Repairing the clan's yurts was important, she knew, but she did not feel its importance. Her

---

stories in song, accompanying themselves with a stringed instrument, called a Sarangi. "Customs of the Tharom Tribe, Third Edition".

needle stabbed repeatedly, drawing the coarse thread of goat-wool through and closing the tear.

"No dear, not like that." Neeta's tone was reflexive, born of repetition. "Our yurts need to protect us from wind and rain, and not let the air in, as your mending will."

Neeta continued to explain how to fold the rent sides of the material to seal the occupants from the elements. Anya, well used to such lectures, her interest lost before her mother even began, gazed out of the raised tent flap at the stunning vista of their current encampment.

They had moved for the last three days, following the herd as always, their yurts loaded on beasts of burden. Stoves and other heavy objects were tied up on the sole clan cart while young children found themselves strapped to their mothers, sisters, aunts or grandmothers. The sure-footedness of the elk often made it difficult for Anya's people to keep up with them. They could walk in single file on tiny ridges or slight grooves in the sides of steep climbs bordered by cliffs. Even now, more than a day after the first tent had been pitched, the wagon had not yet caught up with them.

The herd had come to settle in a sweeping valley, girded on two sides by forested mountains, their peaks emerging starkly from the tree line, rocky and proud. The valley floor was carpeted with lush grass, fed by gurgling mountain streams, and the elk were grazing contentedly. The chosen location for the camp was a raised area where three valleys joined, near a pond formed by a brook. The position afforded Anya and the others a view of mile after mile of spectacular scenery.

Anya's needlework slowed, her mind lost in a feeling of satisfaction that this should be their home. The fabled palaces she'd learned of from the times before The Fall could not have matched the valley for splendour. Spread out below, the herd speckled the green, watched over, it appeared, by eagles circling, finding updrafts to maintain their vantage point over possible prey beneath. Above them still, the azure sky was punctuated by occasional clouds, their shadows flitting across the landscape. All the world in perfect peace.

Lost in her contentment, Anya did not immediately register the horn. Its harsh braying was distant, at first, like the background buzz of a mosquito, and it was only the start of the commotion around her that brought it to the fore of her thoughts.

Rahksharu.

The monsters were lethal, and killed indiscriminately. They were rumoured to be long, with three pairs of powerful legs that could propel them to furious speeds and shred anything in their way with vicious claws. It was said that they had both scales and coarse fur and that they had a mane of hair encircling a face covered in eyes and mouths, a madman's vision of despair and insanity. All was hearsay, for to view one was death.

The women's yurt was now in full uproar, fear ratcheting up their voices. Girls were running around, wanting the safety of escape or the comfort of their mothers. Anya could hear her mother calling out instructions in a clear calm voice, to be still, to close the tent, to not be afraid. Anya moved, as if to untie the cord holding the tent flap open, but instead, her eyes scanned the valley, trying to locate the direction of the warning, the source of the danger. Seeing that another girl was attending to the twine, Anya slipped out of the tent. It closed behind her.

Anya darted to the corner of another tent, not caring which, and peered from behind its meagre shelter, watching the scene below. She could see the herd scattering, whether in response to the harsh note of the clan's alarm or their own sense of danger, she could not tell. The herdsmen were also running, but directly to the camp. She hoped that Amman was not among them, not in danger, and already in the relative safety of the clan. An animal scream rent the air. Anya looked to find the source, seeing a fallen elk, ripped apart and spattered with blood and gore, so brutally butchered that it seemed scarcely possible to have occurred only moments before. Where was the monster? Anya knew from watching the boys play kalkakka [4]with their hard, black sticks, that the sound of their clash only reluctantly followed the sight. She could not find the danger by listening, she had to observe it.

A blur of motion caught Anya's eye. She could see an indistinct shape moving fast towards another elk. Something in her mind reeled at the wrongness of her senses, like an itch with no source to scratch. The animal, an older female, had been left by its kin, too slow to keep up, too old to live. Death closed upon it, and where moments before had been a noble, living creature, now an explosion of slaughter filled the air, and still Anya could not see the attacker.

What was it that Ujesh taught them? The words bubbled up inside her. "Beware the Rahksharu, for they may not be seen. They are servants of dark forces, the hounds of evil sent by Death's brother himself to wreak havoc upon the living. They are cloaked in lies, visions of hopelessness, and should you truly see one and be seen, the secrets of their form will be bought by your silence, a price paid eternally." What did that mean, how could it be possible to not see the thing causing such mayhem below? Could these monsters elude understanding?

Another straggler was dispatched, and Anya shrieked inwardly. The herd was the clan's way of life, where were the Defenders? As if in response, she saw them. Proudly walking towards death, the line of Defenders spread out, the

---

[4] Kalkakka is a game played by boys within the Tharom tribe. All the boys form a ring, except for one, who is surrounded by the others. Those in the ring carry two hardened sticks from the Locanth tree, which is known for its black wood and resonant qualities. The boy at the centre of the circle holds a single stick, and uses it to attempt to strike the body of any of the other boys, who may block this attempt with either of their sticks. The block succeeds only if all others within the circle crash their sticks together in unison, otherwise the blocker is 'out'. They are also out if the boy at the centre manages to strike them - possibly for a while due to the bruising that often results. "Games of the Tharom tribe".

wetly sparkling tips of their long spears announcing their arrival to the heavens. Clad in padded vests and leggings, covered by thick tunics, made with coloured wool in tribal patterns, the most striking aspect of their garb were the hoods that completely obscured their vision. Fastened with buttons to the tunic, these were decorated in individualistic fashion with fierce painted eyes, sharp teeth and many feathers. Often passed down through many generations, further decoration was added each time they were used in anger.

Not anger, Anya decided. In need.

Behind the first line of men, there followed another, fewer in number, but carrying barbed harpoons instead of spears, all with a large object strapped to their hips, and behind them all was the Guide, walking backwards, holding aloft in his arms the Reflector, using it to view the battleground behind him, ahead of the Defenders, shouting instructions to each, telling them where to spread and where to draw in. The Defenders in turn called out the names of ancient heroes, each having meaning in their deadly dance, allowing each to gauge the distances between them.

A shout was heard, a new command, and the front row of Defenders began to swing their spears above their heads, slowly at first, but rapidly gaining speed. They swung in time with each other, avoiding clashes, and as they advanced, they tipped the inclination of their swing so that their arc pointed towards the ground ahead, a whirring wall of razor sharp, poisoned weaponry.

On and on they marched, directed by the Guide, choreographed with a desperate precision, until they reached almost halfway to the scene of massacre. Dangerously close, they halted, and the edges of their front line retreated until no longer a line, instead, they now formed a whirling circle around the leader, a second circle of Defenders spread between. The Rahksharu had now killed another two elk, and its bloodlust showed no sign of abating.

Anya feared they had acted too late, were too distant to affect the monster.

Anya saw the blur of the creature surge towards a fifth victim, and was certain it was doomed, when the Defenders ceased their commands and took up song instead. The circle of harpooners revealed the drums at their sides and began a beat. Two strikes, a pause, two strikes again, over and over, a beating heart underscoring their song of life. The Rahksharu stopped immediately, holding its distance from the isolated circle of men, before slowly, perhaps cautiously stalking towards them. Now certain they had gained its attention, a single drummer was chosen, who continued to beat the rhythm of blood while his fellow drummers cast theirs off, the better to wield their harpoons.

Closer to the men, the Rahksharu crept, watched by the Guide using the Reflector, who called out, silencing the singing, allowing the directions to resume. As if on cue, the monster sprang into deadly speed, striking out for the heart of men arrayed before it, ravenously eating the ground between them with its strides until, nearing the spears of the first rank, it sprang. In the same moment came a call from the Guide, and the whole group surged forward, the rear of the formation split, and the enemy landed on empty ground, unleashing a sibilant noise of fury, while behind it the circle reformed, the defenders wrapping around and the front row raising their spinning spears to allow the inner ranks access once again to the centre.

Suddenly cautious, the hazy form before them moved left and right before attempting to dart through the wall of Defenders and suffered a glancing strike. At once, a call rang out and a harpoon was cast, narrowly missing its target. The circle backed off, leaving their adversary to lick its wounds, whether literally or metaphorically, it was impossible to tell. Relentlessly, still, it advanced, moving left and right, and springing forward to be met once more by the strike of a spear. Again, a call went up, triggering another harpoon to be thrown, but it too missed the mark.

Now fully warned of the danger posed by the Defenders, the Rahksharu circled the perimeter. It began to growl, and emitted a wet, tearing sound, a vile imitation of ripping flesh. It had circumnavigated the men twice and was nearing the point where it was on the far side of the ring of spears from Anya's position when she saw it. Perhaps fatigued by the constant spinning of his weapon, a Defender brushed the turf with its gleaming point, disrupting his rhythm and slowing his swing. Swift as an avalanche, the abomination was upon him and the man disappeared in a sickening rain of red, which spattered his comrades as they attempted to fill the gap.

His death an unwanted signal, another harpoon was cast, this time finding its mark. The distorted air that was the Rahksharu backed off rapidly, and for a moment Anya thought she saw some of its form, thrashing in anger at the insult of its injury. Despite herself, Anya strained to penetrate through the cloud of deception, to what her mind refused to grasp. She strained with all her might at the blurred form, willing clarity from chaos. As she watched, the creature stopped abruptly, the fine cord attached to the harpoon doing its job, halting its retreat.

In a sudden movement, the Defender holding the line flew outwards from the circle, falling awkwardly. With shock, she saw his hood had been dislodged. He looked around for it, clawing at the ground. She found her own nails were biting into the skin of her palms as she watched. The distant figure scrambled to his feet and froze. Why had he stopped? He was facing back toward the ring of his comrades but was still, scant steps from safety. Anya's skin crawled. His clothes had lost all colour, leaving nothing but grey.

He had been turned to stone.

Anya cried out. Tears of anger and frustrations were flooding her cheeks. With startling swiftness, four harpoons were thrown simultaneously, three of them striking the enemy. They braced themselves and this time held their thrashing adversary. It was caught, and all the illusion in the world would not save it now. Another signal, and the remaining harpooners moved in to finish the job

Illusion, Anya thought, grasping at the idea. She saw what it wanted her to see, not reality, not what she wanted to see - the truth. "I don't believe you," she said under her breath and, inhaling deeply, cleared her mind and looked directly at the Rahksharu. Finally she saw, and in seeing, felt its gaze in return, and their eyes locked.

She was jolted, and saw below her, Anya, rigid, unable to withdraw from her contact with that thing, blue lines extending from her eyes across her face, spreading towards her heart. It was cold, and she half expected to see her breath form clouds before her, but there was no breath, no life. The world around her vanished, narrowing to a tunnel of vision, and at the end, an inhuman eye. In its pupil, a snake writhed and twisted, eating its own tail. She was rushing towards it, or it was growing larger, she could not tell, until all that could be seen was eye. She disappeared into it and was gone.

Dreams and Visions

They sat together, sharing their food.

It tasted wonderful, but unfamiliar. She glanced down at her hands and saw that they held the remaining stalks of the flower heads she was eating. Though unusual to her, she continued to chew, as they were delicious. Looking around her family yurt, she saw that they had been joined on their seating cushions by Hiranjan, who was staring at her and rubbing his crotch. He appeared larger, somehow, than the others - even her father - and he had too many teeth.

Frightened, she turned, and found herself standing near her sister-in-law, by the cooking stove. She tried to speak to her, but was ignored. Neeta was overseeing the cooking with a critical eye, admonishing Shanoli for having added too much spice.

"Even my daughter Anya wouldn't have used that much," she said. "She needs to save some for her wedding."

"Mother." Anya took a step towards Neeta. "I'm not getting married to an old man I've never met."

"She's getting married later today. Her husband will want some spice with his new wife."

"Mother!" she shouted. "How can I marry, I haven't yet learned how to fly?"

"He will expect obedience, he is a man of influence in clan Fox," continued Neeta. "She is so lucky we arranged this betrothal."

"You aren't listening to me, you never listen." She was frustrated, angry. "I'm not ready. I want more. I have to have more."

Neeta turned to look directly at Anya, her eyes piercing, questioning. "Do you understand?"

"No," she replied.

"I have a gift for you," said Neeta. "Will you accept?"

"I don't know what it is."

"It is what you need it to be."

"What? Why me?"

"You want to know." It was a statement, not a question.

She was no longer in the yurt, but somewhere high. Before her spread the mountains, the world. She could see to the furthest reaches of Sansara, see anything, see everything. She looked out to the lands beyond her home within the Yanuba mountains, thinking she saw something familiar there. She should be able to see, if only she should want it.

"Yes," came Neeta's voice from behind her. Then the question, "Will you accept?"

She moved to face Neeta, but a dizziness overwhelmed her.

"Will you accept?"

She fell.

"Will you accept?"

"Yes," said Anya.

Strong arms caught her. Anya blinked away the vertigo and cleared her eyes. She found they were now in the mountain valley, but no camp could be seen, no sound heard above the gentle caress of a cool wind blowing the long grass, which thrived in this muted world.

Anya stood, turned, and saw Neeta, many yards away, standing on a large circle of dead ground. Nothing grew, nothing lived. Not grass, not insect. No sign of life ever having been here, except the cracked and bleached outline of a tree, rising behind Neeta like a warning, its dead fingers pointing to the sky.

Neeta approached Anya, appearing to glide over the ground between them, as if walking was an option she simply forgot, or chose not to take. As she neared, Anya looked more closely at her mother, and saw someone else, as though another wore her mother like a costume. There was something in her hand, and the figure raised her arm, holding it out to her.

"What is it?" asked Anya, not recognising what was offered.

"It is what you agreed to have. It is yours."

"Where will you put it?" Anya asked.

She advanced, her arm held out still towards Anya. "In your soul."

Anya felt warmth spread throughout her body, as though a ripple had begun in her head, rebounding from her toes. When again it reached her head, she woke.

Anya opened her eyes, feeling as though she should leap around, but finding her body reluctant to respond. Her feelings of warmth receded, like the dimming coals of a fire. She could feel it still in her core, but it was not able to disguise the pain and weariness that crept in from her legs and arms. It crowded her eyes, causing her to blink away the pain in her head.

She was laid on her bed mat in the family yurt in echo of her dreams. Sunlight pierced the comforting warmth of the tent through a gap not covered by the entrance flap, illuminating motes of dust that danced in and out of existence through the shaft of light.

The movement perplexed her. The air was warm, but still. What was it that caused the dust to move, not up and down, as would a thrown ball, but changing direction randomly, as a mosquito did? Could the dust be somehow alive, proceeding of its own volition, or was there something within the motionless air that moved, buffeting the dust as it collided?

The tent was silent. Her mother sat close. Her head was bowed, and her eyes closed. Not asleep, but as though shutting her eyes helped her concentrate on lifting a great burden. She appeared small, her shoulders slumped. She opened her eyes, looking down at her hands, clasped tight in her lap and muttered inaudibly. Neeta turned her head to Anya, and their eyes met. For a moment, Anya felt a connection so profound, it stole the breath from her body.

"Anya," Neeta whispered. Her gaze lingered, and she reached out her hand, but hesitated, as though afraid to touch her. Her hand hovered near the side of Anya's face, almost touching. Several times she seemed on the point of making contact, but she withdrew slightly as though twin desires warred within, until at last, seeing a tear welling in Anya's eye, Neeta wiped it away, and gently caressed her cheek.

Neeta's eyes dropped, and she took a deeper breath. Looking up, once again, she fixed Anya with a glare. "What were you thinking, leaving the tent? I would never have imagined you would be so reckless, you could have been killed!"

Anya reeled. She was in mental freefall, temporarily unable to grasp the abrupt change of subject. All that registered was hurt, and she screwed up her eyes against a new wave of tears she could feel coming. "But…" was all she could manage in reply.

"There's no excuse for that sort of behaviour. You aren't a little girl any more. You know what we need to do when they come, you've done it many times before. I only looked away for a moment to deal with the others. I should be able to trust you."

Neeta's stream of words ran momentarily dry, allowing Anya's anger to fill the gap. "I wanted to see the Defenders. I wanted to see how they can fight those things. They have to wear hoods over their faces, but they still go up against the Rahksharu. If they can be that brave, I thought I could be brave enough to watch from a distance." With spite, Anya added, "If you only looked away for a moment, how come you didn't find me until after… after… it looked at me?"

"Anya!" Neeta exclaimed. "I had to look after the others, most were so much younger than you. I thought you would be responsible."

"How can I take responsibility if I don't know what the danger is?"

"Don't be ridiculous," Neeta said, rising from the floor of the tent. "Let us hope that this news does not spread beyond our clan, or we will never find another suitor for you."

"What? Suitors, again? Is that all you ever think about?" Anya began to cough and attempted to sit up, but the pain in her head almost made her swoon. She lay back on the bed mat, her eyes suddenly heavy.

Neeta looked back and regarded Anya, frowning slightly. "That boy, Amman, has been constantly asking after you. I've had to shoo him away several times as he was becoming a pain." She paused, and said, "He's waiting outside now."

She waited for a moment, perhaps expecting a response, but when none came, turned sharply and left the yurt. Anya heard conversation, before the tent flap opened and someone entered. She tried to raise her head to see who had come, but her skull had turned to rock. Her neck hurt just attempting to move it.

"Your mother told me I shouldn't stay long, as you need to rest," Amman said. He sat beside her.

"I can't argue with her there," Anya said, aware of the irony.

"You look terrible."

"Thanks," she smiled. "But at least *my* looks will improve."

Amman looked down at his hands. "You had us all worried there for a while. I'm glad you're alright."

Silence. "Amman, what happened? I've never heard of anyone being affected from such a distance."

"That's because nobody else is stupid enough to look at them without the Reflector." Amman said forcefully. He dropped his head and sighed. "The distance is probably the only reason you're still alive. You've been asleep for two days. At first, they weren't sure you would make it."

Anya felt suddenly cold, as though she had been placed naked for sky burial, on the very top peaks of the Yanuba mountains. Not knowing how to respond to this new revelation of her brush with death, she said, "I saw one of the Defenders get… he was killed. One moment he was there, the next… oh, it was so awful. They managed to harpoon it, is everyone else alright?"

"No, another was turned to stone."

"That's awful."

"They say no-one else even got a scratch. It's really strange. There have been Defences before with no deaths, of course, but there aren't any stories told where it has been so easy to finish one off. They normally fight like the demons they are until the end. I've heard whispers, some say it surrendered, if you can believe it." Amman looked seriously at Anya. "Others talk of magic."

"Oh, come on. Some people can't stub their toe without crying 'magic' and calling for the Protector[5], as though the warlocks have returned to destroy us, one minor injury at a time." Anya smirked, and glanced at Amman, hoping to see him smile at her joke. His eyes were wandering the tent and he did not react. She began to feel uneasy. "Besides, magic is evil, so why would it target a Rahksharu?"

Amman brightened somewhat. "I guess you're right," he said. He glanced at her, concern - or something else - showing on his face. "You know, your mother has barely left this tent since they found you. I've never seen her looking so worried."

Anya turned her head away from Amman. Pushing aside uncomfortable feelings, she said, "Worried that she wouldn't be able to marry me off if I died, you mean."

Seeing Amman about to respond, and not wanting to hear what he said, Anya continued. "I still don't understand," she hesitated. "I looked at it, and I was fine. It was just a sort of blur, like as if I had too much sleep in my eyes, right where it should have been. I looked really hard. And..." Anya grabbed Amman's arm with all her meagre strength, conveying the urgency she felt at a sudden recollection. "Amman. I saw it."

Amman wrenched his arm free and stood, backing away. "No!" he nearly shouted. "It's not possible. No one can see it, even when they're dead they can still turn you to stone. That's why they always wrap them in canvas before burning them."

"I saw it." Tears glistened in her eyes. In a small voice, Anya said, "And it saw me."

---

[5] One curious exception to the segregation of the clans is the role of Protector. According to tradition dating from after the Gods' sacrifice, the Protector is charged with the investigation and eradication of magic. Operating outside of clan structure, in apparent accord with the wishes of the Gods, the tribe has granted him authority over all clans to conduct his investigations as he sees fit. "The Clans of the Tharom"

"No." Amman said, gently this time. He knelt beside her, looking into her eyes as though to counteract her connection with the monster, seeking the truth. Seeing only total conviction, he said, "What… what did it look like?"

Anya began to speak, but stopped. She looked confused, frightened. Tears began to flow down her face and she looked frantically at Amman. "I don't know. I can't remember."

Words and Meaning

Much to her disgust, Anya was still in bed. She had been lying in her sleeping area for what felt like years. Her only respite had been calls of nature, and for these her mother had made her use a pot, instead of a sheltered area away from the tents. A pot! Having to do such a thing in her home revolted her, the indignity of it made her feel unclean. Neeta had even brought earth and rounded stones inside, so she could clean herself afterwards.

Her mother had been a near constant presence in the yurt as Anya lay convalescing. Even her father had spent an unusual amount of time away from the rest of the elders, leaving them to smoke and discuss the weighty matters of the day without him. He was never close, but neither was he too distant. Neeta had taken on all the cooking duties, and brought cloth home for mending in order to watch over her daughter. When not otherwise engaged, she cleaned the interior several times. Always close, but never too close.

She and Neeta had spoken, but of inconsequential things, the weather, how she was feeling. The subject of marriage had not been broached again.

"Anya, dear," Neeta began. "There are some girls I need to supervise, so I will be gone for a time." She looked uncomfortable. "I don't want to leave, but Aunt Matreyi will come and keep an eye on you."

She was standing just outside the sleeping area, looking in on Anya. The beaded curtain had been tied back, but still Anya felt the separation between them as though an invisible curtain still hung free. Neeta stood, lingering. "I will be back later." She turned and left.

Anya lay alone in the gloom. It was day, but the anaemic light that crept in through the partially open entrance told her the day was overcast at best. The wind buffeted the sides of the tent dutifully, but not energetically, as though its heart was not in it. Anya imagined a work rota for weather, given out to all the elements, and a disgruntled Wind huffing grumpily, wishing he were elsewhere.

After a time, she lost interest in her musings, and propped herself up using her elbows. This, she found, could be managed more easily than before, though the effort briefly caused a blinding pain in her head that passed, almost as soon as it had come. However, the weariness remained. She felt heavy as stone. Absently, she wondered if the Rahksharu's magic had succeeded, at least in part, only turning her innards into rocks.

Anya contemplated resting once again, though she doubted sleep would come to her – its welcome had been eroded by over-familiarity. As she was on the point of reclining again, a shape obscured the entrance, coalescing into the form of her aunt as she moved softly into the tent, a package held under her arm. She tucked some loose grey hair behind her ear, looked at Anya and smiled.

"Aunt Matreyi," Anya said with delight.

"Dear one," Matreyi replied. Her smile broadened further, revealing gaps in her teeth. "What *have* you been up to?"

Anya basked in the warmth of her aunt's smile. It brought with it feelings of security, solidarity and unconditional love. She noted the accentuated lines that radiated from Matreyi's eyes, the wrinkles that formed about her mouth, and wondered how it was that sometimes, a smile could render such flaws beautiful. The biting winds and the closeness of the sun took their toll on all the Yanuba clans, a fact of life seen on every brown weathered adult face in her tribe. Even so, Anya knew that her aunt had aged prematurely, a legacy of a difficult life, appearing much more than merely a few years older than Neeta. At that moment, however, Anya could not think of anything so lovely.

"I heard you tried to out-stare a demon," she chuckled, and lowered herself to Anya's side. "Next, you'll be wrestling a bear, or kissing a snake, no doubt." She took Anya into an embrace, holding her tight, and stroking her hair.

After a while, Matreyi released her, and held her at arm's length, her smile had lost some of its lustre. She said, "I've been so worried. How are you feeling?"

"Bored." It was first in a race of thoughts that strove to find expression. Anya sighed. "I've not been allowed out of bed since..." She pursed her lips and fixed her aunt with a determined look. "Would you help me up?"

Matreyi looked at her closely, nodded and leant forward to allow Anya to put her arms around her neck, supporting her weight as they both rose to their feet. She smiled encouragingly, waiting until Anya caught her breath, studying her closely for signs of undue strain.

Satisfied that Anya could cope, she said, "Let's go outside. We'll wrap you up against the wind and find a sheltered spot where the sun..." Matreyi huffed and waved an arm in exasperation. "Where the clouds can warm you. Then you can unwrap the gift I have brought you." She indicated the parcel lying next to Anya's bed mat and stooped to pick it up.

Enfolding her niece with woollen blankets she guided her carefully to the rear of the tent, and worked loose the ties binding the exit flap there more tightly than the front. Unseen, they slipped unobtrusively from the stuffy confines of the family yurt.

Anya squinted against the unexpectedly bright glare of the overcast sky and breathed deeply. She could feel the cool mountain air enter her lungs, lifting her spirits and some of the fatigue that still plagued her. She glanced around, finding no-one else in sight. They were largely sheltered from view by her family tent, but also by Matreyi's smaller yurt, which, though no longer adjoining, was pitched immediately adjacent to their own, illustrating her status as being under the authority of Sabir, Anya's father.

Matreyi gently supported Anya as they slowly walked, and as they continued, the effort required lessened the further her steps took her, until, not quite realising how she had got there, they arrived to the north of camp at a secluded recess in the rocks, which continued rising to become another low peak in the great Yanuba mountain range. With surprise, Anya found she was sweating. She reflected that, perhaps, the effort had been greater than she thought, her focus had simply narrowed until her entire existence comprised of single steps, and the exertion had melted away from her consciousness.

Sheltered from the wind, they stood while Anya's breathing subsided, Matreyi's arms encircling Anya protectively as they faced the valley, the camp hidden below by outcroppings and distance.

"For sights such as this, it's worth it." Matreyi whispered, perhaps only to herself, though Anya could not help but hear.

"Aunt Matreyi," Anya began. "How come we can look around us and be amazed, and thankful, and full of joy at this wonderful home of ours, but so many others of our clan don't seem to notice it at all?"

"Well, child," said Matreyi. "I have always tried to teach you to see the world with open eyes." She took off her shawl and laid it on the ground. "Come, let's sit." She helped Anya down to a sitting position.

"There are many in our clan who can only see what is right in front of them, and the wonders that frame their lives just… fade into the background. Marvels so commonly seen – for them – cease to be marvels at all.

"For all the beauty around us, life can be hard," she smiled ruefully. "And when things are hard, survival feels more important than the smell of the spring thaw or the laughter of a child, and so their view becomes restricted, until survival is all they can see." She looked seriously at Anya. "The secret, of course, is to make sure you can do both. Survive, yes, but take joy where you can find it.

"Some others are only interested in what they do, and because what they do is all they have ever done, these things become their whole world. It is everything they know, and makes them feel important, or useful, or safe. Any change to their pattern of life is difficult and uncomfortable for them, and they will fight to prevent it." Matreyi's gaze lingered in the middle-distance. "Over time, these things that sustain us are passed on in stories to help generations yet to come, and the things that just bring pleasure? These things remain, but alas, all too often do not find a place in our tribal tales.

"Listen to me," she scolded herself. "Warbling like a Jula bird[6] because I like the sound of my own voice." Matreyi focussed now solely on Anya. "Here, my gift to see you well." She chuckled and said, "Left to my own devices, I would surely have talked you to sleep, and returned to my tent, the parcel still under my arm." She placed the neatly wrapped package in Anya's lap.

Anya placed her hands on the bundle, savouring the anticipation, though she knew what lay beneath the cloth wrapping. She slowly unfolded the fabric, until the present lay revealed to her eager gaze. Books! She lovingly caressed

---

[6] Jula birds are migratory, spending the winter in lowland areas, returning to the Yanuba mountains to breed in the spring. Their green-brown plumage affords them useful camouflage against summer mountain terrain, but they are best known for the song of the male, which though melodious, can continue unbroken for hours at a time. Because of this long duration, they are sometimes used by the mountain people for target practice using their slings. "Life in the Yanuba mountains".

their covers. In her mind, the feel of the worn leather lent literal weight to their literary contents.

"Oh, they're wonderful!" she beamed. "Thank you Aunt Matreyi."

"But, sweet child, you haven't yet looked inside." Matreyi laughed.

"I don't need to," Anya said. "They're books." She lifted them to her face and inhaled deeply, as if by so doing, she could draw their very words into her heart. "They smell so wonderful," she said.

"They smell like the dusty old temple they came from, you mean," said Matreyi, her laughter twinkling in her eyes as she regarded her favourite niece. "Open them, little one." Anya glanced up with mock outrage, and with a sigh, Matreyi amended, "Not so little one."

Anya held up the first book for examination, opening it at random and scanning the pages. "Intrepid: fearless and brave. Intricate: very complicated. Intrigue… Why, it's a book of words, how perfect!" she exclaimed. "This would have been very useful when you first taught me to read, Aunt Matreyi."

"It was, though I never let you see it. You would have chewed the pages." She smiled at the memory. "The monks tell me that they have many similar books, that such things used to be commonplace."

The second book was filled with descriptions of animals and plants, often accompanied by little illustrations inked with painstaking detail. Anya's face shone with delight as she greedily absorbed both words and pictures.

She came to the final tome, glancing at its title. Her mouth dropped and so, very nearly, did the book. "But, this talks about the time before The Fall. It can't be that old, surely?" she asked in amazement. "I don't trust myself to have it."

"Peace, Anya." The use of her name startled her into seriousness, and she gave her full attention to Matreyi. "Very few are the books from before The Fall. This was written some while later." She paused in contemplation. "Though I think whoever wrote it hoped to make it appear so."

"Nevertheless," came Anya's response, her animation showing in the speed of her chatter, "the author was closer to The Fall than we are." She hugged Matreyi tightly. "Thank you, Aunt, these are a treasure."

They periodically read and talked for a time, relishing the words, both written and spoken, but most of all, enjoying each other's company, until at last Anya began to shiver under her blankets. Matreyi noted this with a guilty sigh, taking up the books and ushering Anya to her feet. Together, they walked unhurriedly back to the family tent.

Unseen, they arrived back at the family yurt, and re-entered the way they had left. Neeta was waiting, a fierce expression on her face. She looked up as they entered, glaring at Matreyi.

"What do you think you are doing, taking Anya out of bed? She needs to rest."

"The poor child needed a change of scenery," Matreyi replied, the lightness of her tone betrayed by the clenching of her jaw.

"A change of scenery? She's not well, and you took her out into a gale." Neeta was shouting now.

"It's alright mother, I'm fine," Anya said.

"I should have known I couldn't trust you." Neeta's face was red with fury, her eyes drilled into her sister's. "What was I thinking, leaving you to look after her?"

"Perhaps that the girl might appreciate some alternative company?" Matreyi countered, biting the words off in her anger. She looked down at the ground. "Neeta, this is not the time or place for this."

"You're right, get out."

Matreyi bowed her head and began to place the books near Anya's sleeping mat, but Neeta interrupted. "And take those books with you." She spat the word 'books' as though the taste of it was foul in her mouth. "I think Anya has had quite enough of those."

"Mother!" Anya pleaded.

Matreyi looked as though she had been slapped. Slowly, and with exaggerated care, she collected the books and began to move towards the exit. "Why I let you continue with that nonsense, I don't know," Neeta said. She moved to place herself between Anya and her aunt.

Almost at the exit, Matreyi paused, and turned to regard her sister with a weary expression. "Perhaps because she loves it as much as you used to." She turned and left them with the silence of the tent ringing in their ears.

Games

Anya read. After much complaining, Neeta had relented and allowed her the books Matreyi had brought.

All was at peace. Her boredom relieved, Anya devoured the words with her eyes. She read, and re-read until she lived inside their covers, walking the pages, and seeing with the authors' eyes, the book of words a constant companion and trusted friend on her journey.

Anya saw cities, huge collections of built dwellings filled with people, each with their own role to play in a chaotic dance that continued, day and night for hundreds of years with never a break. She saw loud, colourful markets filled with food, clothing, animals, and many other things that were bartered in exchange for discs of metal. She saw herd animals, restricted from roaming, kept as slaves, and penned in by barriers of constructed wood, and land deliberately made to grow eating plants, circumventing the need to forage.

Most of all she saw people. Some had brown skin like the Tharom, others black as night. There were even tribes who lived in the far north of the world who were pale of complexion, perhaps to help them hide in the frozen wastelands they inhabited. There were those who sounded like her kin, who venerated the Gods of nature and kept carvings of them in their homes. Others she found who worshipped the elements, fire, earth, wind, and water. There were those who followed a religion of the sun, with holy days according to the times of the seasons. Of course, all respected Death, for to do otherwise might invite his unwanted attention, but strangest of all were those who gave their lives to Vajnata, some of them quite literally.

Anya was unsure exactly what Vajnata represented. Whispered mentions of his name appeared following outbreaks of disease, disasters, and murders. His followers were few, but feared, and rumoured to be cruel and powerful. Anya found and dismissed references to gaining eternal life by giving one's life to him, but that was apparently the motivation behind two ritual suicides she encountered. Anya was appalled that anyone would choose to worship such a God.

All too soon for Anya, her sojourn through the pages of her books ended, for even Neeta was urging her out of their tent. Anya knew she had recovered from her ordeal but had found pleasure in the last few days. She had spent some enjoyable time with her mother, and Matreyi had visited, her relationship with Neeta strained, but intact, though Neeta had not left her alone with Anya.

Anya stood blinking in the sunshine. The warmth of summer had returned briefly to the heights of the mountain range, interrupting autumn's hold. She gazed down at the grazing land as she wandered, and could see that it would soon be time to move again. The elk had eaten the grass down to its rough stalks, patches of brown marred the sweeping green.

As she moved through the camp, she heard the percussive rhythm of hand-clapped beats and the low, half-singing of a Defender practice session. With a thrill, she set off towards the source of the sounds, soon finding that the site was already surrounded by onlookers. She cast about for an opening in the throng - she was no longer small enough to wend her way through without jostling, or comment - and was on the point of giving up when a sharp whistle above her caught her attention.

She looked up at the wall of rocks against which the site of their camp was located, and saw Amman perched happily, swinging his feet and waving to her. Anya cast about, assessing the rough face of stone for a way up. She easily found a route, and climbed swiftly, even for one such as herself whose birthright was to live, play, and climb in the rocky places of the Yanuba.

"You've been let out, then," said Amman.

"How long have they been practicing?" Anya asked.

"Not long," said Amman. "They always start with the clapping and singing, like we do with the Ghandarva's stories."

Anya looked down from their vantage point. They had a good view of the Defenders as they all clapped and sang, relaxed and ready to begin the exercises. "Why do you suppose they clap, instead of drum?" she asked, an answer already forming in her mind.

"Maybe they don't want to wear out the drums?" Amman mused. "Make sure they're in good condition when needed."

"When I watched them against the Rahksharu…"

Amman winced at the mention of her foolhardy escapade.

"… They used the drums and the singing to attract its attention." Anya looked at Amman. "I think they only clap just in case one is nearby, to make sure they don't draw it here." Amman shivered in response.

The Defenders had ceased their song and were spreading out in a line, donning plain hoods and holding unsharpened spears. The Guide began his calls, and the line of men took up their practice weapons and swung them over their heads. Anya listened carefully, matching the calls to the movements, building up a picture of commands and responses, seeking an understanding of the dance. She started whispering the actions she knew to be coming before they unfolded below, and Amman grinned, elbowing her gently in the ribs whenever she got one wrong.

Amman said, "Look," and pointed beyond the men practicing. Further down the slope, a Defender was instructing some boys, who were inexpertly mimicking the controlled movements demonstrated above them. "Hiranjan," he hissed.

Anya saw him, her lip curling in distaste. "What?" Her eyes blazed. "That cretin will never be able to follow the instructions. Look, see how he tilts his spear left, and not right as the Guide told them." She watched, her eyes boring through the boy as he was put through his paces. "I would do better than that," she said softly, under her breath. "Why shouldn't I?"

"I don't know how you can tell what the instructions are," Amman said. "I just hear nonsense," Amman indicated the Guide. "He just said 'Earfly', or some other random rubbish."

"It was 'Ire-Fly', which means the spear-wielders should spin them above their heads, while all harpoons are thrown at once by the second ring." Anya said.

"You got all that just from watching them?" Amman looked amazed.

"I've watched them a lot." She looked accusingly at Amman. "So have you."

"Yes, but I'll never be chosen to be a Defender," he was momentarily wistful. "Not that I'd want to be. It's way too dangerous for my liking, and as Ujesh won't be testing me on my knowledge of Defender signals, I'm content just to sit here with you and admire their skills." Amman looked briefly at Anya, whose eyes were once again narrowed viciously on Hiranjan. He pursed his lips, returning his attention to the men below.

The practice had finished. Anya and Amman were eating some spiced bread he had liberated from his family yurt, where his mother had piled them on a wooden plate to cool.

She had chased him out of their tent with amused threats while he'd run, laughing, to re-join Anya.

"You know, she says you're a bad influence on me," he said in a matter-of-fact tone. "Says I always used to be such a good boy."

"Your mother likes me," Anya said in response. In the back of her mind, the spectre of her Aunt loomed. How much would Amman's mother like her if she followed Matreyi's path?

Seeing a game of gaganni [7] in progress, she said to Amman, "Come on, let's join in." She began to run, Amman following behind.

As they approached, Anya slowed. The game was almost over. Hiranjan, his shirt discarded, revealing a well-muscled torso, and two other boys were facing off against a single player. Knowing his only chance was to raid, the boy advanced hurriedly, taking a quick shot at one of the other boys and missing. His only chance now was to reclaim the ball he had lost.

Hiranjan called out to his team-mates, "Wait! Leave him to me." The others obeyed.

Hiranjan ran towards the boy, blocking off his raid. The boy retreated, but Hiranjan followed. He tried to dodge past, but was grabbed by his sleeve and grappled to the ground. Hiranjan sat on top of the prone boy, taunting him, finally rubbing the gaganwa ball in his face, laughing as he did so. The game was over.

He returned to his friends, who crowded around, congratulating him and clapping him on the back.

---

[7] Gaganni is a game played by the children of the tribe where the aim is to hit the opposing players with a ball made from a stuffed gaganwa fruit. When a 'hit' is scored, play resets and the player is 'out', but only if hit in their own half of the area. For this reason, raids into the opposing half are common. "Games of the Tharom tribe".

"Fancy a real challenge?" Anya called. "Or are you enjoying the attention of those idiots too much?"

Hiranjan sneered over his shoulder, "A challenge, from where?" He turned, looking Anya up and down with a sneer. "Go, cook some food, or something. Girls don't play gaganni."

"You're playing it, aren't you?" Anya said. Amman could not suppress a chuckle, but the other boys' faces were masks of stone..

"Funny." Hiranjan scowled. He turned from Anya. "Don't waste my time, it's too easy."

"You never found it too easy when we were kids."

He turned, a crooked smile on his lips. "It's warm," Hiranjan was leering at her. "I'll play you if you go topless too." He clutched at his own chest suggestively, looking around at his cronies, who were loudly shouting their approval.

"What's the point? It looks to me like you prefer the feel of your own body."

"Go away, loser," Hiranjan said with contempt.

"You should know," Anya said. "You're the one who's too scared to accept a girl's challenge."

Hiranjan stared at Anya for a moment before shrugging his shoulders. "Fine, but it's your funeral if you get hurt."

Anya resisted the urge to insult him again, instead attempting to persuade some of the boys to play on her team. Amman agreed immediately, as she had known he would, but the others required some encouragement. Most refused, and Anya ended up with a team of five.

She gathered them around her. "Ok, Hiranjan is going to want to get me 'out' first, so – "

"Who made you the captain?" asked another boy. "When was the last time you played?"

"Hiranjan made me the captain, when he accepted *my* challenge." Anya softened her tone. "We used to do alright, though, didn't we, Paras?"

"Yeah, I guess." the boy reluctantly acknowledged.

"So, if Hiranjan wants me out first, let's give him a chance." Anya outlined her plan.

The game began as usual, with both teams taking up position at the base of their squares. Hiranjan kept back, his team spreading out, while Anya's walked forward in a line, Anya ahead of the others, keeping always on the balls of her feet.

Anya threw her ball first, but instead of aiming at the opposition, she hurled it up into the air above her, and backed off. One of the opposing players stupidly followed its arc with his eyes, and seeing their cue, Anya's teammates all launched their balls at the same target, more than one finding its mark.

Hiranjan looked furious. He berated his now former teammate by shoving him to the ground, and, like Anya, gathered his team together for the tactics of the next play.

Hiranjan arranged his team more cautiously than before, while Anya's team rapidly advanced without her to the opponents' half of the pitch. Anya moved behind them, as if using them as a shield, but stayed in her own box, watching as they advanced on Hiranjan. She pretended to be focussing all her attention on the feint ahead of her, but was in reality waiting until one of Hiranjan's teammates tried to flank her, which before long, one did.

Anya called, "Now!" Paras aimed a good throw at their opponents' captain, but Hiranjan caught it easily. Paras turned immediately, passing through his own line. As he did so, Anya tossed him her ball, and immediately began to dodge. The attacker, so intent on sneaking up on her, did not even notice Paras until he'd been hit from behind.

Anya's team regrouped for the next play. They exchanged grins, as all could hear Hiranjan shouting at his own players, in equal parts insulting and threatening. They had a good numerical advantage now, if they could get the next hit, the game would be almost over.

Amman was the next out. He had never been especially good at gaganni, Anya reflected, he was neither fast, nor agile, and was hit in the side by Hiranjan. It had been a good hard throw, Anya admitted to herself, but he should have seen it coming.

One by one, her fellow players were hit, Anya escaping narrowly on more than one occasion, until she was left alone, facing Hiranjan and one more boy. Annoyed by the performance of her former teammates, Anya concentrated all her attention on Hiranjan. She could lose, for all she cared, as long as he was out before her.

They began again, and Anya raced forwards, seeking to gain her opponents' box. She paused suddenly, and took fly with her ball, hoping to surprise Hiranjan, but all his attention was on her, and he dodged easily. She knew she needed to cross the dividing line, and raid, or the game would be over. She sprinted, with sudden changes of direction, hoping to confound the boys who faced her.

A sound like a whip singed Anya's ear. She had barely seen him draw his arm back before his ball had passed her head. She was grateful Hiranjan had missed and increased her speed, hoping to retrieve her ball and get back in the game.

Anya angled her run away from the other boy, bringing her closer to Hiranjan. She was raiding now, so the game was safe, for the moment. Hiranjan was irrelevant to the play, Anya directed all her attention on the ball she was trying to recover, and the remaining armed opponent.

As she moved to pass him, Hiranjan took a fast step towards her, using his body to knock her over. She spun and fell to the ground, her mouth open in shock. The move was not allowed in all but the most physical versions of gaganni - neither of them were armed - but she doubted she could successfully argue her point.

Her ball was near her toes, but the other boy had reached her, hand poised to throw, looking to his captain for guidance.

"Just throw it," Anya said, disgusted by the deference he showed to Hiranjan.

"No, give me the ball," said Hiranjan. "I'm going to enjoy —"

Seized by sudden inspiration, Anya positioned her toes underneath her ball. As the boy tossed his to Hiranjan, she flicked her foot and her ball tamely hit the boy's leg.

Anya laughed. "Looks like it's just you and me," said Anya. "Not too easy, I think."

"No wonder you can't find a husband." Hiranjan spat. "What man would want to put up your constant attitude? Take a good look at your weird aunt, you bitch, because that's you before long."

Hiranjan turned and walked away back to his starting position and was passed another ball by one of his cronies. Anya stood, stunned for a moment. Comments of that kind were not unknown to her, but coming as it did, so soon after a moment of triumph - it threw her.

The game restarted. Anya looked at the boys around her as they followed the game. How many of them felt the same? Was that how they all saw her, as some kind of harridan, a shrew destined to nag her future husband to death? Maybe they were right. Why should she lie down for them or anyone, like a rug for cleaning their shoes?

She was knocked to the ground, stars exploding in her vision. She had not seen, had not been paying attention, and Hiranjan had rushed forward and ended the contest with a clean throw to her eye. Anya could feel it swelling already.

"Like I said. Loser!" Hiranjan yelled, before turning to his friends, already coming on to the field to congratulate him. "Keep this up, and you won't even have a pretty face. Not even a Rahksharu will want to look at you."

Anya sat, numbed by the humiliation, feeling nothing. Feeling everything.

Thoughts and Prayers

Anya sliced inexpertly at the roots. Neeta supervised her food preparation while she weaved a basket, simultaneously lecturing Shanoli on her tasks to be completed that day.

Though she had little skill for it, Anya had fond memories of time spent with her mother helping her prepare their meals. She smiled as she recalled stealing fruit intended for baking, the dough on her hands leaving ample evidence for her mother to catch her thieving. The comfort and safety of such things was coming to an end, lost with the passing of her childhood. Perhaps they must inevitably be discarded, remnants of youth to be grown out of, a stepping stone of emotion, of no consequence to her future adult self.

Anya forced a smile to clear her head of melancholy daydreams, and looked at the root in her hand, gradually shortening as she sliced. A thought struck her. "I wonder how small I could cut these?" she asked, without filtering the thought as it revealed itself.

"Just cut them to the thickness of your thumb," said Neeta, misunderstanding the question. "It will be cooking for much of the day, if you cut them too small, they will lose all their texture."

"Yes mother," Anya said, and was silent for a moment. "But if I did carry on cutting them, and had the sharpest possible knife, how small could the smallest bit be?"

Neeta looked up from her weaving, regarding Anya with a frown. Shanoli, passing through the cooking space, said, "If it got too small, you wouldn't be able to see what you were doing."

"I know, but if I had an eagle's sight or better, and could see the tiniest things, smaller than anything that any man ever did see, how small would the smallest piece be?"

"What does it matter?" Neeta scolded. "It would be too small for our food long before." She briefly appeared to consider it, and blew out her cheeks dismissively. "Enough questions, you're losing time by this chatter, time needed to soften them."

"I suppose you would just carry on cutting forever," called Shanoli from the main section of the yurt, where they would sit to eat their food.

"But could you?" Anya mused aloud. She continued to chop more absently, until she nearly cut her own finger.

"Suppose you did cut forever. Each time you sliced it, it would be smaller than before, until it would be so small that there would be no size at all to divide any further." Anya sucked her finger thoughtfully. "But if your piece has no size, you could put a hundred, or a thousand of these pieces next to each other, and it would still have no size."

Neeta looked carefully at Anya, a weary curiosity vying with her obvious annoyance. "Don't you see?" said Anya. "If you can put thousands of these pieces together and still have a piece with no size, you'd never be able to put enough of them together to make a piece as big as this root." Anya's eyes were lit with excitement. "So, the smallest piece *has* to have some size, otherwise you could never have enough to make up anything, not this root, or the knife, trees, mountains or even us."

"I don't think we're made up of pieces of vegetable root, Anya," Shanoli said, laughing.

Anya sighed, and turned to face Neeta. "You can see what I mean, Mother."

Neeta was shaking her head. "You are a strange girl," she said. "You come home one day with a black eye, after playing rough games with boys, games that girls have no place to be involved with." She looked significantly at Anya. "And another day, you waste time daydreaming, imagining chopping roots up into the most tiny pieces instead of actually chopping them to prepare our food."

"But, how can you not wonder how things are, or how they work?" She dipped her eyes, before returning her gaze to her mother. "You do understand what I'm saying, don't you?"

"Yes, Anya." Neeta pursed her lips, her frown still in place as she studied her daughter. "But what good does that do us, it won't help us prepare our meal, will it?" With that, she clapped her hands. "Go on, or it will never be ready."

Deflated, Anya returned to her duties.

The elk had moved on and, as ever, the clan had followed. The herd had travelled for several days, down rocky slopes and difficult terrain, until at last they rested much further down the mountains, closer to the foothills than usual. The wind blew warmer here, and autumn receded, the change in altitude giving Anya the feeling that the clan had somehow reversed the seasons' order. The move had another benefit. They were near the temple.

Anya joined a small group that included Matreyi, who were making the two-hour trek to visit the monks' abode. Their route followed an alpine river that bounced and swirled over a boulder strewn bed, providing a background chatter to the journey.

"What's it like?" Anya asked her aunt, raising her voice to be heard over the rush of the water.

"The temple?" Matreyi looked thoughtful. She did not answer for a time. "It is considered important to the tribe. The monks are thought to dedicate their whole lives to the contemplation of the natural world." Matreyi paused again, and said with less reserve, "They have statues and carvings that venerate the Gods. It is a very peaceful place. When our migration takes us near, it is customary for some of us to visit and pay our clan's respects."

"And to borrow books?" Anya said. She looked at the goatskin sack her aunt wore on her back, its cord crossing her chest, the tension in the string keeping it closed. In places it bulged with sharp protrusions, betraying its contents.

"Yes, child, to borrow books. At least, for me." Matreyi's eyes were lit from within. She smiled at thoughts she kept to herself, before turning her head to regard Anya. "I was surprised your mother agreed to let you come. I'm sure she could have found you some other chores."

Anya laughed. "Chores?" She stared with mock incredulity at her aunt. "There isn't anywhere in the world I would rather be than here, on my way to the temple."

Matreyi observed her niece's exuberance and sighed, again becoming thoughtful. "You are by far the youngest of us," she said, indicating the motley group of pilgrims that walked ahead and behind, always maintaining a discrete distance between themselves and Matreyi. Most had greying hair, or in some cases, little hair at all. "It appears that your fellow youngsters don't share your enthusiasm for pilgrimage."

Anya looked sheepish. "What you mean is that none of them shares my enthusiasm for books."

"Yes, dear, though it's hardly surprising," Matreyi said. "Seeing as very few of them have been taught to read." She walked in silence for a while. After a time, in a quiet voice, she said, "I sometimes wonder at the wisdom of it, myself."

"Aunt Matreyi!" Anya scolded. "How can you say such a thing? Reading, losing yourself in the wonders found inside the pages of a book is the most amazing feeling I know." She fixed her aunt with a serious expression. "And the only reason I know this, is because you showed it to me."

"I worry for you, young one," was all she replied.

"But you feel the same way," Anya said. "I know you do. Why would you worry about me?"

Matreyi did not reply, but continued walking, her sight fixed on the river's edge. Anya tried to see what held the older woman's attention, and Matreyi, realising what she was doing, pointedly looked at the space around them. Anya saw nothing and looked quizzically at her aunt. Seeing this, Matreyi stopped and waited. The other clan members moved around them, not coming closer than the height of two men.

"Oh," said Anya. "I don't worry about that and neither should you. You're better than them, and they just don't realise, that's all."

Matreyi gave the girl a stern look. "Anya! I am no better than anyone. No-one is," she said, "except as proven by their deeds. What have I done that is better than anyone here?"

"You taught me to read," Anya said simply.

"Yes, there is that," Matreyi said. "But what if by doing so, I have condemned you to endure the scorn of your clan, as I do? Then surely this 'gift' would have been better had it not been given at all."

"But Aunt Matreyi, it isn't because you read that…" Anya did not feel able to complete her thought. She refused to see her beloved aunt the way that others did and so her voice ran dry.

"No?" she asked. "If I had not had my eyes opened to the knowledge found within them, would I have wanted, would I have expected more than I found?" Matreyi reached out and put her arm around Anya. "I'm sorry, child. I don't wish to dampen your enthusiasm, but I also don't want to see you suffer - this." Her voice was bitter. She gestured about her, at the distance maintained by the others, devoid of conversation or any attempt to engage with her. Devoid of contact.

"If you were to marry," Matreyi began cautiously, her voice sounding taut to Anya's ears, "you would be spared this isolation." Her eyes were distant. "You could still read to your heart's content, with the understanding of your husband."

"But what if he didn't understand? Wouldn't that be awful?" Anya said plaintively. She contemplated this dire possibility. "And why should I need his understanding?" Her temper began to rise. "Why should I need permission to do something so harmless? Reading, learning doesn't hurt anyone. Why would they want to stop me?"

"Because it's unusual, unnecessary in their eyes." Matreyi's eyes fell. "Because it's aberrant."

"Oo," Anya's excitement flared. "I know that one. That means…" she bit her lip trying to remember the definition from her book of words.

"This is not a game, young one. You need to think seriously about your future." Matreyi clenched her jaw and said no more.

Anya was confused by the unusual display of conformist attitudes from her aunt. What was wrong? Why would she talk like that? A fly buzzed near her eye and landed, Anya rubbed at it to shoo it away, forgetting the bruising that still lingered, and brought her head quickly back, away from the pain caused by her hand. Neeta had rubbed some ointment in before they left, perhaps that was attractive to insects, she thought.

"Wait a moment." Anya was gripped by a sudden suspicion. She stopped and put her hands to her hips, indignantly glaring at her aunt who had walked a few steps further and now half-turned to face her, regarding her warily. "You've never before told me to be anything other than myself. Did Mother put you up to this?" her accusing look bore into Matreyi.

Matreyi sighed and continued walking. Her posture sagging almost imperceptibly as she trudged away. Anya fumed, not sure who deserved her anger more, her mother or her aunt. She let herself be swallowed up by the group behind and stomped onward, folding her arms belligerently across her chest, dark thoughts swirling about her.

She was startled out of her grim contemplation by a shout from the lead group. Anya was irritated by the interruption to her sulk, but pushed through the adults around her, seeking the cause of the cry, unable to dampen her curiosity, and suddenly saw how the ground ahead fell away. Now that she was not so absorbed in her own thoughts, she could hear a deeper rumbling sound rising from beneath the rushing of the river, could feel a growing moisture in the air.

The pilgrim's voices were alive with excitement and wonder. Anya squeezed between their bodies with the unintentional, oblivious rudeness of the young, until she stood near the edge of a cliff. Adults either side of her placed their hands on her shoulders protectively, preventing her from going right to its lip.

Anya looked below her and marvelled. The land dropped into space, revealing a vista of concentric rainbows, suspended in the mist that rose majestically from the bottom of a crashing waterfall to meet the rays from the sun behind them. Half concealed behind this stunning visual display was a bright, azure mountain lake teaming with white birds.

Roughly in the centre of the lake rose a rocky island, thrusting upward from the placid surface, protected for most of its perimeter by a sheer rock face of stone. On one side, the natural stone barrier had collapsed and Anya could see a rough jetty protruding into the clear water and boats moored against it, resting peacefully in the calm lake.

Atop the highest tier of the island sat a low, rough, rambling grey-stone building with an undulating roof of faded orange tiles. Anya could see brown-robed figures milling about, tending to rows of plants, or picking fruit from the trees that completely encircled the temple. She looked about her, seeking Matreyi, all thoughts of annoyance with her forgotten. She found her aunt leaning against the gnarled trunk of a long-dead tree, a faraway expression on her face as she watched Anya.

Anya skipped over to Matreyi. "Oh, Aunt. You never said." She did not finish the thought. There was no need.

"It has seldom looked quite like this," Matreyi replied. She waved Anya away. "Drink it in, child, make the most of this moment while it lasts."

They had rested for a while, basking in the scene, before embarking on the precarious route down to the land surrounding the water. Now they stood on the banks of the lake, preparing to make the crossing using boats moored on the shore for that purpose. Anya gazed across the water, gaining a different perspective on the island and the surrounding lands. In the distance, she thought she saw a column of smoke rising beyond the far shore and frowned. Fires were rare in the mountains and it was wise to wary of them. With the moisture in the air from the falls, it was hard to be sure. She dismissed it as a trick of the light.

Predictably, the boat that Anya and Matreyi occupied was less full than the others. Anya snuggled close to her aunt near the bow, seeking warmth from the chill of the spray in the air, and hoping to compensate for the distance of the other clansfolk in their boat, who huddled in the stern. A lone man of the tribe occupied the central thwart, using oars to propel the boat gradually closer to the waiting island. Even he had his back to Matreyi.

As the boat lazily approached its destination, they escaped the mist and felt the sun more fully, basking and warming themselves in its radiance. Anya trailed her hand in the water, and could see fish wriggling away at their approach. The cold between her fingers felt delicious and a wild desire to plunge herself into the lake flooded her heart. She shifted herself and leaned over, the better to further entertain the idea, but felt Matreyi's hand on her shoulder.

Anya looked back at her aunt, who shook her head. "It looks inviting, dear one, but monsters don't only live on land."

A shiver passed through Anya, transmitted via her reflection in the chilly water. She probed its depths more fully with her gaze, her delight cooled to a wary admiration of its tempting perfection. She thought she saw movement below and imagined nameless creatures sliding beneath them, biding their time, waiting to bring death to the unwary.

They were closer to the island now and Anya could see a double shelter formed of pointed roofs on stout wooden supports emerging into view, containing an upturned boat in one, and in the other a firepit above which hung strings of fish, smoking as they gently waved in the updraft. A skinny figure stood on the pier, awaiting their arrival. He wore a rough looking brown robe cinched at the waist with a woven cord, and leg wrappings above wooden sandals. Anya noticed that, although he shared their complexion, his hair was noticeably lighter than her fellow clansfolk, displaying brownish tones amid the usual black.

Steadily, the distance to the island closed and soon their boats were bumping gently against the sides of the pier. The monk swiftly, but without haste, caught the bow ropes, and knotted them around the mooring posts, lending his arm to aid them out onto the unmoving wooden planks of the jetty. In her excitement, Anya eschewed his help and climbed clumsily out without assistance while he was still dealing with the boat ahead of theirs, her boat rocking alarmingly as she did so.

At last on the shores of the temple's island, Anya could barely contain her anticipation. She wanted to seize hold of the monk's robes and demand to be taken to their library, but with difficulty maintained her control and instead diverted her attention by inspecting the island itself.

Even before she had set foot on the soil of the land, she was enveloped in the most delightful aromas. She recognised the scent of spices familiar to her from her mother's cooking. These were laced with others unknown, exotic to her untrained senses, suggestive of far off lands and distant cuisines. Softly pervading all of them, was the background woody fragrance of the smouldering chips, slowly burning to preserve the fish.

Ahead of her, she saw stones placed in a rough, broken path, leading from the pier, towards steps that were hewn from the island's rock, leading to the upper level. Anya crouched amongst the plants surrounding and interrupting the stepping stones, running her hands through their blooms and leaves, releasing a medley of heady perfumes. She looked around her and realised that every available patch of earth was devoted to the cultivation of plants of use to the monks. There were herbs and spices, as well as climbing vegetables and other leafy plants she recognised from when her chores required foraging.

"What we can, we grow on our island, or draw from the lake to eat." The monk was standing behind Anya, and she rose with a sudden, startled lack of grace. She noticed his arm was linked with Matreyi's. His voice was warm and gentle. "We gather what else we need from the land about, and welcome exchanges with pilgrims, such as yourselves." With his free arm he indicated the bundles of animal skins carried by their fellow travellers.

Anya considered this, and in slight alarm said, "But Aunt, what have we brought to trade?" Her distress at the prospect of leaving empty handed tasted unpleasant in her mouth.

"Company, and a different perspective." Matreyi smiled enigmatically. She inclined her head gently to the robed figure beside her. "The monks welcome a satisfying discussion, I imagine they must sometimes grow tired of the same opinions from the same people, limited as they are in number." She smiled warmly, and said, "Anya, this is Bibek. He is the Acharya, the current leader of their order."

They climbed the steps to the upper level and Anya discovered that, like below, all was dedicated to the production of food or the general upkeep of their temple. Rows of unfamiliar plants grew in patches of earth, kept devoid of grass or unwanted greenery, while the temple's walls were covered in vines laden with as yet unripe fruit. Wandering about the island, pecking and scratching at the ground were several of a type of plump flightless bird that Anya assumed would serve to supplement their diet of fish and vegetables.

Anya ducked under a low branch from one of the trees that lined the upper area and bumped her head on its round fruit. She looked about her and saw that every one of the trees was a gaganwa. Their ubiquitous fruits dangled like decorations from the branches, promising both sweetness and entertainment to her young, ingenuous eyes.

Bibek walked forward to stand in front of the travellers on the single stone step that marked the entrance to the temple. He was framed on each side by pillars set into the adjoining walls, supporting the lintel above the doorway. The walls of the temple were built of uneven stones, roughly layered, the spaces between filled with what looked like solid sand to Anya's untutored sight. Above him, and around the entire perimeter were wooden struts, which extruded from the walls at an angle halfway between horizontal and vertical. These supported a roof that extended a great deal further than the walls, providing shelter from rain or sun to those beneath its protection.

"Welcome all," began the monk. "Many of you have visited before and our hearts sing with our reunion." He looked directly at Anya. "For others, this is your first visit, and we hope that you will be as charmed with our modest hospitality as we are to greet you." Bibek motioned them all to enter. "Come. Please rest yourselves after your journey, and share with us our food."

As Anya passed through the thick walls, she felt the heat of day give way to a cool tranquillity. The sudden transition from the glare of sunlight to the less well-lit interior afflicted her with a temporary blindness. As her eyes adjusted, she realised her hands were outstretched, as if she had been playing Enhaldai[8], and she laughed. Bibek, well-used to this phenomenon, waited patiently by another door, and indicated to them to go through.

Beyond the doorway was a hall lined with old wooden tables on which rested a glorious selection of food - so much that Anya imagined the tables groaning with the weight of it. She breathed deeply, savouring the aroma of freshly baked spiced bread alongside pots of curry. Scented wild rice with fried vegetables and fermented chutney vied for her attention with momo dumplings and dipping sauce, and Anya found she was salivating at the smell of it. Some of her fellow travellers were already seated, and Anya noticed several brown-robed figures standing, apparently waiting for their guests to sit. Not knowing the proper etiquette, she looked questioningly at Matreyi, and at the monks, not wishing to offer them any offence.

As she scanned the monks, she was struck by their unusual hair, which varied in shade from black, as was that of her tribe to an almost coppery brown. Most of all, she wondered at how unusually elegant one of the men was, her smooth brown skin free of any sign of beard or stubble. Anya realised with an audible gasp, that the monk she regarded was a woman and not a man at all. How could this be? Anya had always assumed the monks to all be men, perhaps with

---

[8] In Enhaldai, one player is blinded with a scarf, which is tied over their eyes. All other players seek to touch the blinded player, while stating their name. If they are all successful, the blind player loses. However, if the blind player succeeds in touching any other player with their hands, they must then assume the blind role. "Games of the Tharom tribe".

boys as apprentices, and here before her incredulous gaze was a woman, performing the same role as those about her, or at the very least wearing the same robes of station.

Stunned, she had to be guided to a bench by Matreyi. Anya could not take her eyes off the female monk, who smiled at her momentarily, while politely pretending that the girl's stare did not demonstrate a lack of manners. Seated at last, she continued to study the woman in brown, noting her short hair that had led to much of her own confusion, and, now she looked more closely, a much clearer indication of her womanhood in her slim, but obviously feminine figure.

"Eat, child," said Matreyi quietly. Anya realised that hers was the only plate as yet untouched by food. Her hunger came back in a rush and she eagerly helped herself to the feast.

The monks were now taking their seats among their guests, Bibek placing himself opposite Matreyi. In her barely controlled excitement, Anya both hoped and feared that the female monk would choose their table, but she chose to sit in near isolation at the far end of the hall.

"But aunt," said Anya, her mouth still half full with food. "She's a woman!"

"Yes, she is," Matreyi said. "Her name is Pramiti."

Anya turned to regard her. Her aunt appeared to be engaged in a silent conversation with Bibek, their words articulated with their eyes. Apparently satisfied with Bibek's contribution, Matreyi lowered her eyes, and smiled at Anya.

"Though they are fewer in number, it is not unusual for women to become monks," said Bibek. "We had hopes that your aunt might join us." He stopped and briefly but tightly closed his eyes, as though privately admonishing himself. He recovered himself quickly and continued. "Though we understand the difficulty that this can sometimes cause."

Sensing that this was not the right time to ask the questions that overwhelmed her, Anya turned her attention to her plate and ate in silence.

Anya sat in the temple's central shrine, fidgeting as her eyes looked through the wooden statue of The Bear, not seeing it or the devotion of her clansfolk, who sat or knelt with heads bowed in contemplation.

The shrine was small. It was filled with the monks' craft, carvings and paintings covered every surface of the holy place - the statues, the benches, and the walls. The shrine was also so full of pilgrims that no seat was free, many of her party choosing to prostrate themselves on the floor in dedication of the Gods.

The problem with piety, Anya thought, was that it was so boring. She was no fool, and knew to venerate the Gods. But did the Gods honestly care if people spent their days in meditation to the wonders of nature instead of being out in it, revelling and experiencing it first-hand? This small space was hardly crowded with monks when they had entered, in fact, Anya realised, the room they had passed through to get here was larger, with more of the brethren present, engaged in repairing or copying books. It seemed to Anya to indicate the shrine had a lesser importance to the monks than the books, a view in keeping with her own.

Something else briefly engaged her attention. Along with various representations of the Gods, Anya noticed a particularly accurate carving of a goat on the wall to her left. It occupied a position among other similar carvings, but whereas she could identify tribal clans that revered the others, she could not remember having heard a single reference to a clan Goat, or any of Ujesh's stories that referred to such a God. She pursed her lips in puzzlement and huffed a sigh born of tedium.

Matreyi whispered something to the man sat next to her and nudged Anya to indicate that they were leaving. She stood eagerly, delighted that her ordeal was finally over. Her aunt put her arm about Anya, guiding her firmly to the door and through it, to the scriptorium.

"One more sigh and you may have found yourself an unwanted sacrifice," Matreyi said sternly, though Anya could see lines of amusement radiating from her eyes. "I'm sure we must have caused offence, leaving so soon."

"Who cares what they think?" Anya absently responded, her attention already on the volumes being worked on by the monks. She moved to look over the shoulder of a man carefully illuminating a book with an image of a walking skeleton. The inks were so bright, they leaped off the page into life. On another table Anya saw a monk with skin so tanned, her mind immediately thought of the fabled Numenons, who had lived south of the mountains in a land so hot, it baked their skin until it was almost black. Her own brown skin looked pale in comparison. He was working to replace the cover of a large tome that had been affected by mildew, painstakingly separating its hard backing from the pages within. Anya leaned in as close as she dared, appreciating the craft that went into its assembly, noticeable in the smallest details. Anya tried to absorb it all, always trying to unlock its mysteries with her mind.

Bibek emerged from the shrine and spoke briefly with Matreyi. He nodded, and sauntered up to Anya. "I think what you're actually looking for is through there," he said, pointing to another door they had not yet used, his mellow voice spiced with amusement.

Anya cast her gaze where he had indicated, and glanced back questioningly. Bibek smiled, while Matreyi nodded in confirmation. Anya restrained herself from skipping, but walked swiftly to the door, pausing slightly before opening it. She realised she was holding her breath.

The room beyond was a library.

Shelves full of books lined every wall from floor to ceiling. Anya marvelled at seeing so many in one place. In the middle of the room was a table surrounded by chairs with stuffed cushions in an established seating area. "Are these waiting for repairs?" she indicated a section of shelving exclusively stuffed with decrepit tomes in extreme states of disrepair, some suffering from mould, others missing their spines. All, without exception were old, ancient to Anya's eyes. She cast her gaze around at the other shelves, and could see not a single book even nearing their condition.

Bibek nodded. "We place any in need of work together. These others have been worked on, but have yet to be returned to their place." He pointed to another shelved area on the other side of the doorway. Many of the books he indicated looked as if they were freshly made.

Anya looked at both sections, the beginnings of a frown showing on her forehead. She moved away from them, walking along another row with her hand out, touching every spine on display. An odd feeling was crawling its way down her spine. She put her hand to her mouth, tapping her lips with her finger, before asking, "Can I choose any to read?"

"Yes, except those in need of restoration," said Bibek.

Anya selected a shelf at random, and scanning the spines, found one called 'Numena and its Vassal States'. Thinking of the dark skinned monk, she took it from its place and moved swiftly to sit down, resting the large tome on the table. She opened and began to read.

"Anya, I have some things to discuss with Bibek in private," said Matreyi. "If you need any help, you may ask any of the other monks." She lingered momentarily, but seeing Anya absorbed in her own world, left with Bibek in tow.

Anya was in paradise. She accumulated book after book, skimming their contents, skipping between their contents as whim took her. The images painted by their words breathed excitement in her like a summer breeze, its currents stirring wonder and heartache at all that was gone. She lost herself within them, existing outside of time itself in worlds she created from seed carried on the wind.

Each time she opened another book, she would run her hands reverently across its covers, taking her time turning to the first page, relishing the feel of the leather, noting its firmness and acknowledging the skill involved. Anya had just taken a newly repaired volume and was following the same routine when she was struck by a flash of insight. She moved her finger along the edge of the inside cover, following it with her eyes, and leaving that book, returned to another still lying on the table. She repeated the same action, feeling more sure of herself than ever.

Anya turned her head in puzzlement as her previous uneasiness returned, revisiting her but refined by intuition. Carefully she looked around the library, counting the gaps where books had been removed, and bringing her attention once again to the table and counting the works she had placed there.

She sprang up from her chair and ran back to the scriptorium, where the dark-skinned brother was working on the same book as before. The old cover lay discarded on the worktable, and without seeking permission, Anya seized it, turning it over, and scanning its edge.

"That's a rare excitement for a mere book-cover," came a voice from behind her.

Startled, Anya spun around guiltily. "I, I'm sorry, I was just—"

"Don't worry, you are not in trouble." It was the woman monk she had seen earlier in the eating hall - Pramiti, Matreyi had called her. "It's unusual for anyone to run in the scriptorium. I don't think we should encourage it, but I enjoyed your enthusiasm." She looked closely at Anya. "What is it?"

Anya was bursting with ideas and stumbled in her reply. "You… what… I mean…" she drew a breath and continued with more coherence. "I saw this book being worked on earlier. I... I know it's a bit mouldy, but I could see the clever way its covers are wrapped with animal skins and the detail that goes into making it." She pointed at the inside of the cover. "I thought how wonderful that the makers of this sought to decorate even the most insignificant parts of it." Where she pointed, the leather had been imprinted with a textured pattern of intertwined leaves.

She looked back at Pramiti. "In your library, I noticed that all your books are decorated in the same way, all with different patterns, or so I thought." Anya steeled herself for one final rush of explanation. "That is, until I opened a book, newly re-covered and saw the same pattern repeated that I saw here."

The monk working on the book cast a sharp glance at his sister-monk. Anya stepped forward and took hold of the new cover being attached to the parchment contents. "The inside of this new cover is decorated in exactly the same pattern." Anya craned her neck around the man's work area, seeking something to fit the notions forming in her mind. Her eyes widened, and she grabbed one of the monk's devices and held it up for all to see.

"See? Here is the tool that makes the pattern." It was a wooden wheel attached to a handle. About its circumference were distinct metal decorations in the shape of leaves. Anya moved to the old cover and ran the tool along its edge. Once she had lined it up correctly, she ran the tool along the imprinted pattern without error. "The same tool made the pattern on this old cover as it did on the new." She looked around her. "*All* the books in the temple were made by you. Well, not you exactly, but by the monks that have gone before you."

"It is a useful skill," said Pramiti.

"And I saw that the only books with any kind of wear were those waiting for repair," Anya interrupted, unable to hold back her thoughts. "There aren't any in your library that are even nearly as bad as this one was, which tells me that your library doesn't hold all the books you have. There must be others that are approaching this state, but not quite ready to be mended." She waved at the old discarded cover. "And besides, if you have a whole shelf of books in need of work, where are the gaps in the shelves that they must have been taken from? Somewhere else," she answered her own question. "So, if this room, the library and another area I haven't seen are all dedicated to books, and only that tiny little shrine is devoted to the Gods, what exactly is this temple really for?"

Absolute quiet descended on the entire room as all those in it turned their heads to Anya. Pramiti looked startled, before sweeping her gaze around the whole room. Satisfied by what she saw, she exchanged glances with the others before saying, "I think we ought to find your aunt, so she can keep an eye on you." Her features were set firmly, brooking no argument. "Why don't you take a seat in the library while we wait for her?"

It was not a request.

The Quick and the Dead

They had allowed her to read. Anya was not quite sure if she was in serious trouble, but took that as a good omen.

Anya felt more frustrated than she could ever remember. She tried to focus on the wealth of words in her hands, but found her concentration interrupted by questions that demanded her attention. She had not been left alone and more than once gave voice to her queries, but always her minder met them with silence and a gentle shake of the head.

Occasionally another monk would enter, exchanging hushed words in a whispered exchange, often accompanied by a surprised glance in her direction. She felt like a dragonfly she remembered watching as a young child, a thing of curiosity that demanded examination. She had caught it in a net, but when she tried to release it, she found that she had damaged its wings and it could no longer take off.

At last, Matreyi arrived with Bibek, both looking flustered, as if they had run some distance to get here, Pramiti following them into the library. Matreyi dropped to one knee in front of Anya and enveloped her in a tight embrace. She leaned back, examining her face, amusement in her eyes and barely contained laughter on her lips.

"Well, little one," she did smile now as Anya pulled a face. "They tell me you've been saying some interesting things." She contained her mirth and looked Anya in the eye. "Pramiti is going to ask you some questions now. Answer her honestly. I'll be waiting just outside." She left.

Pramiti sat on a chair opposite Anya, Bibek positioning himself somewhere behind Anya, out of her sight. "Am I in trouble?" Anya asked.

"Hmm, do you think you are?" said Pramiti.

"Well, not really," Anya said. "Aunt Matreyi looked like something was pretty funny."

"What you were saying earlier." Pramiti hesitated, biting her lower lip the way Anya sometimes did when she was thinking. She leaned forward towards Anya, placing her hands on her knees, supporting her upper body. "What has your aunt said to you about the temple?"

"Only that it's sacred, that the tribes always send pilgrims whenever their clan is nearby to show their respects."

"Has she told you anything else?"

"I... I don't know what you mean."

"Did Matreyi say anything that might have led to your display earlier?" Her expression was serious, her eyes intense.

"What? No, I just can't help myself when I get excited about something that pops up in my head." Anya was worried now. "I'm sorry, I didn't mean to upset anyone."

Pramiti leaned back, once again biting her lip. "Before you came here, what else did you know about this place?"

"That it's where she gets her books from." Anya smiled in reflex at the thought.

"What has she said about our books?" Pramiti's tone was different somehow. Less aggressive, the hard edge had gone, replaced with a softer curiosity.

Anya was thrown. She searched her mind for anything significant. "I don't know. She said that they, I mean you, like to lend them to the tribe, because it's important that some of us can read and write." A thought occurred to Anya. "She did say that there weren't many from before The Fall."

Pramiti fixed her with a serious look. "In fact, there are none," she said flatly.

Anya recoiled in shock. "What? Why not? There must be some," she insisted. How could they have kept nothing from a whole world of books?

Pramiti did not answer immediately. She looked over Anya's shoulder, nodding once in acknowledgment of some signal Anya could not see. She breathed in deeply, exhaling through pursed lips in a deliberate fashion. "We don't have any books from before The Fall because the first to inhabit this island had fled here to escape certain death in the world outside." She licked her lips. "They came with the clothes on their back and children in their arms and nothing else, keeping one step ahead of the devastation."

"We don't even think they knew these mountains would be safe. Why would they? No-where else was." Pramiti hesitated, looking uncomfortable. "We have books, records from those early days that say they were saved by the Gods. The language is quite old, and open to interpretation, but they say that They spoke with them, and Their servants gave them seeds that would protect them. They planted those seeds around this island and they are still there today."

"The gaganwa trees?" Anya gasped. "But how is that possible? The gaganwa fruit give no seeds, not any of them along the whole route of the elks' migration. It's a great mystery how they came to be - why there are so many throughout the mountains. Ghandarva Ujesh even has a story about it." She smirked. "He says that they grew from the droppings of The Great Elk - he's our clan's totem, you know - and that's why there are long lines of them wherever the herd roam."

"Well, be that as it may," Pramiti said. "We have no more seeds to plant, and so we take the greatest care of our gaganwa trees." She sighed. "Our predecessors took their experiences very seriously and the shrine to the Gods was the first part of the temple to be built, the first permanent structure on this island. So, our shrine may be small, but it is very definitely not just for pilgrims."

"But, you are right." Bibek said as he circled the table from behind, seating himself to Anya's left. "The primary purpose of the temple isn't the worship of the Gods."

Anya held her breath until Bibek continued, "It exists to preserve as much as possible of what came before The Fall. The early monks spent their entire lives recording their own knowledge and experiences, writing all day, every day to try to preserve some of what would have been lost. What they didn't have time to write they passed on to their children, who in turn wrote down what they had been told." He sighed. "They sacrificed themselves in memory of a world that had gone."

Anya was wide-eyed. "So, all the books you have *were* written by monks."

Pramiti nodded. "They must have rubbed their fingers raw in their work. They wrote so much in such a short time, but inevitably they could not write it all, and so the most recent works are considered the least accurate, having been written by the second or even third generation." She shook her head. "Most of what we do here today is preserving the volumes they created, sometimes reproducing them in full. Some of the early writing was not very legible. A victim of their sense of urgency, I suppose."

"There are new books written," Bibek said. "Mostly about the mountains and the life that's found here. Sometimes we write books of philosophical ideas, or record our thoughts and conjecture about the world before The Fall." He chuckled. "Navel gazing, mainly. It's frustrating, knowing that our information is so limited, that there is so much that we've lost—"

"Couldn't someone go out and get it?" said Anya.

"What do you mean?" Bibek looked puzzled.

"Why not go out of the mountains and bring back the books that must still be out there?"

"Some have," said Pramiti darkly. "None returned."

"'Death walks abroad'," quoted Bibek.

"Pay no attention to our esteemed Acharya," said Pramiti with a roll of her eyes. "That's a phrase we find a lot in the older works here. Some of our number use it like a mantra." She looked mildly embarrassed. "It's sort of a joke, a catchy phrase that you hear a lot around our community."

"But what does it mean?"

"There are differing opinions on that, but most likely it merely refers to the death that came to the world outside of the Yanubas," Pramiti said. "Literally, it is death to leave these mountains."

An eerie cold poured itself down Anya's spine and she shivered. The thought of every living person being confined to the mountains forever, appalled her. Even though she loved her home, and had never thought to leave, she had always assumed that it was at least possible. To hear that chance denied to her, to every last human in all of creation was like the death of a dream on waking.

"I think we can let Matreyi in now?" Bibek directed his question at Pramiti, raising an eyebrow.

"Yes, of course," said Pramiti. Bibek speedily gained his feet. He opened the door and very soon Matreyi was sat beside Anya, looking in her eyes for answers to questions she had no words to express.

"I'm alright," Anya said. She looked at the two monks, but they gave no indication that she needed permission from them for anything. "They told me what they do here. What they really do." She paused. "You knew." It was not a question.

"Yes, dear, but I wasn't at liberty to tell you," she sighed. "I'm sorry, Anya." Matreyi gathered her close, claiming comfort for herself more than for her niece.

The monks had shown Anya their vaults. Behind one section of shelves, which opened into the library like a door, there was a set of rough steps leading down into the rock of the island. Below was a large space devoted to the rest of their collection, with vaulted arches carved directly from the stone helping to support the weight of the temple above.

She had been permitted one last look at whatever books she chose, and she moved carefully around the whole room, not wanting to miss a single volume. As she was scanning their spines, basking in the titles, she found one named 'A True History of the Attack on Temple Isle'. Anya stared at it in surprise. Grasping hold of it and taking it to a waiting table, she moved the lantern closer, the better to see what lay inside.

The language was stilted to Anya's tastes, but there was a rhythm to it that one could adjust to. She opened it at random and read.

> And our foes didst stand on the shores of the lake, gathering unto themselves their power. Their chains didst tighten about their hostage, and from him they tore a scream that floated to us across the water. A light too bright to behold didst form in the hands of one of their number and he didst cast it, as an arrow at our dwelling.
>
> We feared our doom had come, but at the last, their magic vanished, crackling in a most fearsome rage about us as though a shield invisible didst protect us. We watched, most fascinated and afeared as the grass and plants around the wizards blackened and died. The wild energies used were seized from the world around them, and thus stolen, the world around them died.
>
> We since have determined this: That energy is held in all life and that it is possible - by force of will or some method unknown to us - to extract this energy and form it into weapons for use against—

Anya finally tore her eyes away from the pages. Breathing heavily, she swallowed, attempting to wet her suddenly parched throat, but her mouth was dry with fear. Surely these 'wizards' were the warlocks from Ujesh's stories? The monks had been attacked by them, but something - it must have been the Gods - had protected them and their island. She felt repulsed, sullied by the act of reading the passage.

Her clan's most important teaching was that magic was banned by the Gods, and here was a book that described it being used, that even attempted to understand it. The Protector should be informed, she thought. After all, it was his duty to eliminate any remnant or taint of magic left behind after the Gods' sacrifice. She closed the book and left it where it lay on the table, not wanted to touch it any further and left, hoping to find Matreyi. Her aunt would know what to do. She would make things better.

They were leaving now. Matreyi had promised her that she would discuss the contents of the book with Anya's father, and he would most likely take the issue to the elders. She had calmed Anya by reminding her that knowing of something was not forbidden. No magic had been used, and no laws had been broken.

Anya had been required to swear an oath in the shrine to never reveal the secrets the monks had told her. They had indicated that there had never been anyone so young who had taken the vow, that it was a great responsibility to be entrusted with their confidence.

She was thoughtful as she said her goodbyes to Pramiti. Bibek accompanied them as a courtesy and took up position in the middle of their boat, manning the oars. He was clearly well-used to rowing and they made good time at his easy rhythm. Anya was relaxing against Matreyi, enjoying the sun on her face when her reverie was interrupted by the echo of a scream across the water.

Blinking in confusion, Anya first looked up to see Bibek, who had twisted in his seat, urgently search the shore over her shoulder. Again, and unmistakable came another cry. Bibek immediately changed direction, aiming for a point to the left of where they had been heading, his strokes rapid and strong. Anya could feel the angle of the boat change with every draw of the oars through the liquid of the lake.

They rapidly left the others behind as they powered to the shore. Finding a natural mooring, Bibek jumped out without hesitation, wrapping the boat's rope around a wooden stump, almost made for the purpose.

"Stay here," he instructed. "Be ready to untie the boat if I give the signal."

He set off in the direction of the continued screaming, and despite his order, Anya leaped out of the boat after him.

"Anya! Come back," Matreyi called, but she ignored her.

As she made to follow Bibek, Anya cast a guilty glance behind her and saw that her aunt was now also scrambling from the small vessel. Anya kept a slight distance between herself and Bibek, whose attention was entirely focussed on what lay ahead. She did not want to disturb him, nor did she want him to send her back. Such was Bibek's pace, preventing the gap from stretching soon became her greater concern.

The monk disappeared into a copse of trees and Anya, worried she would lose him, plunged in after. She looked around, hoping to see even a fleeting glance of movement to indicate where he had gone, but there was nothing besides the screams of terror hanging in the air. As she wavered with indecision, Matreyi, at last, caught hold of her.

"Must you always be so headstrong, child," she said.

"I can't see him through the trees!" Anya said, frantically.

Matreyi looked down at their feet. "A path, young one." She pointed at the forest floor.

Not much more than the smallest of animal trails, it ran off in the general direction of the cries. Without waiting for approval, Anya raced off once again, twigs and leaves slapping her face as she ran. She kept her eyes on the ground, not wanting to catch her foot on a root or other obstacle in her rush and so shot out some distance into a clearing before she had realised the tree cover had ended.

Matreyi called out, "Anya, look!"

Anya raised her eyes and saw Bibek, a woman draped over one shoulder, being pursued by a huge lumbering creature. It was man-shaped with dirty greyish-brown skin, but larger than a man by more than a third, and three times as wide. Rolls of fat rippled over its middle, but its arms were corded knots of muscle. Great plate-sized hands reached reflexively with each step, their worn and broken claws ready to rip flesh and bone. Its head was almost comically small, given the dimensions of the creature, topped with scrubby hair and dominated by a gaping maw of solid teeth. It was an Ogre[9].

Anya stood, gaping at the sight, a rising fear rooting her to the spot.

"Run!" Bibek bellowed at them, his voice full of a power and authority that only terror can grant. Freed from her paralysis, Anya ran.

They bolted to the right, in the direction that Bibek was heading and rapidly closed on a wall of trees that Anya desperately hoped would hinder the monster behind them. She risked glimpsing over her shoulder and saw that the gap between Bibek at the rear and the Ogre had increased. To

[9] Ogres are a race of enormous bipeds found in mountain foothills throughout Sansara. They are much larger than a human and possessed of great strength, being able to break a horse's spine with only its hands. They have their own tongue, though it has been known for them to speak the languages of men. They are considered by most to be stupid, but can exhibit surprising cunning. Beware the Ogre. "Life in the Yanuba mountains".

Anya's horrified mind, the lumbering brute was moving unnaturally, as though its movements were being orchestrated by another. She noticed that there was a large, bloodless gash in its head, and supposed that might be the reason. However, no matter the peculiarity of its gait, its long strides still ate up the distance.

Worried about blundering into the trees they were running through, Anya tore her eyes away and faced forward, seeking any form of safety ahead. She spied a gap in the undergrowth and darted towards it, again checking to see the progress of her companions. She saw the crashing monstrosity snapping branches with ease as it chased them, rather than swerve in its direct pursuit of its prey. The sight was shocking to Anya, she had never imagined anything could be so powerful, so relentless. She could see that Bibek was tiring, the creature now gaining on him and felt hopelessness overcome her.

"Keep going Anya!" Matreyi shouted amongst great gulps of air. Seeing no alternative, she continued her frantic scramble to escape.

On they ran. Anya's legs were burning, and her lungs were on fire. She almost stumbled, but managed to keep upright and plunge on in her unending flight, ripping her clothes and skin on the scrubby growth lining the forest floor. She heard a cry and a thud behind her, and turning her head realised that Matreyi had fallen. Without hesitation, she stopped and headed back to help. She could see Bibek, struggling, ashen-faced with his burden, but steadfast in his determination to save the woman he carried, despite the doom that would inevitably catch them all.

Anya reached Matreyi and grabbed her arm with both hands, using all her weight to help Matreyi to her feet. Together they loped onward. Shortly after, the trees thinned and stopped. Stumps were visible, and the ground began to slope downward towards a slight valley. As the ground began to fall away, Anya saw a settlement. It was positioned on a mountain stream, and protected by a wooden palisade. In echo of the temple, surrounding the defensive wall was a ring of gaganwa trees.

A loud screaming assaulted Anya's ears. She feared the worst until she realised the sound was coming from her own mouth as she incoherently yelled to indicate the village below. Her heart leaped into her mouth as she risked a backward glance and saw the Ogre bearing down on Bibek, almost within reach as they began to feel the meagre benefit of the slope. He could not hope to reach the defensive walls in time.

Tears were now streaming down her face. For tragedy to strike just as salvation appeared ahead of them was unbearable. Anya wept at the hopelessness of the monk's plight, any moment expecting the unwanted sounds of his demise. On they stumbled, and still they somehow continued to avoid their fate. They were within a long sprint of the walls. Anya again looked back. The Ogre was slowing! She blinked in an effort to banish the tears, trying to understand what she could not believe her eyes were telling her.

The huge creature was faltering. No longer running, it spasmed as if in pain, though no expression showed on its face. At last it stopped. Anya could see its leg twitching, as though the monster's commands were no longer reaching its extremities, its body refusing to obey. For a long moment, it stood swaying, convulsions rippling along its length, until as though felled by a hunter's axe, it crashed to the ground and lay still.

Anya involuntarily mimicked the Ogre, and fell to her knees, exhaustion and relief combined in renewed floods of tears, removing what little strength she had left. Matreyi collapsed beside her, embracing her niece tightly, conveying via physical interaction what she had no words and no breath to express.

Bibek lowered the woman he had carried to her feet. He supported her as she stood on one leg, and Anya could see that her left thigh was bloodied from an unpleasant wound, presumably inflicted by the monster still lying uncomfortably close to them. Anya wiped her eyes and forced herself to look closely at the Ogre's body, checking for signs of life, breathing or movement. She saw none, but almost retched at the vile stench that rolled off the corpse, enveloping them. It smelled putrid, like badly preserved meat that attracted flies. Reassured that it was dead, she dropped her head in relief. Their ordeal was over.

They had been helped into the settlement by its occupants, who had recoiled at the sight of the Ogre. Anya was seated next to Matreyi in a room used to prepare food, and they had all been given a warm mug of spiced drink unknown to her. She swallowed and coughed, feeling its warming fluid settle inside her. She refocussed her attention on Bibek as he spoke

"This village is where our families stay," said Bibek. "There is not enough space on our island and unfortunately, it is not what the clans expect from their monks. It is hardly traditional." Anya thought she heard a slight scorn in his voice.

The day was drawing towards evening, and worried about the journey ahead of them, Anya said, "Aunt Matreyi, we had better be leaving now, otherwise it will be dark as we travel." The thought of ascending to the top of the falls in dwindling light held little appeal.

"I've sent word to the rest of your clan to go on," Bibek reassured her. "They know something of our encounter and we will escort you back tomorrow. Meanwhile, you should eat, bread is baking and will be ready shortly." A woman entered, and Bibek rose to speak with her.

The scent of baking had been rising for some while. Anya could almost taste the smell of the dough cooking, its wonderful aroma was so rich that, in her hunger she imagined biting chunks of bread from the air. She drank some more as she considered the community around them, unknown to all her clansfolk. She looked sharply at her aunt, who was talking familiarly with one of the village women, her attention not on Anya. Of course Matreyi had known about the settlement. Anya wondered what else she had not told her. She frowned, feeling hurt.

Another woman entered, carrying a wooden platter of fresh bread, some salted meat and a pot containing honey. Anya realised she was ravenous and was preparing to pounce on the food when Bibek interrupted. "I'm sorry, but I'll be back. There is something wrong with Tanu."

Tanu was the name of the woman Bibek had rescued from the Ogre. Immediately forgetting her hunger, Anya stood and followed in Bibek's wake through a door, across another room to wooden steps that led to an upper floor. Here there were three doors leading off a short corridor. Bibek passed through the first at the top of the stairs. Anya lingered in the doorway, not so sure of herself as to enter with him.

Inside was a chamber with a sleeping mattress that rested on a raised wooden frame, keeping it off the floor. Appearing pale and wan, her breathing shallow, Tanu lay on this contraption, covered in blankets and furs, despite the warmth of the season. A man sat next to her, perched on a three-legged stool, holding the woman's arm by the wrist in one hand. He looked up as Bibek entered.

"I don't understand it. The wound is not so serious, but she is fading." He held his hands up, helplessly. "It is as though her life is draining out of her somehow."

He reached forward and rolled back a section of the covers. Anya craned her neck to see that Tanu's leg had been cleaned, the gouge in the flesh was not bleeding, in fact it looked too dry to Anya's eyes, but there was a grey pallor to her skin that was a deeper reflection of the lack of colour in her face.

Matreyi arrived behind Anya, and gave a sharp intake of breath as she saw the woman laid out before them. "Anya, back downstairs," she said. "You must be hungry. Eat."

Dismissed, Anya set off back down the stairs to wait.

Anya woke with a start from her dream. In it, Anya had once again climbed the stairs and peered into Tanu's room, but the figure laid out on the bed had been hers. Matreyi had been at her side, but when she turned her head to the door, her face had been a skull. Anya shivered to dislodge the disquiet gripping her stomach.

After waiting for long hours, it had grown late, and she and her aunt had been taken to another home and given beds to sleep in. The unfamiliarity of the beds had made sleep difficult to come by, but once achieved, Anya had been dead to the world.

She slid out of bed and hastily dressed. She found there was a brush on the window sill, which she seized and began forcefully removing the knots from her hair. Alongside the brush, there was a metal bowl and water-filled jug. Anya hastily splashed some on her face, making a half-hearted attempt to dry it using her sleeve, before quietly heading downstairs.

The house was silent, Anya walked on tip-toes to avoid disturbing anyone, she knew it was unusual for her aunt to sleep late, but Matreyi may have needed the rest after the trials of the previous day. Imagining herself to be the only one up, she was surprised when she entered the kitchen to find Matreyi sat with Bibek, both looking tired, neither speaking.

Disconcerted at their demeanour, Anya said, "Tanu?"

Bibek looked stony-faced and Matreyi lowered her head. Anya could feel tears welling up in her eyes, and rushed forwards, into Matreyi's soft embrace.

"How is that possible?" she asked when she was again able to speak. "I've seen worse injuries in the clan heal with no real problems."

"We don't know," said Bibek, his voice sounding harsh. "Her wound was cleaned, but it never even began to heal." His gaze was fixed on the fireplace, as though its stones could provide meaning. "She was young and healthy. It was as though she just gave up."

"Was it an illness then?" Anya said. "Sometimes a wound can get angry, and the heat of it can spread throughout the body, burning so fiercely that they die." She felt as though she had to know why, that she must probe further until this wrong thing felt right to her.

"She was cold, not hot." Bibek screwed up his face and looked away from them. "She was cold as death."

"People die, little one" said Matreyi. Anya did not protest the endearment. "Sometimes, we just die."

The whole village followed the cart, accompanying Tanu on her final journey. Anya walked with Matreyi and Bibek near the front of the procession, feeling uncomfortable, undeserving of her place of honour near the wagon. She glanced around, sure that there must be angry, jealous looks being cast their way, but whenever she did, all heads were bowed in grief. No-one took any note of the interloper, the tribal girl among them. She was insignificant compared to their loss.

A shout went up and the gates began to open, granting them leave from the confines of the walled community. At the threshold, the cart stopped and the whole village looked to Bibek.

"Today we say goodbye to Tanu, who was beloved of our community." Despite the strength of his voice, Anya could feel the emotion pulsing beneath, giving further depth and meaning to his words. "Thank your Gods that she has touched our lives. Remember her in your hearts and minds, in the life she led and not as this empty shell." He gestured at the body, lying naked on the wagon. His voice faltered. "Not as this empty shell. She is not there."

They stood silently for an ever-lengthening time, each lost in their own thoughts. Anya peeked through her almost-closed eyes to see what everyone else was doing, gently cursing herself for wondering how long they would have to stay like this.

At last, the crowd began to disperse, most heading back into the village to continue with their own lives, their own commemoration of another's now complete. Anya looked up to see her aunt and Bibek sharing an embrace. Matreyi held out an arm and Anya joined them, grateful to share their contact and for the life they still had to live.

Satisfied that all who wanted to escort her body to the Dakhma[10] were present, they set off once again. Bibek continued with them, and as Matreyi accompanied Bibek, Anya followed in their wake, once again feeling awkward and out of place, an intruder to private sorrow.

Dakhma were not unknown to Anya, she had seen one once, when her clan's migration had passed close to the perches of the Vulture clan. Though unrealistic for clan Elk, whose constant movement resulted in the more practical adoption of any area of exposed rock for burial, they represented a permanent, sacred location for the disposal of bodies where burial in the ground was impossible due to rock or frozen ground, both of which were a challenge in the Yanuba mountains.

---

[10] Dakhma are generally circular stone constructions used by some mountain cultures for the practice of excarnation, or sky burial, where a body is left to be eaten by scavengers, particularly carrion birds. The structure presents a flat area, raised from the ground, where bodies are placed for nature to take its course. "Customs of the Tharom Tribe, Third Edition."

They circled the settlement, heading for higher ground some distance beyond the ring of gaganwa trees. Anya could see the raised structure at the top of some simple steps, carved into the rock of the hill. It was modest compared to clan Vulture's Dakhma, not even twice a man's height from side to side. Anya wondered what they would do if several of their community died at once, perhaps from some invisible illness that could spread from one to another, the space scarcely enough to place more than three bodies at once. The thought of a disease that could pass between people made Anya slow her pace, increasing the distance between her and the corpse leading the way.

She glanced at the shell that had been Tanu, shame warming her cheeks at her irreverent reflections. As Anya moved her gaze away once again, something in the back of her mind rebelled, and she looked once more at the body. She could see nothing amiss at first, but as she watched, thought she saw a finger move. A chill rippled through Anya as the hair on her arms and neck rose and she gasped.

Matreyi stopped and turned to look quizzically at Anya, who pointed wordlessly at where Tanu's whole leg was clearly twitching. Others had also noticed, and a ripple of sharply taken breath passed through the small group, causing the man drawing the small cart to halt and look around for the cause of the rising commotion. He saw Tanu raise her head and let the handles of the cart go in his surprise, causing it to tip away from him.

The crowd stared, stupefied by what they were witnessing as Tanu slid down to rest on her feet, propped upright by the angle of the cart. She shakily pushed herself away from the wagon and stood.

"Tanu!" cried one of the villagers - a relative, possibly the mother, thought Anya - who rushed to embrace the naked woman standing before them, delirious with happiness at this turn of events.

Anya screwed up her face, assaulted by feelings of disgust and revulsion, she could sense bile rising in her throat. Too much was wrong here, she wanted to scream in wordless warning, but could not give voice to the ominous instinct within. Anya ran to her aunt and grabbed her arm.

"This isn't right," she whispered urgently through teeth clenched to contain the nausea building inside her. "Can we leave? Please can we leave?"

Matreyi turned to Anya, her eyes wide, mouth gaping with shock. Anya, knowing something dreadful was about to happen, had returned her eyes to Tanu and the woman holding her tight. Tanu's arms left her sides and moved as though to return the embrace, but instead of a loving caress, they gripped the other woman's upper arms, holding her in place as she opened her eyes, revealing not the warm colour of living orbs, but the cold pale eyes of the dead. The corpse's head moved close and sank its teeth into the older woman's neck.

Panic seized them all. Most of the mourners broke and ran back towards the safety of the enclosed village. The man who had been hauling the cart slipped as he tried to step back away from the horror unfolding before them, slipping and falling into a sitting position. For a moment he could only sit there, looking darkly comical as his thrusting legs failed to gain purchase on the rocky ground beneath him. Anya tugged on Matreyi desperately, pulling her away from the unreal butchery they were witness to.

Having sated whatever hunger drove it to murder, the dead thing let go of its victim, who dropped to her knees, her life-blood spraying it red in beating pulses of gore, driven by the faltering rhythm of her heart. It turned and regarded those who still remained with its milky-white deathly gaze. Its mouth was still open, bits of flesh hanging from its teeth, dripping wetly down its chin and chest.

It took a shambling step towards them. Anya was facing the abomination, walking backwards as she pulled her aunt by the arm and so did not see the ridge of hard earth behind her. She tripped, the strength of the unexpected contact forcing her to let go of Matreyi and she sprawled on the ground. Unable to take her eyes off the advancing killer, she struggled to rise and saw Matreyi step between her and Tanu.

"Aunt!" Anya cried in protest.

Matreyi stood firm, facing the naked horror. "Get up, child," she said. Her voice was quiet, but filled with determination.

Tanu's arm raised high, poised ready to strike. Anya could see the fingers curl like talons, readying the nails to rip into Matreyi's flesh. Anya screamed with anguish, knowing the unavoidable conclusion to come. The hand descended, beginning its attack when Tanu's shoulder disintegrated, and the arm, now severed, tumbled bloodlessly to the ground.

Matreyi spun and collected Anya bodily, assisting her as she scrambled to her feet. Anya, dumbfounded, saw a villager standing behind Tanu, a sword held clumsily in both hands, desperation and need forging his fear into a weapon sharper than the blade in his hands. The living corpse showed no reaction, other than to turn to meet its assailant. Faced with the implacable visage of death itself, he dropped the steel he held and fled.

Now on her feet and no longer the focus of the dead thing's attention, the spell of attraction that had captivated her eyes was broken. Anya turned her back on the monster and with Matreyi, ran as fast as she could, only glancing back to ensure the distance they had created was sufficient for their safety. Bibek ran alongside, watching them with concern, until, apparently satisfied they were safe, he outpaced them back to the settlement. Finally, as Anya and her aunt approached the shadow of the village palisade, with lungs burning once again from exertion, they slowed and checked more closely the progress of the shuffling form pursuing them.

Tanu – the thing that had been Tanu, Anya reminded herself – continued towards them, its steps jerky and awkward. It did not run, merely continuing at the same unhurried pace, not rapid but inexorable. Anya knew it would continue without the requirement of rest until it had destroyed them all. Something about it was familiar to her, but what could it be, this was something so far from anything she had experienced before? She firmly hoped it had no way of scaling the wall of wood surrounding the settlement.

Satisfied for the moment of their safety, Anya prepared to enter the village when the lone figure, naked and terrible, began to falter. Abruptly, it fell as though its legs no longer functioned, its momentum bringing it to the ground. Anya watched as it raised its head once again to face her. She could see that its mouth was hanging limply open at a peculiar angle, it must have been broken in the fall. The thing had not tried, or been able to protect itself as it fell. Its one arm still worked to grip the grass, dragging it forwards, driven by an unknowable compulsion to hunt and destroy the living. At last it stopped, fingers twitching feebly until it moved no more.

Anya took a step towards it, drawn to know, to understand what it was they had faced. Her breath still rasped in her throat, and she swallowed in an attempt to wet her mouth, which had been rendered dry by her terrified panting.

She felt a hand on her arm. "Anya," said Matreyi. Thought quiet, her voice was intense. Matreyi had never been in the habit of telling Anya what she should do, and she did not do that now. There was, however, an unmistakable caution in that single spoken word.

"I have to know what that was," said Anya. "I have to understand."

Seeing some men, led by Bibek, come running from the village with swords strapped to their belts, Anya beckoned them and pointed to where the body of Tanu lay, motionless. They moved purposefully in the direction she indicated, Anya following them closely. They slowed as they neared the still form, the brutal, vivid scenes they had witnessed demanded caution and reduced their speed as surely as a winter snowdrift. They approached with extreme care.

There was no indication of life from Tanu's body, but what difference did that make? Anya's mind was beginning to catch up with the horrors she had seen, and she flinched with every step, in anticipation of sudden movement from the corpse. At last they were within sword's reach of the body. Bibek prodded Tanu's shoulder, piercing the skin, but evoking no reaction. He grunted, perhaps realising as Anya did, that the test had proved nothing.

After a brief discussion with the other men, Bibek and the others managed to turn the body over using their weapons. The cadaver flopped onto its back, its eyes open but unmoving. Dirt had caked in the gore still hanging from its teeth and on its breasts, absorbed in the blood of its prey.

The men entered into discussion, forgetting Anya, who after a moment's hesitation, darted forward to place her hand on Tanu's neck. The skin was cold as the grave and not the slightest heart-beat could be felt. There was no doubt left in Anya's mind. They had been attacked by the dead.

Hero's Welcome

Rough hands grabbed Anya by the shoulders, pulling her fiercely away from the body. Anya, startled, turned to see Bibek, scowling.

"Stay away from her, foolish girl." Bibek was flushed and Anya could see the undercurrent of fear driving his actions. She tried to respond, but Bibek cut her off. "You can't be sure that she won't attack again!"

"Bibek." There was protective warning in Matreyi's voice. "This child is headstrong, yes." She turned to Anya, and her concerned face warmed. "But foolish, rarely. Listen to what she has to say."

All eyes turned to Anya and, unused to the attention, she froze momentarily. "Uh," she started unsuccessfully. She swallowed, gathering her wits, and continued. "I don't think that is Tanu, at least not in any way that you knew her. I touched her, and she's cold." Anya shivered involuntarily, her chill a reflection of what she had felt. "You saw her die in the night. She's dead!" she said with emphasis. "She has been for hours. Something took hold of her body and used it like a puppet..."

"The dead don't get up and attack people," said Bibek.

"'Death walks abroad'," Anya quoted. "That's what you said. Well, it walks abroad no longer. It's here."

"That's just a phrase used to refer to The Fall," said Bibek. "Even I don't take it literally, though I admit, I wondered if—"

"Where is it from?" asked Anya. "Originally, I mean?"

"It's hard to tell." Bibek shifted his feet uncomfortably. He opened his mouth as if to say more, but if so, the desire passed.

Matreyi was watching him closely. "Bibek," she said. "What is it you aren't saying?"

Bibek looked at Matreyi thoughtfully, glancing briefly at Anya. He began to put his arm around Matreyi's shoulders, his body leaning away from her niece, but she shrugged him off, saying, "Don't think to exclude Anya from this." Her demeanour brooked no argument.

Bibek nodded, though he looked uncomfortable. He indicated with a gesture that they should wait, before entering into conversation with the other men. At his direction, some set off, giving the body lying near a wide berth on their way in the direction of the Dakhma, while the two that were left stood guard over Tanu's remains. Bibek returned his attention to the women, both young and old and guided them away from the other men.

"There are gaps in our library. I don't mean that the first of our order didn't record everything they wanted to." Bibek sighed. "I mean, there are references to books that we no longer have and books where pages have been removed - not torn out, but neatly cut using a sharp implement. The earliest books we have that use the phrase seem to be repeating something that originates elsewhere, presumably in those we have lost."

"Why would anyone remove the pages?" Anya was horrified at the thought of anyone desecrating a book.

"That is a fine question," said Bibek. "It is one we have asked ourselves many times, but with no answer forthcoming." He held up a finger to them, but his eyes held Anya's. "Not everyone is aware of these missing volumes. Our purpose has always been to record knowledge and pass it down. To reveal it would be disheartening, some might question our purpose. I must have your word not to repeat what I have told you."

They nodded their agreement. Bibek said, "Now I must see to the bodies." He turned and moved back to the men standing watch over Tanu.

"What will you do with them?" Anya asked, a panicky edge to her voice.

"Sky burial, as is customary," he said. "Though I think we may dispense with the procession."

Anya felt terribly unsettled. There was something she could not identify, a dread certainty of the danger not having passed fully. She tugged on Matreyi's sleeve and said, "Aunt, they must burn them. I can't say why, but I know they need to burn the bodies. Please, can you get him to see?"

Matreyi looked questioningly into Anya's eyes, as though seeking to see into her head, to discover directly what it was that Anya could not put into words. Apparently satisfied with what she saw, Matreyi nodded and walked to join Bibek, saying something to him in a low voice, Anya trailing too far behind to hear.

"Do you think that's necessary?" he asked. "The whole village will be unsettled, without also changing our method of burial. It would be against our custom."

"Funeral pyres are not unheard of," Matreyi countered. "Mountain custom is pragmatic. It may be that sky burial became the usual method because it requires no wood, which can be scarce in the higher parts of the Yanuba." She looked around. "Not so here."

Bibek frowned, looking rebellious for a moment, before finally nodding his agreement.

"Will you burn the Ogre too?" asked Anya, gripping Bibek's sleeve tightly.

"Why not?" Bibek said sardonically, his face set with grim determination. "The more the merrier."

The atmosphere was sombre as they prepared to take their leave of the village. Matreyi's subdued farewells were part goodbye, part condolence. Anya herself had been hugged so often and squeezed so tightly, she felt like a walking outlet for their grief. Grief she was not sure she could feel. Bibek lingered in his embrace with Matreyi and Anya almost imagined moisture in his eyes as they parted. They thanked the villagers for their hospitality and left, accompanied by two monks who were dressed in their usual brown robes, but Anya had seen the flash of a scabbard and knew that underneath they wore swords at their belts.

As they walked, Anya looked back to see smoke rising on the far side of the settlement from the hastily assembled funeral pyre. A detached part of her mind noted that dry older wood would have burned more cleanly than the green timber they had used from freshly felled trees. She tried not to smell the nauseatingly sweet, meaty fragrance on the air, which was mingled unpleasantly with the scent of pine and ash.

For a long time, nobody spoke a word, each absorbed in their own thoughts. Anya felt exposed away from the protection afforded by the palisade, at great risk of attack. She was grateful for the open expanse of grass around them as they skirted the lake, heading for the path that would take them to the top of the falls, she could see nowhere for an assailant to hide. Even so, she started more than once at an unidentified sound or movement.

The day was overcast, the mist and dampness from the falls was a fitting counterpoint to their gloom. The small party veered to the left to head for the beginning of the trail up the cliff and Anya was glad to move away from the murky air around the waterfall. Shadows lurked there in the fog, moving in an unpleasant, sinuous manner, playing tricks on the mind. She shivered.

There was brief conversation as they prepared to climb. The monks would go first and last, flanking them for protection. Anya walked ahead of her aunt, feeling anxious and trapped, with no options but to continue forward, or to go back. She concentrated on her feet and the rocky wall to her left and after an eternity, they reached the top of their climb, close to the lip of the falls.

In need of a rest, they sat with their backs to a tree and shared some bread they had been given for the journey. As she ate, Anya felt some tentative shoots of optimism begin to emerge in her stomach, settling her frayed nerves. She looked at her beloved aunt, who was with her when she needed her and leaned in to her, resting her head on Matreyi's bosom.

Matreyi draped her arms comfortably around her niece and kissed the top of her head. After a companionable silence, Anya at last gave voice to her thoughts. "Aunt Matreyi, you've made a lot of friends at the temple and its village." She moistened her lips with her tongue. "It suits you, being there. Why didn't you choose to become a monk?"

When no reply was immediately forthcoming, Anya propped herself up in order to silently question Matreyi. Her aunt was looking into the distance where the spray from the waterfall climbed into view, but she shifted her gaze to meet Anya's eyes.

"I would have." Her tone was reflective, sounding sad to Anya's ears. "I wanted to, but my departure would have had serious consequences for your father's standing within the clan." She smiled wanly. "I don't think your mother would have ever forgiven me."

"But you would have been happy," said Anya.

"Perhaps." Matreyi again looked distant. Anya felt certain she was imagining her life as it could have been. Her aunt closed her eyes, as though unconsciously trying to avoid the images from her mind's eye. A cruel trick, thought Anya, as they would be strengthened with the shutting out of the real world around them.

Matreyi swallowed. "Perhaps," she repeated. Her smile deepened, and she opened her eyes to look fondly on Anya. "Though, if I had, I would not have had the pleasure of sharing in your childhood, and for that, I would not have changed a thing."

In that instant, Matreyi's love was for her was palpable, and Anya basked in its warmth. She settled closely to her aunt once more, wishing this moment would last forever.

The return journey was uneventful. They again followed the river for much of the way, this time walking against the flow. Anya could almost feel it pulling on them in an attempt to persuade them to go back. She would be pleased to see Amman and her family again, but she could not savour the expectation, the prospect of returning held less flavour to her than the richness they left behind.

Occasionally Anya would notice a gaganwa tree. They now stood out in her vision in ways they never had previously, as though what she had learned about them made them more significant to her eyes. They truly were widespread, their ripening fruits dangling with invitation. She realised she had always taken them for granted, their ubiquity had shielded them from her scrutiny like magic. Anya shivered. Perhaps it was magic, she thought.

At last they left the river, climbing a long rise that led to the location of their camp. As they crested the hill, they saw the clan busying themselves in preparation to move on. All the yurts had been dismantled, they were being placed into carrying sacks and wrapped up in readiness. The cart was almost full with those objects too bulky or heavy to carry. Anya scanned the clan for her family, finding them quickly, her mother presiding over their arrangements with a watchful eye.

Anya waved, catching her mother's attention. Neeta acknowledged their arrival with a barely noticeable inclination of her head, immediately returning her focus to the task at hand. A poor greeting, Anya thought, considering the events they had endured. Her mood immediately dipped. How typical of her mother to ignore her in favour of some unimportant, menial task. She scowled briefly, before tramping the remainder of the distance between them.

When they had reached them, Neeta bowed to the monks, as was considered proper, thanking them for the care they had shown her family. She offered them her Uphara[11] as a gift, which they refused in keeping with ages-long custom. They accepted water, and after exchanging unremarkable pleasantries, they left. One of them smiled at Anya, winking as they set off.

"Well, you took your time," Neeta said. She looked Anya up and down before giving her the briefest of hugs. "You seem to be in one piece, though why you would set off into the woods by yourself is beyond me."

"There was a scream— " Anya began.

"They said you got yourselves cut off from the rest of our clan." Neeta looked unfavourably at Matreyi. "What was it?" she asked, not waiting for an answer. "Wolves?"

Matreyi silently regarded her sister while Anya again attempted to speak. "No, it w— "

Neeta interrupted again. "Well, you had a nice adventure, I suppose, but while you were tarrying, the herd have moved unexpectedly. Come and help gather our things, we will be leaving soon, and we don't want to have to catch up." Neeta

---

[11] It is considered polite for clansfolk to offer a gift - called an Uphara - when visited by outsiders. This is usually a wood carving, or small ornament that can be kept in a pocket or pouch, ready to present should guests arrive unexpectedly. By tradition, the gift is refused. As a result, gifts are often passed down through the generations, becoming a type of family heirloom. "Customs of the Tharom Tribe, Third Edition".

moved away to attend to their cooking tools, leaving Anya and Matreyi speechless in her wake.

"What do you suppose the world was like before The Fall?" said Anya. She was walking alongside Neeta as they followed the route the elk had chosen, watching the bobbing of the heads of the clan as they snaked off into the distance. She was struck by how similar they all looked, something before her visit to the temple that she had always taken for granted. With the exception of the elderly, all had raven black hair.

"I expect it was much as it is now." Neeta did not look at Anya, and she answered without giving the question her full attention.

Anya screwed up her face in mild exasperation. "For us maybe. I mean the world outside the Yanubas."

"What does it matter, Anya? That world is gone."

"They had settlements with thousands of people living in one place, and buildings filled just with food - they would give it away to those who wanted it, so they could spend their time making music and writing books, or even just thinking." Anya's eyes were alight with the wonder of it. "Imagine that. Being allowed, being able to spend your whole life thinking, telling everyone what it was you found out."

"You can't find anything out just by thinking." Neeta made a dismissive sound. "They had their ways, and we have our own. Our stories tell us that their ways led to their downfall. They forgot who they were and so the land forgot them."

"That depends on which of Ujesh's stories you mean," said Anya. "Doesn't he have another one that says they worshipped evil Gods and were punished?"

"Anya, I'm sure you're going somewhere with these questions."

"Well, it's just that we spend all our time following the herd, gathering food, milking our goats, or mending our tents, or any of the same things we always do." Anya felt there were possibilities bursting to break free from inside her. "What if we knew a better way? What if we stopped for a while and thought of things that would make it easier? If we did, we might have more time to think of other things to help us. Wouldn't that sort of snowball, giving us more and more time for other things? We could teach each other to write and record all these ideas and wouldn't have to rely on Ujesh and his stories."

"So, we should abandon our stories?" Neeta's voice was sharp. She looked at Anya with her eyebrows raised. "The stories that have kept us safe, protected us and carried our heritage across generations of our clan? What good is reading if it makes us forget who we are? You would do well to pay more attention to our lives here than the lives of those who are no more out there."

Neeta stopped and regarded her daughter. "It was a mistake to let Matreyi teach you to read. You would have been more content without."

With that, Neeta turned and continued without her, the hopes Anya harboured lying still and heavy in her heart.

Trials and Tribulations

"So, what do you think really happened?" said Amman.

"I told you what happened, you dimwit," said Anya. She moved her head close to his and looked into his ear. "Wait a moment, I can see the problem, you have a grub in your ear."

Amman flinched as she put her finger into his ear and wiggled it. "Got it," she said. "No wonder you didn't hear me with that in there." Anya stiffened suddenly. "Oh no!" An overblown look of mock horror on her face made Amman smile. Anya looked again into his one ear while reaching across his face to wave a hand over the other. "I can see straight through. I think that must have been acting as your brain."

Amman pushed her away and rolled his eyes. "Hilarious," he said. "You know what I mean. The dead don't attack people, they're well-known for not doing it." His face became serious. "If she attacked you, she wasn't dead, was she?"

"You're not listening." Anya could feel her temper rising. "She was cold and dead, her eyes were clouded, like a… No, not like, they were cloudy because she *was* dead."

"Couldn't it have been some kind of illness that just made her go crazy?"

"She had no heart-beat!" Anya was exasperated. "She died in the night, she'd been dead for hours." She rounded on Amman, subjecting him to the full force of her glare.

"How do you explain her reaction to having her arm cut off, or rather, her lack of one? She didn't react at all!"

"But—"

"Where was all the blood?" She pinned him with her stare.

"Alright, I get it." Amman held up his palms to calm her down, before looking sheepish. "I'll just ask one more thing before I give up. Couldn't you have been so scared, that in the confusion, you saw things differently to how they actually were?"

Anya took several deep breaths to calm herself. "I told you before, Aunt Matreyi put herself between that thing and me. She was facing it when the man hit it with the sword." Her face turned sour. "Why don't you ask her the same stupid questions you're asking me?"

Amman shifted uncomfortably, looking down at his hands as he twirled a stalk of rough vegetation in his fingers. Anya said, "I thought you'd believe me." Amman tried to speak, but Anya continued over him. "Mother won't even listen. She says I have an over-active imagination. She blames it on the books I read, says they've put strange ideas in my head, made me lose my grip on reality." She kicked at some pebbles, sending them spinning from the rock ledge they were sat on.

Anya stared at point where the stones had begun their fall to the earth below, Amman looking at her cautiously. "I believe you," he said. Her eyes were still fixed on the stone at her feet. "It just sounds..." He searched for a word. "Incredible. It sounds incredible. But if you say that's what happened, then that's what happened."

Anya's head was still lowered, her face shielded by her hair. With no warning, she turned and threw her arms around Amman, hugging him fiercely, saying nothing. He looked startled. His face became flushed and he belatedly raised his arms to return her embrace, closing his eyes and patting her back tentatively.

The elk had stopped their migration on a gentle saddle of grass higher up in the mountain range. The clan had pitched their tents on a scrubby bit of ground away from the best grazing and near to the rocks where Anya and Amman had been climbing[12]. There were challenging rock formations and deep crevices hidden among the folds of mountain stone and the pair were sweating from exertion when they reached the ground.

They had reconciled before embarking on some more climbing. Anya felt happy and relaxed, laughing at one of Amman's animal impressions when they were interrupted by a whistle above them.

"Look at the loser lovers!" Hiranjan called out. He was perched on a difficult looking section of rock, looking down at them scornfully. "All hot and sweaty. What have you been doing?" He shivered in feigned disgust. "Ugh, I dread to think."

"We're not— " began Anya.

"Yeah, who cares, anyway?" Hiranjan was rapidly descending the awkward route down, but still found the breath to cut across Anya's denial. He dropped lightly to his feet. "Who else would want you?" Despite his words, he leered at Anya and she could feel his eyes on her like a physical touch, lingering on her chest, where the thin material of her shirt clung to her breasts. They flicked briefly to her crotch. "You deserve each other."

---

[12] Rock climbing is accepted as a way of life by many in the Tharom tribe, but of all the clans, the Elk have taken it most fully as their birthright. It is common, when chores and duties allow, to find children and men of all ages scaling the many rock faces found in the Yanuba mountains. "The Clans of the Tharom".

Anya crossed her arms protectively and shrank from his penetrating gaze, too embarrassed to respond as she would normally. She felt like an animal being chosen for slaughter, not even when her mother had dressed her up in her best clothes and paraded her for inspection by suitors had she felt so keenly anyone's scrutiny. She was filled with a desire for protection and glanced at Amman, wanting him to defend her somehow from whatever it was she was feeling. Amman's cheeks were flushed, his head lowered fractionally. He regarded Hiranjan with loathing, but had not noticed the exchange between the other two.

Hiranjan turned his attention to Amman, lunging forward suddenly before stopping himself and laughing when Amman took a hasty step backwards, fearing an attack.

He spat contemptuously at their feet. "See you, losers," he said, before turning his back on them and walking off towards the camp. "I've got more important things to do than waste my time on you," he called over his shoulder. "Defender training." His pride was obvious, as was his intent to belittle them.

"What a prick," said Amman, when Hiranjan was safely out of earshot. He turned to Anya and was surprised to find her silent. "You're quiet. You'd usually have sent plenty of insults back at him." He stopped and looked intently at her. "Are you alright?"

Anya, realising that her reaction might reveal her discomfort and not wanting to discuss it, walked briskly past Amman in the direction Hiranjan had gone. Amman followed after, a puzzled expression on his face.

"He makes me so angry." Anya stomped down the slope, her hands bunched into fists by her side.

"Don't let him get to you," said Amman. "You know he just wants a reaction."

He would not understand, thought Anya. What Hiranjan had done was wrong in ways that men just could not grasp.

If women belong to men, they can do whatever they like with us and if women can never be elders, we will never have a voice with which to tell them why this is wrong. Why should I need to explain, anyway?

Anya imagined a dozen fanciful scenarios where she humiliated Hiranjan in the presence of the whole clan. "If only I was a man, I'd make him look so foolish," she said to herself.

"Just forget about him." Amman put his hand on her shoulder. "Why would you want to be a man, anyway?" he said, shyly.

"Why?" Anya was lost for words. The enormity of his ignorance was both astounding and completely predictable. Unable to articulate the myriad reasons adequately under pressure from the well of anger rising within her, she stamped her foot and screamed, "Men!" With that she turned and resumed her march down the hill. Amman followed after, shaking his head in bewilderment.

Soon, Anya threw herself down on a patch of grass overlooking the camp and began tearing up clumps with her hands. Amman cautiously lowered himself to join her while maintaining a discrete distance. From where they sat, they could see some of the Defenders drawing out loose-fitting padded tunics and plain hoods and preparing long wooden practice poles in readiness for training. Their ritual was familiar to Anya, the trainees would take some of the gear and change, while the Defenders marked out an area for their session.

A sudden thought gripped Anya, and she reached out to grab Amman by the arm. "Find Paras, quickly. I have an idea." She grinned wickedly.

Anya fidgeted in Hiranjan's baggy tunic and resisted the urge to take off the hood to wipe away her sweat.

The Defender Prabhav strode along the line of boys that Anya had infiltrated, checking their uniforms with a critical eye. When he reached her position, he paused, frowning, and fixed the feather in Hiranjan's hood with a glare. She heard him grunt and cursed herself for not removing the ridiculous thing. Feathers were earned and no student deserved to wear one.

Prabhav shrugged and moved to stand facing them all. He clapped slowly. "Line. Show. Breeze," he said. They all shifted their feet, presenting their practice spears and began their slow swing, following the beat of his hands. "Lull. Swell. Flat. Peak." The commands continued, warming them up, and they obeyed with little to fault, varying their tempo and the angle of their arc in synchronisation with each other.

Gradually, the orders became more difficult and mistakes crept in. "You, position two, that means follow your spear and turn to face behind!" Anya rolled her eyes, boys were so lazy. How could you mess up such an easy command? Several times, Prabhav barked out, admonishing students, correcting them until they could regain the synchronicity that was so important to their task. Anya grinned. Never once to her.

She saw him glance at her and smile. He shouted out further orders, each more difficult than the last, which she executed with as much precision as she could. Several times, he would have to correct the others. Never her. More and more, she found Prabhav's gaze on her, his eyes narrowed and thoughtful. What would she do when they had finished? He would discover her and what then? She should not be here, this had been a mistake.

Anya wracked her brain, trying to think of a way to escape, when she realised Prabhav had stopped issuing instructions. The students continued in their current pattern as they had been taught. She heard raised voices, seeing their instructor looking in that direction.

"I don't know who you are, but you're going to wish you'd never been born!" Anya turned and swallowed. Hiranjan was storming towards her, dressed only in his undergarments, laughter following in his wake.

"You can't interrupt a practice, Hiranjan," said Prabhav. "Where have you been and why – "

"Who are you?" Hiranjan paid no heed to his instructor and grabbed a spare practice weapon as he continued to advance on the mystery boy.

"Put that weapon down!" Prabhav shouted. Defenders were accustomed to obedience, and the lack of respect being shown him was indefensible.

Before he could intervene further, two things happened simultaneously. The boy next to her stopped his exercises and attempted to lift his hood, lowering his head to do so, while at the same time, Anya took a step back, away from Hiranjan, who was still flinging curses at her.

There was a crack. Anya's practice spear shuddered in her hands and she dropped it in surprise. She glanced to her left to see the boy next to her keel over and lie still. Prabhav rushed to the fallen boy, while Hiranjan seized Anya and ripped off he hood, drawing back his other fist to strike. Anya's long hair cascaded free, confusing Hiranjan.

"You!" he cried. Instead of striking her, Hiranjan shoved her off her feet, standing over her as though daring her to get up again. "You'll regret this, bitch. What did you do with my clothes?"

Anya stood in the centre of a circle of elders. Her mother stood near Sabir, her expression a mask of disapproval. Her father was much older than Neeta and grizzled by long exposure to their mountain climes. Their marriage had been arranged many years ago and had been successful. Anya had many brothers and sisters, most of whom had left to marry from without their clan. Sabir's age was clearly not a factor when it came to siring offspring.

The air was beginning to chill, and the evening fire was shielded from Anya by the human ring around her, so she gained little benefit. Her arms were prickled with bumps like the flesh of a plucked bird. She was aware of the gaze of curious onlookers peering over the heads of the assembled elders, waiting to see clan judgement meted out. Though the centre of attention for so much of her clan, Anya had never felt so alone.

Defender Prabhav was speaking. "It was at this point that the trainee, Hiranjan arrived."

An elder interrupted his testimony. "Are you saying that this girl," he waved his hand shakily towards Anya, "had stolen his clothes and pretended to be a Defender in training?" His scepticism was tangible.

"Well, yes— "

"How did you not notice before?"

Prabhav hesitated. "I must admit, I did wonder who it was, but I had no idea it was a girl." Several of those around laughed incredulously.

"She had no technique, of course," he continued hurriedly, "but she was reasonably— "

"For a girl to try to take the place of a Defender, even a beginner, is scandalous," the elder said.

"We have the Defenders to protect our women and children," said another elder. "For a girl to think to put herself in harm's way insults the sacrifice they make for us all."

"Yes, yes," Bibhu, the eldest of the clan spoke. "This is so. Let us get back to the incident." Although his voice was not strong, it had a rasp of authority that quietened all others. He inclined his head to Prabhav to continue.

"When Hiranjan turned up, he was angry, and frightened the girl—"

"I was *not* frightened," Anya interrupted, her irritation at being discussed without giving her side of the story boiling over. "I was worried the idiot—"

"Anya," her father said, sternly. Neeta was stood behind his shoulder, whispering softly but urgently into his ear. "You know women may only speak when asked by this council to do so."

Anya was on the verge of objecting again, but the firm look on Sabir's face and the glare she received from her mother stopped her tongue. She knew the rules of the council and knew that any further breaches would reflect badly on her family. Anya nodded her acquiescence.

Prabhav cleared his throat and said, "The girl was frightened and moved to escape from Hiranjan, but that took her too close to Gaurang and her pole struck him in the head."

The crowd noise increased dramatically. "This is what happens when women forget their position," said a voice.

"Females are not suited to roles that require seriousness or stoicism in the face of danger," said another elder. "The fact she shied away from the boy tells you everything about their temperament."

"Can you think of any reason why the girl would have done such a thing?" Bibhu directed the question at Prabhav, but at his perplexed shrug, he raised his eyebrow towards Sabir.

Again, Neeta muttered in Sabir's ear. "I think there is an antagonism between them," Sabir said. "Possibly something that has persisted since they were young."

"Hmm," began Bibhu. "This may be some form of attention seeking, but the consequences are serious. How should we deal with this?"

The crowd hushed, wanting to hear the deliberation of the elders.

"She is unmarried, so cannot be paraded," said one.

"Thrash her."

"I would say it is an issue of education." All eyes turned at the distinctive quality of the melodious voice. "We have our tribal values, and in this girl, they have not been sufficiently instilled," said Ujesh, his eyes fixed on Sabir, who indicated his discomfiture by rubbing the back of his neck. Other voices rose in agreement with the clan Ghandarva.

Neeta edged closer to her husband, gesticulating automatically as she continued instructing Sabir.

"I beg the council's indulgence," he began. "I may only make a suggestion to my fellow elders due to my clear interest in this matter." He looked around at the others on the council and appeared to weigh his next words carefully. "If this child has not been properly instructed, the fault is mine, having left such things in the hands of my wife." He cast an arch look at Neeta behind him.

"I suggest that she be placed under the direct supervision of Ghandarva Ujesh, so he may reinforce the values the clan require of her."

Anya was mortified. For her own parents to suggest such a thing was an admission of failure on their part. She had brought shame on their family and she lowered her head to hide the hot tears welling in her eyes. There were mutterings within the circle of elders as they discussed the suggestion, but Anya could not tell what their decision might be, so lost was she in her own misery and disgrace.

At last they quieted, all eyes were now on Bibhu as he began to speak. "It is the decision of this council that the child, Anya, be instructed by Ghandarva Ujesh in the proper values of this clan, and in particular, her place in our tribe as a female, and young woman of marriageable age." He looked directly at Anya. "Have you anything to say?"

It took Anya a moment to realise he was addressing her personally and she blinked rapidly to clear her eyes before raising her head and returning Bibhu's gaze.

"How is the boy I hit, Gaurang?" she asked.

Bibhu sucked his teeth and breathed deeply through his nose. "He will live."

Life Lessons

"And so was given unto woman, children, hers for so long as they shall be unmarried, to care for and to nurture—"

"But it doesn't say that women shouldn't also be animal-tenders, or scouts." Anya was careful not to add 'Defenders'.

Ignoring her question, Ujesh said, "And the rest of the passage is?"

"To care for and to nurture them at her breast. To shape them and mould them, each to their appointed role." Anya parroted without difficulty or feeling.

"Hmm, that is so," said Ujesh.

"Why shouldn't women hold greater positions in the clan?" asked Anya.

"What greater position is there than the care and cultivation of the young?"

Anya snorted, before remembering herself and putting on a contrite expression. "If that's true, why is it that you're a man?"

"I can hardly be held responsible for that."

"What I mean is, you've been given the task of cultivating me. You're our Ghandarva and the Ghandarva is always a man!" Anya gestured towards Ujesh. "Why couldn't a woman be the clan story-teller?"

"We don't simply tell stories," said Ujesh. "We hold the truth of them in our hearts. Understanding of such things is a serious responsibility requiring a level head. Women are intuitive and prone to emotional responses that are unsuited to the role."

"Prone to emotional responses?" cried Anya in dismay.

"As you have just demonstrated," said Ujesh with a slight smirk. He sobered his expression and continued, "Besides, the position of Ghandarva commands a place on the council of elders, and a woman cannot be an elder."

"Yes, but that's like saying girls can't climb because the top of the mountain is reserved for boys," said Anya. "I'm a good climber."

Ujesh frowned in disapproval, clearing his throat. "Always questions and challenge with you. Every lesson, it is the same."

Anya's cheeks coloured. "I just want to know why."

"Sometimes it is enough to know that things are, without knowing the why of it." Ujesh looked Anya in the eye. "You should leave the why to your father, the elders and to me."

Anya climbed. She could feel the frustrations of her lesson ease as she surrendered to the feel of the stone under her fingers and toes. She concentrated on the face of the rock she clung to, her mind clearing of everything except the hand and footholds she required to get where she wanted.

It was not even that she did not enjoy the lessons. She knew most of the stories and could often steer their conversations to more interesting subjects, and Ujesh, being clever, was a good verbal adversary. The problem was that ultimately, every discussion led back to tradition, the way things had always been. If our teachings have served us for so long, Ujesh would argue, why would we seek to question them now? Besides, many of the stories were said to been given to the tribe by the Gods, and passed down through the generations. Anya could hear Ujesh in her mind - by what right did she question the will of the Gods? And, of course, to that she had no answer.

Anya's supporting leg slipped as she sought another outcrop for her free foot leaving her hanging momentarily by a single hand. Her heart leapt into her throat as she dangled over the crushing drop. She hastily found another handhold and scrabbled urgently with her legs for another point of purchase. At last her toes caught a crack in the rock, giving her some support and aiding her in seeking firmer footing. Satisfied that she would not fall, Anya cursed herself for letting her mind wander. On a climb like this, such a mistake could easily prove fatal.

She stayed in position while her heart calmed, its beat slowing to reasonable levels. Anya cast around for a safe place to rest and saw a grassy area, hidden from the ground below by stone walls on all sides, which was large enough to pitch a small yurt. Knowing that her arms and legs were still shaky after her scare, Anya chose the easiest route and carefully climbed down, reaching the grass and lying on her back, breathing heavily and staring up at the blue.

Anya closed her eyes and let her mind wander. She had arranged to meet Amman after she finished with Ujesh, but the session had been shorter than usual, and he was nowhere to be found. Anya had needed some activity to unwind so had gone climbing on her own. She was glad she had, because she was able to take more difficult routes in his absence, to challenge her limits and feel free.

A sound disturbed her daydreaming, and she peered about her, squinting in the bright daylight. A voice inside her urged her to vigilance, signalling danger. Suddenly alert, she sat up, ready to spring to her feet and saw a shape drop lightly to its feet from the rock face. It straightened and turned to look at her, and she saw it was Hiranjan, a strange, intense look in his eyes.

"What do you want?" Her voice sounded too high in her ears and she cursed herself for projecting the unease she was feeling. He gave no answer, but walked calmly towards her, never taking his eyes from her form. As he approached, he leered, breathing in deeply through his nose. Her instincts now screamed to her that she was under threat and giving in to it, she sprang to her feet, turned, and ran, leaping at the stone wall ahead and finding some grip in its uneven surface, she reached for a higher handhold.

Hiranjan grabbed her roughly around her hips and tore her forcefully from the rocks. She tried desperately to cling on, but his strength was far greater than hers and she fell to the ground at his feet. He loomed over her, blocking out the sky, and she scrambled to get up, to escape.

The blow caught her by surprise. Anya was so shocked, she did not even cry out. Stars swam in her vision and it was a moment before she realised she was again lying on the ground, which had come up to meet her as she fell. She blinked in confusion. Hiranjan seized her hair and dragged her forcibly away from the rocks to the middle of the grass, away from her only route to safety. She tried to prise his fingers off, but he swatted at her hands and kicked her until she stopped.

Anya's mind raced. How could this be happening to her? She knew they had always disliked each other, but though she despised him, she had never thought him to be a monster. Was that what he was, or was that too easy a thing to believe? She was overwhelmed by her desperation to flee, her eyes darted around her, seeing nothing but a prison of stone. Hiranjan released her hair and she immediately twisted in an attempt to roll away. Hiranjan hit her again. Anya tasted blood in her mouth and for an instant her whole world was the sensation of it on her tongue. Everything else was detached, almost as though it was happening to someone else.

But it was happening to her.

Hiranjan tore off her loose blouse and leg coverings. Anya began to thrash, but his strength was unbelievable to her. She was strong, but nothing she did was able to break his hold on her, it was like trying to push over a mountain. She knew what was coming and screamed with frustration, with rage and with fear. She poured herself into the animal cry, a primal plea to the world. He clamped his hand over her mouth to stifle the noise. Anya could taste the sweat of his hand, the smell of his odour filled her nostrils and she retched drily. Her stomach churned as her whole universe shrank to the inevitable, unstoppable fate ahead.

Anya scratched at Hiranjan's face and drew blood. He snarled, the only sound his voice had made since he had begun his attack. Again he struck her, and Anya's world spun. She could feel him pulling down her undergarments. She tried to clear her head and blinked, looking down to see Hiranjan, his lower clothing removed to his knees, exposing himself, readying himself to violate her.

A blurred shape drifted behind him, she heard a thud and Hiranjan fell across her, blood welling from a wound in the back of his head. Anya scrambled out from underneath him in horror and disgust, backing herself up to the wall of rock behind her and hugging her knees. She looked up to see the shape coalesce into Amman, a snarl etched into his face and a large stone in his hands.

They burst into her family yurt, Anya crying with relief as she finally let the shock of her attack wash over her. For the whole journey back, she had kept the feelings trapped within her, but now they were free. She was gripped by uncontrollable sobbing, which produced tears that streamed down her face. Amman helped Anya to some seating cushions, and she collapsed onto them before anyone in the tent could react. He hovered near, looking between Anya and her family as they burst into sudden action.

Soon they were both surrounded by her mother, aunt, brother and his wife.

"What on Sansara is the matter?" asked Neeta.

Anya was still wracked with sobs and did not appear to have heard her mother. Amman said, "She was attacked by Hiranjan. He… he tried." He stopped and cleared his throat. "He was going to rape her."

Pandemonium broke out in the yurt. Everyone raised their voice with questions and exclamations made unintelligible by their combined cacophony.

At last, Matreyi made herself heard as she knelt next to Anya. "Is she alright?" she said to Amman above the hubbub, seeing that Anya was still in the throes of her ordeal. She put her arm around Anya's shoulder, and hugged her tight.

"And what of the boy, Hiranjan?" said Neeta. Her voice cut through the noise, causing all except Anya to become silent.

"I… I hit him on the head with a rock."

"What?" Neeta's eyes blazed. "Where was this? How is he?"

Amman's responses did not appear to satisfy her, and she said, "Go, find some men to take with you and bring that boy back." She looked intently at Amman. "And pray that you have not killed him."

Neeta fixed Anya's brother with her gaze. "This is not your concern. You don't need to be here." She had been careful not to phrase it as such, but it was clear that this was not a statement, it was a command.

"Why are you still here?" Neeta said to Amman, who was still rooted to the spot, apparently unable to process the new turn of events. "Go!" Neeta gestured to both males, shooing them from the tent.

"How is she?" Neeta asked Matreyi, who was still soothing her distraught niece.

"She is overcome," said Matreyi. "She hasn't yet said a word, but there is swelling on her face and her clothes are ripped..."

Neeta knelt in front of Anya, placing her hand underneath her chin and raising her head to bring her daughter's eyes level with hers.

"Anya, this is important," Neeta said. "There will be a meeting of the council of elders. We need to know what happened," she hesitated. "If the boy... penetrated you."

Anya stared at her mother blankly at first. Her eyes darted around before looking down at the floor of the tent. She shook her head and closed her eyes, squeezing more tears from them to follow the paths of so many that had already been shed.

Neeta looked thoughtful, and said, "Lie back, Anya. We need to be certain."

"Is that truly necessary?" hissed Matreyi.

Neeta turned her head to face her sister, her eyes burning with intensity. "If that boy has succeeded, Anya will be unmarriable. No one from any tribe will ever touch her." She spat the words like daggers at Matreyi.

Matreyi lowered her eyes in submission and acceptance of Neeta's words. Gradually, they persuaded Anya to lie flat, before the woman raised her knees and conducted their examination.

Anya's mind cleared briefly despite her shock and the indignity she now suffered and she at last found the power to speak. "He didn't... Amman stopped him." She closed her knees and sat up to hug them once again. "He was so strong."

"It's alright, child," Matreyi said, soothingly.

"It is most definitely not alright," said Neeta, the fire in her eyes was still blazing. The others all turned to regard her.

"If that Hiranjan boy is gravely injured, or worse, the consequences for us will be serious."

"But— "

"Anya, the boy is in training to be a Defender. His grandfather is on the council. They will make things difficult for us and for that friend of yours, Amman."

"He protected me."

"You should be protected by marriage!" Neeta shouted, her anger now fully on show. "If you had been married, he would not have dared lay hands on you as it would have been *his* life he risked for his bit of fun. As things stand, it is ours."

Neeta stood now, facing Anya, her authority obvious and unquestionable. "All these matches I have found for you and you turned them down. If you had but agreed to do your duty, this would not have happened."

Anya was stunned. She had been attacked in the most vile way, but it was she who had been in the wrong? Could it have been her fault? She found it difficult to concentrate, to take in this new perspective. It felt wrong to her, but her mother was insistent.

"Neeta, the poor child has been through an ordeal," began Matreyi.

"Enough of my indulgence." Neeta cut across Matreyi. "She will marry, if only I can find another suitor. Hopefully news of this will not spread. If the other clans hear of it, there will be few who would touch her, despite the small mercy that the boy didn't manage to defile her."

She turned her attention once again to Anya, who was staring open-mouthed at her. "And what were you doing alone so far from the rest of the clan? No-one would have cast any blame on that boy if he had taken you, a girl of marriageable age, unprotected and alone, in the full bloom of her youth." Her voice was low and precise. "They would have clapped his back and congratulated him, and the others would have been queuing up to follow where he had been. What were you thinking?"

"I, I—"

"Neeta, that's enough," said Matreyi.

"Enough?" screeched Neeta. She faced her sister now and spat the words into her face. "You are to blame for this. It is you and your books that have corrupted her, made her think she can flout the ways of our people. Your encouragement that made her believe she was somehow different and free from the consequences of life. That the reality for us was not her concern."

Neeta drew herself up to her full height. "Go. You are no longer welcome in our tent."

Silence descended, smothering breath and thought and tears, leaving only consequences. Matreyi swayed as though struck with a physical blow, looking between Neeta and Anya. The meaning was clear as crystal, but confusion was written across her face. She swallowed and opened her mouth, but no words issued from it. Matreyi's eyes dropped to the floor and she staggered drunkenly at first, then with resignation towards the exit.

Reputation

Anya rarely left the tent. The safety she had assumed existed within her clan was shattered. The world outside threatened her, and she would not enter it alone.

Amman sat, occasionally glancing at Anya, acutely aware of Neeta's presence between them.

Neeta insisted that Anya dress in a full sari to emphasise her womanhood, that she was no longer a girl. Anya did not object, but secretly knew it would restrict both her movement and access to her 'womanhood', unlike the more usual loose blouse and baggy slacks. One fewer freedom in the wake of her ordeal.

"So, Hiranjan is awake and talking," Amman said. "Luckily, he's going to be alright." He saw the expression on Anya's face and trailed off.

Anya said nothing as she could not see the good fortune in the news. She wished Hiranjan had died. Her stomach knotted itself as the awkward silence stretched thin. Anya knew that Amman was trying to catch her eye, and so was studiously avoiding his gaze. She supposed he wanted to reassure her, but all she could think of was the state in which he had found her. Any contact, any silent communication they might have while sitting here in her tent would not have been able to evade their shared experience, her personal degradation. She was more grateful to him than she could say, than she ever wanted to say, but his presence would always be an unwelcome reminder. She wished he would leave.

"There will likely be another council of the elders now," Amman said. "They told us they would wait until Hiranjan's fate was known."

Again, silence echoed in the space between them. Amman shifting uncomfortably, coughing just to fill the void. "Perhaps you won't need to attend?" he ventured hopefully, without genuine optimism.

"The council will require Anya to be there," interrupted Neeta. "Now that they know he will recover. Now that they know the consequences of that *incident*." Neeta had only rarely referred to Anya's attack since that first day, and when unable to avoid it, she always chose oblique language.

This time, a silence was avoided by a polite cough that came from outside.

"Please excuse me for the unwanted disturbance," came a formal greeting from the entrance flap. The voice was youthful and something of its accent was unfamiliar to Anya. Not as unusual as those in the temple community, thought Anya automatically, with little real interest, they were probably from another clan.

Neeta rose and approached the entrance, smoothing her sari. "Enter, please. There is no disturbance when guests are welcome," she intoned, completing the ritual.

She opened the flap to admit a tall young man, who, despite his youth, wore years as yet unlived in the weathered lines of his face. He stooped to enter, his rangy frame was lean, but well-muscled. As he was a guest, Neeta followed tradition, and offered him her Uphara, which he politely refused.

"Is this the home of Sabir and his most well-respected daughter, Anya, of whom he is deservedly proud?"

Anya recognised the official inquiry of a suitor, she had heard it several times before, but she could not muster the interest or indignation to glance up at their visitor.

"It is," said Neeta. "Welcome and be seated. You must be tired from your long journey."

"That would be most kind. I have travelled far, for news of Anya has spread throughout our lands."

Anya felt her mother stiffen at these words, even though they were a mere continuation of the ceremony. The news of her attack could not have reached any other clan before this man had left. Neeta guided their visitor to some cushions placed away from where Anya and Amman were sitting. She brought him food and excused herself politely.

Coming to where they waited, she said in an exaggerated tone, "Boy, you must leave your *sister*, as we have things we must discuss."

Anya risked a glance at Amman as he stood, and saw that his face was stiff, his lips set in a line. Neeta barely acknowledged him as he set off for the exit, instead coming to Anya and guiding her to the sleeping area, drawing the beaded curtain shut behind them.

"You must stay here, while I discuss your suit," Neeta said. "Let us hope he did not see your face. Perhaps I can persuade him you are another daughter, so as not to put him off, your face is still bruised and swollen." She rambled, driven by the clear excitement of possibility.

Anya sat, saying nothing, looking down at her hands as she twisted her fingers together.

"Anya, I cannot tell you how important it is for us to respond positively to this offer." Anya knew what Neeta meant but did not say, was that they must accept this offer before the suitor became aware of Hiranjan's attack. "Clan Vulture[13] are an old and honourable clan and you are of an age where—"

---

[13] The Vulture clan, as their name suggests, claim the vulture as their totem deity. They are the only clan within the Tharom tribe that is

"I agree, Mother," said Anya.

This was greeted with stunned silence. Anya wanted to see the presumably shocked expression on Neeta's face, but did not trust herself to keep her tears in check if she did. She felt tired and ashamed. She had been fighting with her mother forever and this was where it had led them. She would fight no more, she no longer had the energy.

"Well… I…" Neeta began. "Thank you, Anya." She stood, patting her daughter gently on the head before leaving to rejoin their guest.

Anya wondered vaguely what it would be like to live with his clan, perched on the top of the world.

The elders listened as Amman gave his account. "I waited for a while, but she didn't show up." He fidgeted as he stood, his words barely carrying. His lowered gaze avoided Anya. "I thought she might still be in her lesson, so I wandered over to the rocks, thinking that I could climb a little and maybe sit somewhere high, where I could see our meeting place.

"I was still climbing when I heard her scream." His voice sounded tight to Anya's ears. "I climbed as fast as I could, but I couldn't hear her anymore, so I was guessing where she was."

"So, she stopped screaming?" said an elder.

"Y… yes. Well, it was like it had been cut off," said Amman. "Smothered."

"Could it not have been a playful scream, such as girls are prone to do?"

---

completely non-migratory. Their village straddles the rim of a large bowl-like formation found at one of the highest points of the Yanuba mountains. In summer, the tribe gather animals suitable for food and place them in the depression where they can graze. In winter, they keep the frozen bodies there, packed in snow, ready to be eaten. "The Clans of the Tharom".

Amman looked up, risking a glance at the elder, puzzled by the suggestion. "No. That wasn't it at all," he said, "it wasn't like that." He shivered and paused. Hearing no further contributions from the elders, he continued. "As I moved towards where I thought it had come from, I could hear other sounds, like a struggle and I looked down and saw him. He had his hand over her mouth and was tearing off her clothes." His voice caught in his throat, sounding an oddly high note that hung in the air.

"I rushed down to where they were and grabbed a stone and hit him." Amman's fists were clenched, and his voice was full of emotion. "I stopped him."

Bibhu said, "It is well for you that Hiranjan did not die, for to take the life of another of our clan is a serious matter."

"If I might interject, Bibhu," came the voice of the elder who had previously spoken.

Anya glanced up for the first time, and saw that it was Soren, Hiranjan's grandfather, who spoke.

At Bibhu's nod of the head, Soren continued. "Why did you decide to interfere?"

The expression on Amman's face made it clear he thought he had already explained. "I... he was—"

"Why not let them have their fun?" Amman's face flushed and Soren laughed mirthlessly. "Alright, let's assume for the sake of argument that it was as you say, and the girl did not want the attention. What of it? Why get involved?" Amman just stared at him, his mouth open. "Well?" said Soren.

"She... she was being attacked!"

"Yes, yes, so you say. But she belongs to no-one, why should it matter to you?"

Amman's face was colouring as he forgot his nervousness and said, "She's my friend!"

"Hmm." Soren tapped his chin with his index finger. "Her friend. You are often in each other's company. Perhaps it was simple jealousy that roused you? You didn't want to share her. Perhaps she has already given herself to you, secretly?"

"Of course she has," came a shout from the watching crowd. Other voices could be heard muttering agreement.

Amman's blush deepened. "No, we haven't, we aren't. There's nothing like that."

Soren whispered to his fellow council members, pointing to Amman with a cynical smile playing about his lips. Anya saw one nod in accord.

"Isn't it true that what you saw was this wanton slut begging to be taken by your rival?" He indicated Anya scornfully. Soren's voice became quick and urgent. "Your anger overcame you and that's why you reached for that rock?"

"No!" Amman almost shouted. "That's not—"

"I'm told that she prefers to play games with the boys instead of activities more becoming of a young woman. Look at her. A girl like that has probably serviced every other lad in the clan." He looked encouragingly around at the throng for support.

"Whore!" cried an anonymous member of the watching clan.

"It's not true. Why are you saying—"

"My grandson says she took him in her mouth while he was dozing!" Soren's mask of calm authority had slipped, and he reined himself back, addressing the men of the clan directly. "What man among us would have been able to stop himself in such a situation?"

The world had become vague and insubstantial to Anya. At the first accusation, her anger had briefly flared, but the insecurity she felt had restrained her, reminding her of her place in this council. She must not speak unless asked to do so, so she remained silent. As Soren had continued, pain and hopelessness has swelled within her and she retreated from its sharp edge. All her fighting, her rage at the injustices of life was pointless. Each time she fought, it only made things worse. She was ready to give in, to accept whatever fate she was dealt.

"Who indeed?" From amid the distant drone, a voice echoed down to Anya. It was her father, Sabir. Somewhere deep inside her, a tiny guttering flame fluttered, but did not go out.

"You paint a picture of culpability with no more than suggestive comments and the word of a would-be rapist." He spat the words at Soren. "Where is your grandson to deliver such accusations? Such testimony is not to be considered from a mere second-hand source."

"He is not well enough to appear before the council."

"How very convenient," said Sabir. "For, if he were here, all would see the scratches on his face where my daughter tried to fight him off."

The crowd buzzed at the ongoing drama before them. A few within the council muttered at his contribution to their deliberations.

"Yes, I understand the likely consequences for me, but until such judgement, I am still a member of this council and you must consider my words."

Amman stood in the midst of them all, forgotten and uncertain. Bibhu looked up, as though surprised to see him there. Clearing his throat, he said, "We thank you for your testimony, young man. That will be all."

The council had finished. Anya sat, alone, uncaring of the knowing looks she was given as the people dispersed. They had stripped her father of his position on the council, breaking their family's influence within the clan. Matreyi's peculiarities had been tolerated due to Sabir's good standing, but though they had overlooked Anya's incident with the Defenders, this could not be ignored.

As the knot of elders unravelled, Sabir approached Anya and lowered himself gingerly to the ground to sit next to her. He sighed.

"I'm sorry, father," Anya said. It was little more than a whisper.

"There are days when I am proud of our clan," he said. "Sometimes I am so grateful for the life I have had that giving thanks to the Gods does not seem adequate." He looked at Anya, his shoulders slumped. "Today is not such a day." For a while he said no more, and they sat side by side, together, but separate.

"You should not have had to suffer this. I am too old to have been a good father, too involved in the council and my own importance to spend time with you." He shifted to face Anya, reaching out to hold her by the shoulders. "I have always been proud of you, Anya."

Tentatively, Sabir pulled his daughter into an awkward embrace. As they watched the sun begin to set, a magnificent elk turned its head to regard them, its shadow long, pointing into the distance.

A Wealth of Stories

Anya trudged on, the burden she carried on her back far lighter than the burden weighing down her soul.

For the second time in succession, the elk had moved on earlier than had been expected. The grass was still plentiful at the site of their last camp and speculation was rife among the clan as to what had prompted their premature migration. Some suggested that the grass tasted bad to them, others that the wind was in the wrong direction, unsettling the herd. All the gossip washed over Anya without touching her. She had no interest in it.

Sometimes the topic of their conversations changed when she was near. She heard many whispers referring to her promiscuity or her mental state. Others supported her innocence in her encounter with Hiranjan, but only because they believed that her tastes were not inclined to men. More often, they merely fell silent, avoiding her gaze, her company, her disgrace. Anya had slowed her pace, bringing herself to the rear of the procession in order to avoid these encounters. The Defenders who guarded the end of their convoy took great pains to ignore her.

Matreyi was still unwelcome in their tent, and this clearly extended to any contact with Neeta's family, even when relocating. She had not been allowed to see Anya, and Anya had not asked her mother to reconsider, knowing the response she would receive. Sometimes, she would catch a glimpse of her aunt looking back for her, concern clearly visible on her face, even at a distance.

Anya knew that Amman would be working to ensure the safety of the goats and other animals, as well as making sure they did not lose them on the journey. Strangely, it was his absence she felt the most, while at the same time dreading any prospect of his presence. Seeing him would require her to relive experiences she was trying to avoid. She could not reconcile herself with the memories inside her and she was using all her energies to shut down anything that might trigger their recollection.

Anya spent most of the time looking down at the ground beneath her feet, avoiding the possibility of eye contact. She only looked up to make sure she maintained a sufficient distance from everyone, to evade any kind of physical interaction with the others of her clan. She could see that it was her mother who kept closest to her, whether to confirm her good behaviour or to keep Matreyi away, Anya could not tell.

Their route was peppered with huge boulders, causing the clan to weave between them, twisting along the valley like a snake, slithering around the abandoned playthings of the Gods. Anya was approaching twin rocks, side by side, like the gateway to an alternate route away from the path followed by her people. As she passed, Anya was distracted from her brooding by the sound of falling stones, a skittering suggestive of something having been dislodged from between the giant monoliths.

She turned, lifting her head up to see the most glorious, noble elk she had ever encountered. Its antlers swept back from its head in a regal crown. The autumn sun shone from behind, causing them to glow with majestic splendour. The animal was looking directly at Anya, and their eyes met, one pair clouded and tired, the other at ease with all creation. Anya felt something stir inside her, a loosening of her hold on her emotions and she was filled with the wonder of its beauty. She could only stand and stare, captivated by the creature, only vaguely wondering why it was not with the rest of the herd, such an animal would normally lead the rest, not follow on behind.

At last, before the trailing Defenders could catch up to her, the elk snorted and raised its head in salute, before turning and bounding effortlessly away, to be obscured by the boulders strewn about. Anya's face was wet with tears she had not known she was shedding. The elk's breath hung in the air for a moment, swirling into eddies before dissipating and Anya stirred herself, as if waking from a dream, feeling more refreshed than she had in days.

"There came upon the sacred site, a Jula bird, who saw in the desolation and lack of life, a place of sanctuary, of safety. She knew of the sacrifice of the Gods, but nevertheless gathered twigs and tufts of fur, fashioning a nest on the dead ground in which to lay her eggs. She congratulated herself on her cleverness, saying to herself, 'I am a good Mother. No creatures stir or crawl or hunt in this place. My eggs will hatch in safety.'

"In time, the Jula bird laid her eggs and sat upon them, keeping them warm. She ate and slept and did not keep watch, only waiting on the day when her chicks would emerge, hungry and grateful to their clever mother. However, the eggs did not hatch, and the Jula bird said to herself, 'They are just late, I will wait a little longer.' She sat, and sat, and sat for days that turned to months, until at last, too fat and lazy to move, the Jula bird died. To this day the male Jula sings his lament as a warning for all to hear."

Anya recited her lesson in uninspired fashion. She remembered Ujesh's story word for word and repeated it dutifully. Despite some reluctance on his part, Neeta had persuaded him to continue teaching Anya and they now sat on the trunk of a fallen tree, wrapped up well against the cooling evening air.

Ujesh smiled in delight. Lessons were progressing much more predictably than they ever had before. "Yes, yes. That's very good," he said, looking closely at Anya, who kept her eyes in her lap.

His smile faded a little, and he said, "But what are the lessons we can draw from the story?"

"We should never forget the sacrifice of the Gods."

"Yes, of course." He paused, waiting for her to continue. When she did not, he prompted, "Is there anything more we can learn?"

Anya's mouth twisted in a half-smile. "It's stupid to get so fat you can't move?"

"Hmm." Ujesh frowned, his disapproval plain. "The Jula bird thinks that she is clever, that she can ignore the words and actions of the Gods. She seeks to take advantage of the obedience of all other things to the wishes of the Gods. In effect she places herself above the other animals and suffers the consequences."

"It seems a little unfair on the chicks."

"Nothing grows there," said Ujesh. "Not plant, nor animal. Nor egg."

When Anya offered nothing more, Ujesh shifted his weight on the trunk. "Do you realise we are now very close to the place of sacrifice. The elk have passed up reasonable grazing while we've travelled, they appear intent on continuing to the lands about it. We are very fortunate, for they rarely travel this way."

Anya knew this was true. She could not remember ever having passed this stretch of mountains in her life. She supposed she should feel excited, or blessed, but those feelings eluded her.

"There will be ceremonies," Ujesh said. "One for the whole of the tribe where we make camp, and another for those elders who can make the climb and other men of importance, at the sacred site itself."

A tiny spike of irritation pricked Anya. It was typical that women would be excluded. Clearly, her position of disgrace would deny her the opportunity to attend, but were there no women of importance to the clan? She attempted to shrug off the feeling, but it settled in her belly, its aggravation a familiar source, almost, of comfort.

As Ujesh predicted, the elk continued until they had reached the grazing lands beneath the climb that led to the holy site of the Gods' sacrifice. Arriving late in the day, the clan made camp in dwindling light, using the light of torches to aid them in their efforts. Exhausted by the long journey, Anya finally collapsed onto her sleeping mat, and fell into a deep sleep.

Her dreams were peculiar. She heard a voice welcoming her, but could not see from where it came. She asked others from the clan, who laughed at her or ignored her. Those who did answer claimed not to hear the voice at all, but it continued to sound in Anya's ears throughout. At last she tracked the sound to an unusually tall tent she did not recognise. Anya reached out, pulling the entrance flap wide to reveal another Anya inside the tent, arms outstretched in greeting.

Anya woke, puzzled, with a strange sense of anticipation buzzing gently inside her. At breakfast, she ate little as the food did not settle easily in her stomach. Her family traded eager conversation, clearly excited to be so near the sacred site and looking forward to the celebrations, so Anya supposed she must be sharing in their enthusiasm.

Anya's brother, Rahul and his small family had joined them, his young son drawing much attention and laughter. In such a carefree, relaxed atmosphere she felt Matreyi's absence even more keenly than usual, and contributed little to any discussions. As Neeta played with her grandson, poking his middle, much to his and everyone else's amusement, Anya decided now might be the best time to broach the subject of her aunt.

"Mother," she began, "now that things are settling down, would I be able to watch the ceremony with Aunt Matreyi?"

Her mother's silence gave an immediate answer to Anya's question. Neeta's face hardened instantly as she turned her attention from her grandson. She looked at Anya, her lips tight with disapproval, eyes narrowed with displeasure.

"Anya, I am trying to protect you," she said, her tone suggesting this should have been obvious. "I know that you are fond of her, but you have to see that your difficulties have all come as a result of her influence."

The others of her family reacted as if in response to a command and began to clear away the breakfast things, leaving Anya and her mother alone.

"I blame myself," Neeta said. "If I had not indulged her so much with you, this idea of independence, your endless questions…" Her words petered out.

"But I thought that now I have agreed to a suitor—"

"I will not jeopardise the small steps we have taken." Her words were edged with steel, their consequences immovable as mountain stone. "She is not welcome, and you will have no more contact with her. Soon you will be married and living with clan Vulture."

The words hit Anya like a hammer. She had assumed that things would blow over like they always did. She sat, speechless with sorrow, grief welling up inside her for the loss of her beloved aunt who was as dead to her as any given the sky burial. Anya gasped, finding it difficult to draw breath, her throat constricting the flow of air to her lungs.

"I've tried to be good," Anya said tearfully. At last she drew in a great gulp of air, but it only triggered sobs that wracked her body. "I'm sorry I've not been the daughter that you want me to be. I'll do anything you want. Please," she begged. "Please can I see her?"

Neeta hesitated, her eyes looked into Anya's and softened, until at last she broke the contact, looking down, before rising from the cushions and moving towards the cooking area.

Without looking back at Anya, she said, "No. I'm sorry, but I won't let her drag us down anymore. That's an end to it."

"But, that's not fair," said Anya. A heat was rising within her, as the combination of all the pain and injustice she had suffered piled one on top of the next, their mutual energy uniting into a single flaming fury that could no longer be contained.

"Anya," her mother said, a warning note clear in her voice.

Anya stood, her body tense, her hands clenched with rage. "You never listen to me!" she screamed at Neeta. "It always has to be what you want."

She began striding towards the exit. Neeta moved to intervene, reaching out to grab her arm. Anya twisted her body and wrenched it out of her grasp.

She screwed up her face and shouted with all her force at her mother, "I hate you!" Anya stormed out.

Anya marched, her anger fuelling her determination to get away. Reckless thoughts flooded her mind, muting the sounds of her mother's cries in her ears. Such was the violence of her temper, that those few people she encountered backed off instinctively. She was possessed by it, and her whole being radiated the passion of her displeasure.

She walked without aim or purpose, but gradually Anya became aware that she had been moving uphill. Her exertions were stealing her breath, demanding her energies and sapping her tantrum of its power. She slowed, choosing to continue uphill, and carefully cradled the fire within, maintaining the core of its heat as a charm to ward off the frustrations and inequities of the world. At last the rising ground gave way to a steep face of rock, and Anya transferred her momentum into a climb. Barely pausing in her movement, she began to ascend.

Her mind was tight with focus, identifying suitable outcrops for her hands and feet and highlighting her route, plotting her course up the mountain. She climbed quickly and easily, only stopping when she found a suitable area, wider than a ledge, on which she could rest. She sat on the edge, shaking her hands and dangling her legs, seeking to ease the fatigue that warmed them.

They were very high in the mountains and the view from her vantage point was breathtaking. Almost directly below her, the yurts of the clan clustered close to the rock face on a relatively flat piece of land. As Anya looked out, she could see the herd clinging to the steeply sloped mountain grassland with effortless ease. Beyond them, the slope increased, disappearing out of view until the lands below were blanketed with cloud, pierced here and there in the distance with lower mountain tops. The rising sun shone low in the sky, orange and swollen, highlighting intricate patterns in the cloud and exaggerating the shadows of the emerging peaks.

Anya soaked in the scene before her, its beauty and tranquillity in marked contrast to the feelings inside her. The feelings to which she still clung, that drove her here to take in this spectacle. She glanced down once again at the camp, and briefly considered returning to face the inevitable consequences of her outburst, but the flames inside her flared at thoughts of her mother and she dismissed the idea, resuming her climb.

After a while, Anya found she was breathing heavily from exertion and the altitude. The sense of expectation she had found on waking had returned, vying with her cooling anger for control of her mood. It gradually strengthened, and Anya imagined herself humming audibly in response to its vibrations. She hoped she was nearing the top and wondered idly what course the elders would take, surely this was not the only path to the sacred site.

It was only at this point that Anya realised where she was heading. The site of the sacrifice of the Gods! Should she be here? Would her presence sully the holy place? Why had she not realised sooner where her anger was taking her? Why did she always end up doing something provocative? These and other questions raced around inside her head and for a moment, all she could do was freeze with indecision.

She imagined that the way above her flattened out in anticipation of the top of the climb. She must be near the crest of the rock face, but to visit the sacred site without permission, before the elders and men of the clan, would be viewed dimly, at best. At worst, she would again find herself paraded before the council.

She was on the verge of descending before anyone realised she was here, when a voice inside told her to stop. Her worth was not measured by others. It was not determined by who or what she was, but by what she did. She was doing nothing wrong. She drew a deep breath and continued to climb.

It was not long before her suspicions were confirmed, the end of her journey up the escarpment was imminent. The ground was levelling out, but Anya still concentrated on finding sure footing, all too aware of the drop beneath her. She finally crested the top of the rock face, still on all fours and rolled, exhausted, onto her back, drawing in great lungfuls of air.

She lay there for a while, the thrill of her exertions confirming her own vitality, the joy of being alive momentarily banishing the complications of living. Gradually, she became aware of a hush around her. It felt like the whole world held its breath, not a sound could be heard. Even the wind was still.

Anya lifted her head and turned, seeking to view the sacred site for the first time, knowing what to expect from Ujesh's stories. Before her lay the blackened earth and rock with not a single plant growing within an enormous circle of ground. Forming an intermittent ring around the parched earth were tall sentinels of stone, called The Watchers [14]by the tribe, no two the same, each standing guard over the holy place. These things Anya noticed only in passing. What captured her undivided attention was the tower that rose from the centre of the scorched landscape.

Anya stumbled to her feet, unable to take her eyes from the unexpected sight before her. A thrill of excitement and fear shot through her as she stared, dumbfounded, her mouth hanging open in wordless amazement. There was nothing in the old Ghandarva's tales that told of any buildings here. None of her relatives had ever mentioned such a thing, not even her father, who she knew had visited the sacred site at least twice before.

Unbelievably, the tower was real. Incredibly, impossibly real. It rose to a height taller than any building she had ever seen, and thinking of the homes of the settlement near the temple, she estimated it must have space for at least five levels, for it was more than twice the height of the houses they had built.

Her thoughts of the temple community triggered a recognition in Anya's mind. The style of the building, with its grey coloured stone and fading orange tiles was similar to that of the temple. It even sported the same type of wooden beams, fixed into the outer walls to support its overhanging

---

[14] Called 'The Watchers', eight standing stones are positioned around the perimeter of the sacred site. If one were to draw straight lines between opposite stones, joining each in pairs with one other, all lines would cross at the same point, the very centre of the circle. The stones pre-date the time of the tribal Gods' sacrifice, but their original purpose has been forgotten by the clans. "Places of Power in Sansara".

roof. There, however, the similarities ended. Where the construction of the temple had appeared rough to Anya's inexpert sight, the stones of its walls haphazardly placed to form an uneven outer surface, this was the result of a master of their craft. Each stone both purpose-made for its position in the tower and, at the same time, entirely natural. The tiles that covered the roof were perfectly aligned and laid, not leaving even the slightest of gaps to allow in the wind, rain or snow, they looked weathered, but were without wear.

The structure was circular, its lowest level forming a wide ring that completely surrounded the central, narrower column that emerged, thrusting high into the sky, its tip catching the morning light and scattering it like a crystal. Its high walls were pierced regularly by tall windows, which were filled with a flawless glass, Anya could see in them perfect reflections of the surrounding mountains.

Facing her directly, was a large double-door so dark in colour, Anya imagined they must be fashioned from the wood of the Locanth tree. The sturdy doors were reinforced with thick iron bands, and metal rings hung from each, acting, she assumed, as a type of handle. Something inside Anya sang with joy, and she felt a sense familiar to her, almost akin to a homecoming. Anya found herself walking calmly towards the tower, without any recollection of her first step.

As she approached, Anya could hear the ground underfoot crunching where she stepped. She looked down and saw that where the rock was not exposed, the soil, if it could be called that, was equal parts fine grey sand, like ash, and course gravel, Anya was not surprised to see that no plants of any kind grew in it. The location of the Gods' sacrifice was a wasteland and she shivered at the thought of the power unleashed here.

The tower loomed over her now, but rather than make her feel insignificant, instead she thought of Matreyi and the sense of being special she always had when with her. It was a welcome sensation, in marked contrast to the hopelessness she had felt of late. As she neared the door, the building's central column was obscured by the lower floor's extended roof and soon Anya sheltered beneath it, standing on a raised step, her eyes fixed on the handles in front of her.

She tried to swallow, but found it difficult, her mouth was so dry. Anya raised her hand, hesitating slightly as though she feared the tower might disappear like a dream if she touched it, and grasped one of the metal rings. It was strangely warm to her touch, but it turned easily in her hand. She could hear a mechanism click on the other side and she pushed. The door opened smoothly and noiselessly, and she caught a slight breath of air from inside, its scent tickled her nose with the promise of discovery.

Anya stepped in and found herself in an entrance room, closing the door behind her as her eyes adjusted to the lower light inside. Two windows set either side of the door illuminated the space with natural light, showing her two stone seating areas, each set along the walls. Above each was a mural, depicting mountain scenes in such detail she was awestruck by their realism. On her left, the picture there showed the mountains at night, the sky covered with stars, rendering the peaks in silhouette and when she moved her eyes, Anya was struck with the illusion that the stars were twinkling.

Directly ahead was a large single door of the same dark wood as those behind her. Anya opened it eagerly, rushing in to find herself face to face with an Ogre. Panic-stricken, she screamed and stumbled backwards, falling onto her backside on the stone floor. Scrabbling to get back up and escape, she glanced hurriedly over her shoulder, expecting to be crushed at any moment by the monster's fearsome arms but saw that the creature had not moved at all. Finally, regaining her feet, Anya ducked around the side of the doorway and peered cautiously at the beast. It was merely a statue carved from stone, but of incredible quality. She thought the precision of the artist's work must have contributed to her fright.

Unnerved, Anya found a door to her right and rushed through, closing it rapidly behind her. She leaned against the door, waiting for her heart to calm and took in the sight before her. Ahead of her was a large table, placed near a fireplace, a large round stone rested on a stand set in the middle, she supposed for decoration. Surrounding the table were seats of animal hide, but stuffed like sleeping mats until they were tight, stretching around the nails that kept the material attached to its frame.

To her right were shelves, crammed full of books, perhaps as many as could fit in the temple library. Anya stared in amazement, walking aimlessly away from the door and turning slowly in an effort to take it in. As she turned, she saw that the central area of this level of the structure was ringed with great arched pillars, supporting the tower above. Within, the stone floor was raised in a path that completely encircled a large patch of earth. Anya moved closer but could see nothing growing there. She wondered what it could mean, what could be its purpose.

Dimly, on the far side of the tower hub, Anya could see a regular pattern of large shapes, obscured by the light from the windows behind them. Intrigued, she skirted the soil using the path, and entered the space beyond. Anya stopped suddenly, as though she had hit an invisible barrier. She looked around wildly, unable to process the reality of the scene. This entire section of the tower, almost half of the space available on this level was filled with books.

They lined the walls to a height far above her own reach, only interrupted by the regular pattern of windows and by the shapes she had seen, themselves large bookshelves that extended out from the walls like the spokes in the wheels of the clan's cart. Free from her paralysis, Anya darted between them, caressing them and scanning their spines with her gaze. Occasionally she would pull one from its shelf, flicking through the pages with wonder, feeling like a small child at her first taste of honey. She saw books about the world, about far-off lands such as Numena, even the Yanuba mountains of her home, books filled with words and language she did not know, with explanations as to their meaning. One volume she examined was full of numbers, with strange symbols joining one to another.

Anya danced through the library, laughing, unable to contain her delight and her astonishment at the sights around her. She wanted to consume it all, to digest all the knowledge on display. She stopped, struck by the realisation that she could never read it all, not if she lived for a dozen lifetimes. Humbled and even more awe-struck than before, she settled at a nearby table, piled high with books she had grabbed in her mad dash from shelf to shelf.

She leaned back in her chair and puffed out her cheeks, still baffled with amazement. Anya was almost convinced she must be dreaming and pulled on her hair to see if she might wake up. Satisfied of the reality before her, her eyes flicked from spine to spine, reading their titles once again. Several books referred to places beyond the mountains, places lost to men. She imagined what Bibek and the other monks would give to see this and to study here.

The thought jolted her out of her blissful stupor. The temple had been founded as a repository of all the knowledge rescued from before The Fall. The refugees who had made their home on that island had recorded everything they knew, and what they had written was insignificant compared to the vast store of information around her. Where could it have come from? Who could have created all of this since the last time any of her tribe had visited the sacred place? It was impossible, but she could not dispute the existence of this very real space around her.

Anya jumped up with a start. How long had she been here? Snatching a book at random, she ran towards the exit. Worries over the possible consequences of her coming without permission to the holy place of the Gods vied with the need to announce to her people the presence of the tower. Thoughts struggled against one another inside her head, circling until Anya felt dizzy with them. At last she reached the double doors and burst out in the fresh air, swiftly closing the doors behind her.

Anya was unsure whether to climb back the way she had come or to search for another route. Deciding there must be a different way down that might be quicker, she turned - and found herself the subject of the dumbfounded scrutiny of a delegation from her clan, here to enact their ceremony in memory of the sacrifice of the Gods.

Fire and Fury

Anya wanted to run. Her eyes darted around, looking for a way to escape, but it was hopeless. The attention of the elders and Defenders was fixed unbreakably on her. She was reminded of vultures perched in the trees, staring unwaveringly at a mountain lion's meal, waiting patiently to feast on the remaining carrion. Anya clutched the book in her arms tightly to her chest like a shield, her feet shifting guiltily beneath her.

"What is the meaning of this?" came a breathless question.

Anya turned her head, recognising Bibhu's voice, trying to find him among the gathering crowd. Her appearances before the council came flooding back to her and she lowered her head in recollection of her shame, stopping her mouth as was proper. More of her clansmen were arriving, circling the tower from both sides. She imagined, like her, they had been stunned to find it here and had been inspecting it, walking around it in a daze.

A figure approached, Anya glanced up and saw it was Bibhu, looking exhausted and fearful. "Speak, girl. Have you done this?" he said.

Anya was startled and confused. Why would they think she was responsible? How on Sansara could she have created the tower? "N-, no," she stuttered.

"It is Magic!" came a cry, answering her unspoken questions. "She's using dark magic."

"What?" she protested.

"Evil magic!" Voices were now assaulting her from all sides. All accusing her of using the forbidden dark arts, banned by the Gods themselves.

"It wasn't me!" Anya was frantic now, desperate for them to understand. Her growing panic loosened her tongue and she talked over their hubbub. "How could you think I could do this? I can't use any magic. I climbed up here because I was angry, I know I shouldn't have. I, I..." Anya ran out of words once again.

The clamour subsided as Bibhu turned to them, raising his hands, indicating quiet. He turned to face Anya.

"What do you know of this abomination?" he said.

"It... it's not evil. It isn't magic. It's just a library," she said. The words sounded unconvincing once she had uttered them, even to her.

"How did you get in?" asked another. It was Prabhav. "I couldn't open the door."

Anya blinked, uncomprehending. "Maybe I locked it somehow, accidentally?" she said.

She turned and tried the handle again. Again, it opened easily. Anya pushed wide the door for all to see.

There were muted gasps from the watching delegation. Anya saw some take a step back, as though expecting a fearsome threat to emerge. When no imminent danger presented itself, Bibhu cautiously approached Anya, some of the other men following in his wake. He waved his hand at her, indicating the book she still carried in her arms. Anya had forgotten she still had it and held it out for him.

He studied it for a moment. "What does it say," he asked, pointing at the cover.

"The Clans of the Tharom," said Anya, surprised by her own words. She did not remember taking a book by that title from the shelves.

"Soren, I believe you read," said Bibhu. "What do you make of it?" Bibhu gestured to his fellow elder to take the book. Anya noticed he carefully avoided any contact with it, himself.

Soren looked less than enthusiastic, but after a slight hesitation, took and opened the book. His eyes flicked over the writing inside and he rapidly turned over several pages. Anya could see the heading 'Clan Elk' where he had stopped.

Soren huffed in a disapproving manner. "What it says appears to be mostly accurate." He shoved the tome back towards Anya, who caught the book eagerly just as he dropped it.

"Why anyone would waste their time writing such obvious facts is beyond me." Soren skewered Anya with a penetrating look. "You girl, what else is inside?"

"I can show you," said Anya backing inside the door.

Some of the gathered dignitaries looked away, shifting their weight uncomfortably, but Prabhav said, "I would see the inside of this place."

Anya was suddenly aware of a noise that had been gradually building, but which had not registered until now. The elders and dignitaries around her noticed it as well, and they craned their necks to see over those gathered behind them. Swarming up to the holy place were many clansfolk, mostly men and most of these young. They were crying out in alarm and anger at the sight of the tower. As more and more arrived, the heat of their feelings rose dangerously.

Shouts went up, and Anya could see men lifting rocks above their heads, running and launching them at the walls of the building. Others joined in or cheered on the offenders. Those who had gathered for the ceremony were jostled as the crowd built and surged around the structure. Anya realised they were now surrounded by an uncontrolled, raging mob.

They were trapped with nowhere to go, the mass of people showing little respect for the elders, and the Defenders present automatically formed a ring around them for their protection.

"It's open!" Anya heard a yell from angry throng.

The cry spread, and the pressure built on the wall of Defenders, until, unable to hold them back any longer, Prabhav said, "Inside! We must go inside, or risk being trampled."

Relieved of their caution and desperate for safety, they rushed into the tower, carrying Anya with them. They flooded inside, swept through the antechambers by a rising tide of young angry men. The jostling abated a little once they had burst into the spacious interior as each newcomer took in his surroundings, gazing around them in bewilderment at the unexpected sights.

What little lull there was did not last long. Groups began rushing through the library, pulling books out and throwing them to the floor. Anya could see them attempting to topple the shelves on which they stood, but they would not move. Frustrated in their rampage, they began turning over tables and chairs, looking around for anything else to destroy.

Men were still pushing their way into the tower through the entrance. "Is there another way out?" Anya turned to see it was Prabhav who had spoken, steady and composed, a rock of calm amid the chaos.

Before Anya could answer, he pointed to an area across from the entrance that divided the library from an area set aside for the preparation of food. "What about there? Surely there must be access to the upper levels?" His voice was raised to carry above the clamour engulfing them.

Anya looked more closely. There was a section of the tower that extended to the hub, but one side she knew was lined with shelves, and from their position near the seating area, she could see that the wall facing them was hung with pots and pans and fitted with a wooden counter that extended for its full length. The only remaining space for a door was directly off the raised walkway around the hub, but the stone formed a regular and unbroken wall. No door existed.

Anya shook her head and shouted, "There isn't a door on the other side, just more bookshelves."

"What manner of place is this?" shouted Prabhav. Not expecting an answer, he moved to shepherd the elders away from the mayhem raging around them. His eyes were alert, flicking around, seeking for any signs of trouble.

Several men rushed between them, further separating Anya from the reassuring presence of the Defender. She found herself standing on the far side of the seating area she had seen when she first entered, backing towards the food counter as more and more of the men descended on the fireplace and the furniture, using knives to shred their coverings, spilling their stuffing of hair and wool onto the stone floor.

They snatched up wood and kindling, which was stacked by the side of the hearth and swarmed back towards the library. Anya's instincts shot a warning jolt through her and she shouted incoherently at the mob of people as they surged mindlessly on their path of destruction.

Anya rushed forward to remonstrate with one man. She screamed above the tumult, grabbing his arm for emphasis. At first, he barely noticed her, but when she persisted, her efforts pierced the fog of hatred that engulfed him, and he turned to glare at her. He tore free of her grip with ease and stood facing Anya as if seeing her for the first time. She thought she saw unpleasant possibilities written in his face, reflecting dark thoughts circulating behind, and felt suddenly vulnerable, her mind taking her back to Hiranjan's assault.

She backed away rapidly and held her hand up between them as both ward and apology. The man blinked, before snatching the book she still held, looking around and re-joining the others in their rampage. It was only when he had left that Anya realised the man was Paras' father, his face had been so transformed by the intoxication of destruction that she had not been able to recognise him.

Anya stood stock-still, gripped by an uncontrollable shivering that coursed throughout her body. Her breath came in shallow pants and cold sweat ran down her back. For a time, she could do nothing beyond trying to slow her heart, which was hammering against her ribs. It was only the smell of smoke that interrupted her paralysis.

Anya focussed, looking around desperately, and saw the library on fire, sending flames up to lick the ceiling. She coughed as the fumes built around her. Covering her mouth with her sleeve, she moved through the central hub, getting as close as she could to the library, transfixed with horror by the unfolding scene. Anya searched wildly for something, anything that might make it right, that might fix the terrible wrong being committed by her people.

The mob, meanwhile, was dwindling. Some remained, basking in the proof of the triumph of their rage, the light of the flames flickering over them, transforming their faces indescribably, rendering them as hideous creatures from ancient legend. As the fire built, even these wavered, joining their fellows who were slinking out, their thirst for destruction slaked and their pride diminishing as the danger to themselves became apparent, the consequences of the riot finally penetrating their fogged brains.

Anya saw that the elders too had gone, presumably shepherded out by Prabhav. She knew that she must also leave before she was cut off by the flames, and cast one last despairing glance about her, determined to capture in her mind the terrible price of their ignorant fear, to somehow honour the purity of this place with her witness.

She was about to turn and leave with the last of the rioters when she saw a shape lying on the floor of the library, partially hidden by a pile of burning books and furniture. She peered through the smoke and shimmering air and saw that it was a body. She gasped, which caused her to cough heavily once again, her eyes watering in the increasingly foul air. Anya blinked, clearing her vision and saw that everyone else had fled, no-one was left to aid her. She was alone.

She contemplated running to get help, but the fire was still spreading. There were no other options available and Anya instinctively ran into the fire. The heat was astonishing and vicious. She would not have believed it was possible for anything to be so hot and she cringed from the power of it. Crouching, the better to see through the thick, dirty air, she stumbled to the side of the figure on the floor and saw an older man. This was not a man fuelled by youthful passion to cause chaos, but an elder of the clan. He looked familiar, but no amount of blinking would clear the murk from her eyes, deposited there by the smoke.

The ferocity of the flames assaulted her, and she worried that she could smell burning hair. She frantically patted her head, hoping to put out any smouldering, but had to snatch her hands away, as the heat she found there was blistering. Breathing was becoming difficult, the smoke and the temperature of the air she drew inside her lungs made her feel light-headed.

Urgently, she seized the ankles of the man on the ground and pulled, to no avail. She could not move him, and panic threatened to overwhelm her. She tugged in desperate, futile bursts, but still he would not shift. In her mind, a voice seemed to whisper soothing words, granting her a small measure of calm, and she channelled her terror into furious action, lending her strength she had never before felt. She heaved, screaming in frustration and despair, and at last, she succeeded. The body shifted, sliding free of the burning debris on top of him.

Slowly at first, but with steadily increasing speed, she moved him. Anya leaned into the pull, the whole weight of her body aiding in her efforts. Ignoring the minor bumps in the floor, but aware of the elder's head bouncing as she dragged him, she pulled him gradually to safety. Panting with exhaustion, she paused near the statue of the Ogre, taking in the complete immolation of the library. Cold fury took hold of her and she cursed those who had done this. Her face was twisted in a snarl as her anger held her tears in check.

Anya used her temper to fuel her flagging energy as she hauled the dead weight of the clan elder at last through the double door to safety. She continued until she had moved some distance from the building, wanting to get far enough away in case the central tower were to fall. Some of the men who had ransacked the interior were standing around gazing at their handiwork. Anya shouted nameless insults at them, pouring all her rage into her screams until finally, she was spent. The men laughed at her.

It was only when she caught her breath that the shock of the cold hit her. Sweating from the heat and her exertions, rivulets of soot ran down her face and arms and these were now chilled in the mountain air. As the heat drained from her skin, the anger dissipated from her soul, leaving nothing but desolation and anguish. Anya turned to face the tower, which had promised her so much, and whose mysteries she would now never unlock, and fell to her knees and sobbed. Through bleary eyes, she saw the eerie dancing red of the raging fire peak through tower windows blackened with soot, a kind of dark light emanating from dark deeds.

Anya dropped her head, and closed her eyes against the world, against the evidence they presented her of the futility of her life. She became vaguely aware of people around her, the urgency of their voices dampened by her misery. Someone shook her, and she briefly looked at them, uncomprehending. They shouted something at her, but the words were as meaningless as the roar of the fire. Men were gathered around the elder, but it meant nothing to her. Crumpled beside his still form, she released the hold she had placed on her emotions, keeping them in check, and let her despair pour from her in rivers of tears.

Heart's Desire

"Elder Bibhu sends his regards," Neeta said, as she entered their tent. "I'm told he is recovering well from his ordeal."

Anya did not react in any way to the news. Neeta looked at her daughter, concern and unease playing across her face. Anya had not said a word beyond automatic replies or routine pleasantries since she had been carried back to the camp. She was listless, spending most of her time in their yurt. When Neeta insisted she go outside, she sat, unmoving, near the entrance, staring at nothing.

A council of sorts had been held. Amid much shouting and consternation regarding the tower, two salient points had been raised concerning Anya. First, she had gone without permission to the site of the God's sacrifice before the clan ceremony had been performed, unbefitting of a girl, particularly one in her position. Second, she had pulled Bibhu from the fire at considerable risk to herself and saved his life. With the latter point in mind, the council had agreed to waive any sanction for the former.

Neeta wavered, her expression conflicted. She sat on a cushion next to Anya and said nothing for a while, simply watching her troubled child.

"I want you to know that I'm proud of what you did," she said. A tiny ghost of a smile flickered briefly on Anya's lips.

"But you should not have gone to the sacred site," Neeta continued and Anya's smile faded as though it had never been. "At least pulling Bibhu from the fire has done a little to restore some of our lost reputation."

Anya's eyes became more unfocussed, she looked beyond her hands on her lap, which she rubbed together absently, fingers interlaced. Occasionally she raised a hand to her mouth and chewed on a fingernail, a habit from her early childhood. The silence stretched between them like the skin of a drum, taut and poised to be struck, neither willing to interrupt it with the crashing sound of ill-judged words.

Some time passed, each saying nothing, before Neeta sighed, softening the tension at last. She looked to the floor at the rug on which their seating cushions lay and said, "Perhaps you might like to visit your aunt."

It took a moment to pierce her mental fog. Once it penetrated, Anya's head flicked around like a whip to face Neeta, her eyes scouring her mother's face for signs of reservation, or disapproval. Eager, but fearful of an instant change of heart.

"Go," said Neeta. "It's what you want." She turned her face, meeting Anya's eyes. "Just this once, though. Nothing else has changed."

Not trusting herself to speak and feeling that for her mother this was no cause for celebration, Anya merely gave a gentle smile of thanks before leaving the tent at a brisk walk. Neeta, abandoned in the muted light, frowned, and a shadow seemed to cross her face.

Once out of the yurt, with the entry flap safely closed behind her, Anya sprinted the short distance to Matreyi's tent, which had been pitched precisely to the rear of that of Anya's family. Anya had always assumed this was some form of deliberate symbolism, but at that moment she cared not at all. The thought of seeing her aunt overwhelmed her and all her energies were focussed on finding her as quickly as possible, before her pent-up emotions broke free.

Anya burst in through the entrance, with no announcement and little effort to push aside the flap, which trailed into the tent after her.

"What?" Matreyi was startled, lifting her head up from the book she had been reading. Seeing Anya hurrying towards her, she dropped the book and tried to get up, but her niece was too quick, and rushed into a tight embrace before she could rise.

"Sweet child." Anya was weeping into Matreyi's shoulder. All of the effort, the strategies Anya used to keep her feelings at bay had melted away, leaving no resistance to the force of her emotions. She clung to Matreyi, letting her soak up her sorrow, just as her clothes were soaking up her tears.

Matreyi held her for a long time and gradually the initial frenzy of her grief abated. "Should you be here, little one?" she said, gently. "Your mother made it quite plain – "

Anya nodded vigorously, swallowing hard in an effort to gain control of her voice, while Matreyi waited patiently for her to speak. "It's alright," she said through her continued sobs. She sniffed. "But only this once, she said."

"Well, in that case we had better make good use of it," Matreyi said brightly, her light-hearted tone a deliberate counterpoint to Anya's misery.

"I'm sorry," said Anya. "All I've done is cry."

"Crying is as good a use of time as most. Pity the poor soul who will not do so. Tears can be a great release."

Matreyi held Anya, waiting for her crying to reach its natural conclusion, rocking her gently and kissing her hair. At length the tears dried up, Anya yawned deeply and snuggled closer to her aunt.

"You've heard about the tower," Anya paused. "About the library?"

"The clan are talking about little else." She looked fondly at Anya. "You did a very brave thing, child."

Anya smiled reluctantly at the compliment, unable to muster much pride when thinking about the destruction of the library.

"Why are people so foolish and stupid?" asked Anya. "To destroy something so wonderful."

Matreyi sighed. "They are frightened by what they don't understand." She hesitated, looking uncertain. "So am I," she said.

"Oh, there's nothing to be afraid of." Anya's eyes sparkled at the memory. "Just row after row of books, about… well, about anything you could ever hope to know. So many, it was like they went on forever."

"But where did it come from, child? Who built it, and why?"

"Does it matter now?" Anya said bitterly. "All of those books, all of that knowledge waiting to be discovered. It's all gone, and for what? Because a bunch of idiots would rather stay ignorant."

Matreyi watched Anya, concern apparent on her face. "How do you think it got there?"

"Someone built it."

"Who?"

"I don't know."

"How?"

"I don't know. The same way anyone builds things, I suppose."

"But how could they do it so quickly? To build something so large would take a lot of people a great deal of time. And where did all the books come from?"

Anya could feel an eerie, creeping sensation begin at the back of her neck. She thought she knew what her aunt was suggesting, but her stubborn defensiveness would not allow her to acknowledge it. She released Matreyi, sliding off her lap to sit on a cushion, so she could face her directly.

"There must be another tribe somewhere in the Yanubas," she said.

"Hmm, how is it possible that not a single clan has ever encountered them?"

"I don't know. Maybe they live underground or something."

Matreyi pulled a face. "In which case why build it on the surface, and why in such a holy place?"

The unease Anya felt, deepened under Matreyi's relentless arguments. Backed into a corner, Anya was forced to consider her aunt's position.

"So, you think it's magic, just because we don't know the answers?" Anya retorted. "Well, what if it is? It was full of books." She shivered inwardly at what she was saying.

"Anya! Magic is banned by the Gods."

"If that's so, how come they let it be built on their holy ground? If it's bad, why would they allow it?" At last finding a solid argument, she pressed her advantage. "They wouldn't, would they? So, it can't be bad." She thrust her chin out and leaned back, pleased with her own logic.

Matreyi did not reply. She looked into Anya's eyes with concern. Anya stared back defiantly. "Well, I suppose it doesn't matter anymore." Her expression softened. "It must have been an amazing sight."

"Oh auntie, you have no idea," said Anya. "There were so many books, more than you could count, almost." She told Matreyi all she could remember of the wonders of the tower, her words tumbling out of her in her desperation to share her experience with the one person who would understand. As she spoke, her face lit up, and her aunt smiled affectionately at the sight.

Inevitably, it did not last. Anya was driven to continue her story, as though recounting it would lessen the power it had over her. She described the fear she had felt at the mindless destruction of the mob. Her words slowed, and her melancholy returned.

"What will they do with it?" she asked.

"Do with it?"

"With what's left."

Matreyi gave her a quizzical look. "Anya, the tower still stands."

"But how could it? The fire was so hot, it could have melted stone."

Matreyi smiled an indulgent smile.

"Can we go and see it?" asked Anya.

There was a pause while Matreyi considered and tried to ignore the deliberately large eyes and pleading look her niece gave her. "Well, we will have to ask permission," she said, giving in Anya's wheedling.

They found Bibhu sat on cushions in the sun, well wrapped up in blankets against the chill of the autumn air. He was being attended to by members of his family, who had fashioned a kind of seat in a hollow for him, made of tent poles and material. About the hollow there grew a sweet-smelling plant called chikitsa[15], lending a fragrant air to his recuperation. It proliferated on the mountain slopes where the elk grazed.

Not wanting to intrude, Anya and Matreyi lingered nearby, until the old man's daughter noticed them waiting

---

[15] Chikitsa is a hardy mountain plant that flowers throughout the year. It has a pleasant scent and is often picked by the women of the tribe and brought into the clan's yurts to freshen the air. "Flora and Fauna of Sansara, volume 1".

and pointed them out to him. After a brief conversation, he raised his hand slightly, beckoning them over.

When they had approached, he spoke to his family members. "Please leave us for a moment. I would very much like to speak with this young lady in private." Looking affronted, they moved far enough away to not hear their conversation, but close enough to intervene, should they be needed.

He chuckled. "It amuses me to imagine what they will think we are talking about." He started to cough, and for some moments they stood patiently, waiting for the fit to pass. Now they were close, Anya could see that a poultice had been applied to the skin on the far side of Bibhu's face. His arm on that side also looked over-large and Anya realised it must be wrapped in bandages.

At last, his coughing subsided, and he dabbed at his mouth with a cloth, looking up at his visitors with watery eyes. Anya was startled by how much frailer he looked than normal.

"Don't look so shocked, girl," he said. "Have you never seen a dying man before?" His breathing was laboured, but rapid, as though from exercise.

Anya was confused. "But," she stuttered. "My mother told me you were getting better."

A sour look crossed Bibhu's face. "My family," he said. "They are being somewhat liberal with the truth." He paused, drawing in tiny gulps of air that produced an audible rattling. "They think they are being protective, but I have lived a full life, and to die in this place, well..."

His words drifted away, and his eyes closed. Anya was sure he had fallen asleep, but his eyelids flickered, and he blinked before looking at her with a squint.

"What?" he said, looking puzzled. "I was saying something."

Matreyi said, "You were saying you have lived a—"

"Yes, yes," he interrupted her. "I will die here. A good place, but for our mysterious… structure up there." His eyes flicked up in his head as emphasis, before looking directly at Anya. "What do you think of it?"

Anya stammered at the unexpected question. Why was he asking her opinion of the tower? She exchanged a look with Matreyi. "I don't—"

"I may have been hasty," Bibhu said suddenly, not waiting for her answer. "To call such a thing an abomination. Certainly, I wish it had been built elsewhere, but once inside, I was touched by a strange sensation." He gave Anya a calculating look. "I wanted to get a better look, to see it for myself." He coughed several times again, before swallowing. "I watched as they started pulling out those books and throwing them to the floor and I was irritated. We should have dealt with it correctly, in the council. When they prepared to set a fire and I tried to stop them." He looked sour. "They did not even notice me, and I was knocked to the floor. Something broke, my hip, I think, and I could not rise."

He lapsed into silence, his eyelids drooping and his breathing ragged. At length, his eyes refocussed and he fixed Anya with his gaze. His expression soured and he loosened his blankets. "It's too warm for the time of year. The snows should already be here at such a height. Time was, when the summer season was much shorter in these mountains." He worked his mouth as though rolling a nut around inside. He cleared his throat and said, "I should thank you for pulling me out."

"You don't have to—"

"Well, I do." Bibhu grimaced, whether from the pain of his condition or from the discomfort of the discussion, Anya was not sure. "You may have extended my life for just a few days, but I am not ungrateful."

Anya stood, not knowing what to say. She decided to say nothing, instead fidgeting awkwardly.

"Elder Bibhu," began Matreyi.

Again, the old man interrupted. "The question I have is why? Why save my life?"

Anya felt constantly wrongfooted by Bibhu, and opened and closed her mouth, speechless that he should have to ask such a question.

"You could have left me there. No-one would have known. You must have thought of it, of getting your own back on the most senior elder of the council that has found against you so often of late."

She was indignant that he could think her capable of such a thing. Was that what he thought of her? Inside her, a tiny flame grew larger, warming Anya with the beginnings of anger.

"Why save me, when you have been so much on the receiving end of the council's justice?"

"Justice?" Anya was incredulous, her disbelief finally overcoming her reticence and loosening her tongue. The coals of her anger fanned by his casual ignorance of her position, of that of every woman in the clan. "You call that justice? Why is it that if a man is brought before the council, he may speak on his own behalf, but a woman cannot? Why should it be that the judgements against me should deprive my father of his place on that council, when all he has ever done is serve the clan? If a man is punished, the punishment is his alone."

She was in full flow now, her ire burning brightly. "Oh, don't answer that, because I know why. It's because women are the property of men, not able to make our own choices, not able to be what we want to be, and if we try, men like you punish us for our temerity." Matreyi put her hand on Anya's shoulder, bringing her back to herself and she stopped her tongue.

Bibhu looked at her sternly from underneath unruly eyebrows. To her amazement, he started to laugh, a low chuckle at first, which grew until it transformed into another wracking coughing fit. Anya stood, perplexed by his curious behaviour. She saw his daughter-in-law looking their way, on the point of intervening.

This time, the coughing soon dwindled, and Bibhu wiped his mouth with his cloth. "I'm sorry, that was unnecessarily cruel." He looked keenly at Anya. "I see, however, that your spirit still burns. I am glad of it, for you have the makings of a good man." He smirked impishly at her confusion, waving his good hand dismissively. "For what it's worth, your recent actions have given me cause to think. Perhaps there is something in what you say, maybe we are doing ourselves a disservice by not making the most of the talents of all members of our clan, but it is too late now, of course." He looked pensive. "Well, what do you think of it?"

"I thought it was wonderful," said Anya with passion. "But now it's all gone."

"Elder Bibhu," Matreyi repeated, trying to gain some control of the conversation. "I would like to escort Anya to the place of sacrifice to help her come to terms with what happened there. Will you give us permission?"

Bibhu turned his head to look shrewdly at Matreyi. His gaze flicked between Anya and her aunt as he considered the request. "That is something few would grant, I would think, particularly to the two of you." Anya felt her heart sink. "You say you want to come to terms with the threat you faced in the fire, or is it more about the loss of the books I believe you covet?"

Anya did not respond. She could not deny his suspicions without lying outright, something she had not been brought up to do.

"I see," he said, clearly reading her silence. He coughed gently. "I am curious to know what fate has in store for you, my girl, and I don't have much time to wait for it." He paused. "Very well, you have my consent."

Anya and Matreyi looked at each other in relief and surprise.

"You know, there is no lock on the inside. I checked." Bibhu's look was piercing. "That tower opened for you, and for no-one else. I believe there is a connection between it and you. Why do you think that is?"

"I… I don't know what you mean," said Anya.

"Hmm, well that is interesting in itself."

As they passed through the tents of the camp, they caught snippets of different conversations. All talk was about the tower.

"…gives me the creeps."

"...it didn't even leave a mark…"

"I heard the fire warped the doors, no-one's been able to get inside."

They rounded a yurt as they wound their way between them and Anya found herself face to face with Amman. He had been walking with his head down and looked up, startled.

"Anya!" he said. "Are you alright? I haven't seen you for ages."

Anya felt the colour rise in her face and she looked away, anywhere but at Amman. "I'm fine," she said.

"Are you sure? It's just that I thought your mother was keeping me away, but…" he looked thoughtful. "Maybe we could watch a Defender practice sometime?"

"Yeah, maybe," said Anya, evasively. "Um, we've got to be somewhere. See you around?"

“Yeah, see you around,” said Amman, a crestfallen look on his face as they walked away.

As they continued, Anya kept her eyes on the ground, avoiding looking at her aunt, who she could feel was watching her. They took a different route to the holy site, one that the elders must have taken, she thought. Perhaps they had carried her back this way, though she had only the vaguest recollection of it. By the time they reached the top, Matreyi was breathing heavily.

Anya, out of breath herself, looked at Matreyi with concern. She said, “Are you alright, auntie?”

“Yes child,” said Matreyi. “I am not as young as I used to be, or as active. Just give me a moment to catch my breath.”

While Matreyi rested, Anya turned her eyes to the tower. It still stood, solid and strong, a physical challenge to the capriciousness of men, looking just as it had the first time she had found it. If she did not know better, she would never have believed it had burned at all.

At length, Matreyi gained her breath once again. She took out a small flask from a pocket and drank, not offering any to Anya. She smiled, appearing refreshed and held out her arm for Anya to take. As they walked, Matreyi stared at the structure in amazement, while for Anya, a sense of dread was growing. She knew she wanted to see inside, to see for herself the library’s final chapter, and hoped that what they had heard was true, that it would not be possible to open the doors.

They circled the whole tower. Anya remembered the clansmen hurling rocks at the walls, but could see no scars, no sign of their fury beyond the stones themselves, lying still where they had fallen. How remarkable was its construction to withstand such an attack with no damage? At last, they reached the doors, and Anya searched the Locanth wood for traces of charring, but saw none. She supposed it would not show easily on such a dark surface.

Matreyi stepped forward and tried the door suddenly. Anya's heart was in her mouth as conflicting desires warred within. It would not open. She breathed a sigh of mingled relief and disappointment. The tension she had not realised she was feeling eased, and Anya visibly relaxed.

"It appears they were right. They are stuck," said Matreyi.

Anya stood, her eyes fixed on the doors. A voice inside her was urging her to try. She tried to counter it by telling herself it was pointless, why should she be able to open it, when her aunt and all her clansfolk could not? The voice in her head would not be silenced, however. Anya continued to fight it, paralysed into inactivity by the conflict within.

"Are you alright, child?" said Matreyi, looking closely at her niece.

The yearning to open the doors was growing stronger. Anya felt an almost physical ache, a longing to give in, but she was terrified of what she might see. It built to a crescendo until at last, she gave in. Anya walked up to the doors and placed her hands on them, feeling the texture of the wood under her fingers, running them over its knots and grain.

The world disappeared. All that existed was Anya and the tower, alone in all creation. She was drawn to it in ways she could never describe. She was overwhelmed with a certainty that it would open for her, and her heartache returned in anticipation of what she would find inside. Her hands found the handle and she closed her eyes as her fingers closed around its ring. Once again, it felt warm to her touch. Anya breathed deeply, willing herself to calm, bracing herself.

She turned the handle and the door opened.

Anya imagined she was in a waking dream, in which everything was hers to command. She pushed the door and it swung open easily and silently on its hinges. All was quiet and as Anya prepared to enter the tower, she felt a hand on her shoulder. The world came rushing back to Anya, its sounds, its smells, its textures all battering her senses as though a bubble had suddenly burst around her. She shivered in sudden cold and frowned in irritation at the interruption of her trance, turning angrily.

She saw Matreyi, wearing a wide-eyed expression of concern, who stepped back when confronted by the venom in her face. "Anya," she said, startled.

Anya stood for a moment, staring at her, then blinked and stepped forward to throw her arms around Matreyi. "I'm sorry," she said. "I was…somewhere else for a moment. Somewhere peaceful. Forgive me."

"There is nothing to forgive, child." Matreyi returned the hug, kissing Anya on the head. "Are you sure you want to do this?" she said.

Anya released her and turned to face the open door. "I'm going to go in. I need to see." Without waiting for a response, Anya entered the tower.

The first chamber was exactly as she remembered it, the colours of the murals bright and undamaged. She heard a gasp from behind as Matreyi took in the splendour of the wall art. "Close the door, auntie," she said, a strange note of authority in her voice.

Knowing what to expect in the second chamber, Anya held out a warning hand to her aunt, before opening the door. To her surprise, the statue of the Ogre was gone. She passed through the doorway, looking around in bewilderment, but aside from the plinth on which it had stood, nothing of it remained. Anya supposed it might have been destroyed in the riot - she thought she had seen it, but might not have noticed its absence as she left, concentrated as she had been on dragging Bibhu from the fire - but she was puzzled at the lack of rubble in its place. The floor was clean and free from debris.

Now that she was not hurrying to avoid the Ogre's threatening presence, Anya looked around at the second chamber in more detail. Here also, the walls were painted with a glorious mural around every wall, which showed the interior of the tower as it had been before the fire. Even in the dim light, she could see the library in incredible detail, the books so clear and crisp she almost believed she could draw them from their shelves. To her right, the art portrayed the seating area as she remembered it, though the fire was lit. The part of the mural depicting the centre of the tower showed a tree growing in the circle of soil. Its shape reminded her of a gaganwa tree, though its bark was silvery-gold.

Anya braced herself for what she would find beyond the door to her left, which opened directly to the library. She closed her eyes to mentally prepare, and found herself buoyed by a curious sense of hope.

"Something here is not right," said Matreyi. Not taking her eyes from the door facing her, Anya again held up her hand, this time indicating quiet. If Matreyi had intended to elaborate, she failed to do so.

In a swift motion, before she could change her mind, Anya grasped the handle, turned it and opened the door wide. Beyond, instead of the charred and smoking remains of her dreams, they saw a perfect library, intact and full to bursting with books, pristine and nestled comfortably in their spoked array of shelving.

Anya gasped, her eyes wide with wonder. Without hesitation, she dashed through the doorway before the impossible sight vanished and reality returned. She pulled books at random from their places, opening them and flicking their pages, seeing sheet after sheet of glorious words. Satisfied at last that this was not a hallucination or a dream, Anya skipped with joy, finally coming to stand in the middle of the library. She spun around in delight, watching the tower rushing past her vision, going faster and faster in her growing excitement.

As she spun, she could see the blurred shape of Matreyi approach in fleeting glimpses of her colourful sari.

Something cooled inside her and she slowed, coming to rest facing her aunt, the room around her still spinning oddly. She repeatedly tried to focus on Matreyi's face, but her eyes kept turning away, until at last the dizziness faded. The giddiness in her stomach, however, remained.

Matreyi regarded her with a look of fear. "This is not possible, child," she said urgently, gesturing around her. "All this, all of it was destroyed. It cannot be here."

"But it is," said Anya.

"It's magic, Anya."

Finally, with no other option than to accept the truth, Anya deflated, her shoulders sagging. Her head dipped, before she raised it slowly once again, looking up at Matreyi with raised eyes. "It's just a library," she said, noticing the pleading tone in her own voice.

"You know what this means." Matreyi fixed her with a grave look. "The Protector will come here."

"How will he know if no-one tells him?"

"He always knows. He is probably on his way here now."

"But— "

"Anya, child, this is serious," said Matreyi. "If we do not report this and send for him, there will be difficult questions for us to answer." She sighed. "It would not go well for us. You do not play games with the Protector."

"But look around you. This is not magic, at least not the kind of magic that we know from the Ghandarva's stories." A glow was returning to Anya's eyes. "What do you think the people will do if they hear of this? Think of it, the sheer waste of knowledge. You're right, of course, the tower must be magical, but what of the books? Surely they are just objects, nothing more. If something is created by magic, does that mean the thing itself is also magic?"

"Little one, this is an argument over the difference between rock and stone."

"No, it's the difference between happiness and misery." Anya's expression was serious. "Our clan has already declared the tower to be magical. Messengers have probably already been sent out to find the Protector. What harm could it do for us to stay here and read? Just for today?"

Matreyi said nothing, her expression at once both thoughtful and full of unease.

"If we tell everyone about this," she waved emphatically at the shelves around them. "They will destroy it once more, and this time set a guard that will make sure we never again have the opportunity to learn the secrets kept here." Anya's words dried up, the prospect of losing her heart's desire forever had constricted her throat. She coughed to clear it. "I would never forgive myself for that."

Matreyi looked around her, taking in the quiet details of the tower properly for the first time. She sighed, and looked her niece in the eye.

"Neither would I," she said.

Behind Closed Doors

Anya was filled with gratitude for the love and constant support of her aunt. She ran to her, wrapping her arms around Matreyi and being enfolded in return.

She led her in among the shelves, showing her the huge variety of topics on display. They gathered volumes as they strolled, eventually making their way to a table to lay them down and sit. Anya noticed that there was already a book waiting for them when they sat. She picked it up and scanned the cover. It was the same book she had been holding when she was confronted by the group of elders on leaving the tower, 'The Clans of the Tharom'.

Puzzled, she placed it on the table before her and read. At first, she was inclined to agree with Soren that the book was accurate but full of information obvious to anyone from the tribe. She skipped to read of the Vulture clan, curious, despite herself of what would await her there when she married. For a while, she was content discovering the peculiar differences between their clans, but after a time, boredom loomed, and she skipped to the end.

> The Tharom tribe, isolated as they are, face an uncertain future. With no interaction from without the clans, they have turned inward, revering custom and tradition over innovation. When faced with disruption, they will struggle to overcome the challenge, and as conditions on Sansara worsen, they will not have the skills to make it right.

Anya was unsure she had understood, so she read it again. She flicked backwards in the text, looking for more information, but found little else that was similar and nothing that elaborated further. Matreyi was similarly nonplussed when she passed the book for her opinion of it. Anya sat, quietly, looking around the tower, musing on a strange feeling that had taken hold of her. She reached again for 'The Clans of the Tharom' and resting it on its spine, she opened it at random and read again.

> Shortly after the first appearance of the Rahksharu, clan Elk discovered a collection of artefacts, which they presumed originated from before The Fall. Though each had a unique design, their purpose was the same. They were mirrors, each with a highly burnished metal plate set in the middle. It was found that these plates were incredibly resistant to scratches and no mark could be made upon them. They were named 'Reflectors' by the tribe.
>
> Knowledge of how it was discovered that the Reflectors would protect the viewer from the gaze attack of the Rahksharu has been lost over the years[4], but once discovered, Reflectors were sent to all the clans. Their power has been utilised and integrated into various forms of defence against the monsters with great success, and the mysteries of their magic passed down by the Defenders in great secrecy.
>
> ---
>
> [4] See 'The Oral Tradition of the Tharom', chapter 25 'The Weakness of Oral History'.

Anya frowned. 'The mysteries of their magic'. Was this merely a turn of phrase? Everyone knew that they protected the Guide from the Rahksharu as he directed the ring of dancing spears around him, so what was the secret they kept? She blinked as the realisation hit her. How stupid of them all, she thought. Everyone in the clan knew that you could look at the Rahksharu using the Reflector, but no-one had ever suggested that the Reflectors were actually magical. They had been so blinded by the absolute knowledge, drummed into them with every tribal story, that magic must be evil, that no-one ever questioned it. Anya herself had never questioned it.

She sat, stunned at the thought. The implications were huge, and she reeled from vertigo, induced by the yawning chasm that had opened before her. The Gods had banned the tribe from using magic, but they had not stopped this tower from being built here. If this book was correct, neither had they punished them for using magic against the Rahksharu. Perhaps not all magic had been banned. Anya closed her eyes and tried to recall the phrase used by Ujesh. At last it came to her, 'Let no man, from this day forward be granted our magic willingly'.

Anya grinned, maybe Amman was right. Maybe she could recite Ujesh's stories word for word. The thought of Amman sobered her, and her smile faded. She pushed him aside in her mind, not wanting to deal with the discomfort caused. 'Our magic', the story said. So, what magic was the Reflector and the tower, or whose? Anya continued to puzzle over the words. She was fascinated by the possibilities and scared in equal measure, but could not quite shake the feeling of suspense that still enveloped her.

She realised that Matreyi had wandered off to investigate the tower and skipped over to join her. Matreyi was stood near one of the bookshelves that projected out from the walls towards the central space, looking up at a strange device or decoration that was attached to the end, protruding out into the empty space above them. Its base, attached to the wood of the shelf was iron, Anya supposed, but shiny and free from rust. It was finely decorated as a plant stalk and formed a graceful arc. At its end, the metal opened like the sepals of a flower, protecting and supporting an opaque glass sphere, itself decorated with a pattern of petals. Anya was entranced.

"There are many of them, positioned at regular intervals throughout the library," said Matreyi, bringing Anya out of her contemplation.

Anya looked and saw that every spoke of shelving held a similar decoration. They were also attached to the walls high above, projecting over sections of books far too high to reach.

"I wondered how anyone might reach those." Matreyi had followed Anya's gaze. "I thought it cruel to place knowledge entirely out of reach, before I realised that these are actually steps leading to arched walkways." She indicated small extensions of shelving that jutted out from the shelves themselves, forming a rising, angled pattern. Anya had assumed they were simply a novel place to rest your books as you gathered them - she had used them for this purpose already herself - but now that she looked again, she could see that their arrangement was actually a set of stairs, leading diagonally upwards to a walkway that ran along the walls for the full length of the library.

Anya ran up the side of the bookshelf, smiling at the ingenuity of the arrangement. Once she had gained the top, she saw many more of the glass spheres hanging over her head and also attached to the walkway itself, curving out, away from the wall. She walked over to the nearest and saw that the detail of the craftsmanship was astonishing, even the veins could be seen in the petals of the globular bud. On an impulse, Anya walked along the top of a bookshelf and looked more closely at the decoration there. Although similar, there were subtle differences. She whistled in admiration. However these had been made, the attention to detail was astounding.

"Come down, child," called Matreyi. "I would like for you to show me the rest of this marvel."

Anya descended to join her aunt, and arm-in-arm, they headed towards the inner hub. As they passed under the arches that supported the central tower, Anya said, "Here is the patch of earth I told you about. There is nothing growing in it, but see, it has a sort of path that runs around it, and on the other side—"

"What about that door?" Matreyi cut in. "I'm sure you said that section of the tower had no entrance." She pointed to a section of curved wall almost opposite the entrance chambers.

Anya stared. Positioned to the right of centre in the wall Matreyi indicated was a door. Also made from locanth wood like the others in the tower, it had images carved into its surface in exquisite detail, forming a relief picture. Anya ran her eyes over it, seeing a mountain scene at the bottom so familiar, she gasped in amazement. It was the view she had seen when resting on her initial climb to this place, carved so accurately, she half imagined someone peering into her head while they sat working with their tools on the wood.

Above the mountain scene, overlaying a v-shaped division in the image, was a carving of a tree. Some aspects of it reminded Anya of a gaganwa, like the mural in the second chamber, but in many ways it was different, somehow more real and full of a majesty that captivated her. Above the tree, wings spread wide, was carved an owl, its large piercing eyes looking down on them with both wisdom and warning. Surrounding everything, forming a border around the whole door were illustrations of books, some in shelves, others open, displaying pages that Anya could almost read.

"But… that wasn't there before," Anya said at last. "I remember Prabhav asking during the riot if there was another entrance." She began to walk towards it, following the circular path.

"Be careful, child." Matreyi's voice was different, somehow. Anya could feel the tension in it. With a distant, automatic part of her mind, she recognised the sound of fear.

Strangely, though she knew magic must be involved, Anya was not afraid. She felt calm, but excited, as though she were out in a lightning storm. She remembered once she had run out from the camp to dance in the warm rain during a summer storm, thunder bouncing around her as the jagged bolts of blinding light had illuminated the valley where they camped. She had never felt so alive, so captivated with the power of nature. When she had returned to the family yurt, her mother had been furious. She had felt different from all her clansfolk that day. She felt different now.

Anya stood before the door, studying it, drawing every detail of it in her mind. There was something about it that bothered her, something wrong, or out of place. Somehow, however, she knew that behind this door lay the key to the mystery of the tower. How ironic, she thought, that she should have to open a door to find a key. She glanced around, realising now what it was that troubled her.

The door had no lock and no handle.

Putting her face close to the surface of the door, Anya scanned it to see the rise and fall of its surface, looking for anything that might be a handle, or could be used as one. There was nothing. Anya tried grasping at various parts of the carving, trying to get a purchase on it, enough of a grip to shift the door, but despite all efforts, it would not move. She ran her hands around the edge, pushing the tips of her slender fingers in the small gap between door and stone and pulled, tugging desperately to no avail. She knew it would not open, she could feel it deep inside. It could only be opened another way.

She felt, rather than saw her aunt join her. Her eyes were still fixed on the barrier when Matreyi placed her hands on Anya's shoulders and kissed her hair.

"Perhaps it is not meant to open," she said. Anya detected a relieved, or hopeful note in her voice.

Anya kept her silence. She did not think Matreyi would want to know her suspicions. For a while, she stood, facing the door, running possibilities through her mind. At last, she resolved to come back another time, but without Matreyi. She felt almost as if her aunt had shown her the way, but that where Anya went, she would be unable to follow. She experienced both sadness and guilt at the thought, as though even thinking it was some form of betrayal.

She turned, and feigning brightness, said, "Shall I show you the rest of the tower?"

Anya took Matreyi by the hand, and together they explored at leisure. In the nearest area to them, as well as pans for cooking, they found knives for the preparation of food and cupboards full of wooden plates, cloths and tools whose purpose was unclear to them. On the counter were ceramic jars for storing spices, arranged in an orderly line below the pots that hung from hooks attached to the wall. Leaning nearby on a wood burning food stove was a broom, made from a sturdy pole and fixed using twine with many lengths of strong, flexible twigs, useful for sweeping the floor.

On the wall further along, Anya saw a frame in the stone, as if for a door or window. Intrigued she moved closer and followed the stone arch with her eyes. It was quite plain and functional looking, which made the lack of an actual portal all the more peculiar. The wall within the border was blank and unadorned with decoration, it looked like nothing except a seamless continuation of the walls around, if not for the surrounding arch. She looked at Matreyi, who shrugged, sharing in her puzzlement.

As they moved on towards the seating area, Anya noticed for the first time a statue near the antechamber door on this side of the entrance. Looking more closely, she realised that it was the sculpture of the Ogre that had been missing when they entered, somehow looming larger than before. Intrigued, Anya rushed over to examine it more closely.

Now she was closer, she saw the statue was life-sized, the enormous monster loomed over her like a bad memory. Anya could see the ugly wound in its head that she assumed had finally killed it during the chase. Its eyes stared blankly towards the hub from its tiny head, its posture paused in mid lumber. Anya heard a sharp intake of breath behind her.

"Anya, this is not just any Ogre," said Matreyi. "This is the very same one we ran from." The fear Anya had noticed before was again apparent in her voice.

"I know," said Anya. "But this changes nothing. Just because this statue was made with magic, doesn't mean the Ogre itself is magical."

"No, that's not it at all." Matreyi was looking at Anya intently. "This Ogre clearly links the tower to us, to you. No-one else could open the door. Bibhu was right. This tower is here for you."

Confession

Anya stared at Matreyi while a tingling sensation ran the length of her spine. She wracked her brain, trying to find something to help her refute her aunt's assertion, but could find nothing useful. Not because she did not want it to be true. It was, she admitted to herself, quite the opposite. She wanted so desperately for this tower to be special to her that she had pushed all the signs away, fearing the ultimate disappointment - a rejection of her dreams.

How had she been so blind? It was not like her to be so stupid. At least, not where logical reasoning was concerned, she conceded to herself with a rueful inner smile. She felt suddenly tired and drained after all she had been through recently, and shook her head, feeling the need to clear it.

Matreyi mistook the gesture. "Little one, you cannot deny it. I couldn't open the door and from what you said neither could any of the elders." She looked at Anya with concern. "You found this tower, or maybe it found you."

Anya swayed on her feet, feeling more weary than she could ever remember. Her aunt moved swiftly to her side, supporting her with her arm, and directed them towards the cushioned seating. Once there, Anya flopped onto the long, stuffed seat in exhaustion and let waves of pent-up despair wash over her, attempting to reconcile her feelings of personal and family disgrace with Matreyi's revelation.

The idea that she was special in some way had been with her as long as she could remember, but she supposed that was often the case. Everyone wanted to believe they were significant, unusual or extraordinary. To hold otherwise was to admit to mediocrity and insignificance. Now she had evidence that she was different, now that something unique had happened to her, perhaps even for her, the fears she had been carrying were released. Anya let them go, imagining them flowing from her just as her tears of relief ran from under her closed eyelids. She felt Matreyi sit close beside her.

"Oh Auntie, I've been so scared," she said. "Of getting married, of the council." She swallowed. "Of Hiranjan and men like him." She breathed deeply. "Most of all, I've been scared that I was wrong. Not that I was wrong about something, but that something about me, or in me was wrong. I'm so different from everyone. Everyone, that is, except you," she added. Matreyi put her arm around her, and gave a gentle squeeze.

"I've been in so much trouble lately. I know I can be a bit wild sometimes, but I cause problems even when I'm not doing anything, when I'm just being me." A barrier within had cracked, and her words came tumbling out. "Mother is never pleased with me and I've not been able to see you, and you're the only one I can talk to."

"What about your friend, Amman?"

"I can't," she said quietly. "I just can't."

Matreyi was silent, waiting for Anya to continue.

Anya wrung her hands, twisting them until they hurt. "I… you don't understand. He saved me, he was there when I was… when he was about to…" She trailed off. "I just couldn't face him." She hung her head.

She heard Matreyi draw breath but before she could speak, Anya said, "I won't be able to see you again, either. Mother told me it was just for today," she said. "I think she only let me because she was feeling sorry for me."

Matreyi tightened her arm about her niece and for a long while they sat in silence, finding comfort in each other's presence.

It was time to leave. Anya worried that their long absence would have been noted and hoped they would assume they had been in her aunt's yurt all this time. She had few visitors, perhaps no-one had checked on them.

There were so many volumes she wanted to take with her, but if she appeared in the camp, her arms laden with books, it would be impossible to still the wagging tongues. Anya looked around in frustration, desperate for some kind of solution. Maybe if she only carried one book, she could hide it under her sari.

She was about to ask Matreyi's opinion, when she spotted something hanging on the back of a chair around another table. She had not noticed it before and walked over for a closer look. As she rounded the table, she could see a strong strap looped around the chair back, supporting a brown leather satchel. It was very similar in style to those she had seen traded from clan Vulture, plain, but sturdy. Anya clapped with excitement. It would fit several books without anyone thinking anything of it. Anya seized the bag, and clutching it in her arms, she skipped back to the table where Matreyi waited.

"Auntie, look, a satchel for our books," she announced happily. "I bet we could get four or five books inside with anyone saying a thing. Which ones would you like to take?"

A little line formed on Matreyi's forehead, and she held still for a moment, before exhaling deliberately. Anya hesitated, wondering if she should not have announced her find so readily, until her aunt began a discussion on the merits of the various books that littered the table in front of them. They chatted contentedly, finally deciding on the final four to take.

As they prepared to leave, Anya looked around her in the fading light, savouring the hope she felt the tower represented. She imagined coming here openly, lighting the fire with no worries about revealing their presence inside, sharing food and knowledge with others who wished to learn. She thought again of the monks at the temple, but stopped herself before her mind could run away with her. The reality was that they were here in secret, and to return would be difficult. She vowed that she would find a way. With a sigh, Anya looped the satchel over her shoulder, and linking arms with Matreyi, they left.

Although the sky was overcast, they emerged from the tower blinking in the light. They had grown used to the dim illumination afforded by the library windows and took a moment to adjust while Anya carefully closed the door behind them. They looked around, and not seeing anyone at the holy site, they set off, the peculiar ground crunching beneath their feet.

They were nearly at the start of the path that led down to their camp when they were halted by a shout.

"What are you doing?"

They turned to see Amman stepping out from behind a standing stone, his face a mask of anger.

"Amman, it's alright," said Anya. She nervously checked that there was still no-one else around.

"I've just seen you coming out of a building created by who knows what sort of dark magic, and you tell me it's alright?" His disbelief was obvious.

"It's not like that," said Anya. "The tower wasn't created by dark magic."

Amman scowled. "How can you say that? It must have been magic, everyone says so." He planted his feet apart in challenge. "How *was* it made then?"

"There is nothing evil about this tower. It's just a library."

"Libraries don't grow all by themselves," he shouted.

Anya bit her lip, upset at Amman's tone and the position he was taking against her. She did not want to say more, worried it would confirm his fears.

Matreyi attempted to explain. "You need to listen—"

"Wait a moment," he interrupted her as though she was not there. Amman's face opened in astonishment. "The fire, everything was burnt in the fire, so what were you doing in there?" He was closer now and reached out, grabbing the satchel at Anya's side. She instinctively clutched the strap, but he did not try to take the bag, he merely opened it.

"Where did these books come from?" There was a panicky edge to his words. He dropped the bag and grabbed Anya's wrist with both his hands, turning hers over, looking at it closely. "Your hands are clean."

He leaned in and sniffed at her. The action made Anya recoil in revulsion. Something about it echoed in her mind and she had a sudden image of Hiranjan just before he tried to rape her. For the first time in her life, she felt afraid of Amman, her constant, reliable friend throughout her whole childhood.

"You don't smell of ash or smoke. Why don't you?" His voice cracked, and he backed away from her.

"Amman, calm down. Everything's alright, I need you to trust me."

"Something's not right here. I thought your mother had told you not to spend time with me, but that's not it, is it? I can see now, everything they say about you is true." He pointed his finger directly at her in accusation. "You've been avoiding me because you're drawn to this tower, drawn to its magic, sneaking up here with your bhakta[16] aunt and you didn't want me to find out."

---

[16] Bhakta is a derogatory term, used to insult any member of the tribe - though it is usually aimed at women - who has acted inappropriately,

At his insult to Matreyi, something sparked in Anya. "And what exactly is it that *they* say about me?" Her eyes flashed with a fire born of anger.

"They say that you brought it here, that you knew it was there when you went alone to the holy site."

Anya laughed, a harsh, forced bark, hurled sarcastically in his face.

Amman's expression tightened. "Some even say that you created it with your own magic." His chin jutted out defiantly.

"My own magic?" Anya repeated incredulously. "Listen to what you're saying, you're talking like I'm some kind of evil warlock. Is that what you think I am?"

"I don't know what to think anymore," he wailed.

"It doesn't sound like you're thinking at all, as usual." She bit off the words angrily, aiming their sharp edges to cut at Amman.

He dropped his eyes briefly, but when he raised them, they had changed. Although they registered the pain of her wounding jibe, they were harder and more distant than she had ever seen them. He walked past her down the path, brushing his shoulder against her as he went. The steep track doubled back, giving him a clear view of Anya and Matreyi.

"I'm going to tell the elders about you, about the books. I'm going to tell them everything." His mouth twitched. "I don't know you anymore."

Anya's anger evaporated in an instant, the fire snuffed out by his words, replaced with a fierce knot in her stomach. For a moment, she watched him go, wishing more than anything for him to turn and laugh, to tell her it was all a bad joke, to be her Amman. At last, realising she was not concerned about his threat, but of losing his friendship, she ran down

---

according to Tharom social standards. "Customs of the Tharom Tribe, Third Edition".

the path, following him. Matreyi called after her to be careful, for though the path was easier than the climb Anya had taken previously, the route was still steep and difficult in places.

She scurried after him, moving too fast for her own comfort, thinking it was unlike Amman to go so fast, to take risks on a dangerous path like this. But of course, it was also unlike him to be disrespectful to his elders, to raise his voice, to let his anger show or to insult anyone. Anyone except Hiranjan, she thought. Hiranjan. Why did her thoughts have to return to him? Everything changed with his attack. Not for the first time, she wished that Hiranjan was dead. Perhaps if her were, everything would go back to normal. Perhaps, Amman would go back to normal.

The trail rounded an outcropping of rock, and ahead Anya saw Amman as he disappeared down a climb in the path. She was not sure he had seen her, and rushed to where he had vanished, stopping to look down and seeing him nearing the bottom and a resumption of the track.

"Amman, stop!" she called.

He glanced up, before jumping the last short distance to flatter ground. He turned and said, "I'm not your tame animal, I don't have to do what you tell me."

He began to walk off once more, and Anya pleaded with him. "Please don't go. Don't go to the elders, you don't understand."

"As usual," he mimicked. "Maybe I never did." He started to move off once more, but stopped and turned to look up at her. "All your questions, the criticism and constant doubting of our stories. I thought it was just your way of understanding them, of getting closer to the truth they hold. But now, I can see that you don't hold them as sacred at all.

"You found this thing, this tower standing on the place where our Gods sacrificed themselves for us. It's desecrating our most sacred place, but you didn't even stop to think, to question if what you were doing was right, you just went straight in. What were you thinking?" Anya thought she could see moisture on his cheeks. His jaw clenched and he continued in a quieter voice. "I'll tell you, you were thinking of yourself, nothing else."

"Amman, please!"

"What did you find in there? Just books? You must have known it was magic. Was that what you were really after. Is it magic you want?"

Anya hesitated, and Amman saw it. His eyes widened, and his face collapsed in something approaching grief. Anya found some words at last. "I wasn't looking for magic, you have to believe me. I just wanted to see what it was."

"It was magic, dark magic!" he shouted. "Isn't that enough? Isn't that obvious to you?"

"It's not dark magic." She was begging him now. "I don't know exactly what it is, but it isn't what the Gods sacrificed themselves to save us from."

"You keep telling yourself that," he said, "while I tell the elders the truth." He turned and strode away.

She knew she was losing him, maybe she already had. Her desperation finally breached her shame and guilt, she could feel it give way inside her and she called after him. "I'm sorry, Amman. I'm sorry." She crumpled onto the ground, her head bowed, tears welling in her eyes.

"It wasn't Mother who kept me away from you, and it wasn't because I was hiding anything either," she sobbed. "You're my best friend, we do everything together, but… but you saw me when that bastard was going to… was going to rape me, and there's nothing I can do to change that, to make it better." She was completely blind with tears, they dripped directly from her eyes onto her lap, making weird distorted images in her sight. She knew that Amman was gone now, but the dam had burst, and the words continued to gush through the breach.

"I couldn't face you. I just couldn't. I was too embarrassed. I never wanted you to see me like that, and now, whenever you're around, it's all I can think about." Anya wiped her eyes, pointlessly. The tears continued to come. "I've been avoiding you because the memory of it would have been floating in the air between us, unspoken, and I just didn't want to talk about it, ever. It would have always been there."

For a moment, she was overcome and unable to speak. She swallowed, and haltingly at first, as though from a distance, she continued. "I… I tried to run, but he caught me. He was so strong, I couldn't fight him off. I always thought I was strong, but no matter how hard I tried, I just couldn't stop him. I was helpless and weak, powerless against him."

"I've never felt that like in my life, so vulnerable. I had nothing left to fight with." She paused, and her breath came in little rhythmic pulses. Anya swallowed and said, "And you saw me like that. I sound so ungrateful, I know, but I'm not. I could never thank you enough if I spent the rest of my life telling you." She sniffed. "But you saw me. It wasn't just that I wasn't clothed, though that's part of it. You saved me. I was vulnerable and *you*, saved *me*."

Anya lapsed into silence. After a time, she continued, "I didn't want you to be the strong one. I always wanted to be in charge and I wasn't anymore. How could I thank you without admitting that I needed saving, without talking about what happened?" She lifted her legs, hugging her knees. "I didn't want to be the weak one, the one that needed to be rescued."

There was a sound, below, on the path. Anya stiffened, worried for a moment that someone might be there, listening to her secrets. At length, after no repeat of the noise, she relaxed, blinking slowly as the tears dried up. She sighed.

"And now you're going to tell everyone, because you're right about me. I am drawn to it." Her voice was quiet now, but it carried in air suddenly still, as though the mountains themselves strained to hear. "I want something more, more than this life is prepared to give me. The tower is my chance. It's not like the warlocks' magic, it's not."

"It can't be," she said.

Unwanted Truth

The herd showed no sign of moving. The available grazing was steadily diminishing, close-cropped areas of brown were beginning to dominate the slope, and many within the clan were anxious at their continued presence and the elks' stubborn refusal to leave.

Conversation in the tent washed over Anya as she read, sitting by herself on her sleeping mat.

"I just wish they would move on, so we could leave that abomination behind," said Shanoli. Bibhu's description of the tower had caught the clan's imagination, and now everyone described it as such.

"They'll move soon enough," said Rahul, placing a reassuring hand on Shanoli's shoulder. "They will need to find more grazing when the snows come."

Shanoli continued to clear the breakfast things as Neeta played with her grandson, the sounds of his burbling and laughter a background noise of the morning.

Anya had braced herself for a visit from a representative of the council, but none came. She was sure that if Amman had informed them that she had again entered the tower and taken some of the books it miraculously still contained, she would have been banished or perhaps declared untouchable, like Matreyi. The fact they had received no such visit, she took as a hopeful sign.

She was reading absently from a book titled 'Flora and Fauna of Sansara, volume 1', skimming over much, but noting especially mention of any species found in the Yanuba mountains. The entry about chikitsa, which was abundant in their present location, was causing her to grow increasingly absorbed as she read.

> As well as its pleasant fragrance, the chikitsa plant has some useful medicinal properties. When ground into a fine powder and suffused in hot, but not boiling water, the fumes given off have within them a powerful healing agent, useful in cases where lungs may have been damaged by breathing in unpleasant air. The patient should place his face over a steaming bowl and breathe deeply, drawing in the vapours that they may begin the healing process.

Anya beamed in delight. To discover such a thing about the apparently mundane was like unlocking a door and finding behind a great secret, a hidden part of life just waiting to be uncovered. She wondered how much more there was to learn. She looked around her, could everything have similar mysteries hidden within?

As she pondered, her smile faded and a voice in the back of her head urged her to think. She frowned in concentration. What was it that was bothering her? She tapped the book with her finger as she waited for the feeling to resolve itself. Finally, with a rush of relief, she realised what it was she sought. Bibhu.

She knew that Bibhu had broken bones and burns, but it was his breathing that had upset her when they had met him to ask for his blessing to visit the place of the Gods' sacrifice. What if it was the smoke he inhaled that was causing it? Anya leapt to her feet and dashed for the exit. She slowed as she neared the flap, breathing deeply. She braced herself, still wary of exposing herself to the stares and gossip of her clansfolk, before plunging through, out into the open.

The ground in and around camp was flattened, the grass and other plants trampled into the earth. Anya rushed down the slope to where it became steeper, leading to the herd's grazing land, and smiled with glee at the profusion of little white chikitsa flowers on display. Excitement bubbled up inside her and she began tearing up clumps of the plants, until her hands were full, and she could hold no more.

Anya pelted back up the slope, past her brother who she guessed had been sent out to keep an eye on her. He turned around in confusion, before following slowly behind her, an indulgent, wry smile on his face. She flung open the entrance flap, depositing the chikitsa on the floor inside, and ran to grab a container of water, pouring some messily into a pan before placing the pan on the cooking stove.

"Anya, what—"

"No time to explain. I need to grind this up," she interrupted her mother, recovering the plants from the floor. Anya wrenched the roots off the rest of the chikitsa, depositing the remainder in the stone mortar and began grinding them with a pestle. As she worked them, they gradually broke down to form a thick, dry paste.

"I'm not sure that smells better than it does whole," said Shanoli. She moved closer to sniff at the ground plant, bringing her head back suddenly and wrinkling her nose. "Oh, it doesn't. That will never do, Anya, it's too sharp."

"I hope I can clean those enough to rid them of the smell," said Neeta, indicating Anya's tools. She came to stand over her daughter. "What are you up to?"

Anya took the mortar to the water heating on the stove, and first checking the temperature with a dip of her finger, she tipped the mixture in, stirring it around with the pestle.

"I need to take this to elder Bibhu," she said, the urgency clear in her voice. "I think it will help him."

"How would you..." Neeta stopped and glanced at Anya's sleeping mat, where her book lay discarded. She returned her suspicious gaze to Anya.

"Please Mother," she said. "What harm could it do?"

Neeta did not answer immediately, appearing deep in thought. "If it hurts him, or hastens his departure, there will be consequences." Seeing Anya's determination, she sighed, and said, "Of course, if it does help, that wouldn't do our standing any harm." At last, she nodded and indicated to Rahul to accompany her.

Anya impulsively kissed her mother on the cheek before snatching up the pan and carrying it from the tent. She moved as fast as she could without losing too much of its precious contents and soon came to Bibhu's yurt, where his grandson sat at the entrance on a stool, whittling a piece of wood to a sharp point. The flap was open, allowing fresh air into the interior. Anya could smell an unpleasant odour emanating from inside.

The grandson looked up at Anya and her brother and scratched at his beard. "What is this? Where are you taking that?" he indicated the bowl using the spike in his hands.

"Please, I have something that I think will help our most revered elder Bibhu," Anya said, using the formal words of respect.

The man stood, his face full of scepticism, and bent to take a closer look. He caught the sharp scent and reared back. "I don't think so, girl. He wouldn't thank me for shoving that under his nose."

"My sister is sure that it could help," said Rahul. "She's very—"

"What is going on out there?" Bibhu's voice was painfully thin and fragile, but he made it carry. A small coughing fit followed, and Anya waited anxiously for it to pass.

"It's that girl, Anya," said Bibhu's grandson. His lip curled as he spoke her name.

"Is it, indeed," came a barely audible response. "Well? Let her in."

Frowning, his grandson let them in. Rahul hung back, waiting respectfully for the elder to speak, but Anya hurried over to where Bibhu lay. She had to hold back her gasp, disguising it with a cough, afraid to give offence. The elder was wasting away, appearing tiny amid the many cushions and blankets engulfing him. She could see the cloth clutched in his skeletal hand was tinged with red. The women attending to him scowled with disapproval at her lack of manners.

"What do you think you are doing?" one said sternly. "You must wait until he calls you over."

"But I have something that might help him," Anya protested.

The woman huffed her doubt. "Or do him— "

"Enough." Bibhu's voice was a mere whisper, but such was his authority, even over his own family, that she stopped talking immediately, heeding his command. He swallowed, and waited to catch his breath, his eyelids fluttering as though he struggled to fend off sleep. "Leave us," he said at last.

Anya ignored the women as they moved away, eager to take her opportunity before the old man lapsed into slumber.

"Elder Bibhu," she said gently. "I have something for you." Anya knelt beside him, holding out the pan she carried so he could see it. She moved her lips closer to his ear and lowered her voice. "I have read of a treatment that may help you." He did not immediately react, and Anya wondered if he had heard.

She was about to repeat herself, when his finger twitched feebly, indicating to her to continue. Anya thought she detected a ghost of a smile on his lips. Without waiting for a more definite sign of agreement, she said, "You just need to breathe in the scent from this bowl." She helped raise him by pushing cushions carefully under his head and back, before holding the still fragrant bowl under his nose.

He wrinkled it in distaste, but Anya said, "I know it's a little unpleasant, but I'm sure it will do you good."

Bibhu reached out with his hand, patting Anya's arm lightly before settling, saying nothing as he breathed, eyes fixed on the pan she held. His breath was painfully shallow, coming in little wheezes, but gradually she heard it ease, lengthening somewhat and deepening. Anya's anticipation was building, excited at the possibilities opening before her, before them all, when she realised that Bibhu's eyes were closed. He had dropped off to sleep. Unsure of what she should do, she remained where she was for a time, allowing him to continue breathing the lessening vapours, hoping a longer exposure would yield better results.

Soon, Bibhu's family stirred, aware that their patriarch was asleep, they returned to his side and made it plain that she and her brother should leave. Feeling awkward under their hostile glares, Anya scrambled to her feet, stuttering her faltering thanks.

"We are grateful for your most gracious welcome," intoned Rahul from behind her. "Please pass on our regards to revered elder Bibhu when he wakes." Anya was immensely grateful to her brother for his calm and gracious words, and clutching the pan in one arm, she hugged him with the other. Together, they returned to her yurt, her arm linked tightly with his.

For a while, Anya had expected a dramatic development, so convinced was she about the treatment. She had paced the family tent restlessly, drawing critical looks from her mother as she often found herself under Neeta's feet.

"Anya, I cannot get anything done with you in my way all the time," Neeta said, exasperated. "Rahul has gone climbing, why don't you join him?"

She was clearly desperate to have Anya out of the tent, and thinking it better than the endless waiting for anticipated news, Anya agreed. She changed out of her sari into blouse and slacks and left for the rocks with Shanoli as her chaperone at Neeta's insistence. She hurried to find her brother, wanting to avoid the inevitable comments that would follow her as she passed her fellow clansfolk. As it was, she soon found Rahul without enduring any barbs, though whether her sister-in-law had acted as a kind of shield, protecting her from remark, she could not tell.

At the rocks, it was not long before Anya became unsettled. Usually, she loved scaling the many rocky climbs found in the mountains, liking little better than to challenge herself to master a difficult route, or to climb faster than she had before. She found a flat area and sat, throwing small stones down the steep bluff below, disgruntled by her lack of enthusiasm.

After receiving an admonishing look from Rahul, who was hanging onto a rock some distance below her, Anya shifted her attention to the horizon, noting the peaks falling away into the distance, melting into the hazy air. She shivered and looked around for shelter from the cold wind on her wide ledge, and realised that this was the same place where she had rested on the day she discovered the tower.

Now that her thoughts turned to it, all Anya could think of was returning to the tower. She knew she was supposed to stay with Rahul for her own protection, though whether that was from potential attack or from damage to her already questionable reputation, she was not sure. If she slipped away, he might get the blame, but if she was quick, she might never be missed.

Anya called down to Rahul, telling him she would rest there a while, that he should carry on. He nodded and continued without her, causing her a twinge of guilt at the deception. But, after all, she would rest, at least until he was out of sight. She waited until he headed down and around an outcrop of stone, before rising to her feet and scaling the last of the rock face.

She peeked her head up at the top, ensuring that no-one was there to see, and scurried over the desolate ground to the tower entrance. Taking a deep breath, she swiftly opened the door and ducked inside. The tower was cool and quiet, Anya's breathing and the echo of her footsteps the only sounds to be heard. She entered the library and felt a gathering charge of excitement build within her.

Anya walked among the shelves, absently reading the spines of the books arrayed before her, but the taste of them was lacking on her tongue, as though they were missing a key ingredient for full flavour. She left them all where they were. She followed her feet as they wandered, knowing where they would ultimately take her. The door.

She had been distracted since leaving the tower with Matreyi, her thoughts returned to it constantly whenever she was engaged in any activity where her mind could wander. When she read, the images she saw were not of the words on the page or their subject matter, but of the door with no lock and no handle. She was absorbed by its mystery, it was a challenge that she would not refuse.

She looked up from her musings and was not surprised to find herself standing within reach of it, its design perfectly matching the image etched in her mind's eye. As she stood, contemplating the door, the picture in her imagination aligned with the physical reality before her, locking into place with an almost audible snap. In an instant, her entire being became focussed on the portal she faced, her senses heightened, her mind free of distractions, feeling clear and sharp as it never had before.

Anya placed her hands on the door, running her fingers over the carvings. She knew every detail, every bump. Even the patterns in the grain of the wood were familiar to her. She breathed deeply and evenly, finding the edge of the door with her fingers, she paused briefly and pulled. The door did not move.

She smiled wryly to herself. She had not expected it to work but thought it worth a try. That was not the way this door would open. Anya stood back from it and looked at it as she had never looked at anything before. The details were crisply in focus, the carvings taking on a quality as real as the scenes they depicted.

"Open," she said.

Again, nothing happened. Anya frowned, forming a thin line between her eyebrows. She knew this door was a test of some kind, perhaps it was a test of magic, but what did she know of it? Only mentions of it in Ujesh's stories, or fragments from books she had read. All of these were of the magic of the warlocks, wielded in opposition to the will of the Gods. This magic was different, it had to be. Reluctantly, she summoned up her memories of what she knew of magic, and suddenly recalled the book from the temple.

> The wild energies used were seized from the world around them, and thus stolen, the world around them died.
>
> We since have determined this: That energy is held in all life and that it is possible - by force of will or some method unknown to us - to extract this energy

The monks believed magic to be an energy in all things, and that to use it, one needed to tap into it somehow. Maybe it was possible to do this without destroying things? Anya took a deep breath and closed her eyes. She could still see a perfect image of the door in her mind and when she again opened her eyes it had not moved, it simply became real. She imagined that she was connected in some way to the stone of the tower, to the earth behind her and most of all to the door, that the energies they contained could flow at her command. She directed her thoughts until all she could see and sense was the barrier she faced. Anya willed their power into the door with one purpose, to open.

The door remained stubbornly closed.

Anya stamped her foot in irritation. "Open, you stupid door," she said aloud. "I want to find out what's behind you." She folded her arms crossly and leaned against it with her back, thinking furiously.

"How can I learn your secrets, if I need magic to open you?" Anya's face was set in a scowl of frustration, her thoughts whirling in useless circles, feeding themselves in endless repetitions of fruitless conclusions. At last, realising this, she decided to disregard her judgement, and instead listen to her instincts. She soon felt the well of excitement within her, waiting still, ignored but present. She knew she was close. What was it she wanted to find behind the door? There was plenty of knowledge, more than she could ever read, waiting in the library to be discovered without ever setting foot beyond this point. What did she think it hid?

The answer was clear to Anya, as if she had always known, but refused to accept it. If all the knowledge in the world was with her, outside, the knowledge within must not be of her world or experience. Magic. She shivered, knowing that to go further was forbidden, that to do so would be breaking the tribe's strongest taboo. Was that what she wanted? There would be no turning back, no return to things as they were and the punishments if she were discovered would be banishment or worse.

She snorted scornfully at her train of thought. No return to things as they are? Without the tower, what was there for her to look forward to? A life in the Vulture eyrie as a dutiful wife, married to someone she had never met, or remaining with her own clan in total disgrace, subject to all the unfair rules of the tribe, with no husband to exercise her rights.

There was nothing for her to fear, except... Amman. Amman had accused her of seeking magic, and here she was contemplating doing exactly that. She knew Matreyi would always be there for her, but the thought of losing her best friend was heart-breaking. Anya closed her eyes, trying to shut out the poisoned choice before her. Matreyi had told her this tower was here for her, how could she choose between Amman and the opportunity the tower offered? She knew she would never get the chance again.

If she denied it, she would either marry, in which case she would never see Amman again, or refuse marriage and live her life in disgrace, Amman a condescending presence, always looking down on her. Her dishonour would taint him, by association. Thoughts of Matreyi flitted through her mind, long-suffering and shunned by all. She knew which she must choose.

She drew a deep breath and addressed the problem she faced. "How do I open this door? I don't know any magic," she said. "That's what I want to learn. I want to learn magic."

A click resounded around her, coming from the wall behind. She turned and stood back, her eyes fixed on the portal as it began to swing open. Anya stepped aside as it swung past her, revealing a dark, unlit space within. She could see a wall stretching away to the right of the entrance, flanking the open doorway, but sensed an open space opposite it. She stepped forward into the room but strained to see anything beyond vague impressions and shapes.

"Why is it so dark?" she said. "I need some light."

Immediately, light appeared inside, fading smoothly from a dim candlelight to something approaching bright daylight. To Anya's delight, she saw it emanated from one of the globular glass flowers set near the top of the right-hand wall of the chamber. She laughed, a bright peal of joy at the wonder of the miracle she controlled.

On impulse, Anya said, "Dark."

Instead of a gentle fading of the light, the chamber within vanished from view entirely. Anya could not even see her hand in front of her face, it was like the darkest, starless night and she was startled by the sudden transformation. In her confusion, she stumbled backwards, falling out through the still open doorway to land awkwardly on the ringed path outside. She was amazed to find that she could now see, the strange darkness did not extend beyond the arched entrance. It fitted it perfectly, like a doorway to oblivion.

Cautiously, Anya crept up to the wall of darkness, fascinated and fearful in equal measure. She reached out with her hand, pushing it into the void, and watched as it disappeared entirely from view. She snatched it back, relieved to see that it was unaffected. It appeared as though there was a barrier, not in the physical sense, but insubstantial. A boundary through which anything might pass except one, it was absolutely impervious to light.

"Light," she said.

Abruptly the darkness was replaced with light, as though it had never been.

"Out." The light faded gently, leaving behind the natural shadow she had first found there.

Anya grinned, delighted with herself. Struck with a sudden whim, she ran into the library and shouted, "Light!"

Instantly, the whole room erupted in a blaze of glorious light, a blossoming flowering of brilliance that swelled, illuminating the shelves of books and tables via the many glowing buds positioned around the library. Anya whooped with delight, laughing as the crazy, incredible light obeyed her command.

"Out!" At once, all the lights faded. More laughter burst from her and she danced around, unable to keep still, or contain the wild happiness she felt. Again, and again she caused the light to glow and to fade, laughing anew each time. As she spun and twirled, a voice inside her urged caution, and she stopped, her eyes drawn to the perfect windows that punctuated the walls. Anya imagined the view from outside, bright light flashing from that flawless glass in mad ominous bursts.

Cursing her recklessness, Anya remembered the mysterious door, now open behind her, and felt her enthusiasm return. She turned and savoured the anticipation, before approaching it in a dignified manner she thought appropriate to the significance of the moment. When she reached the open doorway, she again commanded the globe to light and when it did, she could not prevent a grin appearing on her face.

She stepped through and saw that the space beyond had the look of another antechamber. A sturdy table dominated the room, more shelving containing many volumes of blue-bound books covered the wall to her left and there was another door opposite the entrance she had used. Anya walked over, trying the handle, but it was locked, she glanced around for suitable key without success. There was a single chair and on the table was a kind of portable shelf, itself holding several books and a carved box made from a lighter wood than that of the tower doors.

Intrigued, Anya examined the box's carvings, and saw that the entire perimeter showed images of scenes of nature, including mountains, forests, lakes and great plains of waving grass. On the lid was carved a tree, surrounded by the totem animals of the Gods, the Elk, Bear, Fox and Snow Leopard. Perched on the tree itself was the Vulture.

Anya lifted the box and peered underneath, curious if the carvings extended there. With revulsion, she found the entire base carved with images of death. She briefly saw standing skeletons of men and animals, some with rotting flesh still clinging to the bones, before the shock caused the box to slip from her hands. It fell to the table, where it opened, spilling its contents, a single round seed.

Hurriedly, Anya righted the box and dropped the seed back in, closing the lid and looking around as though expecting a rebuke. She rolled her eyes at herself for her foolishness and, still feeling flustered, picked the first book from the shelf and without scanning its cover, opened it at random. She sat and began to read.

> Hooked chains or other devices can be formed by shaping the raw energies into weapons, which when attached by force to a victim via an attack, can draw their power out against their will, to feed the energies of the wielder. With such a method, one can create a loop, where the gained magic gives greater strength to the assault, drawing ever more power until the victim dies.

Anya staggered backwards, tipping her chair over. The sound of it striking the stone floor was harsh and brittle in her ears. She howled in disbelief, clutching her abdomen at an almost physical pain inside her. The room took on a sinister, sterile edge and she dashed out, slamming the door shut with both hands, leaning up against it, breathing heavily. She doubled up, retching, and fell to her knees, emptying the contents of her stomach on the path. Twice more she was convulsed, vomiting what little was left. She felt her arms shaking, threatening to no longer support her as she leaned forward on all-fours.

She sat back, closing her eyes in despair. How could she have been so stupid? They were right, all of them. This was the very magic used by the warlocks to attack the temple, the same power they used in an attempt to steal magic from the Gods themselves. It was banned by the whole tribe and she had sought it.

Anya lurched to her feet, feeling empty, not just as a result of her purged stomach, but hollow inside as though she were nothing more than a puppet, made to dance for the amusement of a cruel master. The tower around her felt oppressive and her eyes flicked around, seeing details that had previously inspired her, now turned macabre in her eyes.

She ran for the exit, fearing that she might be trapped, that the doors would not open for her, but when she reached the double doors, they opened without difficulty. Anya pushed them closed behind her, and felt her legs quiver and give way. She slid down until she sat with her back to the entrance, slumped facing the scorched ground where the Gods had sacrificed themselves for her, and clutched her knees, her whole body shaking with grief and shame.

Signs of Recovery

Anya was not sure how long she sat there, she wanted nothing more than to curl up in defeat, but knew it would do no good for her to be discovered. Shakily, she got to her feet to return to the camp. For a moment, Anya considered taking the gentler route down, her legs still felt unsteady and the alternative climb was arduous in places, however, she was still under Rahul's authority and protection. She worried he might already be wondering where she was.

Her decision made, she dried her eyes as best she could and headed for the bluff opposite the doors to the tower, checking for signs of her brother as she began her descent. She could see him below, apparently unconcerned by her absence. There were many undulations in the rock face where one might be hidden from view, she supposed he would have assumed she was climbing elsewhere.

Finding the easiest route possible, Anya lowered herself carefully, feeling uncharacteristically unsafe as she climbed, her legs and arms protesting at the exertion. Her mind was not on the climb as it should have been and kept revisiting the room beyond the door with no handle. She tried to shut it out, but her thoughts returned to it relentlessly, probing like the memory of a lost tooth. As she worked, her breathing came fast, and her heart was beating rapidly. She did not think the difficulty warranted the fatigue she felt but could not be sure as her thoughts were too fragmented to rationally assess the situation, and more than once she had to shake her head to dispel a sense of dizziness.

As Anya moved to find another foothold in the rock, her standing leg began to shake violently, before suddenly slipping, leaving Anya hanging by her arms. She lost her grip immediately with one hand and for a moment was clinging to the bluff with just the fingers of the other. She scrabbled desperately for a foothold, but before she could find any purchase, her remaining handhold slipped from her clammy fingers and she fell.

A glancing blow to her ribs knocked Anya's wind from her and spun her around before she landed heavily on her right side. It took her a little time to realise she was no longer falling, and she looked around hazily, at last recognising that she had landed on the wide ledge she'd visited previously. She tested her side with her fingers, finding bruises and abrasions but nothing worse. She sighed with relief and shifted herself away from the edge, resting her back against the stone, she had been very lucky, such a fall could easily have been fatal.

The nook where she had retreated sheltered her from the wind, but even here it whipped around in frigid eddies. Despite the sluggishness of Anya's thoughts, she sensed that snow was on its way. She wrapped her arms around herself in an effort keep warm and to restrain the continued shaking of her arms. Her breathing continued to come in short, quick pants and her head was starting to loll as drowsiness threatened to overcome her.

She heard a voice from within. *Anya, you need to lie down with your legs propped up higher against the rock. Do this now.* Sleepily, she tried to ignore it, but it repeated itself, even more insistent than before. Anya slowly did as the voice instructed and found that her thoughts cleared a little as a result. The wind continued to bite, although the recess where she lay protected her from the worst of the cold. Anya realised that she was in no state to continue her descent, she needed to take the easier route down to the bottom, but to do so, she would have to make the climb back up to the top.

She made herself lie still, for though the breeze still chilled her, her head was clearing, and it helped to have a focus for her thoughts, something to distract her from her brooding. Anya began plotting the best route back to the top, and as she lay, she imagined she heard a scraping sound above the wind, and turning her head to look, she saw a face rise up from below. It was Rahul.

"This is no place to rest, Anya. There is snow on the way."

"I fell." It was all she could find to say. Rahul hoisted himself up and came to inspect her.

"Can you stand?" he said.

With his help, she got to her feet. "I don't think I can climb down."

Rahul nodded, and after a brief conversation, he helped her manage the short distance back to the top. Standing on the edge, her shivering grew more pronounced, and her brother lent her his outer jacket to wear. His lingering body heat enveloped Anya like bedclothes on waking, she imagined the warmth as a physical thing permeating her whole body, returning life to her frozen limbs. Together, they headed for the path.

The journey down was thankfully uneventful. Though not without difficultly, the consequences for any slip were greatly reduced and with Rahul's help, Anya was able to make it down without further mishap. The wind's edge blew more keenly now, the sense that snow was on its way was clear. Anya leaned gratefully against her brother for support and she imagined she looked a sorry sight as she staggered home.

Anya barely said a word as they approached the camp, her efforts focussed on keeping her emotions under control, suppressing the heartache of her discovery. She knew she had been stupid and foolish, and this weighed on her almost as heavily as the death of her dreams. Her desperation to escape her destiny, to believe herself to be special had opened her up to be exploited by whatever dark magic was behind the tower. She only hoped that her recklessness had not endangered the clan in any way.

A figure was hurrying their way, head-down into the wind, not looking up until it became clear they would collide. They stopped abruptly, looking up at last and Anya saw that it was Amman. Briefly, their eyes met, Amman dropping his immediately and mumbling something that Anya did not catch. His typical awkwardness pierced the fog of her thoughts with comforting familiarity and without thinking she rushed forwards, enfolding him in an embrace.

He stiffened in surprise, before lightly returning her hug. "Er, Anya," he said. "I… I'm sorry about..." He fell silent and tried to escape from her arms, but she clung on tightly. His expression widened as Anya's body started convulsing with audible sobs. He looked sharply at Rahul, who returned a look of concerned bemusement.

Amman looked around at the gathering stares. "Let's get her back home, quickly."

Anya allowed herself to be guided to her yurt. They settled her on her sleeping mat under the watchful eye of Neeta, who looked on suspiciously as Anya continued to cling to Amman, who was forced to sit next to her.

"She had a fall, not serious, I think," said Rahul. "Probably just surprised, she usually climbs like a spider." When Neeta offered no reply, he shrugged and left.

Anya continued to cling to Amman, who looked over his shoulder, and saw Neeta sat on cushions repairing clothes in the main section of the tent. In a lowered voice, he said, "It's alright, I never would have told the elders about… you know." She did not respond, so he continued. "I was angry. I shouldn't have been, but it seemed like this was something you could've told me about, but you chose not to. I shouldn't have shouted at you, I trust that you know what you're doing."

His words caused renewed tears to flow. Anya's throat constricted with a painful lump, removing her capacity for speech. He did not know. He was right about the tower, right about her desire to claim its power and here he was apologising to her. She flushed with shame, withdrawing her arms from him and clasping them together on her lap, her eyes gazing though them as her thoughts lingered on the words that had revealed her folly.

Until the victim dies.

Anya drew a deep, shuddering breath, feeling a measure of calm after the storm of her expressed emotions. Keeping her eyes on her hands, she swallowed and said, "You shouldn't trust me. I was wrong."

Amman looked startled but waited for her to continue. "I was so desperate to be different that I was willing to abandon everything we've been taught. I convinced myself that the stories were wrong, that they were simple tales for children, something I had grown out of." She sniffed and not finding a cloth within easy reach, wiped her nose on the back of her hand. "There *is* magic to be uncovered in the tower, but it's the same evil the warlocks used against the Gods. It was there, written on the page, I saw it!"

Her voice, though whispered, had taken on a harsh sibilance and Amman put a finger to his lips. Anya glanced nervously at her mother, who was still patiently stitching the material draped over her legs. She relaxed slightly and nodded to Amman in thanks.

"She'll know soon enough though, because we have to tell the elders," said Anya, urgently. "They need to know the library is restored, that the warlock's magic is there to be learned. Everything. The Protector will come, and he will want the truth."

"We can't," Amman said, giving Anya a desperate look. "If we do, you'll be declared untouchable, just for finding it." He lowered his eyes. "I would never do that to you.

"But—"

"And I would never allow you to do that to yourself," Amman interrupted her. Anya bristled at his interjection, but noticing a firmness in his voice that she was unused to, she deciding not to press the issue.

They lapsed into silence. Anya feared a return of the distance between them and wracked her brain for a conversation starter that would not be awkward or obvious. She was about to open her mouth when Amman said, "I heard what you said, after I left. I know how difficult it must have been for you. I just want you to know, I wouldn't… I mean I didn't look." He blushed furiously.

"You… you should know that you've never been weak." He smiled wryly. "I know. I've been on the wrong end of so many contests with you. I suppose what I mean is that just because you couldn't fight him off by yourself, it doesn't mean you aren't strong." Her head was still lowered, and Amman's eyes were fixed on her hair, an enigmatic smile flickering on his lips. "You're the strongest person I know."

Anya smiled briefly, his words generating a wisp of pleasure that lived and died in an instant. She swallowed. "I didn't go to the tower because I was strong, I went in because I was arrogant and vain."

Anya searched inside herself, finding a hollow void in place of her anguish. She was numb and empty. "I found the books of magic, because I wanted to." She shook her head, knowing that her words were misleading. "What I mean is, I couldn't have found them by accident. If I hadn't decided I wanted to know how to use it, the tower wouldn't have revealed its secrets." A splinter of self-loathing pierced her sense of detachment. "If that was being strong, we're all better off weak. I thought I knew better, I didn't even resist. I gave in so easily to it, to the temptation."

Anya noticed Neeta go to the entrance flap and talk with someone outside. "But you didn't go through with it, did you?" Amman said. "You stopped yourself." He continued, but Anya was distracted, her mind on her mother's conversation.

"Are you sure?" Neeta said.

"I'll always admire that about you." Amman was avoiding eye contact with Anya and did not notice that she was no longer listening.

"That's welcome news, but what does that have to do with my daughter?"

"Anya, there's something that I've wanted to tell you for a long time."

"He insists on seeing her? Of course. Thank you." Anya's full attention was focussed on Neeta now, and she turned her head, looking questioningly at her mother.

"We're best friends, I know, but I've always—"

"Anya, Anya!" Neeta called. Amman fell silent, unable to compete with her urgency or volume. She scurried over to them, gesticulating for Anya to get up.

Anya rose to meet her, leaving Amman still sat behind her, an unseen look of distress on his face. Neeta was beaming and clasping her hands like a young girl at prayer.

"I've had news, he's asking for you," Neeta said. "Elder Bibhu, he believes you healed him."

On the Brink

Anya was quiet as they made their way to Bibhu's yurt.

"If elder Bibhu is truly recovered, this could help us to regain our position in the clan," said Neeta. "Your father could be restored to the council."

Anya cast a sideways glance at Amman, who was tagging along with them while her mother continued to give voice to her hopes for their family's station. His look in return was intense and concerned. Anya was caught between hoping Bibhu's recovery was genuine and fearing what such an unnatural change or influence could mean. She had read the reference to the medicinal properties of the plant in a book found in the library of the tower. The same tower that she now knew for certain was truly an abomination.

If the cure was real, what did that mean? Why would such knowledge exist in a structure built by dark magic? It made no sense to Anya, so she feared the worst, dragging her heels in order to delay meeting with Bibhu for as long as possible. Neeta occasionally shot her a look of exasperation whenever Anya found a pretext to slow them down, admonishing her briefly before resuming her optimistic monolog.

When they arrived at Bibhu's tent, snow had begun to fall and another of his grandsons sat by the entrance. The young man looked up and ushered them in immediately, hesitating when he saw Amman, but deciding against denying him entry. Once inside, they stood respectfully, just within the entrance and let their eyes adjust to the lack of light. Anya hung back behind the safety of her mother, peering around her to get a glimpse of Bibhu.

Remarkably, the old man was animated, chatting energetically with his daughter, sat on cushions beside his sleeping mat. His voice carried and Anya could tell that it had regained much of its lost vigour and strength. Her stomach twisted, both in hope and apprehension.

Bibhu looked over at them, smiling broadly and said, "Anya, please come closer and receive an old man's thanks."

Anya hesitated until her mother tugged firmly on her arm, turning her head so her face was shielded from the elder's view, to give her a stern look that brooked no argument. She followed reluctantly with Amman trailing behind her.

"Why so shy, my girl?" asked Bibhu. "Come, I won't bite." He gnashed his remaining brown-yellow teeth at her unpleasantly, and reached out a bony arm to her in expectation. She looked with trepidation at his shrivelled and spotted hand with its long rough nails, but seeing no other option, Anya placed her hand in his.

"Anya, what you have done for me is little short of a miracle. I am still plagued with my burns and broken bones, but it was my breathing that would have killed me, so I'm told." His eyes found hers, expressing his sincere gratitude. Anya relaxed. This frail old man was not a twisted product of dark magic, filled with hatred and vile intent. He smiled, and said, "As it is, that threat has been lifted. I can breathe more easily than a new-born, and I have you to thank."

Not knowing what to say, Anya said, "Thank you Uncle[17]."

---

[17] Within Tharom culture, it is considered widely acceptable to refer to one's elders as 'Uncle' or 'Auntie', this being an honorific and a mark of respect. In fact, due to the relatively small size of most clans, the use of this custom often reflects the reality of the relationship. "Customs of the Tharom Tribe, Third Edition."

"You have here, a most remarkable daughter," Bibhu said to Neeta. "She has done me, and I trust, your family, a great service. Once I am fit enough to do so, I will raise the matter of your husband's... position with the council."

Neeta nodded gratefully, her barely contained excitement visible in a twitch of her lips. Bibhu continued, "With your indulgence, I would desire a moment of this young lady's time in private, so I might thank her more personally." His manner was light and easy, but to Anya, his eyes were bright and full of meaning. She could see a stiffness in Neeta's manner as she took her leave, issuing the usual formal phrases, and propelling Amman ahead of her with her hands on his back. Anya noticed that the women attending to him left immediately, without a sign of their previous churlish attitude.

When he was sure they were alone, Bibhu fixed Anya with a sharp look. "The treatment you gave me, what was it?"

Anya understood his meaning and flushed guiltily. "It... it was just something I read in a book." He continued to pierce her with his eyes. "A book from the tower," she mumbled.

For a while, he said nothing. Anya looked down at her feet, worried at what he might read from her eyes. "Forgive me, Anya, but how is it that you have a book from that library, when they were all consumed in the fire?" Now it was Anya's turn to be silent, wishing she could leave, to be anywhere but here, facing these questions.

"Speak, my child." When she still did not respond, he said, "Look at me."

Anya looked up hesitantly but found Bibhu smiling gently at her. "I give you my word that I will hold what you say in complete confidence. You may speak freely."

Her mouth suddenly dry, a sense of wretchedness settling in her stomach, Anya licked her lips and swallowed. "The books. When I went back to the tower, the books were… undamaged. It was as if the fire had never been."

Bibhu's eyes widened. "Who have you told?" he whispered, urgently.

"Only my Auntie, and my friend, Amman."

"Tell no-one else." The intensity in his hushed words shocked Anya, and a crawling sensation began creeping up her spine. "The Protector will be found, and when he comes, it would not go well if he should discover this." He breathed deeply. "Was it magic, this medicine of yours?"

"No!" The denial came out louder than she had intended, and she looked around, seeing it had raised several curious glances. Anya feigned a smile, hoping to allay their concerns. She leaned closer to Bibhu, and said, "It was just from a normal book, it wasn't magic, I wouldn't…" She was unable to complete her sentence.

Anya could not read the look he gave her, it made her feel uncomfortable. "Come, Anya. We both know that however that structure got there, it was not built by hand." He paused significantly, glancing around before continuing in an even lower voice. "Therefore, the books that miraculously still populate its library were also not made by hand. They are the result of magic."

Anya winced. She wanted to escape, dreading where their conversation was leading. He did not know, how could he? The turmoil must have been visible in her features, for he said, "You are a bright girl, you know this. What is it that you fear?"

"It's magic."

Bibhu looked thoughtful. "Yet you were happy to come to me with a treatment in one of your 'magic books'."

"That's different."

"Why?" It was a simple question that would lead to difficult answers. Anya hung her head, wishing she could disappear into the ground. "Anya, what is the matter? Something has happened. Tell me."

For a long time, she could not find the words. Bibhu waited patiently, though the way he studied her face made it plain he would insist on an answer. "There is a door in the tower, it has no lock and no handle. It separates the main library, the ordinary books from..." Anya sighed heavily and started again. "I knew I couldn't open it in the usual way. To go past that door, I had to commit in some way. Against all the laws of our tribe I had to declare I was prepared to learn magic despite what that might mean for me. And I did." Anya let her hair obscure her face, a shield from the judgement of the world in the form of the old man.

"It opened for me and I was so pleased with myself. I'd broken our greatest taboo and I congratulated myself on how clever I was, how I was different and special. I'm no better than the warlocks."

"Yes, you are," he said.

"That's just it, I'm not." Anya looked directly at Bibhu, her anger at her own self-serving vanity briefly overcoming her shame. "The first book, the very first one I looked at in the room beyond contained instructions on how to steal magic from others to fuel your own. It was the same power used by the warlocks against the Gods, right down to the chains described by Ghandarva Ujesh in his stories.

"I thought the tower was different somehow from that magic, but I was wrong. I deserve to be punished."

"Well, that was quite a speech. I wonder if you would consider a second opinion?"

Anya saw amusement on the old man's face, and it blew warm air over the coals of her anger. "I didn't come here to be made fun of." She thrust out her chin at him in defiance.

"Anya, calm yourself." He looked around significantly. "I only mean to say that you are too ready to chastise yourself for your apparent crime. But, have you considered everything? What does your Aunt think, or your friend?"

"I'm not permitted to see Aunt Matreyi." It was all she could bring herself to say.

"I see," he said. "Well, I would like you to consider the most remarkable treatment you have given me. It came from the tower, the very same place which you now believe to be evil." His expression was serious now. "Have you read anything else in that library that is suggestive of dark magic? Why would such a wonderful medicine be found in a place of evil?"

When she did not answer, he continued. "I know you are frightened. If you promise not to tell anyone else, I will admit to being somewhat apprehensive myself. But you see, I believe that you *are* special in some way. Everything happens for a reason, and I do not think we have yet discovered the reason behind the tower." Bibhu looked at her with a penetrating gaze.

"I want you to go back."

"The old man is crazy, that's all there is to it," said Anya.

Amman was about to respond, but saw that Neeta was approaching with stoneware cups filled with warmed gaganwa fruit juice, mixed with water. She was humming to herself as she handed them each one to drink, before returning to prepare the fruit's skins for drying.

Anya sipped the spicy drink gratefully, it was a welcome ward from the cold outside. "He doesn't know," said Anya. "He wasn't there."

"But isn't it possible that he's right?" Amman looked uneasy, but continued. "If it is evil, why would it contain instructions for such an incredible medicine?"

Anya looked intently at Amman. "I've been thinking about that. What if it's like a trail of thornberries, little pieces of knowledge that could benefit us all, making us believe that the tower means no harm. It lures you away from what's right until you're too dependent on it to turn away, back to what's right."

"I suppose, but if you were wary of that, you'd be less likely to get trapped."

"There is another possibility," Anya said. "Elder Bibhu is the only person who received that medicine. I know it looks like it healed him, but what if it did something else to him?" She quickened the pace of her words, while also lowering her voice. "It could be that it changed him in some way, maybe it did something to him that let in an evil spirit or… or put him under the tower's influence."

"I guess, but he seemed pretty normal to me."

"He said he wants me to go back."

Amman did not respond immediately, a thoughtful look on his face. "Let's say you go back." He held up a hand as Anya prepared to interrupt him. "Let's say you do. You've already read some of that book, and you're alright. I mean, you're still you, aren't you?"

"So?"

"So, you aren't possessed or anything. You read a book about dark magic and you're not a warlock or crazy or anything. At least, not any more than normal." He smiled a crooked smile.

"I won't go back."

"What if I came with you, maybe I could help?"

Neeta called from across the tent, making them both start guiltily. "I have to go out for a while. You need to finish your drink." She looked pointedly at Amman, who took her meaning and clambered inelegantly to his feet, flustered by her words.

Anya rolled her eyes. "Mother, this is Amman you're talking to. Honestly, I'm perfectly safe." For her mother to be protecting her reputation from Amman was faintly ludicrous to her.

Amman twitched his head towards the exit. "Why don't you come with me?" he said, significantly. "Maybe we could do that thing elder Bibhu mentioned."

"Hmm," she huffed, getting to her feet. "We'll see."

Neeta waited at the entrance flap, holding it open until the children left. A familiar flutter of trepidation tickled Anya before she stepped outside, though she thought it was perhaps a little less than she had been feeling of late. The snow was settling now, the first of the winter, late, but inevitable. It was unfortunate for the clan to be caught so high in the mountains at this time of year. Usually the elk would travel to the lower slopes in late autumn and remain there until spring, reducing their need to forage through a blanket of snow.

Aside from a few young children enjoying the snow, and their parents, there were few people outside. Ahead, they were approaching some men, sat under an awning, smoking from a hookah, which they passed between them. Instead of the usual rowdy arguments, their muted discussion was serious.

"This snow will make it difficult to get to lower ground when the herd move on," said one man.

"If they move on," came a response. "It's the abomination that's keeping them here, you mark my words."

"Or the witch," said another.

Anya hurried past them, raising the hood of her woolly coat, protecting her against the snow and recognition. With a sinking feeling in her stomach, she thought she knew who it was they meant, and was thankful they had not looked up at her passing. She kept her eyes on the snow beneath her feet, not wishing for any scene or difficulties.

A tug on her coat made Anya look up at Amman, who jerked his head, indicating something on her other side. He leaned in to her ear, but before he could speak, a voice cut across the silence of the fresh snowfall.

"Look who it is boys, it's the slut with her boyfriend." It was Hiranjan.

Anya shrank from him. Although she had seen Hiranjan occasionally from a distance since his attack on her, this was the first time she had not been able to avoid him.

One of his cronies said, "How about I persuade your boyfriend to leave and you and me find somewhere private? I know you want to." This provoked general laughter and suggestive whistles.

"She doesn't want privacy. She pleasured Hiranjan out in the open," said another.

"We can all take her. She'd like that." This last from Hiranjan. Amman steered Anya around, to head back the way they had come, but they found it blocked. Some of Hiranjan's gang had circled behind, preventing them from leaving. The rest spread out ahead of them. They were surrounded.

All Anya could think of was the sense of helplessness she had endured when he had attacked her. The world had collapsed around her, conspiring to leave her trapped in a permanent cycle of humiliation. She searched desperately for a means of escape, but none presented itself to her.

Amman stepped in-between her and Hiranjan. It was a useless gesture, they were encircled by his friends, exposed on all sides. Anya felt hands grab at her.

"Let go of her," shouted Amman.

As he turned to help her, Hiranjan took full advantage of his distraction, stepping forward and slamming his fist into Amman's face, knocking him to the ground, where he lay sprawled in the snow, moving feebly.

Anya angrily wrenched her left arm from the hand that held it and spun around to her right, her elbow out. She was lucky, it caught the boy behind her on his jaw, and he staggered backwards. Her success brought a sense of elation and for a moment, she forgot her situation and revelled in the fire that was fuelling her, burning from within. It suggested the possibility of retribution against her enemies, against all oppression, a righteous fury that would burn all that stood against her.

The look on her face caused a couple of the boys to step backwards in alarm and she briefly savoured their fear. Anya made to move towards them, seeking somehow to press her slight advantage when she was seized from behind by strong arms that clasped together in front of her, pinning her arms to her sides.

She squirmed and thrashed to no avail. She looked up, catching a glimpse of Hiranjan before her vision exploded with stars. The speed of his slap astounded Anya and she stopped struggling, shaking her head to clear it, trying to focus on Hirajan and ignoring everyone else. He leaned in so close she could see a patch of stubble he had missed when shaving earlier, and licked her face, slowly. Anya's heart was hammering in her chest, its energetic beat in marked contrast to the fearful paralysis she felt. She fought against the dread that threatened to take her dignity. Whatever happened, they would not see her cower. She stoked her anger, holding it in reserve for when an opportune moment presented itself.

Out of the corner of her eye, Anya saw clansfolk pass behind the ring of boys, either too frightened or too disinterested to intervene. Perhaps they believe I deserve it, thought Anya, maybe the whole clan are cheering them on, hoping they mete out deserved punishment to the witch in their midst. She considered crying out, but feared another blow from Hiranjan.

"What, no clever words, bitch?" he said. Another man passed by, slowing his step to take in the scene, and Hiranjan looked around, clearly considering his next action. He leaned in again, whispering into her ear. "I'm going to taste you before you leave for their Gods-forsaken shithole with your husband. He's going to seem pretty tame after I've finished with you."

To the others, he said, "Come on, let's go." He directed a swift kick to Amman's ribs as he tried to rise, sending him writhing onto the ground once more. The tight grip in which she was held loosened, releasing her. She spun around, her eyes like daggers aimed at her attackers as they retreated to vanish into the falling snow.

Why had no-one intervened? Was she so far beneath the clan that she no longer counted as one of them? She knew that she had deliberately broken the tribe's primary taboo, she had sought out magic, perhaps she had marked herself in some way they recognised instinctively and this had placed her outside their concern. She cursed them inwardly. Her thoughts turned once more to the door in the tower and what lay beyond. If the clan would not protect her, she would protect herself. There was magic there to give her power over others, over Hiranjan.

Until the victim dies.

Amman was trying to regain his feet once again and Anya reached down to help, pulling him up by the hand. He scooped up some snow in his gloved hand and placed it against his face, flinching against the pain or the cold.

"Let's go," she said, inadvertently echoing Hiranjan's words. She indicated the path to the sacred site with a tilt of her head.

"Are you sure?" said Amman. He looked at her closely, and she turned away, wary of what he might read in her eyes. "Are you alright?"

"I'm fine," she said, tersely, before setting off, not waiting to see if he was following.

The path to the tower was made treacherous by the snow. It disguised unsafe footing and coated everything in a slippery blanket of frozen water.

"I'm not sure this is a good idea."

Anya did not turn to face Amman. "Go back if you want, I'm carrying on." Driven by anger though she was, a small part of her registered the risks she was taking, but she disregarded them as easily as batting away a fly, they held as little meaning for her. At the pace she set, it was not long before she crested the final rise. The tower loomed up from the concealed sacred circle, a blemish of darkness pointing skywards in a silent world of white.

Not a single footprint could be seen marring the perfect cover of snow, no-one had visited since it had begun to fall. Wary of the tracks they would leave, Anya waited for Amman to catch up. "You need to cover our tracks behind us, they'll point straight to the tower."

"Uh, are you sure you want me to come in with you?" he said.

Anya was not sure, but said, "Of course, you can't just stand out here in the cold."

Amman nodded and walked backwards following Anya, brushing the snow behind them to conceal their prints as they made their way to the cover provided by the building's overhanging roof. Once in its shelter, he looked back to examine his work, pulling a face indicative of his dissatisfaction. He shrugged and trailed after Anya, who was already skirting the tower wall towards the entrance.

Very soon, they stood at the double doors. Without hesitation, Anya reached out, opening the door and they slipped inside, out of the snow. Amman closed it behind them, the sound of the latch as it clicked into place reverberated throughout the building. Hurriedly, Anya passed through the second chamber into the library.

The illumination from the windows was muted by the falling snow. Anya felt irritated by the gloom and called out in a loud voice. "Light." She heard a gasp behind her from Amman as the entire library was lit by the magnificent floral globes. She continued without breaking her stride until she once again stood before the carved door with no handle. She placed her feet wide, facing the door proudly.

"I want to learn magic," she said.

The door opened wide without a sound, Anya made to enter, but Amman's hand on her upper arm caused her to turn, fixing him with a glare.

"Anya, you're acting strange. This is so..." he waved his arms around at the strange sights that he was seeing for the first time. "What's the matter with you?"

"What's the matter?" she repeated. "Don't you see, doesn't anyone see what's wrong? A woman can be attacked, not even out of sight, but right in the clan camp. People walk by and no-one does anything!"

"We just need to be more careful. Avoid Hiranjan."

"Why? Why should I need to avoid him? Why is it that I have to change, just because that... that bastard..." She pinned Amman with a hostile gaze, breathing rapidly, her inner flame surging up to her brain, inflaming her thoughts until they rushed forth in a blazing streak of fury. "I want to make him pay. I want to hurt him." She bit the words viciously off as she spoke. "If I know magic, he will never hurt me again. I'll... I'll burn him from the inside until nothing remains but ash."

"But, Anya—"

"But what?"

"That's not why we came here. Elder Bibhu believes this place might be here for good."

"And you think it wouldn't be a good thing to deal with that shit? I'd be doing everyone a favour."

"Anya, you know that's not what he meant." Amman looked frightened. "Don't do this. You're talking about willingly seeking to learn the warlocks' magic to hurt someone, kill them even. You know that's not right, not even for Hiranjan." He met her eyes, matching calm resolution to blazing anger. "That isn't you. Please, you must see that."

Anya raised her hand to strike at him, to remove him from her path. He looked at her and did not move. Instead of an irritating obstacle in her way, Anya at last saw Amman, her friend who was looking out for her, as always. In her mind a draught of soothing water cooled her raging thoughts and she paused to consider what she was doing. She dropped her arm and looked down, suddenly weary, the inner fire quenched abruptly, leaving behind only the uncomfortable residual heat of shame.

Her eyes still on the floor, she said, "I'm sorry, Amman. I… I just don't want to have to be afraid of him anymore, to be helpless…" A single teardrop spilled down her face and she wiped it away with her hand.

"You won't be, I'll be with you." He reached out his arm for her. After a slight hesitation, she took it and hand-in hand, they entered the room together.

First Steps

The room was as she had left it. Anya noted the table with its peculiar portable shelf and box, the upturned chair still lying where it had fallen and the book, open, its forbidden text waiting for the unwary, waiting for Anya.

Her stomach tightened, and she shied away from its pages, knowing the contents were staring out, exposed for all to see. On a sudden impulse, Anya stepped up to the table and swept the book onto the floor with her arm. She righted the chair and sat on it, breathing heavily.

"Thank you, Amman," she said.

He was looking around the room at the shelves filled with yet more volumes. "It really is a library, this whole building. Can there truly be enough words in the whole of Sansara to fill all these books?"

Anya smiled, a small thing, but precious to her after the tumult of her maddened rage. "Enough and more, apparently. Imagine all the things ever said in the whole history of the tribe, written down in books like these." She indicated the tomes lining the wall. "Well, perhaps not quite like these, but they would fill the entire building to spill out onto the place of sacrifice."

Her smile turned wry. "I expect there would be an awful lot that's repeated, and yesterday's would read much the same as one from a hundred years ago."

Her eyes were drawn to the remaining volumes on the table, she wanted to reach out for one, but was distrustful of their contents and her ability to choose right from wrong.

"Go on, pick one," said Amman.

Anya took a deep breath and selected the nearest one. Its title was 'The Theory and Use of Precise Formulae to Control Magic Forces'. It did not sound like warlock magic to her, but still wary, she opened and read.

> This treatise addresses the use of precise formulae, or spells, to harness those forces that, invisibly, permeate the universe around us. Through rigorous study, research and practice, one can come to an understanding of how these forces may be manipulated and channelled into very precise effects, to the benefit of the magic user.

Anya looked up at Amman, a look of cautious optimism on her face. He had been regarding her warily, but relaxed visibly at her reassuring demeanour.

"I'm going to have a look around, there isn't a chair for me in here anyway." He indicated the solitary seat in which she sat. "Give me a call if you need me." Giving Anya an encouraging smile, he left. She watched the empty doorway thoughtfully for a while, before turning her attention back to the words on the page.

> Inherent in the universe around us are forces arising naturally from the essence of reality. Though there are many theories and methods one can use to manipulate these forces, such as sorcery, clerical magic or more tailored approaches such as the gifted magic of the Tharom Gods, this book seeks to take a more rational approach, one that will further an understanding of the nature of magic itself and provide a broad base for the creation of the most powerful spells.

Anya frowned, puzzled by a phrase. What was this 'gifted magic of the Tharom Gods'? The only references to magic in the clan tales involved the warlocks. There was something familiar to her in that expression and she wracked her brain, trying to recall what it was. Her eyes widened as a snippet from Ujesh's telling of the Gods' sacrifice unfurled in her mind. 'Let no man, from this day forward be granted our magic willingly'. *'Our magic'*. Had the Gods granted magic to her people? She continued.

> Through the application of demonstrable and verifiable principles devised from experimentation, one can learn the fundamental techniques that may be combined to allow the magic user to control magical forces in order to accomplish a variety of tasks. Depending on the requirements of the student, these forces can, for example, change the nature of objects, present illusory images and sounds or summon entities from this and other dimensions.
>
> It will be demonstrated that although the use of prescribed movements, phrases or materials can channel magical energies, the true key to mastery of this type of magic is one's mind. It is necessary to prepare the brain to store the energies themselves in the form of spells, themselves a codified representation of the understanding required to invoke the transfer of power. Once the triggering sequence of components are complete, the energy stored in the mind is released and the caster will require rest before he or she is able once again to store the energies required to cast this or any other spell.

She blinked, re-reading the obtuse text several times, finding herself no clearer as to its meaning.

> The more accomplished the user, the greater is the capacity of their mind to store these energies, allowing for a larger number of spells or those of weightier magics to be controlled. Key to this, whether a beginner or accomplished mage is the training of one's mind. Accompanying this volume are several works relating to beneficial practices such as meditation, critical analysis and exercises in conceptual understanding.

Anya blew out her cheeks, worried that if she had so much difficulty grasping the introduction, she would never succeed in understanding how to use magic itself. Perhaps she would not be able to. Maybe that would not be such a bad thing. *Do not be put off by the newness of the concepts, persevere and you will find your reward.* No longer questioning the voice in her head, she ploughed on.

> It should be noted that, for primitive societies, such concepts may be difficult to accept, indeed, the lack of magic on some worlds can be directly attributed to an adherence to tradition over discovery. To be a truly civilized society, it is necessary to be adaptable at least in this: knowledge is progress. Indeed, the search

for knowledge begets more questions, guiding the search further. If one does not seek, one cannot progress, it is as true for a civilization as it is for an individual.

One further point needs to be addressed. If all knowledge is progress, what of that which can cause harm or kill? Is there not a moral element, both 'good' and 'evil' magic? Magic is a tool, and as such has no more moral bent than a hammer, knife, pillow or sword. It is the wielder who creates the spells and who uses them. Such morals as there are, for good or ill are brought to its use by the mage.

Anya was intrigued. Was there truly neither good, nor evil here? Was Bibhu's cure merely the application of knowledge and not noble in itself? There was so much she was ignorant of and, it apparently, so little time to learn. She refocussed on the book and dived in, immersing herself in its words.

"Anya, we have to go!"

Anya looked up, uncomprehending from her study, surrounded by piles of books on topics such as geology, physics, phonics and mathematics.

"But I haven't finished," she said. Anya grabbed 'The Theory and Use of Precise Formulae to Control Magic Forces', pointing to the open page. "It says here that there are training spells that a beginner can learn, which allow them to practice the most basic underlying principles of magic. I need to know how to use them, it will lead to—"

"Anya, it's late. If we don't go back, where will we say we've been? What will they think if we are both missing overnight?" He looked seriously at Anya. "We need to go, now."

She looked around her desperately. She wanted nothing more than to stay, to forget the world and have it forget her. With so much to do, so much to understand, to be reminded of the rules and standards of her people, to have them interrupt her study, galled her. New concepts hummed inside her, resonating so energetically she could feel them expanding her mind. She was so close.

"Anya?"

She sighed, realising that Amman was right. With great reluctance, she nodded, and together they left the tower. Once outside, in the fading light, they saw that the snowfall had stopped, the depth of settled flakes no deeper than when they had entered. They crossed the sacred circle of ground the way they had come, trying once again to cover their footprints, with little success.

"This is useless." Anya looked at the obvious trail behind them. She smiled ruefully. "Maybe if I knew magic, I could just say 'cover our tracks', and it would happen by itself."

She bent once again, to carry on, when Amman shook her by the shoulder. Anya looked at him, questioning him with her eyes. He pointed. Anya looked and saw the snow between them and the tower move by itself, blowing and fluffing from the surrounding area to land, apparently pristine, over the dints they had made in the snow.

"How did you do that?" said Amman, his eyes wide.

"I… I don't think I did." She stared in amazement and backed up as the moving snow approached their position. They set off again, with their eyes fixed on the bizarre phenomenon in their wake. Amman kept glancing at Anya, as though she were suddenly a stranger to him.

"Amman, this isn't me. I don't think this is how magic is supposed to work." Her thoughts scrambled to make sense of what was happening. "I've had an idea. Stop," she said. Immediately, the snow settled, moving no more.

"Cover our tracks," she repeated. The eerie movement of the snow began again, continuing until they reached the perimeter of the circle of blasted ground where the Gods had died, at which point it ceased as though it had never been.

"It is you," Amman said.

"But I'm not using magic. You know the light globes inside the tower? I can command them without doing any magic, maybe this is like that?"

"How can you make magic happen without doing magic?" Amman asked, bewildered.

Anya thought fleetingly of the Reflector. "I read about things you can create, items that perform magic for you on command, maybe this is like that?" she said.

"So, where is the thing, the item you're commanding?" said Amman.

For a while, Anya had no answer. With sudden realisation, she turned her head. Amman followed her eyes with his own. They both regarded the tower, thrusting up from the earth, a beacon of mystery amid the frozen peaks.

Anya was restless. She had not been able to return to the tower since visiting with Amman, Neeta had kept her busy with menial chores and instructing her on the correct behaviour when meeting her betrothed from clan Vulture. She carried out her tasks as well as she was able, much to the annoyance of her mother, who criticised her regularly on her cooking skills or her stitching, but the truth was, her mind was elsewhere.

Finally finding some time to herself, Anya inevitably returned to the books she had borrowed from the tower. She read from a book titled, 'Sansaran religious practices'.

> We should not question the definition, 'God'. In all cases where people worship, their appeal is to a higher force. It is not necessary for this force to have personality, or even power, it is enough for it to represent something beyond the worshippers, who may seek understanding, aid or comfort.

She looked up as Sabir entered the tent. It was unusual to see him here during the day and she knew that lately he spent much of his time smoking with the other older men of the clan. Neeta went to him immediately, she, like Anya, recognised this as atypical behaviour. As Anya watched, her mother's manner became visibly excited and very soon Neeta rushed over to her side, Sabir following behind.

"Anya, your father has been restored to the council," she blurted. "Elder Bibhu has been meeting with the others while he recuperates, and his good word has persuaded them of the value of your father's wisdom." Neeta gave her a significant look.

Anya gave Neeta the slightest of nods. She stood and said, "I'm so pleased Father, you should never have been removed in the first place." She cast her eyes down at the floor of the yurt. "It was my fault."

Sabir glanced between his wife and daughter, a thoughtful look fleetingly on his face. "There was no fault on your part, Anya, but today is a new day and we can move forwards once more." He walked over and embraced Anya gently.

A sense of relief welled up inside her, as a guilt she had not realised she was carrying fell away, its presence so routine that the discomfort it caused had faded into the background. She squeezed tightly, smiling at her mother who beamed back at her with delight.

"And I have more good news," he said, releasing Anya and holding her at arm's length, smiling warmly. "A messenger has just arrived. Your husband-to-be is on his way and will be here in only a day or two, depending on the snow."

The warm feelings within her instantly cooled, and her smile vanished as the reality of her situation hit her. She was desperate to please her family, but to have such a limit on the time she could spend at the tower was crushing. Possibilities were opening up before her and she had a sense that she stood on the brink of an understanding that no-one in her tribe had ever had before. How could she abandon it when she was so close? Anya resolved to return to the tower today, to make the most of the time left to her.

Anya glanced up, catching Neeta's eyes upon her. She was watching her closely, wearing a concerned expression. Anya feigned a lighter mood and smiled to allay her mother's fears.

"Come on!" Anya looked back at Amman, she could see his breath misting in the frozen air as he laboured to match her pace. It had not snowed any further and the way was easier than before, cleared by those who had made the journey to the place of sacrifice since their last visit, but he perhaps did not share her sense of urgency. She fretted about the limited time available before her world changed forever, it had taken some time for her to manufacture an excuse to leave the family yurt and her contrived good mood had collapsed into its reverse.

At last they crested the final rise, preparing to make straight for the entrance to the tower when, their attention elsewhere, a voice halted them in their tracks.

"It's good to see young people so keen to visit the sacred site of our Gods' sacrifice." It was Soren, his voice sneering to Anya's ears. "Such dedication is unusual, something to be cherished." His eyes flicked suggestively between her and Amman.

Anya automatically clutched at her bag, blushing guiltily and saw Soren smile slyly. The old man would take her flushed face as a sign that his innuendo was justified, and she cursed herself for her embarrassment.

Looking somehow pleased with himself, he headed for the path down to the camp, but before he reached the slope, he turned to face them once more. "How rude of me, I almost forgot." His smile reminded Anya of a wolf's. "Congratulations are in order on your upcoming wedding. I hear your betrothed is scant days away. You must be so pleased." With that, he left.

Anya stomped off in the direction of the tower. When she was sure the old fool was out of earshot, she cursed. "Stupid old man, he'll spread his silly gossip to everyone he meets. How ridiculous! It'll be just like the trial." The thought of her ordeal did nothing to improve her mood and she fiercely yanked open the door of the tower, causing it to bash the stone of the surrounding wall. Amman, a crestfallen look on his face, cast around fleetingly, before following his fiery friend and closing the door behind them.

Anya studied for hours. The sheer volume of information she apparently needed to grasp staggered her. She had taken a break from the daunting piles of books accumulated on tables throughout the tower and sat on the over-stuffed furniture next to Amman.

"It's too much!" she complained. "How will I ever take it all in? I don't think I can do it, I'm not smart enough. Every spell there is to learn has a foreword that talks about its requirements. I've learned about different types of energies, what fire actually is, even the different planes of existence that connect to all the elements." She paused, puffing out her cheeks and grinning. She turned in the seat, the thoughts in her head giving her animation once more. "Different planes of existence! Just think about it, every time you light a fire, you're opening a connection to another world, though 'world' isn't the right word for it, depending on the plane, they might be like the inside of a ball, or floating islands, or completely flat, like a piece of parchment."

She stopped herself. "There's even a plane of magic, which links to our world in some way." She huffed in exasperation. "There's just so much I need to know!"

"Why don't you forget what you think you need to know and just try?"

"Try what?" said Anya.

"To use it. The magic spells, the training ones, I mean. Just try to use one."

She screwed up her face in protest. "But I don't understand half of it."

"Who cares?" said Amman. "Just because whoever wrote this stuff thinks you need to have all the knowledge in the world, doesn't make it true. That might just be their way of doing it. Do it your way."

Anya looked at Amman as though she had never seen him before. "Amman, that might just be the single most insanely brilliant thing anyone has ever said to me." She kissed him enthusiastically on his cheek and ran, skipping back to the study.

She searched the table for the book of training spells, clearing the rest to create a space for it. She thumbed through its pages until she found one that piqued her interest. Satisfied, she sat back and closed her eyes, attempting to clear her mind of everything, her constant monologue of questions, her eagerness and instead to focus on herself. Anya had read of the benefits of this technique and the instructions came back to her easily. In order to produce magical effects, an energy needed to be stored in her mind in the form of a very rigid and defined code. By repeatedly reading and memorizing the spell she desired, those energies would be laid down in her brain - but only if her mind was focussed solely and completely on the effort.

She was gripped by a rising excitement. Alarmed, she tried to banish the feeling, but this served only to highlight both it and her desire to be calm. *Relax*. Anya released her thoughts and concentrated on her breath, its regular motion reassured her and as her mind dwelt there, all else fell away, leaving her calm and balanced. Without hesitation, Anya opened her eyes, finding the passage she needed and began to read.

Again and again she repeated the same phrase, until she no longer needed the book in front of her. Still, she continued, undistracted by the expanding sensation in her mind, like the arrival of a brilliant or inspirational idea. At last she stopped and held still, intent on her breath until the alternating feelings of hopefulness and anxiety drifted away, leaving her full of peace, and light, as if a feather suspended in the air.

As with most spells, she had discovered through her study, there were triggering words and gestures, movements and sounds that for reasons unclear to her channelled the magic and completed the ritual. The spell she was attempting should enable her to see energy within a target object or space, and was intended to further a student's understanding of the energies that could be manipulated with magic. Anya prepared to recall them, in readiness to release the energies she had attempted to store in her mind.

She stood, opened her eyes and contemplated the table, as good a subject for the spell as anything else. She fixed it in her mind and vision and began reciting the words of the incantation she had memorized, moving her arms in peculiar patterns through the air as prescribed by the spell instructions, a requirement for the correct application of the energies involved.

As she uttered the final syllable, she was at once filled with a rush of euphoria. Nothing she had ever experienced in her life came close to the feelings that now cascaded through her. Her mind soared, transcendent, more powerful than ever before and uplifted with joy. Laughter burst from her, erupting in disbelief at the thrill of the controlled forces within. Anya was a crystal in the sun, casting glittering shafts of insight throughout the room. She gasped lightly as the energies stored in her mind poured from her, evoking a sensation of flight, her view transformed as if from a great height, observing the room around her.

With difficulty, Anya remembered to focus on the results of the spell, and she glanced down, seeing the table, as if for the first time. Standing there was not a mundane and static object, but a dynamic creation of swirling, coruscating energies that were constrained by, or themselves somehow generated the shape of the table. She could see lines of force pulsing along the grain of the wood, spiralling around its knots. She ran her hand along the edge, transfixed by the new reality beneath her touch. She bent close and watched as her hand followed the surface of the wood, sending minor ripples out from the contact. She was fascinated, but somehow expected more.

These energies, she knew, must be present at all times, only to be revealed to her by the effects of the spell. What was unclear to her was what the energy represented. Was it chemical energy that would be released by burning, thermal energy that flowed within and could be altered by interactions with the environment, magical energies, or a mixture of all of these?

Anya frowned in frustration, she needed to know more, perhaps the answers would come to her if she studied the glowing image for longer. What if it did not? The spell would fizzle out soon and she might be left with more questions than answers. Perhaps if she changed the focus of the spell? She reasoned it might reveal distinguishable differences to the patterns she saw, so why not? Anya was about to examine a book from the library when, on a whim, she chose instead to concentrate on the spell itself. She did not know if that was even possible, but began by searching within her mind, looking for the spell she had stored, but it was gone, wiped from her mind by the casting process. In its place, however, she felt instead a tiny thread, a connection that she followed, like a cord in the dark. She imagined it extruding from her brain through the front of her head.

She looked, seeing nothing. Anya could sense the start of a bubbling of anxiety, the fear of failure, immobilizing her for a moment. She fought to control her breathing and closed her eyes, searching for the energies of the spell, and at last, found them. She concentrated, finding that she could produce a visualization that persisted, even when she opened her eyes.

A tiny silvery trail of ghostly, twisting, pulsing light weaved through the air from her forehead, before distorting weirdly near the table.

Anya tried moving her hands as though to grasp the intangible substance, but it had little effect, beyond a slight waver. She tried waving fast and slow, but the reaction was similar each time and certainly unrelated to the breeze she generated with her flapping arms. Glancing down at the spell description, she noticed the instructions that detailed the precise patterns required in the casting of the spell. Holding her breath, she again repeated the movements. Immediately the flow of the silvery cord altered, responding to her obscure gestures.

She combined them with the triggering words and was amazed by what she saw. The entire length of the tenuous thread formed a pattern in the air, but not one that represented the air or its currents, it was something else. Briefly, Anya saw little extensions shoot off from the main channel, forming glowing tangles like the roots of a plant clinging to unpromising rock. Near to the table, the area of distortion glowed bright. Anya lowered her eyes and peered curiously at it, trying to follow the lines of energy, but finding that the effort hurt her head, as though her eyes were being drawn from her skull.

Drawing a deep breath, Anya looked hard at the mysterious glow, seeing more root-like tendrils that formed shapes she could not describe, it was as if they moved in places the eye could not follow. From this place, more and stronger energies flowed, enveloping the table in a shimmering blanket of magic. Where was it coming from? It was clearly related to the connection in her head, but somehow also somewhere else.

A flash of inspiration struck her. What if it was a connection to the plane of magic? Spells channelled magical energy, why not from the planes themselves? Perhaps spells were a kind of instruction to the world around them to release energies already in existence, shaping the link between this world and another, and by the shaping, dictating the effects of that connection? She needed more evidence.

She flicked the pages of the book to other spells, trying out the movements and words described there, and found that each manipulated the energy stream in different ways, ways that to Anya began to form a pattern of its own. In her mind, she constructed a language of movement and sound, testing her ideas with each gesture or chant, knowing that she was on the right path, desperate to continue, to confirm her theory.

Abruptly, the spell winked out of existence, and Anya was left with nothing but the after-images of memory and ideas that filled her with excitement. She would cast it again, and again until she understood. Thrilled, she turned and without warning, the world around her titled as a wave of nauseous fatigue flooded her body. She staggered to the chair, seeking support, missed her grasp and fell to the floor.

Heightened Tensions

Somehow, they had made it back to camp. Anya was weary down to her bones, as if she had been climbing a challenging rock formation for days without rest, her mind as tired as her body from the demands of plotting her route. They were resting at the base of the path from the tower, waiting for her to regain her breath.

"Are you sure you're alright?" Amman said once again. Anya had woken to find he had carried her over to the long seat and laid her down, covering her with his thick coat for warmth.

"I'm just tired, that's all," said Anya, breathing heavily. She had been confused and bleary, unable to focus on anything for any length of time. Amman had sat by her, talking about everything and nothing, until she began to show a greater coherence.

"You know," he said tentatively, "I… I didn't say earlier, but I was standing in the doorway when you collapsed. You were behaving pretty strangely, muttering and waving your arms around and stuff." Anya had not argued when Amman suggested it was time to leave, and appreciated his patience when she had been slow to respond, insistent on packing more books in her satchel.

She looked up at him, wondering what she could say that might make sense to him. "There are movements and sounds you can use that… that unlock possibilities from the word around us. I think it's a bit like pouring water on a sloping bit of dry ground, it will follow a path down to the bottom that is least resistant to its motion." She bit her lip, before starting again. "I mean, if you looked at the ground, it would all look pretty much the same to us, but the water will naturally want to go downhill, so it will turn left or right, depending on the tiny bumps in its path, so its motion isn't just a straight line."

"Casting a spell is a bit like that, but in reverse. You have to know the path you want the water to take, but because the world is normally pretty chaotic, the path isn't just there, it has to be made. The things I was saying and the arm movements kind of… change the nature of the air, no, not the air, the space in which the air floats, or the ground lies so that a pattern is created down which magic energies can flow, only the patterns themselves make a kind of sense that, that…" She exhaled wearily, puffing out her cheeks with her breath.

"I'm sorry, I get carried away." She flashed Amman a wry smile. "But I felt I was so close to working out the reasons behind the patterns and the spell ended. What you saw was me trying out different trigger movements and words from other spells, watching their effect on the path of magic in the air."

"Er, but there was nothing to see." Amman awkwardly shifted his weight. "You looked a bit crazy."

Anya looked at him in irritation. "You couldn't see the magic effects?" He shook his head. "Not even the glowing table?" Amman's eyes betrayed concern, Anya even thought she saw him take a small step away from her. She imagined him watching her as she peered at empty air, leaping around like a lontal monkey and wondered how he had kept a straight face. She sniggered, unable to control the swell of amusement at the picture in her head, began to laugh in a great cascade of mirth.

Amman hesitated, he was clearly worried at first by this new symptom. Eventually a smile found its way onto his face and he joined in fully, though Anya suspected, not understanding the joke. They laughed together, tears streaming down their faces, losing themselves in shared amusement.

"No wonder you look so worried," said Anya when she could catch a breath, pantomiming outrageous motions with her arms. This only served to stoke her laughter and she broke down again, almost falling off the rock she was perched on, which in turn caused Amman to redouble his convulsions, holding his sides as if to keep them from bursting open with hilarity.

At length, their laughter subsided, and they looked at each other with wide grins before Anya again sagged with fatigue, her smile transforming into an enormous yawn. They dried their eyes and guessing that Amman was about to nag her once again about moving on, Anya rose sluggishly to her feet, gesturing for him to come near. Together they set off, Anya walking with his help, her arm across his shoulders, clinging on for support.

They were moving among the second rank of canvas dwellings when Anya became aware of raised voices, and rounding one of the bigger tents, she saw a large crowd of people, blocking their route to Anya's family yurt.

"We need to move on," came a call over the general noise of the throng. "We shouldn't stay here."

"We go where the herd take us, and at this moment, they aren't taking us anywhere." Anya recognised Bibhu's voice and looked around, getting her bearings. The crowd had gathered near the entrance to his tent. She craned her neck, trying to catch a glimpse of him, but of course, he would still be reclined as his broken bones had not yet mended, and the cluster of men was too thick for her to see.

"It isn't natural, they should have left days ago."

"And what are they doing this high in the mountains at the start of winter?" interjected another man.

"But they haven't—"

"Where are they getting their food? They should have grazed that slope out by now, even if it wasn't covered in snow." Different voices rose and fell, peppering the elder with questions and complaints.

"Calm down. For all we know, they will move on tomorrow." Despite his words, their tempers remained high. Anya started circling the crowd for a better view, pulling Amman behind her.

"My son was rolling balls of snow on that slope with his friends. They made them so big that it all came up, stuck to their ball. They could see the grass underneath, he says that the grass was long, like it hadn't been eaten at all."

"It's not right!"

"For all we know, that grass might have been too close to our camp, the elk won't forage too near, or maybe a small area they missed when grazing."

"It's not natural, I tell you." From her new vantage point, Anya could see the speaker was Paras' father, his voice gravelly and rough, as though he'd been shouting for some time. "It's that thing up there." He pointed up at the escarpment. "It's keeping them here."

"We cannot just leave the herd. We need their meat to see us through the winter months, have you thought of that? We will not be leaving." Anya had wriggled through some of the crowd now, and could see Bibhu, encased in blankets in the entrance to his yurt. A flush of anger mottled his face.

"It's against the Gods!"

Another voice inserted itself into the commotion. "What our esteemed elder Bibhu is saying is that even in these trying times, our way of life must be maintained." Anya scowled as she recognised the smooth tones of Soren. "I think we could perhaps send some scouts out along the elks' likely route, to help ease our way when the herd does move off." Some in the throng made approving noises, reacting positively to his meaningless placation.

"There's no bloody poi—"

Soren continued without a pause, louder than before to drown out Bibhu's protests. "Or perhaps the abomination will simply disappear, as mysteriously as it arrived?" His voice grew and too late, Anya realised he must be approaching her place in the crowd, obscured from her view by the bodies around her.

A hand seized her coat by its hood. "What do you think, girl? You're curious about our visitor, aren't you? You discovered it, and weren't you up there this morning?" He bared his teeth at her in an unpleasant approximation of a smile. "Speaking of which, where have you been hiding away all day? I believe your mother was looking for you."

The general tone of the mass of men about them darkened, and Anya tried to pull her hood away from Soren, anxious to escape the threatening atmosphere. "I... I was paying my respects to the Gods," she lied desperately, fear overcoming her reluctance to deceive.

"All day?" sneered Soren.

"Well, uh—"

"We've been visiting Anya's aunt Matreyi," said Amman, his voice carrying over the unpleasant muttering of the mob.

"Is that so?" Soren had picked up on Anya's guilty posture.

"She didn't want her mother to know, that's all," continued Amman. "Anya's not supposed to see her. It's my fault, I was the one who suggested it." He hung his head sheepishly, remorse written large on his face, causing Anya to stare at him in amazement at his glib deception.

Soren gaped, briefly looking like a fish in a mountain lake.

"Anyone see you there?" came a voice from the throng.

"Aunt Matreyi doesn't get a lot of visitors," Anya spat the words, their irony unpleasant on her tongue. "Besides, I don't have to justify my movements to you. What am I accused of that I should have to defend myself, assuming I'm even allowed to?" She stared around her at the mass of angry men, meeting their anger with her own, the defiance of her gaze lowering that of any who would challenge her.

"This isn't the council, let me go." She yanked her coat at last from Soren's grasp and pushed her way through the crowd, Amman following on behind.

Anya slipped quietly from the tent. It was early, the sun had not yet risen, though the moons cast a silvery light that sparkled off the frozen snow, easing her progress. She walked as quietly as she could, being careful to avoid stepping anywhere that had not yet been compacted by the tread of others. Her breath misted in the frigid air, whirling in curious eddies before drifting away in the gentle breeze.

Although craving more sleep, Anya felt refreshed after her early night. She had been ravenous at her evening meal, eagerly devouring every available morsel, but suddenly tired had been unable to keep her eyes open. She had retired immediately to her bed-mat, aware despite her fatigue, of Neeta's concerned scrutiny. Now, she pushed thoughts of her sleeping parents aside and concentrated on ensuring her footsteps were as silent as possible. After a long, cautious dart through the camp, she reached the start of the path to the sacred circle, and found Amman already waiting for her, as agreed. She returned his smile and, neither speaking, they set off at once, keen to avoid notice.

Their journey to the top was uneventful, their only difficulty was in keeping their hands warm, it was considerably colder than before. Amman was leading as they made their way up the final slope to the sacred site when Anya caught sight of something unexpected. She grabbed him, dragging him down level with her own crouched stance. He was about to protest when she put her glove to his mouth to indicate silence.

"Someone's there," she whispered.

"That's weird," he said. "Only animal handlers and scouts should be awake at this time of day, and there aren't any animals up here. What's he doing?"

"Nothing, just standing there, but whoever it is, they're standing right in front of the door."

The beginnings of a nagging suspicion rose in her mind, and she scuttled to the side of the path to hide behind an outcrop of rock, peering around it at the figure blocking their way. Anya thought he had the look of a defender, though it was difficult to tell under his many layers of clothing, despite which, he was stamping his feet while he paced to and fro in an effort to warm them.

Amman crept up to join her. After watching for a time, he said, "We'd better leave. It doesn't look like he's going anytime soon."

"No." Anya was adamant. She had little time before her husband arrived and she was determined not to waste it. "All we need is a distraction."

"I could try to get his attention somehow," he said. "Maybe tell him I've hurt myself and need help getting back to camp."

Anya shook her head. "I've got a better idea. Stay here and keep hidden until I give you a signal." She waited until the figure by the tower was pacing away from her and scrambled over to stand behind one of the Watchers, the large sentinel stone providing more than adequate cover for her. Move a little snow, she thought, focussing on an area near her feet. She grinned when a small clump moved by itself where she watched. This will work, she said to herself.

Picturing the area around the double doors, she sent a verbal command to the tower. She heard a strangled cry from the other side of the Watcher and clapped her hand over her mouth to contain her giggles. Knowing that the man's attention was elsewhere now, Anya peeked around the stone at the scene.

Spinning in the air before the tower doors, was a vortex of ice crystals, drawing up more and more of the snow as it moved slowly away from where Anya watched. The Defender was crouched low in a defensive posture, his eyes fixed on the eerie sight before him. Grinning to herself, she sent a further command and from inside the spinning twister shot a ball of snow, narrowly missing the horrified man.

Anya worried the man might run, but was relieved when she saw him draw a knife instead. She ordered the whirlwind to move around to the far side of the building, watching and hoping that the Defender would take her bait. The man moved off, and Anya realised she had been holding her breath. She turned and waved for Amman to follow and stepped inside the sacred circle, looking for a trail of footprints to disguise their own, that would lead them to the shelter of the tower's over-hanging roof.

At last she found them, and gaining Amman's attention, waved for him to follow her. With that, she moved as fast as she dared, speedily arriving at the door. Anya yanked it open and they tumbled inside, swiftly closing it behind them, breathing heavily more from the suspense than from exertion.

"I'm not sure that was a good idea," whispered Amman. "How will we be able to get out again?"

Anya's face darkened with self-recrimination. How could she have not thought of that? "I don't know," she said, and stomped off, moving directly towards the study.

"Anya, stop." She turned, eying him in irritation. "I know what you're like, you'll bury yourself in those books for hours. You need to eat something, I've brought some food for both of us." He began taking off a bag, slung diagonally across his chest, while walking towards the stuffed seating. "Come on." Reluctantly, she followed.

Amman sat and produced fruits and vegetables, as well as a collection of dumplings, left-overs from yesterday's main meal, arranging them on the table by the round stone ornament. They ate in silence, for the most part, Anya giving mono-syllabic responses to all his attempts at conversation, her mind elsewhere, worrying at the problem he had highlighted. At last, Anya offered her barely adequate thanks, and set off for the books and their magic.

Once again, Anya studied the book of spells, but found she was still distracted by the issue of the guard outside. She placed her elbows on the table and repeatedly banged her head into her upturned palms, as though the act might physically loosen its grip on her thoughts and made a determined effort at clearing her mind, utilizing a meditation she had learned, focussing on her breath and nothing more. After a time, satisfied that she was ready, she looked down and began memorizing, repeating the same phrases and committing the energy of investigative spell to her mind.

The procedure, which had exhausted her previously, this time felt easier to Anya and she flicked to another page, trying to also commit the spell she found there to memory. It took some time, but after one failed attempt, with a rush of satisfaction, she succeeded. Not daring to risk any more, she calmed her mind and prepared to recall the trigger words and actions for the spell she had cast before. They came easily to her, and momentarily, her mind began working on the theory she had begun concerning patterns she believed she had seen in the words and movements, which she was sure would help her understand how magic worked. Realising her lack of focus, she stopped, returning her attention to the preparation of the magic. Taking a deep breath, she brought her thoughts back to the spell and cast it.

This time, she was ready for the overwhelming feeling that washed over her. Ready, but not prepared. A shudder passed through her as the energy was released, accompanied by the same feeling of triumph, almost supremacy at the control she exerted over these fundamental forces. She again concentrated on the spell itself, repeating the movements and incantations of other magics contained within the book. As she did so, her theory transformed from rough instinct, to something more solid. Anya clapped her hands with excitement, but the proof she needed would only come by experimentation. She would cast the second spell, using the first to test her theory.

Anya muttered the words, gesturing precisely, watching as the path for the magic was forged, finding that both felt right to her. Once again, she channelled the magical energies to do her bidding, observing their flow closely and matching them to the theory she had built. The joy that flooded through her in the casting was exhilarating, but distracting to her concentration. She savoured its ecstasy, wondering how she ever could have lived a life without it. Though the same, there were aspects of it that differed, as though it were somehow another flavour of pleasure. She controlled her emotions, watching with fascination as connections were formed, until the spell was complete.

She sought an image in her mind, smiling as it formed in the air, scowling unpleasantly. It was Soren. To her eyes, it was a whorl of radiant energies of light, connected to her by a tiny thread and obeying her commands, but to anyone else, it would appear as though Soren were there in person. Anya knew that it could not make a sound, but if that was not noticed by Amman, she could give him a fright. Carefully, she directed the illusion from the study, making it walk towards the seats near the fireplace. She peeked around the open door, seeing Amman's back as he reclined in an armchair.

She positioned the image of Soren behind his chair and coughed in what she hoped was a gruff manner, thinking to herself how inadequate the sound was. Amman turned around, looking for the source of the noise and immediately leaped out of his seat, crouching as though he might either run or attack the old man. Anya laughed, making her vision of Soren caper like a lontal. Slowly, she saw Amman relax, a mistrusting frown on his face.

"Is that you?" he said, shivering at the eerie sight.

"I'm sorry, I could resist," said Anya. Coming to stand behind the illusion, she waved her hand through it. "It's all just light, generated by magic to simulate the real thing. I can control it to make it do anything I want." She stepped to the side and grinned as Soren began picking his nose. He removed his finger and licked his lips in apparent anticipation when the spell ended and the image vanished.

Amman stuck out his tongue and feigned being sick. "That's gross."

Anya was about to respond when a familiar enervation took hold of her. She staggered, reaching the chair in which Amman had been reclining and fell over the cushioned arm into its seat, her eyes fluttering in the grip of her exhaustion. Amman rushed close, his face anxious, but Anya smiled weakly, holding up her hand in an effort to reassure.

"I'm alright," she whispered. "Just give me a moment… so tired." With that, she slept.

"I've got it."

Amman had been looking at the false doorway in the wall when Anya spoke. He turned, looking at her curiously. "You're awake then. Got what?" he said.

"I know why the movements, why the sounds do what they do." She looked at him, her eyes bright. "There's a pattern. If you piece each bit together, you can do pretty much anything you want. I don't think I need the book of spells, I could make up my own."

"Anything?" he said.

"Well, in theory, anyway." She bit her lip, frowning in concentration, before continuing, "What I don't quite understand are all the ways you can tap into the connections - to the different planes, fire, water, magic and others. Whatever you want to do, it requires a way of connecting, so, for instance, if I wanted to light the fire there, I'd need to find a method of creating a connection to the fire plane that lit just the wood. If I got it wrong, I could burn myself to a crisp, so it's pretty important to only try what you can handle."

"What do you suppose this is for?" Amman said, changing the subject. He gestured at the blank wall of stone, framed by what looked like a doorway, as though the builders had simply changed their minds about adding a door.

Anya offered no reply. She'd wondered herself, but could come up with no convincing explanation. If the tower had been created using magic, surely it could have been made to appear, fully formed to the exact specifications of its creator, so to add something, anything with no purpose rankled her. Perhaps it was some kind of joke, something to satisfy an unknown sense of humour.

"And that circle of earth in the middle, why would you need it in a building like this? It doesn't even have anything growing in it." He wandered back to the seating area, settling himself on the long seat facing the fireplace.

Deep in thought, Anya's unfocussed eyes were looking through the hearth, the round stone ornament resting on the table occluding part of her view. A glint of light on its exterior drew her attention from her musings and she looked more closely at the orb. It was smooth, and polished to a shiny perfection, reflecting warped, coloured versions of the room and objects around it in its surface. She had previously ignored it, but in the light of her speculation, was now intrigued.

"What about this stone?" she said, and reached out to place her hand on it.

As soon as her fingers touched the glossy rock, the room around her vanished. All Anya could see was the back of the

Defender outside, obscuring her view of the sacred circle. Surprised, she jerked backwards and the interior of the tower reappeared as her hand broke contact with the orb. Anya stared, breathing heavily, her eyes flicking between her hand and the stone.

"Anya?" Amman was looking at her with concern.

Once again, Anya placed her hand on the stone ball, this time prepared for the vision. Once again, her view altered, and she saw the man pacing left and right as he guarded the entrance. She tried to look behind her and the view changed naturally, as though she were actually standing there turning her head, until she saw the entrance to the tower. The man, now 'behind' her, stamped his feet, clapping his hands together in an effort to warm them. Anya turned, realising that this illusion, this vision, provided sound as well as sight, but not the sense of touch, as despite the cold of the scene around her, Anya did not suffer the wind's bite.

She looked down, finding nothing supporting her vantage point, no body or anything but air. Amazed and enchanted, Anya laughed. Immediately, the guard whipped around with his knife in hand, his eyes darting around for the source of the sound. He had heard her laughter. Seeing nothing, his wide eyes above the scarf covering his face betrayed his obvious fear, and he backed away, scanning left and right for something that would explain the noise. Feeling guilty, Anya withdrew her hands and turned to Amman.

"I think I know how we can get out without being seen."

Anya had read more in the last few hours than she had ever thought possible. Using her new theory, she devised a way of channelling magical energy so that the words on a page could be read at a staggering pace. Though at last she flagged under the weight of all the new information she was trying to digest, she had read more of magical items, which, like the Reflectors, sometimes worked at all times or otherwise might require a word of command to be spoken. She had learned of magic that could animate corpses using negative plane energy, a source that was somehow equal and opposite to the forces that drove all life. The idea of such magic was repulsive to her, a desecration of life's sanctity.

She also learned that Sansara had no real history of magic use, beyond the natural gifts of certain creatures, such as imps [18] or unicorns and the powers of the Gods. One reference she found alluded to the existence of other worlds, where magic was commonplace and taught freely to those with the talent to learn. So many questions formed in Anya's thoughts and she found herself longing to visit such a world, wondering if there was magic to achieve such a thing.

"Are you ready?" Amman restlessly occupied the open doorway, clearly keen to leave.

She nodded, and hurriedly stuffed several books into her satchel, looping it over her shoulder before walking with Amman to the orb of stone. Seating herself, Anya ran her plan through her mind, picturing its success and imagining possible complications.

"Be prepared to run," she said, and reached out to place her hands on the round stone.

Once again, her vision was transported to the tower entrance. A different Defender now stood guard, but realising this changed nothing, Anya peered around her for signs that other people were near. As she looked towards the path to camp, her point of view moved in that direction. How wonderful, she thought! Immediately changing her plan, she searched for a suitable spot out of sight of the entrance, instructing the tower to begin moving snow as if someone was struggling underneath its cover.

---

[18] Though few in number, imps still frequent the Yanuba mountains. They tend to be solitary, and try to avoid contact with humans. On those occasions when by inattention or chance they find themselves close to members of the Tharom, they will use their magic to distract. Loosening items of clothing and temporary amnesia are common tricks of these tiny winged creatures. "Life in the Yanuba mountains."

Turning her point of view so that the animated snow was between her and the tower, Anya began screaming for help in what she hoped was an altered voice. The whirling snow would hopefully be brought to uncanny life by the sound of her cries. After a moment or two, she saw the Defender rounding the tower to investigate and let him approach while she continued to cry out.

She let go of the orb. "Now!" shouted Anya.

They both hurtled to the exit, flinging open the door in their haste. Anya closed it again, as quietly as she could manage, and they dashed away, not daring to look back until they were sure the path had taken them out of sight of the tower. They dropped down into the remaining snow and listened for signs of pursuit. All was still. Anya carefully crept back up the path until by raising her head, she gained a clear view of the double doors. As she watched, the guard shuffled back into place, looking around him with fitful movements.

She ducked down and smiled at Amman. His face broke into a relieved grin and together they made their way down the path, reaching the camp without complication. Amman insisted on accompanying her back to her yurt, and they moved cautiously between the tents, wanting to avoid any possible trouble in the fading light. The met no-one, and Anya gave her friend a quick hug before darting into her tent.

"Where have you been?" Neeta turned as she entered, glaring at Anya, her eyes narrowed in suspicion.

"Oh, you know," said Anya airily, still giddy with their successful escape from the tower. "Out and about."

Neeta's eyes took in the satchel hanging at Anya's side. "What have you got in that bag?" she said.

Her mood instantly dampened, she clutched it defensively. "Uh, I… nothing," said Anya, hating herself for the feebleness of her reply.

Neeta walked over to her, and reached out to grasp the satchel. "Let me see, Anya."

"No!" Anya tugged on the bag, resisting her mother's demands.

"I beg your pardon?" There was ice in Neeta's voice, and her posture brooked no argument. "Give it to me this instant."

Anya dropped her head, releasing the bag. "It… it's not what you think, I can explain…"

Neeta flipped it open, peering inside. Confusion flashed across her face, and she reached in, as though searching with her fingertips for something she could not see. She closed the bag, stiffly returning it to Anya. "Very well. I don't know what all that fuss was about, young lady," she said.

Anya stammered, not knowing what to say, as confused as her mother had been a moment before. How had she not found her books, the books of magic that would incriminate her?

Recovering herself, Neeta said, "It's not good enough, Anya. You need to be ready for tomorrow."

A cold chill ran down Anya's back. "What?" she said.

"We've had word that the party from clan Vulture will be here tonight." Neeta's expression was stern. "You will be married at noon tomorrow."

Marriage Vows

Anya found it difficult to move. All morning Neeta and the other women of the family had been busying themselves about her, adding new layers of clothing to her already tightly-wrapped frame, or applying pinches of crushed berries to her lips and cheeks. Rings and bracelets of gold adorned her hands and arms, a dazzling, jangling array of borrowed riches, sending her levels of self-consciousness to new heights. The wonderful scents arising from the prepared food wafted out into the snow through the opened sides and front of their yurt, unappreciated by her, while smouldering braziers kept the chill at bay. All was ready.

A constant stream of clan women and girls passed through the tent, bestowing their blessings and gilding her head with the traditional red stain of all tribal weddings. It was claimed to bring luck and prosperity, though Anya suspected its true origins were lost to history. She resolved to look it up in the tower library before remembering that she would never be able to return, and within her, an ache intensified at the thought. Often these and other rituals would be performed for days prior to a wedding, and one or two old crones complained as they passed, muttering about ill omens under their breath, thinking she would not hear. Neeta had been buzzing around, trying to alleviate these fears with explanations of snow and altitude to account for the ceremony's haste.

Amman's mother was next in line, wishing Anya blessings and happiness, reaching out to her cheek to wipe away a tear she had not realised was there. The gesture brought more moisture welling to her eyes and she bowed her head to hide her sorrow, unable to express her thanks. It was common for brides to cry at weddings, she knew, after all, for many this would be the last they would see of their clan before leaving with their husband for a new life elsewhere. Anya's grief was not limited to the impending separation from her family and she felt its edge all the more keenly.

In the background Ujesh inexpertly played the Sarangi, his lack of skill causing the instrument to resemble more than ever a wailing human voice. It was traditional for the Ghandarva to maintain the practice, but the clan were always grateful for his restraint. All who engaged him in conversation were granted a sheepish look and a muttered apology.

Loud cheering interrupted the music. The groom and his small party were approaching the yurt, processing past each tent in camp, receiving the noisy congratulations of the clan before completing the journey to claim his new bride. Beside her, Sabir rose awkwardly to his feet, he often complained of stiff joints when sitting for long periods. He gave Anya a melancholy smile before moving off to meet with her new husband.

Anya shifted uncomfortably, straining against the tightness of her outfit, which constrained her to the point that breathing deeply caused the fabric to contract alarmingly. She raised her head, curious despite herself to catch a glimpse of her husband-to-be. The well-wishers, also aware of the procession's imminent arrival, stood back, leaving Anya exposed to clear view on the pile of cushions arranged for her and the groom.

Gradually, the sounds of the party grew louder, until finally, they rounded the last tent into view. Leading the parade, Anya saw the tall young man who had travelled to arrange her suit, dressed in formal splendour and festooned with decorations. He moved easily, laughing along with the others, and for a wild moment, Anya found herself hoping that this was to be her betrothed. She looked him up and down, finding him pleasing. When he glanced her way and their eyes locked momentarily, he coloured, and quickly looked away.

Behind came the rest of the party, surrounding one man who Anya realised must be the actual groom. For a while she could not get a glimpse through the throng around him, but as they approached her position, they slowed and parted, like a flower presenting its nectar. The metaphor caught in her throat as she saw the man she was to marry. Wearing the robes of a groom, the man revealed was old and grey, he might once have been muscular, but if any was left, it had settled around his midriff.

Anya's spirits fell, and a flush found its way onto her face. It was common for girls to marry older men, but usually this meant a groom in their thirties, old enough to be established in his position and a confident master of his new wife. This man was much older, perhaps as much as sixty, how could her mother have agreed to this? Her embarrassment deepened as the answer became clear, with her reputation, no-one else would have her.

Again, she lowered her head, this time to hide her shame. Perhaps they will assume I am coy, she thought, before the ridiculousness of the idea pierced her hopes. What young girl would be flattered by the prospect of marriage to such a man? Anya did not dare to look around her, not wanting to see their looks of pity. She kept her eyes fixed on her hands, following the lines of henna tattoos on her hands and fingers, which flowed in endless loops.

Anya was abruptly aware of the hush around her, all was silent but for the voices of her father and the groom, discussing the price of her dowry[19]. She found it difficult to

---

[19] By tradition, the Tharom groom will pay a dowry to the father of the bride to take ownership of his daughter. This will often include domestic

hear what they were saying and frowned. In most weddings, this ritual was conducted boisterously and with great boasting from both sides, lauding the virtues of both bride and groom. The price was always agreed in advance, however, and the mock bartering served as a source of great entertainment to the guests. She risked a glance, seeing expressions of discomfort on those guests nearest the two men.

Straining to catch their conversation, Anya looked at her father, who was clearly agitated. As she watched, Sabir gestured emphatically in her direction, his face stern. The groom merely waved a single finger from side to side before spreading his hands in a gesture of helplessness.

"Two handfuls," he said, firmly, his reedy voice carrying across the yurt.

Sabir's face was dark as storm clouds, his eyes hard with loathing as they regarded the man before him. With a shock, she realised this was no charade, the two men were literally bargaining over her worth in front of the assembled members of her clan and that of clan Vulture. She stared, open-mouthed at the unfolding discussion, acutely conscious of the unwanted attention focussed on her. Despite her embarrassment, Anya was grateful beyond words to her father for clearly valuing her so much higher, humiliating though it was to be publicly traded, given her situation, she considered he had done well to have negotiated two handfuls of saffron for her.

"Cinnamon!" hissed Sabir, incredulously.

The world fell away beneath Anya, and she reeled as though hovering on the edge of a precipice. Her value had been set at two handfuls of cinnamon, a paltry quantity

---

animals, such as goats and items made of gold, but will, in truth be measured in spice. Saffron is considered by many to be the true measure of a bride's worth, with as much as twenty handfuls exchanged in some weddings. "Customs of the Tharom Tribe, Third Edition."

amounting to a mere gesture, a blatant fulfilment of tradition only.

"You tradesman, you're nothing but a counter of beans." Sabir's words carried to the uncomfortable ears of those around.

The tall young man stepped forward, saying, "You will treat my father with respect. He has come a long way in difficult conditions to marry your daughter, and when he arrives, he learns that..." He glanced momentarily in Anya's direction, before dropping his eyes and avoiding her gaze. Despite the rising heat in her cheeks, she cast about the wedding guests, her eyes stopping on Soren, who was smiling contentedly at the exchange. The warmth of her face was joined by the spark of her temper igniting within, and blood began pounding in her ears.

"A long way for someone used to perching all year long on his fat—"

"Sabir!" Neeta moved close to her husband, clutching his elbow. "You will…" The rest of her words were hushed and did not reach Anya.

"I have no wish to offend," said the groom, his voice smooth, but insincere to Anya's ears. "I am in no need for more children and merely wish my new wife to look after me in my declining years. Three handfuls," he said, a derisory increase on the already meagre dowry.

Anya's mother forcefully struck Sabir's shoulder. "Very well," he said, stiffly, clearly not happy with the arrangement. Neeta retreated to her place behind him, her face tense, but grimly satisfied.

"Good, good. Now that our business is concluded, it is time for me to claim my prize." Her betrothed turned to face Anya and his eyes widened in surprise. Anya found that she had risen to her feet, unable to remember how she had got there.

"Your prize, bought and sold before all present, like a beast of burden, only less valuable." Anya's voice was low, but its scorn carried in the crystalline air over the shocked silence of the tent.

"Anya!" cried Neeta. "It is not your place to speak. This arrangement is between your father and Khagendra, your husband."

"He is not my husband yet, Mother. Still seeking to avoid embarrassment, even as your own daughter is traded for the price of a goat?" She stared at Neeta with incredulity, shaking her head with disdain. "The shame is all yours." Neeta recoiled as though physically slapped.

"Is this how she behaves, at such a time?" said Khagendra in urgent low tones, uncomfortably addressing Sabir as though Anya had not just spoken to him directly. "Perhaps I was too generous."

"Generous? I'll bet even your close family wouldn't claim that of you." Anya looked openly at the man's son, who could not meet her eyes. She smiled in bleak satisfaction. "You insult my father, and you insult me with your grasping, miserly disrespect."

"Shrew!" cried Khagendra, finally turning to acknowledge her, mopping his forehead with a brightly coloured piece of cloth. "You will learn obedience and decorum."

In the air she sensed a pattern lingering, the magical energies she could summon waiting on her command, her anger sought their use against this pompous man. With a great effort, Anya instead drew a deep breath, leaning in towards Khagendra, her face dangerously close to his.

"But not from you, you fat old man," she whispered. Anya turned to those assembled, and said with venom, "I am no-one's property to be bought and sold. No woman should be, it is to our disgrace that we hold to such traditions. Shame on us all."

She spun around and began to stalk from the tent, tugging at her clothes, frustrated at the restrictions of her costume. The air buzzed as the gathered attendees gave voice to their astonishment and surprise. She approached the circle of onlookers and at the fury in her glare, they parted without a word.

"Anya!" Again, Neeta called out her name. Anya stopped, exhaling deliberately before turning to face her mother, who had followed in her wake and now stood, hands clenched at her sides, her knuckles white with suppressed anger. "You will come back and apologise. Maybe, with luck, he will still have you."

"No, Mother, I will not." The steadiness of her voice surprised her. After her outbursts, a calm enveloped her, and her thoughts held a peaceful clarity.

"You will do as I say. We are your parents and know what's best. This is not just about you." Neeta had lowered her voice, though it held no less passion for its lack of volume. Anya knew her mother would not choose to discuss such things in public, but her desperation to avoid scandal had been overcome by the urgency of the moment. "If you refuse this, your last chance at marriage, you will be cast out of our family in disgrace, untouchable, like Matreyi."

"I will, but by whom, Mother?" asked Anya, her eyes searching Neeta's, full of sadness.

"You think we have a choice? This is our tradition, our life. It is not our place to question it." Neeta's control had evaporated, and she exploded her words at Anya.

"I question it."

"Your father will be stripped, once again, of his position on the council because of you."

"I'm sorry. But you're wrong. All of this is wrong." Anya's temper stirred once again, and she aimed her word like knives at Neeta. "You choose honour and respect over the wishes and happiness of your own daughter."

“That’s enough!” Neeta’s voice cut through the entire assembly, the silence that followed was brittle and sharp. “You will beg forgiveness and accept this marriage, even if we must give you away for nothing.”

The moment swelled, and the air crackled with tension. All was still, every eye fixed on Anya.

“I will not,” she said, her voice quavering.

“Then you are no child of mine.”

The words were like a hammer to Anya’s soul. Though she had known the consequences of her choice, the reality of her disgrace was more painful than she could ever have anticipated, it washed through her in waves of nauseous grief. Her lip trembled as Neeta turned her back on her, and she looked around frantically, as though searching for succour. She found none. Tears began to prick her eyes, and she fled, out into the cold.

Crime and Punishment

Anya ran, heedless of her destination. Conflicting thoughts surged through her, blinding her to her surroundings. She fell in the snow, Neeta picked her up, lifting her above her head, dandling her in the air and laughing, before placing her on Sabir's shoulders while Rahul watched with a wry, fond smile. She realised she had snow in her mouth, and spat it out, like when her sister had deliberately sprinkled too much hot spice in her favourite food. Her sister, who was married and living with clan Bear, just as she should now belong to clan Vulture.

On and on, a thousand memories of a life she had lost flashed across her mind. Lost forever, and for what? Was it worth it? She had stood up for her right to be herself, not to be anyone's property, to make her own decisions and her prize was a life without choice, subject to the decisions of others and protected by no-one. Anya slumped in the snow and cried, her legs under her, sitting on her heels as if praying to the Gods.

After a time, the chill of the mountain air penetrated her bridal outfit, bringing her some measure of awareness of her environs. She looked up and through her tears saw her flight had taken her once again to the site of the Gods' sacrifice, and to the tower. She laughed bitterly. Without its influence, without the hope and belief it had fostered within her, Anya would never have faced down Khagendra and her mother. Without it, she would have married.

Her laughter died. In a sense, what had she lost? A life of servitude in a loveless marriage. But Khagendra would have died long before she, and she would have been left respected, perhaps even with influence. Now, as a result of wanting to control her own destiny, she was destined to weather the scorn of her own people, without agency in the decisions others made on her behalf. Either way, the promise of the tower would be denied her.

She wiped her eyes and glared accusingly at the stone edifice, rising above her from the centre of the sacred circle. A bitter cry burst from her. "Is this what you wanted, a pitiful, broken girl? Is this why you came?"

As if in response, a voice in her head spoke to her. *Danger!* Anya thought she heard a sound behind her and wheeled around, seeing Hiranjan sauntering towards her, shaking his head, his cronies forming a circle around her.

"I'll tell you why I came. To try out the bride." He struck her almost nonchalantly with the back of his hand before bending down and grasping her by the throat. "There's no-one who's going to protect you now. No friends, no husband and no family. I thought I'd lost my chance and here you are, all dressed up just for me... well, me first, anyway." He looked around at his gang significantly. They laughed eagerly.

"Stupid bitch, you should've married the old fart when you had the chance." Hiranjan let go of her neck and in the same motion slapped her hard across the face. Anya reeled, her vision swirling in dizzying fashion. A sharp pain in her head brought her back to her senses and a frightened yelp escaped her lips. She was being dragged through the snow by her hair, towards the far side of the tower, that slight bit more concealed from any unwanted interruptions, assuming any would choose to intervene on her behalf. For a moment, Anya was paralysed with fear, she closed her eyes, as though she could shut out the world, and deny her inexorable, inevitable fate.

But only for a moment.

Opening her eyes, she saw the windows of the library passing by, and her thoughts returned her to the study behind the door with no handle and no lock. Her thoughts returned to magic. Anya's eyes closed again, not to block out her pain, but to control her breathing, and focus her thoughts. In her mind she sought a pattern and she imagined the energies around her and how to tap into them. She could feel the structure of the world around her and the path down which the magic must flow. She waited calmly for her moment, ignoring the throbbing in her scalp, the words she would use ready on her lips.

At last, the pressure on her head eased as she was released from his hold. Immediately, Anya rolled to her knees, Hiranjan was slowly turning, expecting to find a quivering helpless girl. Instead, he frowned in confusion as before him, he saw a woman in control of herself, chanting and waving her arms with precision. He laughed with derision.

"What do you think you're doing, you crazy bitch?" he jeered. "Is that supposed to scare me, or freak me out? No, wait, you think it's some kind of spell to ward off evil."

Anya's arms ceased their motion and she raised her eyes to fix him with a stare. "Yes, it is," she said.

He lashed out at her and despite herself, Anya almost flinched at his brutal speed. However, the blow never found its mark, Hiranjan howled with pain as his fist hit an invisible barrier between them. She registered something else in his eyes as he cradled his injured hand, looking at her aghast. Fear.

"What?" He glanced at the others in confusion.

Anya rose serenely to her feet, never taking her eyes from the would-be rapist. "You will never hurt me again," she said. Once more, she began a spell, drawing from the ground beneath her feet, requiring the force of the solid, static earth.

Hiranjan lashed out again with his foot and again found a shield thwarted his blow. His face contorted with rage and he rushed at her in a frenzy of suppressed terror and violence. Anya held her arm outstretched with palm facing him and Hiranjan immediately stopped, frozen in place, like the ice that hung from the eaves of the tower, unable to move, except for his eyes, which were alive with dread. She regarded him with loathing and contempt.

"If you ever try to harm me, or anyone that I love, you will suffer worse than this." With that, Anya stepped forward, swinging her foot with all her might and connecting viciously with Hiranjan's crotch. To her satisfaction, his eyes bulged in agony, the tiniest moan escaping his confined throat.

She became aware of a muttering around her, as his friends belatedly reacted to the events before them. Anya looked up, scanning their eyes and body-language for a likely response. Some were backing off, others standing their ground, clenching their fists. All were scared.

"Dark magic!"

"She's evil!"

She saw them reach for knives, calling out to their fellows to do the same, and driven by fear they ran at her. Desperately, she realised she had considered nothing beyond this moment. Anya reached instinctively for something to frighten them still further - fire - and formed the simplest, strongest pattern she could to directly channel the energies of that plane.

Her hand erupted with flame. It roared outward, stunning Anya with its ferocity. She raised her hand into the air reflexively, knowing that anything in its path would be roasted in moments. Before her attackers could react, she pointed it at the ground between them, spinning in a circle around the frozen Hiranjan. Where flame met snow, a hissing, furious cloud of steam exploded into the air.

Hiranjan's gang skidded to a halt, shouting in horrified alarm, scrambling desperately to escape, and pelted away headlong, back to camp. Anya laughed in triumph, before she was enveloped in excruciating pain, radiating out from her left hand. She looked and saw her skin burning, scorched by her own fire. She cancelled the pattern, the flame ceasing abruptly and plunged her seared hand into the snow at her feet, sobbing as the slush stung her burnt flesh.

The shock of her injury brought her mind into sharp focus, she had broken clan law in sight of a crowd of witnesses. The council would judge her severely. Anya staggered to her feet ignoring the living statue beside her and stumbled towards the entrance to the tower, and sanctuary. Waves of fatigue threatened to overwhelm her, and she fought them, desperate to keep herself above the sleep that would claim her in their depths. The double doors came into view as she drunkenly rounded the walls of the building. One thought drove her as the world dissolved and unconsciousness took her - to be found guilty of magic was death.

Anya woke abruptly with freezing slush-filled water sluicing off her face. She gasped, coughing as fabric in her mouth threatened to be drawn into her airways, blocking her throat. Finding her arms bound behind her, and unable to use her hands to wipe them, she blinked the wet out of her eyes. At last able to see, she stared, terrified around her, her eyes darting about in panic at her situation.

Pointing directly at her from all sides were the razor-sharp points of Defender spears, so close she could see the discolouration that marked the tips as poisoned. Standing implacable in a surrounding circle, the men themselves watched her struggles vigilantly, no trace of emotion visible on faces so grimly set, they could have been hewn from stone.

Anya risked an attempt to sit up, which elicited no response from her guards, and winced as her movement eased the pressure of the bonds on her wrists, allowing fresh blood to return to her hands. Her left hand blazed in a fiery echo of her injury, throbbing unbearably at the renewed circulation and bringing tears to her eyes. She tried to investigate the extent of the damage with her other hand, and to her surprise, found it apparently wrapped in bandages. A fly landed near her eye and she shook her head to dislodge it.

Animal smells assailed her nostrils, and she looked around her in the gloom of the dark tent, noting the evergreen branches strewn about the ground, dotted here and there with the droppings of goat or donkey. Clouds of flies swarmed around the excrement, producing an ominous background drone. The clan livestock had been removed to make way for an animal of a different sort, their sanctuary against the ice turned to a prison for the girl who threw fire from her hands.

"Get up," came a voice from the rank of Defenders, Anya thought it sounded familiar to her.

Anya tried to speak, to question, but her intended words were reduced to a high muffled note of apprehension.

"The prisoner will be silent." The entrance flap opened, casting cold light on the face of the speaker. It was Prabhav, his face stern and unreadable.

She tried to rise, but with both hands behind her back, it was difficult. No help was forthcoming and after two failed attempts, Anya gained her feet from a kneeling position. The formation around her changed, the circle mutating to form two lines either side, with a channel that led directly to the exit. With no choice and no inclination to resist, she walked towards the light, shivering as the warmth of the tented stable gave way to the frozen air outside, easily penetrating her tight bridal outfit.

Once outside, her eyes adjusted rapidly. The light which had pierced so brightly the dim confines of the tent, was muted with fresh snow, falling peacefully in large flakes, settling on the already frozen ground. The Defenders formed a moving cage of spikes around her, directing her towards an area of open ground beyond the tents of the camp where Anya could see smoke rising from a clan fire. A large crowd parted as they arrived, allowing them ingress to the cleared space within.

The gap closed behind them as jeers and insults began to rain down on her. Anya searched fretfully for a friendly face, anyone who might be there with sympathy in their heart for her. All were hostile, wearing faces twisted with hatred and baying for her blood. Khagendra was visible, standing next to his son, a look of satisfaction on his face.

Anya's eyes found her parents, locking onto them for courage, seeking, if not support, then love. Neeta's features were hard and unforgiving, she looked back at her daughter with apparent loathing, a vision of condemnation. Sabir kept his eyes on the ground, his shoulders slumped. Alongside her mother, to Anya's eyes, he looked defeated, a man crushed by loss of position and prestige, here to see the perpetrator punished for her crimes.

Anya trembled, though from apprehension or cold, she could not be sure, the heat of the blazing fire did little to warm her from this distance.

"You may stand back." It was Soren. Obediently, the Defenders retreated and raised their spears high as though in mocking salute to her.

"We are here today, gathered so all may see clan justice meted out to this brazen slut, concubine to the brother of Death." He strutted inside the clearing, all attention now focussed on him. "Her actions have violated the very heart of the clan who once nurtured her in its bosom. She has used dark magic, calling forth the abomination upon on our most sacred site, the place of our Gods' sacrifice, where they fell to protect us from those who used magic against them. She has used this sorcery against her own people, in contravention of our most fundamental law." He paused dramatically. "She seeks to be a warlock and to use their power."

Although they all knew the reason for the council, Soren's words caused a baying cry to rise up from those assembled. Several gobs of spit were launched in her direction, falling short due to the size of the cleared area maintained by the ring of Defenders. Anya did her best to block out the hate-filled screams of those who, not long ago, had been her fellow clansfolk, if not her friends. She was not successful. Soren strode around her, skirting the crowd, the falling snow rendered him less substantial to her, like a ghostly apparition. He allowed the intimidating torrent of outrage to continue unabated. Anya imagined he savoured the sound, music to the ears of one who believed she had somehow wronged his family.

"This whore, who earlier today snubbed the protection of our honourable cousin from clan Vulture in order to preserve her promiscuous ways, in anger at the deserved consequences of her insult, attempted the murder of several of our finest young men using magic granted her by the darkest of Powers." Though not as fine an orator as Ujesh, he was preaching to the converted, and the throng lapped it up, eagerly. He gestured to somewhere over Anya's shoulder and she looked down at her feet, unwilling to turn and see for herself. "Come forward, boys, let us hear your testament."

Hiranjan's friends traipsed past, keeping well away, their eyes fixed unwaveringly on Anya, wide with fear. Initially, her lip curled in derision at their act, but she soon conceded to herself that their apprehension was genuine, they were honestly scared and probably unaware she had not sought to harm them with her flames. A bitter humour rose up in her, of course they were unaware, people saw what they wanted to see, a witch, a slut, a target for their fears, and an outlet for the simmering tensions, which had been increasingly on display within the camp. She looked at the people with fresh eyes. They wanted someone to blame for the behaviour of the herd, for having to live under the shadow of the abomination.

"Please my friends. Let us hear what these young men have to say." He held his hand aloft to calm the crowd and turned to face the line of boys. "Go, on, don't be worried, she cannot hurt you anymore."

"She… she used magic," said one, hesitantly. Anya almost laughed at the obviousness of the statement, but caught herself, some part of her recognising the mania behind the impulse.

"She tried to freeze Hiranjan solid, like ice," said another. "And tried to break him with a kick."

"Then she threw fire at us. It was like a gate to hell had been opened. I thought we were dead, for sure." The boy began to cry, unable to continue his testimony, causing renewed expressions of anger from the watching masses. Anya was transfixed with a confusing sympathy, she was the cause of his distress, and despite what she knew they were all prepared to do to her, she fervently wished she had not been responsible for his tears. Here, surrounded by his elders, shorn of Hiranjan, his leader, he was revealed as nothing but a frightened child. Her shivers intensified as the flakes of snow swirled around.

Soren turned away from the boys, briefly, as though composing himself. Anya was almost convinced, until she caught a glimpse of firelight reflecting off his teeth, bared slightly as he smiled to himself in satisfaction at their words. Composing his features and returning his attention to the boy, who was wiping his nose on his sleeve, he said, "Thank you for your bravery. To face this witch must be very difficult for you. You may go, all of you."

"My grandson is once again recovering from injuries sustained at the hands of this wicked creature," continued Soren, wantonly ignoring that it had been Amman who had stopped Hiranjan's first attack on Anya. "You have heard the testimony of her victims. She caused the flames of hell to target them, issuing from her very hand." He strode over to her, and roughly removed the bandages covering her wounds. Anya cried out at his callous treatment, a muffled sound, lost in the snow and general mood of discontent. Her hand was exposed now, the cold wind and touch of snow a peculiar blessing against its searing pain.

Soren dragged her around the circle. Anya stumbled backwards as he paraded her injury for all to see, clear proof of her wickedness, the dark magic that would consume them all if they were not vigilant. Beneath her numb dread, a small part of her considered that hers was the greatest injury sustained, the line of boys on display were unmarked by her sorcery. A ball of snow hit her on the side of her face, finding the swelling bruise left by Hiranjan's blow. The suddenness of its strike was shocking to her and she flinched. Emboldened by this, more snow and ice were hurled at her, but this was no child's game, these people wanted her dead.

By now Anya was wet through, shivering uncontrollably, her teeth chattering in her skull. She stumbled, falling to her knees, her legs so cold, the snow enveloped her like a warm blanket against their chill.

Soren looked down at her, his face twisted, hard with disdain. "By ancient tradition, all who seek the magic of the warlocks shall die. I propose that this creature be stripped and tied to the rocks, where she will be a living sky burial. It is a greater mercy than she deserves, the weather will claim her before she is eaten. What say the council?"

At once a chorus of 'ayes' filled the air. The world receded from Anya's senses, becoming no more than a dull backdrop to her misery. Her last hope extinguished, Anya was filled with despair, her shoulders wracked with sobs.

"Hold!" came a voice from the surrounding onlookers. Anya looked up vaguely, to see the people part, admitting Bibhu, who supported himself with two sticks as well as the help of his grandsons, well-wrapped up against the cold. His face was creased with exertion and sweat glistened on his forehead. Leading them all was Amman, who saw her and rushed forwards, removing his coat and draping it around her. He lifted her up out of the snow and she leaned against him, her tears renewed by this final act of kindness. His arms held her firmly, keeping the coat closed against the wind and cold.

"We recognise elder Bibhu's right to speak, but the council has made its decision." Soren's oily tone was cautious.

"Until I am heard, that decision must wait," said Bibhu.

"Even your esteemed voice is not enough to change the verdict of this council," said Soren. "We are unanimous, do you dissent?" There was a new note in his voice. Amid her wretchedness, a new trepidation began to stir and she looked fearfully at Bibhu, sure that he was somehow in danger.

"The decision is not flawed," said Bibhu. "But I was not present, and I would have argued differently." An angry murmur grew in the air. "Yes, yes, our law is clear, to use magic is punishable by death. I would only choose a different kind of death."

Soren said nothing, but eyed him watchfully. Bibhu continued, "This child is, or was one of us. There stand her mother and father." Her parents lowered their heads, Anya imagined they would not wish to suffer the disapproval of those present. "Let us show them some mercy, and instead banish the girl to wander the mountains alone, dead to the tribe, and in this renewed weather, to die by the Gods' hands as they see fit, but on her feet."

Soren moved silently around Bibhu, regarding him as one would excrement, inadvertently brought into a yurt on the sole of one's shoe. "You cannot simply choose the punishment, our tradition—"

"There is precedent," cut in Bibhu, ignoring Soren's expression of affront at his interruption. "Banishment has been preferred before, has it not, Ghandarva Ujesh?"

Ujesh, his face unreadable to Anya, nodded thoughtfully. "That is so. There is a story, but it tells that the accused was a Defender, the son of a prominent elder. That is not the case here, and she is a girl."

"She has no family, so I will take her as my own," said Bibhu to gasps from the crowd. "Will that suffice?"

"But she is untouchable, would you destroy the good name of your family?" Ujesh was aghast.

"You cannot make my whole family untouchable."

"No, but— "

"This is irrelevant," cut in Soren, reasserting his position of dominance over the proceedings. "It changes nothing, the decision has been made. Amending the sentence would still be at the behest of the council. We reject your proposal." Cries of assent followed this declaration and Anya's heart sank further in her chest.

"You leave me no choice. I will over-rule it, by dint of my position as the most senior elder in the clan." He tugged his arms from the grip of his grandchildren, disdaining their support and stood unaided, shaking with the effort. The surrounding mob erupted in fury at Bibhu, incensed at the prospect of their victim escaping justice. Anya closed her eyes, not wishing to deal with any false hope.

"That privilege has not been used for— "

"But it has been used!" shouted Bibhu, cutting Soren off, the sharpness of his tone even quieting the crowd. "I am entitled by our clan tradition, am I not?" He turned a questioning look at the Ghandarva.

"Yes," said Ujesh. "But you would forfeit your position as elder." Bibhu nodded his understanding.

"And it is only the method of punishment that you can change, not the verdict of death." Anya was strangely grateful for Ujesh's calm and dispassionate appraisal, his vote against her had not been personal.

"So be it," said Bibhu.

"Let it be known that Bibhu is no longer and never again shall be, an elder," said Soren, spitting his words. "The witch, Anya, is hereby cast out from the tribe, to die alone among the frozen peaks of the Yanubas." He faced the people, his back to Anya.

"No, not alone." It was Amman.

Anya turned her head, her wild eyes filled with concern. "No," she tried to say, but the words were muffled and distorted by the cloth in her mouth, too quiet and indistinct for any but Amman to understand.

Soren turned, addressing Amman with scorn. "The verdict is final, boy."

"I am a man," said Amman, his voice too high. In other circumstances the contrast with his words may have been amusing. More forcefully, he said, "I am old enough to marry, therefore I am a man, and as a man of the clan, I do not need your permission to go where I please. I will go with Anya."

There was renewed commotion in the surrounding host, Anya could not bring herself to look for Amman's parents. She imagined his mother, who had always been fond of her, now cursing her name and praying for her death.

Soren's lip curled in disdain. "Do as you will, the witch must be gone by nightfall." He paused, and turning to address Anya directly, said, "Any attempt to return to the clan, or to visit the abomination on our holy site will revoke this amendment of your sentence, and you will be chained alive to the rocks of the Yanubas and left to die. This council is over."

Amid a great murmuring of surprise and disapproval, Amman hustled Anya close to the fire, removing her gag and bonds and rubbing her arms beneath his coat. Bibhu, again supported by his grandsons, hobbled with difficulty to join them as the crowd began to disperse into the falling white.

"I'm sorry Anya," said Bibhu. "It was all I could do." She did not respond. To her, everything was muted, a distant impression of reality, lacking immediacy, like a distant glimpse of the lowlands from a mountain peak.

"It was unwise of you to use magic before witnesses." His tone betrayed a hint of annoyance and it sparked a reaction from Anya.

"Better to let them gang rape me, I suppose?" Her voice was a low monotone and she regarded him with hooded eyes.

"I… they didn't say… I'm sorry," he said again, his face earnest and full of sorrow.

"Not that it would have made any difference to the council's decision, even supposing they had let me speak," she said bitterly. The taste of the rags in her mouth was still on her tongue and she bent to spit. It made little difference. "You didn't need to do that for me."

"Yes, I did." Bibhu's tone was earnest. "You saved my life because you have a desire to understand, and to use that understanding to bring change. None of that would have happened without you, our tradition would not have allowed it. There would be no change, and I would now be dead."

"I didn't mean that," said Anya. She looked around at the heavy snow. "I have to leave soon, I won't last a night in this, you know that. It was kind of you, but unnecessary."

"We'll find a way," said Amman.

"No, we won't. You're not coming with me."

"And who's going to stop me?" Amman asked sharply. "It's not like you get a say in this, you're banished and untouchable besides."

Anya looked at him, seeing grim amusement dancing in his eyes. "You idiot. I could turn you into a frog, or something," she said.

Amman laughed, and Anya could not help but smile, despite the hopelessness of her situation. "Anya, I have a few things to take care of. Meet me in your aunt's yurt, we'll leave from there." He fastened up his coat around her before standing back in assessment. "In the meantime, stay close to the fire, you need to get warm and dry." With that, he left.

"Anya, all is not lost," said Bibhu. "You have power, we know you can channel it to make fire. Use it to keep warm, use it to survive."

She held up her left hand for him to see, the skin was cracked and broken, fluid weeping from the uncovered flesh beneath. "This is what my fire did for me," she said. There was silence for a time, and Anya gave voice to something that had been bothering her. "Elder Bibhu, why were you so keen for me to go back to the tower? It wasn't just the knowledge, like the chikitsa treatment I gave you. You wanted me to learn magic."

"I'm sorry, if I had known where it would lead—"

"No," interrupted Anya. "Despite the consequences, I'm not angry. The tower is a wonder, we just don't deserve it. We're not ready." She gave the elder a penetrating look. "Why did you want me to learn magic?"

Anya watched Bibhu as he lowered his head. At length he sighed, and raising it once again, said to his grandsons, "Would you give us some privacy for a moment?" They retreated beyond the range of their conversation, appearing content to leave him with her.

"There is a… hypocrisy within our clan, within our tribe," began Bibhu. "Our laws are selective, choosing punishment for one act, and praise and gratitude for a different, similar act. I think they are not so different."

Anya frowned at his words, her mind seeking the meaning behind them, the effort brought the world into better focus around her. "The Reflector!" she said at last, remembering the passage she had read. "You're talking about the Reflectors."

Astonishment was writ large on Bibhu's face. "How could you know that?"

"How does it work, what is it that the guide sees reflected in it?"

"I... I cannot say," said Bibhu, with resignation. "It is not permitted. Only the guides and most senior elders know, were the people to find out... it would be too dangerous." He fixed Anya with a serious look, swallowing an obvious fear. "It can do no good to know. Suffice to say, he sees the reality of the monster, and is protected from its magic."

Anya searched her memory of the incident with the Rahksharu. She had been convinced that she'd seen it, but when she tried to remember, the image skipped away from her. With an effort, she controlled her breath, bringing a measure of calm to her thoughts. She imagined a Reflector in her mind, and held it up to the memory.

At once, a barrier broke within her and she recoiled from the vision revealed. The twisted form she saw was a madman's nightmare, a collection of dead things spliced together, multi-legged and lethal, covered with rotting flesh, and mounted on it all... Anya opened her eyes, blinking repeatedly to dispel the insane image, but it remained, holding her mind's eye as it had before. The Raksharu had a human head, its eyes glowing death to all whose gaze they met. What captivated her with horror though, was the rest of its face.

It had begged for death.

Escape

Anya and Matreyi embraced. Anya clutched her aunt fiercely, as though by doing so, she could somehow capture her essence and take her with her.

"I could still come with you," said Matreyi, echoing her thoughts.

"No," replied Anya, she recoiled from the thought of her beloved aunt out in the snow, lacking protection in the midst of winter. "Besides, we both know what that would do to my father." Matreyi had requested of Sabir that she go with her. He had refused, and for her to disobey him would further damage his reputation and standing within the clan, perhaps even to the point of his being made untouchable. It was unthinkable to Anya that she cause her parents even greater misery.

A sound at the access flap to Matreyi's yurt heralded a blast of freezing wind as Amman entered, closely followed by Rahul. Both were loaded with carrying sacks, their arms full of clothes. With a final squeeze, the two women released their hold on each other and turned to regard the newcomers.

"Time to get changed, you should find a good selection of warm clothes here," said Amman. He, along with Rahul, deposited the bundle of furs and other clothing at Anya's feet, before turning away, his ears reddening at the lack of privacy in Matreyi's small abode.

Anya rifled through the pile, choosing a selection of warm garments, before stripping off her wedding outfit, made ridiculous by her circumstances, and, satisfied that she was now relatively dry, pulled on several layers of her most insulating clothes.

"Thank you, Amman," she said, hugging him and her brother. She stood back, examining Amman, who was similarly wrapped up against the elements, her expression serious. "You've made it clear I can't stop you, but you don't have to do this, you know." Once again, moisture welled in her eyes. "I don't want to be responsible for, for your…"

Amman stepped forward, lifting her chin with his hand, his gaze flicking to each of her eyes repeatedly. "We'll make it. We'll find a way."

She did not share his confidence, and fearing another bout of tears, Anya crouched and very deliberately examined the other items they had brought. There were goatskin sacks, empty for carrying spare clothing, a rope, ice hammer, kindling and a bag containing fabric and pegs. Her eyes widened with hope.

"Is this a tent?" she asked.

Amman looked sheepish. "Actually, it's material we use to give shelter to the animals if there's no room in a yurt, or the weather isn't so bad as…" He indicated the snowstorm outside and shrugged. "It's got to help," he added.

"It's wonderful."

The next bag she opened produced a small flurry of flies and she waved them away, seeing inside a selection of food, wrapped where possible in light waxed fabric. She recognised much of it as food that had been prepared for the celebration of her wedding and she choked on the swelling that leapt at once to her throat. Anya looked down momentarily, unable to process the tumultuous events of the day, blinking rapidly. How had it come to this, for her to be preparing to go out into the frozen mountains, banished, in all likelihood to die as sentenced, alongside her dear, foolish best friend who could not see that he should abandon her?

Only this morning she had been resigned, if not excited, to be married. A life of security and safety in the wooden settlement of clan Vulture had awaited her. She closed her eyes, unable to deal with her change of fortune.

Anya breathed deeply, vigorously stuffed some clothes into an empty sack, concentrating fully on the task, hoping to avoid eye contact with the others. She looked back to the mound of clothes, and saw underneath, the leather of her satchel. Her heart leapt with joy, and she shoved all the garments aside and reached for it, holding it close to her chest. She frowned, her hands patting the bag, which had been lying in her tent, abandoned in the flurry of wedding preparations. Cautiously, she flipped open the flap and looked inside. There, before her disbelieving eyes, were the same books she had so hurriedly crammed in before she and Amman had escaped from the tower guard.

How had her mother not seen them? Anya opened the books of magic, finding them as she remembered, before placing them back inside and giving the bag a closer examination. It was well-made, she had known that, but this was something else, clearly it had magical properties. Her eyes caught something small, apparently written in the leather at the top of the front of the bag, normally hidden by the flap that secured its contents when closed. A single word, 'Tavara'. A suspicion arose in her thoughts, but knowing they were short of time if they were to secure themselves a shelter before nightfall, she pushed it to the back of her mind, placing the satchel alongside all the other bags she would take.

At last, and all too soon, they were ready. The many layers they wore were crossed by the cords of the bags slung about them, causing them to sweat in the warmth of the yurt.

"I wish things were different," said Rahul softly as they hugged. Anya looked up at him and they regarded each other through eyes moist with tears.

"Thank you," she said. "Take care of Mother and Father. If she…" Anya trailed off, not knowing what to say that was adequate, unsure even if her words would be welcomed by Neeta.

Anya kissed Rahul and turned to Matreyi. There was no pretending now that this was anything other than a final goodbye. Matreyi, her beloved aunt, all efforts at maintaining her composure abandoned, wept openly, sorrow ageing her by many years as she gazed at her favourite niece with love and pride. Their embrace was more awkward than Anya would have liked, laden as she was, but she wished it would last forever. Together they held each other and together they cried.

"I'm sorry," said Anya, not feeling able to express the reasons why.

"Don't be, I've never been prouder of you. Always remember, you are stronger than I ever was." She kissed Anya's forehead and stroked her hair. "Live, little one," whispered Matreyi. "Live."

They separated, each taking one last look, storing the moment for all time, before Anya wiped her face and turned to Amman.

"Let's go," she said, and strode out of the tent, not daring to look behind her.

Outside, the wind had strengthened, whipping snow into their faces. It was settling quickly, already adding another hand span of powder to the impacted white beneath. Anya tugged up her scarf to cover her mouth and nose, checking that Amman was doing the same. Together they made their way to the perimeter of the camp, the only moving figures out in the cold. Anya was disappointed, somehow, as though she had expected crowds to have lined their way. The significance of their departure was reduced to irrelevance by their isolation.

Soon, they began to crest a ridge in the grazing land, which lay between them and a route down to lower altitudes. The herd below were huddled together for warmth, their newly thick coats providing marvellous additional protection against the elements. Anya envied them.

As they approached the top of the ridge, there was a lull in the wind and snowfall. They stopped briefly and turned to take one last look at the life they were leaving behind. The collection of yurts below barely seemed adequate to house the recollections of her life, the moments that had shaped her, and that ultimately had led to her banishment. Snow had drifted up the sides of the tents, drawing them into the fabric of the landscape, causing them to appear more natural than fabricated with their dusting of flakes.

A shape moving in the snow caught her eye, and Anya strained to see as a man rounded a distant outcropping, approaching the clan from the other side of the camp. Although wearing furs, they were loose, exposing part of his chest, even in the midst of the snowstorm. Despite the distance, she could see his muscles bulging impressively beneath his clothes, a large hunting horn hanging at his side. His furs extended to a cowl, fashioned from the head of an elk, the points of its noble rack pointing brightly at the sky. Intrigued, she took a step back towards the camp, wanting a better view of the newcomer.

The man paused, appearing to see them against the snow, he smiled warmly, raised his arm and beckoned to them - a friendly gesture. Anya glanced to her side, seeing that Amman was similarly interested. He looked at her and grinned. She felt hope build within her, surely this was a man she could trust, who would smooth over the issues between her and the clan. She smiled back, and together, they began to walk back down the ridge.

Anya was captivated by the dignity of the stranger, and though he was unknown to her, something about him was familiar. No, not familiar, she thought, something else. She slowed, working at the peculiar feeling. The man below gestured more strongly to her, as though time was of the essence.

"Amman?" she said, suddenly unsure. He had continued, but glanced back, frowning in irritation.

Anya stood and stared at the man, wavering with indecision. She was being foolish, she thought, this man was a friend to her, to all of them. At that moment, a large elk trotted from the herd, placing itself between her and the traveller, obscuring her view of him. It tossed its magnificent antlers and looked directly at her for a long moment, before lowering its head and turning it towards the camp.

Anya blinked as though from a dream and looked again at the figure of the man. No longer a reassuring presence, his bulky frame now radiated danger, his smile a wolfish baring of teeth, teeth that were somehow wrong to Anya, they looked as though they were pointed, though she could not be sure from this distance. The elk skull on his head was a mockery of their God, its broken spines a twisted challenge to the divine. The arm he held aloft that had previously encouraged her, she saw was stiff and commanding, almost as though he was attempting to draw them to him by force of will.

"Amman!" she called, more urgently than before. He had resumed his walk back towards the ominous figure, and Anya dashed to her friend, grabbing him by the arm. "Amman, this is wrong, something isn't right."

He turned his face and scowled at Anya. "What's wrong with you?" he said. "This man will protect us, he'll fix things, we can stay."

"No, he won't." Anya's voice was insistent. "Look at him, really look at him."

Amman turned, and a beatific glow spread across his face. Anya knew she had said the wrong thing, he was falling further under the influence of the stranger. This was magic, she realised, and tried to imagine what sort of patterns could accomplish such a twisting of the senses. Dimly, she could see how it might be done, but it was complicated, she was not yet strong enough, and she had no time to experiment.

Strength! That was the answer. Anya knew that she was stronger than Amman, he had rarely bested her in the rough-housing that they had often engaged in as young children, but to drag him against his will away from the sinister stranger would take time, time they did not have. Anya let go and weaved her hands firmly in a triangular pattern through the air, chanting sounds she knew would complete the spell. The usual feeling of euphoria coursed through her, but this time it settled in her limbs, prickling with contained excitement.

Reaching out to grasp his arm once more, Anya strode away from the camp, dragging Amman effortlessly behind her. His startled yells grew ever more frustrated and angry as she went. He lost his feet and thrashed around, seeking to break her grip, pounding on her arm with his fists. Anya barely felt a thing, so fixed was she on her desperate need to escape. As she hauled him to the top of the ridge, Anya caught a glimpse of the tower above them and to the side, visible now from their vantage point. She could not help but reflect that Amman was being pulled in different directions by magic forces, quite literally in her case. She hoped he would come to his senses and forgive her.

"Stop, I don't want to go." Amman's voice was frantic. "Let go of me. You didn't even want me to come, why can't you make up your mind? Don't you want to go back? That's it, isn't it? You think you're different, better than the rest of us, and staying with the clan would prove to you that you're not."

Anya almost hurled him back towards the clan. Instead, she marched with increased vigour, and Amman yelped at the sudden increase in pace. "I'm going to pretend you didn't say that," she said between clenched teeth. "You're under the influence of some kind of spell."

"What if I'm not?" he said. "What if you're just seeing what you want to see?"

"You think I want to see danger wherever I look?" Anya was shouting now. "You think I want to live in a world where it's alright for a man to hurt me, just because I'm a girl? I mean, what's so special about men? Does having that thing between your legs make you better than us?" She stomped on in silence for a moment. "Think about it, Amman. We only just saw that man, and straight away we thought he was someone we could trust, that he would help us. Is that normal? It's magic, Amman. Trust me, I should know."

They crested the rise, and made their way down the other side, the snowy ridge now between them and the disturbing figure. Amman calmed slightly.

"Alright, alright," he said. "You can let go now."

"Can I?" said Anya, stopping, but not releasing her hold on his coat. "You won't rush back to the arms of this man you've never met, and abandon your friend to die alone in the frozen mountains?" A pang of guilt pricked her conscience, she knew she was being unfair on Amman, who had volunteered for this hopeless journey with her.

He got to his feet, eying her strangely. "You'd better be right about him," he said, sullenly. "I don't want to die for nothing." Anya let go, and he trudged off ahead into the renewed snowfall, while a lone horn sounded behind them.

They had found an overhanging rocky outcrop within a stand of pine trees that grew where the ground was flatter than the surrounding slopes. The trees provided shelter from the wind, allowing the space under the rock to remain free from drifting snow. Amman had been surly since their escape and conversation had been sporadic, limited to what was necessary to cooperate when erecting the animal screen, to protect their shelter from the elements.

The snowfall was reduced in the fading light of day and the wind blew less fiercely. Nevertheless, the cold and hardness of the ground could be felt even through their sleeping mats. Amman was gathering what dead wood he could find in the uneven blanket of white around the boles of the copse's trees. Anya could hear him clearly as he foraged, the only sound in the world around them, besides the occasional hoot of a mountain owl, perched in the boughs above.

Anya, her bags draped over her for additional warmth, flicked clumsily through the pages of her books, not wanting to remove her gloves to aid her in her efforts. Her thoughts were unsettled, the jarring events of the day intruded on her attempted study. Even her satchel provided a distraction, the secret of its magic a mystery waiting to be uncovered. With a determined effort, she peered once again at the words in the dim light.

> Magic is a force, and as such the simplest forms of use are those where magical force is merely channelled or shaped. As such, elemental magic tends to less subtle effects, while other types, such as the Tharom warlocks' corruption of gifted magic is limited to the creation of temporary tools of energy, controlled by the wielder's will. Though the forces so channelled can be great, such a user acts only as a conduit for unrefined powers, with little delicacy or skill.
>
> When true mastery is achieved, the uses to which one may put magic is almost unlimited, including, though not restricted to; the creation of gateways to other worlds, manipulating time, even the shielding of oneself from death. Only by fully understanding the forces involved can the most powerful magic be controlled.

Anya was once again distracted from the wonders revealed to her in the pages of her book, though this time she could not pinpoint the cause of the interruption. Suddenly tense, she listened intently, but could hear no noise. Her skin prickled with unease and a voice inside her urged caution.

"Amman?" she called in a low tone, not daring to raise her voice. The screen they had set up prevented her from seeing out into the grove, causing her to feel isolated and vulnerable.

She caught the sound of crunching snow, steadily approaching her shelter. Hastily, Anya returned her book to the satchel, and raised herself to crouch in the limited space, bringing to mind a pattern of defensive magic. Abruptly, the screen was pulled aside, revealing Amman, his attention elsewhere, his eyes scanning the trees.

"Something's out there," he said, his voice no higher than a whisper.

Floating almost imperceptibly in the still air, a faint sibilant noise caused Anya's heart to freeze, she had heard the sound once before.

"We have to go. Now!" Anya's whisper was filled with the volume of urgency. She threw some bags at Amman, hastily grabbing what she could. Amman, eyes full of concern began to form a question, but Anya put a finger to her mouth, silencing him. The terror on her face was unmistakable. "Rahksharu," she mouthed.

He blanched, the white of his features an echo of the blanket of cold around them. He scrabbled with the cords, clumsily looping them over his head, while Anya led the way out of the shelter, abandoning the screen and bed mats in her haste, torn between a headlong dash for safety and a careful escape that might give her the opportunity to listen for pursuit. They were barely a man's height from their abandoned cover when the scream of a dying animal split the air, causing the hidden owl to hoot in alarm.

Frozen for a moment, they stared at each other in horror, before their fear took hold, propelling their limbs and they fled blindly through the trees. Anya was unspeakably grateful for the snow around them, which preserved the dying light, giving them a chance to see the flat silhouettes of the trunks as they loomed ahead of them in the semi-darkness. Behind them, an explosive crashing sound preceded the fall of first one tree, then another, and another in a cacophony of splintered timber.

Not daring to look behind them, they redoubled their pace, pursued by an ungodly, unseeable horror. Images of lethal, blade-ended skeletal limbs above a pleading, human visage flashed into Anya's mind, unwanted and distracting. She forced them away, concentrating on the ground ahead, knowing that a single slip could mean death. Ahead, she could see the trees thinning and she risked a glance to where Amman followed in her wake. His eyes were bright with fear, but he was managing to contain it, racing after her in the gloom.

They broke out of the woods into the grey of the night-shrouded snow, Anya heard a muffled sound behind her, and skidded to a halt, just before the ground sloped steeply down ahead of her to disappear into the haze of falling flakes. She turned to see Amman, sprawled in the carpet of snow, thicker here out from under the shelter of the copse, scrambling to get to his feet. Behind him, the monster was closing rapidly, the staccato bursts of disintegrating trees now visible to Anya. It was heading directly towards them.

"Come here, get close to me," said Anya, her voice sounding calmer in her ears than she would have believed possible. Remembering the words of her book, 'The simplest forms of use are those where magical force is merely channelled or shaped', she imagined the simplest shape, a sphere, concentrating on directing the required energies with her movements and words.

Anya kept her eyes away from the lethal blur of the approaching monstrosity, not wanting to risk its deadly gaze, but struggled to maintain her poise as the line of decimated trees grew rapidly, approaching them with fearsome speed. Amman was too slow to rise, the snow too deep to allow him purchase. At last, he gained his feet, and ran, stumbling through the furrows of Anya's own passing, the formless path of destruction behind him blasting through the final trees, a blizzard of disturbed powder and splinters, until it was upon them. Amman fell, cringing at Anya's feet, raising his arm in a hopeless gesture of protection as the thing struck.

A sound like a bell resounded, achingly loud in their ears as they were thrown physically around, tumbling about down the slope behind them, but without touching the snow. They and their possessions were constrained within an invisible ball, crashing about as it pelted, unrestrained down the pristine incline, knocked on its current path by the Rahksharu's attack.

"Brace yourself!" yelled Anya, who had stretched out her hands and legs, reaching to push against the insides of the sphere. With difficulty, Amman emulated her, ceasing his bruising tumble, but although they had gained some measure of control, a loose bag was rattling about, striking them at random. Worse, the ball was spinning, its rotation gaining momentum as it rolled. Dizziness threatened to overwhelm them, until the snow beneath them disappeared, and their weight suddenly dropped away. The sphere's motion stabilized somewhat, and Anya caught a glimpse of a snow-lined cliff, drifting up out of view above them.

They were falling through empty air.

On the Run

Anya snuggled in her bed, still half-asleep, and listened to the distant sounds of her mother cooking. Pine smells mingled with the aroma of roasting meat, unusual for breakfast, she supposed food was running low due to the herd's refusal to move on, and some of the elk had been butchered. She stretched, finding the effort painful. Her brows creased, and she explored the source of her discomfort with her good hand, prodding a bruise she had suffered in their escape from the Rahksharu.

Instantly awake, Anya sat up so rapidly her head swooned and began to throb. There was a large swelling under her hair which was tender to the touch. The space around her swam in her vision, and she closed her eyes, lowering her head until it cleared, worried the queasiness in her stomach might cause her to be sick.

"You should take things gently," a full, rich voice came from behind Anya. She turned her head slowly, taking in her surroundings. They were in a hut fashioned using fresh evergreen branches, a hole above letting in light, exchanging it for the fire's smoke. Amman lay next to her, still asleep. At last, her eyes reached a bearded man, rotating a spitted animal over an open fire.

"Where am I?" she asked.

The man considered her for a moment, his warm brown eyes thoughtful. He was clothed in well-crafted animal skins, and though not new, their good condition demonstrated careful maintenance. Anya tried to assess his age, but found herself conceding he could be anything from early twenties to late thirties. One thing she could tell – he was both rugged and handsome.

"I found you lying out in the snow. Can you tell me how you got there?"

Images of their uncontrolled flight from the Rahksharu came unbidden in her mind. They had fallen for a long time, before a jarring landing on a long steep incline of snow. Once again, they had bounced around inside the ball and Anya realised she had no memory of what happened next. She looked up to discover the eyes of the stranger on her, patient and unhurried. She blushed, what could she say that made no mention of magic? Her mouth opened and closed, unable to find words she felt were safe to use.

She dropped her gaze, feeling her silence was an ill reward for his kindness, and saw that her burnt hand had been wrapped in fresh cloth.

"Let me see how that is doing," he said, moving closer. He knelt beside her and began to unwrap the bandages, Anya found his musk pleasant, like the earth in spring.

"When I brought you in, it was in danger of becoming infected." She watched reluctantly as her hand was gradually revealed, fearing what she would see. As the last of the bandage was removed, Anya gaped in amazement. She held up her hand in front of her, turning it to see the unblemished skin, there was no sign of any damage, beyond a pink hue to the newly healed skin. She laughed in astonishment and relief, beaming at the man as he took her hand, holding it close to his face for a better examination.

"What do you think you're doing," said Amman. He was propped up on his elbows, having clearly just awoken. "Get away from her." His face was flushed, and he sounded petulant to Anya's ears.

Anya turned to face Amman, frowning in embarrassment at his tone. "It's alright, Amman, he…" She faltered, gesturing at the man, and looked at him apologetically. "I'm sorry. You've been so kind, and I've not even asked your name."

"I am called Theelk by those who know me," he replied.

"How did we get here?" said Amman. "I remember after we stopped moving, you were out cold. There was blood on your face, running down from your head, but I couldn't get any snow to clean it with, the ball…" Anya was grimacing furiously, finally capturing his attention and stopping his tongue.

"Thank you for your help, Theelk. My hand is… well, it's amazing. How did you…?"

"There is more than one type of magic in this world," he replied, with a meaningful look at Anya. "Interestingly, when I found you, you were lying at the end of a long channel in the snow, like a chute made by children when they slide repeatedly down a hill." He looked at them, a curious expression on his face. "Except that this chute was almost perfectly smooth." An uncomfortable silence followed, in which Anya and Amman exchanged secretive glances.

He watched them carefully. "No matter," he said, tossing them each a gaganwa fruit, before moving to the fire and carefully removing the spit. "Eat. You look as though you need it."

"We have to tell him about the Rahksharu."

"Why? If he lives out here alone, he must have some way to avoid them."

"Amman! He's been nothing but generous and helpful to us, warning him about the monster is the least we can do."

"Hmm, alright, but then we should leave."

"Leave? How can we leave, we don't have any food, it was all destroyed when we fell." Anya's temper was rising, Amman had been difficult all morning and his attitude towards Theelk bordered on outright discourtesy. They had begun arguing almost as soon as he left to collect firewood.

"I would have cleaned your head wound and found somewhere safe to rest, but that bloody spell, I was trapped inside, snow all around, but impossible to get to." He raised his head, looking as though a new thought had just occurred. "And I remember feeling sleepy. I just couldn't keep my eyes open, it was really weird. I thought I'd lie down for a quick rest, and… and I woke up here."

Her curiosity piqued, Anya forgot her anger. "I wonder," she said, nibbling absently on her lip. "The protective sphere wouldn't let anything in or out, not even the air. You know when Bibhu was sick after the fire? That book where I found the chikitsa remedy said that it was good for damaged lungs if they had breathed in unpleasant air. What if the air we breathe out isn't as good as the air we breathe in? What if it made you sleepy because it's 'unpleasant' somehow?"

"You only have to smell Paras' breath to know it can be unpleasant," said Amman with a grin.

Anya reached for her satchel. "If only I had a reference book, but I could only take a few, and these all deal with magic." She sighed. "If I had the whole library, I'd be able to prove it one way or another." Anya gazed at the open bag, lying across her lap, and noted again, the word, 'Tavara'. The hairs on her neck began to prickle and she swallowed, not wanting to let her growing excitement get the better of her. She emptied the satchel, before letting the flap close and placing her hands on top.

"Tavara," she said.

Amman looked at her curiously, and feeling somewhat foolish, she opened the bag once again and peered inside.

"What?" said Amman, as Anya reached in, pulling another book from within, and laying it down on her lap, her eyes alight with wonder. The book was titled 'A Treatise on the Workings of the Human Body'.

"Do you know what this means?" said Anya.

"It means there is much you that you wish to hide." They both turned, startled by Theelk's interjection, neither had heard him return.

"I... er, we..." began Amman.

"How long have you been listening?" said Anya.

"Long enough." He regarded them seriously. "That is a most interesting bag, what other magic do you have?"

"Magic?" said Amman, the look of confusion on his face clearly hollow to Anya.

"Come, should I treat you like children, perhaps send you back to your clan?" A line appeared on his brow and he narrowed his eyes. At their obvious alarm, Theelk softened his tone. "I presume you would not be out here alone for childish reasons, so I would appreciate it if you did not play games with me."

There was an undeniable authority in his manner, and despite Amman's shake of the head, Anya said, "You're right, we're sorry, we don't mean to be ungrateful." She hesitated. "The truth is... well, the truth is that I've been banished from the tribe for using magic and I cannot go back, they will kill me if I do." Theelk listened solemnly. "In our tribe, to use magic is punishable by death. They accepted my banishment because they don't think we'll survive out here. They're probably right, even if the cold doesn't kill us, we only narrowly escaped a Rahksharu."

Theelk nodded to himself, before looking into her eyes, capturing her in the depths of his own. "You should believe in yourself, Anya. To escape from such a monster shows unusual resources, or good fortune." He stood abruptly.

"You must move on, it is not safe for you to stay here. To where are you heading?"

Amman interjected himself into the conversation. "We haven't— "

"I thought we might go to the temple." Anya cut across him, her attention directed to Theelk. Amman scowled, giving her a wounded look she did not see. "Do you know it? We've sort of fallen off the trail, would you be able to tell us how to get there?"

"I will do more than that, I will accompany you."

"No, you don't need to, we'll be fine." Amman said, sourly.

"Gather your things, we leave at once."

Anya was cold. Each day since they had set off had been arduous and long, making precious little progress through the fresh snow, which though slackened, had continued to fall. The ground beneath them could be treacherous, with sudden drops and voids disguised by the fluffy white cover that blanketed the whole land. They walked single-file, the youngsters following in the older man's wake, their conversation hushed, all too aware of the possibility that their noise could cause an avalanche. Though Amman was sure they were safe from the Rahksharu, Theelk continued to warn of their remaining danger.

"Why would it be pursuing us?" said Anya, her voice low. "Aren't they mindless beasts?"

"You know they are not natural," said Theelk. He did not look at her, but continued to scan the route ahead.

"Well, no, but— "

"They are created, animated from corpses, given 'life' by energy from the realm of Death's brother, Vajnata, and therefore have a purpose, even if it is simple cruelty." He strode on for a moment. "This one, however, I believe is here for you."

"But how can that be?" she said, but Theelk gave no answer and from her position behind him, she could not read his expression. Not that she ever could, Anya admitted to herself. She turned to look behind her, seeing Amman trailing a long way back. He had been surly and uncommunicative lately and she worried for him.

"He suffers under a kind of enchantment," said Theelk, as though he read her mind. Anya returned her gaze to their bearded guide, finding his eyes still on the path before them. "It is testament to the bond between you that he is here at all. It will pass." She hoped he referred to the enchantment, and not the bond.

"Couldn't I use magic to remove it?"

"You could, but dispelling another's magic is difficult. First you would need to understand the spell you sought to banish. You should continue with your current line of enquiry."

Anya bit her lip. Theelk had been encouraging her in her studies, giving some direction to her research and she was learning quickly, as a result. All her efforts were being devoted to the Rahksharu. He believed she could defeat one, and she almost believed it too. She glanced behind once again. Shouldn't I also try to help Amman, she thought. She felt torn by indecision.

The light was waning. Looking around, Anya searched for trees that could provide shelter for the coming night, but the altitude and rockiness of the ground was less hospitable here, and she found none. They were walking along a path caused by a split in the rock of the mountain. To their side and looming high above them, the bare stone of the cleft was burdened by overhanging snow. It amazed her that it could overshadow them so much, and not fall. She supposed that they might find a suitable recess in the wall, around which they could build a barrier of snow, as Theelk had shown them last night, but she hoped they would reach flatter ground before nightfall. The vertiginous drop on her other side made her uncomfortable.

"How long until we reach the temple?" she asked, berating herself inwardly for asking. Once expressed, it sounded to Anya like the pestering of a spoilt child.

"It is many days journey," said Theelk. "It would be so even without the current weather."

"Thank you for helping us, I think it would have taken us far longer to find a route, but you seem to know exactly where you're going."

He walked on for a time, before saying, "I have been there once before, many years ago…" He lapsed into silence, and Anya once again wondered how old he was.

"Did you visit with your family?" Anya was suddenly curious about their guide. "Perhaps your parents—"

Anya! You are in danger. Amman. The voice in her head was intense, interrupting her as she spoke. Immediately, she wheeled around, seeing Amman still trudging some distance behind. He appeared to be fine, what could have prompted her sudden feeling of imminent peril?

"Anya, there!" prompted Theelk. He pointed over her shoulder at the slopes beyond the split in the rock, where she saw not one, but two flurries in the snow, as if the air swirled of its own accord, moving rapidly towards them, towards Amman.

"No! Amman!" she cried.

Amman looked up from his feet at the desperation in her voice and seeing the direction of their gaze turned to glance behind him. At once, he spun, pelting in their direction far faster than was wise. Despite his lack of caution, the blurred shapes were gaining on him fast. He would not make it.

Anya fought down a feeling of foreboding and concentrated on the results of her study. She could not fight what she could not look at, never mind see. The words came to her and she traced an intricate pattern in the air before her eyes, which shimmered before clearing once again. She was ready. As she looked up, she saw Amman skid and fall onto the slippery path, his momentum taking him towards the edge. His arms scrabbled around, seeking to slow his motion, seizing handfuls of snow and little else before he slid over the precipice.

She screamed, desperately searching for a spell to save him, but instead of falling to his death, Amman hung, suspended over the drop, dangling by the cord of a goatskin bag, which incredibly, had snagged on the edge of the path. Anya knew his reprieve would be short-lived if she did not act soon, the first Rahksharu was almost upon him. The things were constructed from the bones of dead creatures. These and the rotting flesh that covered them were connected to Vajnata's plane, full of a kind of anti-life, the antithesis of living things. She would give them a taste of life itself.

Swiftly, she followed a connection from herself to the plane that fuels all truly living things, widening it and drawing a path in the air towards the monster closing frighteningly fast on Amman. Anya spoke the final syllable of her spell and a burst of blinding energy shot from her hand to strike the leading Rahksharu. The blur that disguised the spectre stopped, and wavered briefly on the verge of the lethal drop, hissing furiously.

Anya needed to see, not just where they were, but exactly what they were doing. She remembered her first encounter with them, shuddering at the memory. They used illusion to cover themselves, she had only to accept that fact in order to pierce their covering magic. I will see the truth, she thought. The fog of lies around them unravelled, and she saw the nearest thing swing around to look at her. As their eyes met, the air before Anya's eyes shimmered, dissipating the stony death of its gaze. She could see drops of a thick black fluid oozing from a large wound in its body, and one of its legs hung uselessly from its side. It began to move forward once more, slower and more cautious than before, its attention now fixed on Amman, a captive victim, helpless in its path.

Her second burst of energy caught it full in the face, and she saw its head wither, visibly shrivelling as though time itself was accelerated, before finally crumbling to dust. The rest of its body collapsed, unmoving onto the path. Waves of fatigue crashed through Anya, but she forced them away, dragging her limbs into action as she ran towards Amman. Looking down at him, she could see the cord suspending him was snagged on an icy spur of stone. She reached into her bag, pulling out the ice hammer, and set to work exposing the stone further, to give her feet something against which to brace herself.

"Anya, where is the other monster?" said Theelk. She spun around, as though expecting it to be poised, ready to strike her from behind, and cursed herself for being so careless. She felt so weary, fear was the only thing keeping her alert and awake. Theelk took the hammer from her hand and continued working on the ice, leaving her free to defend them against the remaining Rahksharu.

It was not on the path and she could not see it on the slopes beyond. Where was it? A sensation like a spider creeping along her back made the skin on her neck prickle and she swung about, looking above her. At the top of the looming wall of stone, the second horror perched on the frozen snow, ready to spring. How long had it been there? Why had it not attacked? Anya gasped. The thing was looking straight at her, its face grotesquely familiar to her. It was Bibhu.

Consumed with revulsion, Anya screamed, "No!"

The thing was quivering, as though opposite impulses warred within. Bibhu's face, hideously fixed to the monstrosity, was contorted as if exerting a great effort. Its mouth moved, though no sound issued from it.

"Anya." She could read its lips. Its eyes were wide with terror, and she could see a red glow intensifying within. "Kill me," it mouthed.

Anya shook her head as though she might deny the request. Not daring to take her eyes off the monster, she said, "Theelk, hold on."

Summoning a simple burst of force, Anya cast it at the overhanging snow above the path, breaking its icy grip, loosening it to fall, sparkling over the cliff, taking the twisted form of the Rahksharu with it.

Tumbling snow continued to fall around her, and Anya squeezed herself against the base of the broken stone until at last it ceased. She brushed herself free of snow, looking around her for her companions. All was white. Her vision swam, but she forced herself into action, digging in the snow where she had last seen them, but they were not there.

A sobbing cry escaped her. Why couldn't I have destroyed it, like the first one, she thought? It wasn't Bibhu, not truly, what have I done? Anya slumped on her knees in the snow, her head in her hands, when she felt pressure on her shoulder. She turned, seeing Theelk, and behind him emerging from the fallen snow, Amman, weary, but alive. In a flash she pushed past Theelk, to wrap her arms around Amman.

"I thought I'd lost you," she said, before sleep finally claimed her.

Discovery

The morning was crisp and clear. The brightness of the new day heralded a change in the atmosphere surrounding them as they travelled. Anya and Amman walked together, laughing at shared jokes. Anya hoped their troubles had fallen away with the Rahksharu.

At the thought of the monster, a cloud passed over Anya and she lapsed into silence. Amman, noticing her change of mood, looked at her and asked, "What's wrong?"

She glanced at him and forced a smile. "I just can't get the thought out of my head. It was Bibhu's face on the Rahksharu. What could do such a thing?"

"Maybe it doesn't mean anything, maybe it's just part of their illusion."

Anya did not reply. She was unnerved by the memory, sure it had been real. She thought of her family, of Matreyi, and felt guilt at her feelings of freedom, now mingled with concern over their safety. If Bibhu was truly dead and had been used in such a manner, they could all be in terrible danger. Anya shuddered. What could she do? If she returned, she would be killed herself. The thoughts nagged at her constantly, never far from her mind. She had to find a way.

Theelk signalled to them to stop. Ahead was a narrow saddle between two peaks, heavily laden with snow. On either side the land fell away sharply. "Now we must descend." He indicated the vast slope to their left. "The way ahead is steep and there will be little opportunity for rest."

He sat on a snow-covered rocky protrusion and reached into a bag, slung across his shoulders, producing gaganwa fruit, which he tossed to each of them.

"Gaganwa, again?" complained Amman. "Haven't you got anything else in there, maybe some mithowroot[20]?"

"Eat. They will protect you better than mithowroot." He drew another from his bag and bit through the skin, ripping it open with his teeth, before holding it up and crushing the fruit, squeezing its juice into his open mouth.

"Protect you?" Anya repeated. "That's what Pramiti said, she's a monk at the temple. She said the Gods gave them seeds to protect them. Those seeds grew into gaganwa trees." She narrowed her eyes. "How do they protect, and how were there seeds, when the gaganwa have none?"

"Some fruit can be infertile, but still there must have been a seed to grow the tree on which it grew."

"So, where did they get the seeds from?"

"Perhaps the Gods just made them," Amman interjected.

"Seeds usually come from another tree," said Theelk.

"So, where is that tree?"

"That is the most interesting question of all."

Anya pondered the mystery further for a while, but finding no great insight, her mind once again drifted back to the Rahksharu. If she continued her study, her power would grow, and she could return to the clan despite their judgement without fear of the consequences. If they were in danger, she could save them. On a sudden whim, Anya took off her satchel, and said, "Tavara." She opened it, finding inside a book titled 'Flora and Fauna of Sansara, Appendix

---

[20] Among the many and plentiful edible plants of the Yanuba is the mithowroot, also known as sweetroot. Although the leaves are bitter and disagreeable to the palate, its roots may be used for cooking, or eaten raw. The texture is somewhat leathery, but the flavour is pleasant and sweet. "Flora and Fauna of Sansara, volume 2".

1'. She skipped to the index, scanning the lists with her finger, until at last she found the word she sought. She flicked the leaves through her fingers to the page indicated and lay the book across her knees.

> Rahksharu are listed in this appendix as they have no place in the ecosystem. They are neither natural, nor strictly speaking, alive, being warped creations made using the remains of the dead. Extremely dangerous, they always feature a human head mounted on top of a multitude of razor-sharp appendages, which is possibly required to provide some measure of control or intelligence to the monster.
>
> The process of forming these vile animations imbues them with power, both for concealment and petrification, though how this is achieved is not known. Further information may be found in documents hidden at the monk's temple, in the foothills of the Yanuba mountains.

"It is time to move on," said Theelk, interrupting Anya from her study. She looked once again at the words, resolving to continue her investigations when they reached their destination. Amman was gathering up his bags once again, making ready to join Theelk, who was already testing the route down.

"Wait," she said. "I have a better idea."

The wind whipped Anya's hair madly, her exhilaration bursting from her in uncontained peals of laughter to be lost in the air behind her. She looked around at the others, clinging desperately to the invisible sled, their hoods long since blown off their heads as they hurtled down the side of the mountain. Anya turned back just in time to divert their path and avoid a spur of rock, protruding from the snow cover like a tree of stone. She kept her eyes on their route now, guiding them safely to a gentler slope, pleased with herself for saving them hours of careful trekking down the precarious incline.

She revelled in the thrill of her budding mastery of magic. Shaping and directing the energies into an improvised toboggan had been easy, and she reflected that this was the first time in days she had cast a spell when not in danger. Wouldn't it be wonderful to be free to use such power openly for the benefit of others, without ignorant tradition to judge and punish her for it? Anya imagined returning to the clan, showering them with her largess in the form of magic to improve the lives of them all. They would welcome her, granting her a pardon and place on the council, instituting new tradition in her honour.

At that moment, the spell energies dissipated, throwing them all bodily into the snow. They had traversed an enormous distance, reaching flatter ground in a valley flanked by ranks of trees, which clung to the steeper terrain either side. Anya and Amman were spun over, rolling along the top of the white cover, their speed dispersed in flurries of powder amid the cushioned impact of their fall. At last they stopped, Amman frowning at her in consternation, his hair frosted with icy crystals. To Anya, he looked like some kind of burrowing animal, surfacing to find the wintery world not to his liking. She began to giggle at the sight, and Amman threw a ball of snow at her, hitting her full in the face. After a moment of indignation, she joined with her friend in childish combat, laughing with him, until exhausted, they lay in the snow, their heavy breathing puffing clouds of frosted breath into the air.

The rest of their journey was uneventful, a repetition of travel, sustenance, study and sleep for many days. As they descended from the higher reaches of the Yanubas, the snow cover grew thinner, until at last they reached the temple lake where they found none at all. Anya once again had the feeling of a reversing of the seasons, after their frozen trek, the breeze off the lake smelt to her like summer.

"Are you sure you won't come with us to the temple?" asked Anya.

"I have been too long in the wild, I do not fit well in buildings." Theelk gazed across the water, taking in the temple. "I will wait for you here."

She and Amman boarded a boat, and took turns rowing, finding it more difficult than she would have believed, each teasing the other for their ineptitude. Gradually, through trial and misadventure, the temple grew larger, until with a heavy thud, they at last guided the vessel against the pier. Anya jumped out, tying the boat to a post that supported the wooden structure. She helped Amman disembark, he was gawking at the island, and sniffed at the smell of smoked fish in the air, drying in the nearby shelter. Anya's stomach rumbled in sympathy, she would be glad to eat something other than jerky and gaganwa.

"Well, well, what have we here?" came a voice Anya recognised. Walking down the steps from the temple was Bibek. She rushed to him in relief, but slowed before she reached him, unsure of the propriety of embracing an Acharya. A slanted smile found its way onto his face and he reached out, pulling her into a hug.

"I imagine you have a story to tell," he said, stepping back to look her over. Anya opened her mouth to speak, but Bibek spoke first. "Please, come and eat. Then we'll talk."

"Anya, you know I would be delighted for you to join our community, but we are not entirely outside of tribal law." Bibek rubbed his face wearily. "If your clan discovered that you were here, never mind if you wore the brown robes, we would have to send you back."

"I understand." Anya ached with disappointment. If they could not stay, where would they go?

"But you are welcome to stay a while and look for any information on the Rahksharu. You say you think clan Elk are in particular danger from them. Why is that?"

Anya took out the book from her satchel. Although she had not felt able to tell them exactly why she was banished, the tower library was something she knew they would understand and appreciate. She found the section she had read and presented it to Bibek.

"I can't tell you why, it's just something I feel deep inside." She reddened at her own evasiveness. She could not talk of their encounter without mentioning her magic.

"This book, if it is merely an appendix, why, there must be other volumes still in that library." His face was alight with astonishment. "And the craftsmanship, it's unparalleled. Anya, you say there are thousands of such books?" She nodded. "Of course, you must search our poor store of knowledge, but to have such a wonder simply appear… all of us here would do much to see it." He nodded and stood up from the refectory bench, inviting them to do the same.

"I will let Pramiti know she is to help you if she can," said Bibek. He turned to face her friend. "In the meantime, Amman, would you like a tour of our island? You say you are learning to be an animal handler within your clan…"

The men left, and Anya watched them go, paralysed with mixed emotions. She cursed the traditions of her clan, that they should ruin her chance of sanctuary here, but was grateful to Bibek for allowing her the opportunity to use their library. Biting back her frustration, she turned and headed for the books.

As she entered through the scriptorium, several familiar faces looked up as she passed, some waved, but none protested as she walked directly to the library entrance. She opened the door, stepping through and immersing herself in the fragrance and calm of the room beyond. Her worries receded, and the tension she had not realised she carried in her shoulders, eased. Anya pushed the sense of contentment aside, she had limited time.

"Welcome back, Anya." It was Pramiti. She was holding a lantern and looked closely at her, taking in her travel-worn attire. She nodded to herself and said, "Come with me. I think I can show you something that will help you."

Pramiti opened the disguised door, swinging the bookcase wide, and led Anya down the steps into the vault, holding the lantern before her. At the bottom was a table, on which rested several more oil lamps. Pramiti lit one with her own and handed it to Anya, her stern look conveying the care she was required to take with it. Together they walked into the hidden store of books, which once had seemed so vast to Anya, now rendered insignificant in comparison to the knowledge found in the tower.

The woman stopped before a separate bookcase, looking along the large spines displayed, before selecting one and laying it on a table, placed nearby for that purpose.

"We have books that are used to reference other books. They are bound differently, as we may have need to insert new pages, but as a system, it works tolerably well." She opened the tome, turning a few pages before pointing with her finger. "Here. Rahksharu."

Anya looked, and underneath the heading were references to other books, with page numbers or chapters listed alongside.

"What are you hoping to find?" Pramiti's eyes were narrowed questioningly.

"I'm not sure, but I want to know where they come from." She paused, unsure of what to say. "If my clan are in danger, I think it might help to find out."

"In that case, we'll choose the oldest books first." She glanced at the open book, before heading off into the shelves. Anya lingered by the table for a moment, unsure if she should follow, before catching up with Pramiti as she pulled an old book from its place. The monk blew dust and old spiderwebs off the top, frowning in disapproval, before bringing it back to the table.

"Thank you so much," said Anya. Pramiti nodded wordlessly and indicated to Anya to sit, taking another seat and watching her as she began to study. She found the relevant section and read.

> Among the most dread monsters to roam the Yanuba are those which the tribesfolk refer to as Rahksharu. The name was hitherto unknown to us, however their descriptions lead us to believe that these Rahksharu are in fact the very same nameless horror described in 'A True History of the Attack on Temple Isle'.

Anya frowned. Something in the text was familiar to her, but she could not place what it was. With Pramiti's guidance, she found the book referred to in the passage, and was amazed to realise that it was the same one she had read when last she was here. How long ago had that been? She had read of magic used in the attack on the island and recoiled. That same girl would have recoiled from her now. She sighed, skipping through the pages, her eyes dancing across the words, searching for any sign of this 'nameless horror', wishing the monk was not with her, so she could make use of magic to aid her in the task.

Again and again she scanned the words, each long moment stretching to hours, but nowhere could she find the words she sought. "It's not here," she said aloud to herself, prompting Pramiti to draw a breath.

"Perhaps it used to be."

Anya looked at her, comprehension dawning slowly. Bibek said that some pages and entire books were missing from their library. She closed the volume, and peered at it from the bottom. Near the spine, she noticed the smallest of gaps, like a bubble in the parchment, and running her finger along the edge, parted the pages once more and studied the open book. There, she could see it, a page had carefully been cut out. But why? She began to read.

And so didst the foul invaders set foot upon these shores, demanding at once the presence of Dheemant, our Acharya, bestowing most cruel punishment on those of our number whom they met. Our esteemed Acharya rushed hastily from the shrine, where he had been seconded, seeking guidance from the divine. Our foes were most enraged, using their powers upon him

There she encountered the break where the missing sheet should be, and at the top of the following page.

were enraged by its demise, lashing out venomously at our order. Those whom he had charmed, proceeded at once to our library, selecting with deliberation those tomes deemed offensive to their master.

Anya screwed up her face in frustration. To be denied by ages old vandalism was almost unbearable. Why had she been led here if there was no longer any information to further her search? She sat back, scowling, trying to keep a check on her rising anger. Pramiti stood, coming alongside Anya, examining the text over her shoulder.

"Presumably this is where they wrote of the Rahksharu," she said. "I wonder why it was removed, what were they trying to hide?"

"Who knows? But your entire library has been limited deliberately. They must have come back again later to remove this page." A thought prickled Anya's mind, demanding attention. She continued in a subdued tone, distracted. "Or they could have left these 'charmed' monks to continue their censorship."

"I'm sorry that— "

"Wait!" Anya was suddenly alert. "'What were they trying to hide', you said. My book, the one that said I would find more on the Rahksharu here, said it would be found *hidden* in the temple."

"Perhaps it was only a turn of phrase," said Pramiti.

"I don't think so, mostly the books are pretty direct, they don't really use any sort of flowery language. I think it means it is literally hidden."

"But where?"

Anya stood, walking back and forth, biting her lip in concentration, running through the words again and again in her mind. "Are there any loose stones or anything in the temple you could use as a hiding place?" she asked.

Pramiti gave her a condescending look. "Look around you, if there is work to be done, we do it. You will not find anything unrepaired for long."

A thought struck Anya. "Do the Acharya write? Is there somewhere else where their work is kept?"

"Yes, but all their writings are held here, in the vaults. Except for the writings of the incumbent." She rose and led Anya to the end of a row of shelves, indicating a number of volumes with a greenish tint to their covers.

Anya scanned their spines, finding names, not subjects. Assuming them to be the names of all the Acharyas, she moved methodically, searching for the name, 'Dheemant'. It was not there.

"Could it be somewhere else?" she said.

"Sometimes books are taken to the village, but not usually one of these." She waved her arm at the shelf. "It could be that his book is one that was missing."

Anya began to pace, her mind working furiously at the puzzle. "What if he had been writing in it when they arrived at the island?" She turned to Pramiti, her eyes shining. "It said he came to the pier from the shrine." At once, she was off, heading up the steps two at a time in her haste. She dashed through the library and scriptorium, bursting into the shrine, disturbing the silence of a solitary monk within.

Stuttering an apology, Anya began scrutinising the space around her, noting the intricate carvings in passing, her sole purpose to look for potential hiding places for books. The monk, wanting his own solitude, rose, and left her alone with her excitement. The benches, though sturdy, were too thin for any form of hidden compartment, and the engraved wooden containers she examined were used to store books of prayer and ritual worship, and had no space in which to conceal much more than a sheet or two of parchment.

Anya's stomach became uneasy, the consequence of doubt and the possibility that she was wrong. She sat down on a pew at the front of the chapel and found a carving of the Elk.

"If my people are in danger, help me," she said, her words startling in the quiet of the empty space.

No reply came, and Anya cast around, seeing again the wooden sculpture depicting the Bear, also a mural of the Snow Leopard, the lectern fashioned in the shape of the Vulture and several depictions of the Fox. Her eyes rested on the carving she had noticed on her last visit. A goat.

Anya turned to look around the shrine, searching for any other references to goats, and found that Pramiti stood in the doorway, watching her once again.

"Has there ever been a clan Goat?" she asked her. "Might there have been one many years ago?"

"I have never heard mention of such a thing, though it might be possible."

Anya walked over to the carving, noting the quality of the work. Most of the sculptures of the Gods were worn where pilgrims had placed their hands on the deities, this, however, was unworn, except... could the stone be smoother in the middle of its horns? Anya gripped them with each hand and pulled. At first, nothing happened, but when she braced herself, using her body to aid her in her efforts, it moved with a slight crunching sound, to reveal a secret space, hollowed out from the block of stone.

Inside, were books.

Revelations

Anya reached inside, lifting the nearest book out of its hiding place. She examined the front, finding no title, and opened it to the first page. 'Journal of Dheemant, Acharya of Temple Isle', she read.

She turned to Pramiti. "Close the door," she said, before remembering herself. "Please, close the door." Anya gathered her thoughts. "This has remained hidden for, what, hundreds of years? I don't think you should tell anyone about this, except Bibek, I don't believe that anyone else knew about this hiding place besides your Acharya at the time. Is it possible that there are still members of your order who are under this 'charm'?"

"How could that be? The warlocks are no more."

Anya did not answer, her thoughts uneasy. She pushed the unwanted notions aside and took in the details of the book in her hands. Like the others, it was bound in green, the dyed animal skin bright and fresh, well-preserved through lack of handling, perhaps. She knelt before the nearest bench, laying the journal on the seat, turning immediately to the last entry.

> I fear The Fall has come at last to our mountain refuge. One stands on the shores of the lake who is known to me by reputation. His name is called Mordenar, and his deeds at Patann are not spoken of. He is an acolyte of Vajnata, though his followers know this not, having been seduced to his service by his beguiling enchantments and the promise of power. He has corrupted the Gods' servants, just as he has corrupted the magic they gifted them.

The Gods be praised, the gaganwa trees have been a succour in our hour of need, dispersing their magic, which they rained down upon us from afar. Enraged by his impotence against us, Mordenar, using the last of the life force of his captive, didst draw from the earth, bones, and formed them into a nameless horror, affixing the remains of the prisoner atop the multitude of hideous limbs. Once accomplished, the monster vanished from sight, though ever didst its chittering haunt our ears across the water.

They have begun to use their magic to freeze the surface of the lake, and afeared of an invasion, I made haste here, to the heart of the temple, determined to provide witness to these events. Our doom may be upon us, and if so, I implore whoever finds this testimony to go at once to Patann, where, if the books of our forebears speak truly, the key to unravelling this great evil may lie waiting still, for any brave enough to claim it. Alas that we, here, have failed in this, for all who left have not returned. Death walks abroad, and so it has proved. I pray to the Gods it will not claim the lands of the Yanubas.

Dheemant, Acharya.

Anya was stunned. Her mind raced, conflicted by so many revelations it could not settle on any, instead flicking in amazement from one to another. Beside her, Pramiti's face shone white in the dim light, the colour drained by fear.

"This is the horror you believe to be threatening your clan?"

Anya nodded, mutely.

"I'm sorry, if someone has the power to do this to them, they are lost."

"No, they can't be," said Anya, desperately. "What about 'Patann'? The Acharya believed something there could stop this 'Mordenar'."

Pramiti bit her thumb, her eyes darting as she considered the possibilities. "I will speak with Bibek. We may find volunteers brave enough to venture out. If it could somehow reverse The Fall, it would be a miracle." She sighed. "I cannot promise anything, the dangers are very great, but perhaps we could send an armed group on an exploratory foray outside, find out what we might face."

"An exploratory foray? We need to go to Patann!"

Pramiti looked at Anya in surprise. "We? You don't think Bibek would allow you to go, do you?"

"And what authority does he have to stop me?" Anya's temper was swelling.

"Anya, you have brought this danger to our attention, and found this… treasure trove of information. We will always be grateful for that, but your part is done. Perhaps in a few weeks, we may be prepared to go to Patann, but—"

"A few weeks? There is no time to waste with your explorations and preparation." Anya gesticulated angrily. "My people are in danger, and if there is something at this… 'Patann', I will find it and return to help them."

"Calm yourself, Anya." Pramiti fixed her with a stern glare. "All who have ventured outside these mountains have not returned. You are but one girl, what makes you think you can survive?"

Anya wheeled to face Pramiti. "This!" she said, holding her hand outstretched between them. Over her palm, a blazing fire burst into life, illuminating their faces eerily from below. Still staring into the monk's wide eyes, Anya closed her hand into a fist, plunging the room back into a semi-darkness. With that, she turned, and Pramiti, staring, her mouth open wide, watched her leave.

"Patann is, or was a city many days journey from the mountains," Bibek said, somewhat stiffly. His manner had been distant, though Anya was unsure if that was down to his disapproval of her recklessness, or her use of magic. Nevertheless, he had provided food for the journey and directions, gleaned from their oldest books. He had even given them a crude map drawn on a spare piece of parchment, though what use it would be to them was debatable.

"Thank you for your help, Bibek," she said.

His face softened, and he said, "Anya, can I dissuade you from this, perhaps for Matreyi's sake?"

"It's for Matreyi and the rest of my clan that I'm going," Anya retorted, with a touch of heat. She drew a breath, before continuing. "If I don't do this, I truly have no clan, and the council were correct in their judgement of me. I believe they are in danger and this could help them, maybe help all of us."

"But the risks—"

"I'm not afraid," she said, knowing it not to be true. "Besides, I may be the only one who is able to do this, maybe since the time of the fall." Anya sighed. "Aunt Matreyi has lost me already, if I die out there, she'll see me no less than now."

He was quiet for a time, and Amman shuffled his feet, clearly uncomfortable with the exchange between the two. "And how is Matreyi?" Bibek said softly. "I'm worried for her."

"No more than me," said Anya. She looked closely at Bibek, only realising now how deep were his feelings for Matreyi. "When we left, she was well, though after my banishment, my family's influence... well, she's less protected than she was."

Bibek nodded his understanding, displaying again the faint disapproval she noticed earlier. An awkward silence followed. Anya looked at Amman, desperately wanting to make him stay, but, not wishing to repeat a well-worn argument, she swallowed her words and said instead, "We'll go now. I hope you won't be caused any trouble because of me."

Together, she and Amman left the refectory, passing via the hall out into the early winter sun as it dropped towards the horizon, sparkling across the water. The Acharya accompanied them to the ring of gaganwa trees and watched as they climbed into their boat, ready for their return journey.

As they pushed off, he left, and they departed unremarked by any at the temple.

After two days, according to the directions given to them, they were nearing the wastelands beyond the mountains. The sun was at its meagre zenith, and they paused to take a meal of dried fish and gaganwa fruit, Amman complained as usual, but ate it nevertheless. Although the sky was clear of clouds, there was a grit in the air that found its way into their clothes and their food, making eating unpleasant as they crunched the fine particles with their teeth.

The atmosphere was subdued. Though their path was set before them, the possibility of disaster loomed large, and each of them was consumed with their own thoughts. Anya's nerves made it difficult for her to swallow, and she was grateful for the juice of the fruit to take away the dry sensations in her throat. She glanced at Amman, who was gazing unseeing at the remains of last night's fire, his eyes unfocussed, his mind elsewhere.

"It is time to move on," said Theelk. The bearded man had not acted surprised by her decision to venture beyond the mountains, and agreed to accompany them as though to do so was of no greater consequence to him than returning to his life among the frozen peaks. Somehow, he seemed older now to Anya, though he looked the same to her. The stoicism and solemnity of his bearing in the face of the unknown dangers did not belong to a younger man.

Shortly after they set off once more, they crested a rise, beyond which they observed a great line of the largest gaganwa trees Anya had ever seen. They stretched into the far distance, beyond the range of her vision, as though they might ring the entire Yanuba mountain range, protecting the lands within from the world outside. Amman whistled in amazement, while Theelk merely stood, his eyes fixed on their mighty forms. Anya imagined a look of satisfaction in his calm features.

They set off down the slope towards them, the vegetation beneath their feet changing to scrubby, coarse tufts of grass that protruded increasingly infrequently from sandy soil. As they approached the barrier of gaganwa trees, they gradually became aware that beyond their cover the ground rose, as though the trees themselves grew inside the lip of an enormous bowl in the land. Anya frowned, looking left and right to see that this ridge extended as far as the trees, and in fact… she squinted against the fine dust in the wind. Yes, she had not imagined it, the ridge undulated forwards and backwards, forming a pattern like waves, each peak stretching towards the gaps between the trunks, retreating again as though repulsed by the reach of each tree's branches. Intrigued, she moved ahead of the others, determined to unravel this mystery.

Half running, half walking, Anya made her way to the nearest gaganwa, and soon found herself under the vast canopy above. She ran her hand against its bole, the texture surprisingly smooth to her touch, and considered the vast line of similar trunks, curving into the distance. For them to be found so, could not be by chance, someone hundreds of years ago had planted them all. How far did they extend?

She continued walking until she came out from under the overhanging branches, and stopped, taking in the sight of the land waiting outside their cover. The ridge was nothing other than an immense dune of sand, obscuring any view of the territory outside the Yanubas. Anya could almost believe it represented the end of the world, there to prevent them all from falling off into nothingness, the only world that mattered was inside its formidable wall.

"What could have made it?" Amman drew level and stood beside her, mesmerized with awe and humility.

Anya shared his sense of insignificance against the magnitude of what the ridge represented. She glanced at Theelk, who hung back, a look of profound sadness on his face. She thought his eyes glistened and turned away, feeling as though she was intruding on private grief. Steeling herself, realising she would be leaving behind all she had ever known, Anya took a deep breath and moved forward. The sand grew deeper as she advanced, its surface a rippling static wave, fine particles swept off its many crests by the wind.

At last, she stood at the foot of the rise, as insignificant as an insect beneath the looming wall of sand. She took her first step, pausing to gather herself, and continued, her feet sinking into the dry powder beneath, making walking more difficult. Soon, she became aware of a crunching sound, as though the sand itself was just a coating over something breakable, like twigs. Sometimes her feet would sink suddenly, causing her to steady herself with her hands.

As she neared the top, she heard Amman shout from behind her. Turning, she saw him sunk almost to his hips into the dune, scrabbling to get out, looking for purchase with his hands, finding little to help him. She and Theelk moved to assist him, seeing him grasp something solid as he scraped around. He pulled, but it came away from the sand and he dropped it in instinctive revulsion. It was a bone.

"Ugh, help me out, would you?" he said.

Together, she and Theelk grabbed his arms, dragging him out of his predicament until at last his feet found more solid ground on which to stand. He looked at them, the smile of gratitude on his face fading as he followed their gaze. Their eyes were fixed on the dune. Where they had pulled him from the sand, the ground was littered with bones, one of them a human skull, which lay staring balefully up at them. A creeping dread seized Anya, she knelt and began scraping away the sand, ignoring Theelk's cautionary hand upon her shoulder, until revealed beneath were more remains. She scuttled desperately some distance away and dug once again to find yet more fragments of the dead.

The entire dune was a vast covering for a mountain of bones.

Anya sat back on her heels, staring at the evidence beneath her hands, unable to take in the enormity of the discovery. With a jerking motion, she looked to her left and right, the wall repeated its waving line until it disappeared into the distance beyond her sight.

All bones.

The sheer scale of death overwhelmed her. "It can't be real, it can't be." She was sobbing now, unable to contain the weight of sorrow within, perched on the graves of thousands, perhaps millions of people. To Anya, The Fall had always been a distant thing, lost in the mists of history, a regrettable fact, but one which acted as a cautionary warning of the folly of human conceit. This was no story to tell children, it was too real. Death on a level unimaginable and impossible to convey with mere words. Anya bowed her head and wept.

She cried until there were no more tears. Her head was heavy, too heavy to lift, so she just stared at the skeletal remains she'd uncovered, unable, or unwilling to meet the others' gaze.

After a long time, Theelk said, "This is no place to stay. We need to find shelter before nightfall."

Reluctantly, she stirred, climbing wearily to her feet, seeing Amman doing the same a little way off. His eyes were red, and Anya looked away, giving him the privacy she had taken for herself. The sorrow they all felt was not a personal grief to be consoled, but a lament for countless souls unknown to them, too great and too dreadful a mourning to be healed with comforting words or contact.

They resumed their climb, silent but for the sound of crunching bones as they trudged heavily to the crest of the ridge. The dune dropped away before them and Anya looked up at the land beyond, grateful that she had exhausted her tears. It truly was a wasteland, nothing grew, no sign of life at all to the limits of their sight, the entire vista a barren vision of sand that drifted in the wind, piling up against the occasional abandoned structure, the only hint that life here had ever been.

Exposed as they were, the wind deposited grit in their eyes, causing each blink to grate painfully. Anya felt this was a sign that they should keep their eyes permanently open in witness to the desolation, or else close them forever in grief at the passing of the world. Into this, she walked, clutching desperately in her mind at the possibility of salvation.

The nights were hard. Theelk, who in the mountains had been incredibly adept at utilizing the land around them for shelter, bending trees into huts, building walls from compacted snow or finding hidden caves, was at a loss when confronted with the barren, desolate wastes around them. Worse than that, to Anya's eyes, he aged daily. This morning, she had noticed flecks of silver in his beard and wondered how she had never seen them before.

Apart from the abandoned dwellings they passed, the only possibility of shelter was from the terrain, which was unpromisingly flat. No living trees or plants of any kind were to be found, and Anya had not seen even a single insect or other creature, not even those that thrived on death. Sometimes they would encounter strange vertical wooden monuments, worn smooth by the action of the sand-laden winds. Only by digging around beneath one such structure had they discovered the roots that identified it as the standing remains of a tree, eerily preserved and rendered thin and frail by wind and not decay.

At night, they took what little sleep they could find on the open sand, taking turns to watch for trouble. Today, however, Anya felt they had been lucky. As the day dwindled, they had come across a large settlement, the first such sign of the wondrous cooperation she had read of in Matreyi's books from the temple. All the roofs of the buildings they found had collapsed, but in one, the derelict frames still provided cover enough for the three travellers to shelter beneath. With little fear of danger from wild animals, Anya sparked a fire to life using magic, burning whatever wood they could find. Though not as cold as the mountains, the nights could be bitter, and the flames warmed their spirits as much as their bodies. Weary, they slept.

"Wake up." It was Theelk, his voice low, but insistent.

Anya opened her eyes blearily, rubbing away the sand that caked her eyelids. Her mouth was dry and tasted like the shifting desert around them. "Wha?" she said, not yet fully awake. She blinked painfully, and tried to focus on the bearded man in the light of the moons, both were full and cast a silvery light into their shelter. He raised a finger to his mouth, cupping his other hand around his ear. Anya sat up slowly, leaning her back against the wall to support her as she eased to full consciousness, and strained to listen. Amman was already awake, turning his head slowly, frowning in concentration.

She was about to complain to Theelk about waking her unnecessarily, when she caught a faint shuffling sound, coming from somewhere outside the building they sheltered in. A chill swept through her, the noise was so unlike anything they had become used to in this strangely quiet world. It was the sound of movement, of something or someone. Whatever caused it was nearing their location. The three exchanged looks, Amman breaking off a piece of loose timber from the fallen roof and waving his fingers at Anya in a clumsy imitation of her arcane gestures.

They focussed their attention on the open doorway through which they had entered this building, waiting as the sound grew louder. Anya moved to leave their cover, wanting space in which to work her magic, and as she attempted to straighten from her crouched stance, gasped at a sharp pain in her calf. She fell to her knees, and reaching down to rub her leg, found a skeletal hand stretching from beneath the sand, the bones of its fingers gouging relentlessly into her flesh.

"Anya!" called Amman, his voice choked with fear and concern.

For a moment she panicked, whimpering and prising desperately at the hand as it closed ever tighter around her leg. Blood was welling around the finger bones and Anya was filled with nausea, unable to calm her mind and imagine a pattern she might call on to help her. The pain had grown to almost unimaginable levels when Theelk slammed his foot hard onto the thing's wrist, shattering it and releasing her from its grip. She stood, and moved as fast as she could away from the broken hand, limping, unable to put weight on her bleeding leg.

As they watched, another dead hand emerged from the sand, dragging the rest of the damaged skeleton from its forgotten grave. Before it could stand, Amman lunged in, clumsily swinging the wood he grasped down onto the horror, clipping its skull. Its head jolted sideways, but it showed no sign of inconvenience as it rose and turned to face Amman. He swung again in a wide horizontal arc, catching it in the ribs, which shattered with a darkly comic, almost musical percussion. Again, the apparition continued as though the damage was immaterial. It reached out with its remaining hand, snatching the improvised club from Amman with unstoppable force.

"Anya!" cried Amman again, risking the briefest of glances in her direction.

She looked up, as though suddenly roused from a waking slumber. The scene before her ran slowly. The skeleton raised the timber above its head in a jerking, unnatural action, as though it was a puppet obeying the whims of its master, dangling from a set of invisible strings. Anya traced a pattern of force, moving smoothly in comparison to the world around her, reciting the words that would complete the spell.

As she uttered the final syllable, the world returned to its proper motion. The energy she had summoned shot like a wave into the thing as the wood it clutched began its downward stroke, slamming it backwards into the wall, splintering its bones. The club spun and fell harmlessly in front of Amman, who turned, the grateful smile building on his lips twisting, his eyes wide with alarm.

Anya whirled around. Clustered so thickly they hindered each other as they sought to pass through the doorway were more walking bones. Amman, white-faced, stooped to snatch up the piece of timber, and as he did so, more hands sprouted from the sand beneath. Anya's blood ran cold as she realised they were trapped.

"This way," said Theelk, his face drawn and intense. He indicated the tiles of the collapsed roof and helped Anya as she hobbled painfully, eventually choosing to shuffle backwards on her bottom. Amman swung his club around, in an attempt to buy them time, and caught the skull of one of their assailants, smashing it. The rest of its bones dropped and lay still. Seeing another reaching for him from behind, Anya sent another pulse of force at the evil thing, sending it flying across the room. She saw another skeleton emerge from the sand, this time an animal of some kind and called out to Amman.

He scampered up the tiles, turning to ward off the advance of the mass of animated bones with his swinging club. Anya recalled the pattern she had used before against the Rahksharu, and reproduced it, expecting to harness the energy of life against this living death. As she finished the last word of her chant, instead of a surge of power, Anya felt nothing. There was no flow of energy at all. The horde of the dead was building, and finding the smooth tiles difficult to gain a purchase on, they instead climbed over each other, achieving height through sheer weight of numbers. She tried the same spell again, with the same result.

"I can't do it," she screamed. A new fear was building inside her, even eclipsing her fear of death. Magic had failed her.

They had gained the top of the wall, and casting their eyes around, were stunned to find a sea of moving dead, waves of them crashing against the structure, surrounding the perch on which they stood, rising to drown them all. Amman, the last to join her at the summit of the wall, looked sadly into her eyes, his own full of tears.

"I love you, Anya," he said. "I always have." With that he turned, grasping the timber with both hands, his feet placed wide in preparation for the inevitable.

A sudden glow to her side distracted her, causing Anya to turn, and she saw Theelk, his eyes closed in concentration, head bowed and arms aloft. His entire body was giving off light, building in power and ferocity, until she could no longer look at him. She turned her face away, and closing her eyes against the unbelievable glare, she was startled by a peculiar after-image.

With a final surge, the light faded. Anya was enveloped by a sense of wondrous euphoria and opened her eyes to see the mass of living death around her disintegrate in a wave, crumbling to dust as a silent shockwave expanded around them. Each new victim simply ceased to be, and yet they continued to advance in the face of their own destruction, heedless or uncaring, without emotion even for their continued existence.

At the sight of the last of the dead to fall, the rapture drained from Anya, and she blinked, again seeing that image behind her eyelids.

An image of an elk.

Moment of Truth

Anya was startled by a sound behind her. She wheeled around and called out, "Theelk!" Their guide had fallen from the wall, and lay on the drifted sand outside.

She crouched and jumped, shouting in pain as she landed, the finger wounds in her leg burned with a cold fire. Amman followed her down as she crouched beside Theelk, rolling him over to see how he was. Anya recoiled in shock, the man before her was ancient and wizened, his face painfully thin beneath a beard of grey. He opened his eyes, and she saw within them some essence of the man she had known.

"Anya," he said, his voice rasping and hollow. "I'm sorry, but I have to leave you now."

"You can't!" she cried. "You can't die. You're… you're the Elk!"

He smiled a crooked smile. "Of course I can, but how did you know?"

The confirmation of her intuition nearly overwhelmed her. "You were so bright. When I closed my eyes, I saw a shape, your real shape." She blinked in realisation, before laughing sadly. "Theelk. How stupid of me. The Elk. You were teasing me."

"It was a small thing, but it amused me." His eyes narrowed with pain. "Inconvenient things, bodies, but so precious. They have a habit of failing on you. In this place, there is no connection with life, I was forced to use my body to fuel the magic." He looked into Anya's eyes. "Do not fear for your own magic, it is different. New. Your spell would not work because you sought to channel the power of life." He swallowed. "Those things we faced are undead, fuelled by a force diametrically opposed to life itself. There is no life here, just death. The world itself is dying."

"But how can we hope to reach Patann without you?"

He fixed her with his gaze, his eyes soft. Anya imagined she saw sorrow there, but how could a dying man, a dying god feel sorrow for her? "I cannot tell you what you should do. It will be difficult, should you choose to continue, and for that I am sorry, but it will be difficult for your clan if you do not.

"Be careful. What you find at Patann may not be what you expect. Believe in yourself Anya, you have great potential, but ask yourself, what will you use it for? What do you want from life?"

"I don't understand."

"No, but you will," he said, and for a time he was silent, the only sign of life, the rise and fall of his chest. His eyes flickered open. "Take the fruit," he said, clutching at Anya's arm. "It is important that you eat it, more important than you know." With a final spasm, his grip released, and he said no more.

They shunned all signs of human habitation, avoiding buildings of any kind. At night, they rested on stony ground, where they could find it. Where they could not, they walked through the night, trusting to the Gods to provide safety in the darkness.

More days passed, and Anya's leg would not heal. There was a grey pallor to the skin where the dead thing had held her, and blood continued to drip sluggishly from the wounds it had made. She had pricked it experimentally with Theelk's knife and had not felt a thing. When he thought she was not watching, she saw Amman looking at her leg in concern, perhaps mindful of her tales of Tanu, less sceptical than he had been of the possible consequences. He was always there to help her when she stumbled, providing support when she needed it. He was quiet, and Anya had not raised the topic of his confession, unsure of what she felt in return.

Twice they had encountered isolated undead. Anya had used fire, to little effect, finding a barrier of force more useful to protect them. Amman had broken their bones using a long shaft of metal he carried with him, recovered from a farming tool found stuck into the ground as they travelled. Although possessed of great strength, the horrible things were brittle with age, shattering easily from a strong blow.

After long weeks of tension, at last they stood on a rocky ridge overlooking Patann. It looked vast in the waning light of the sun, a huge collection of buildings straddling a murky river that oozed through the centre, full of silt. The endless sand was less here, the ground more rocky than before and Anya could see stone roads leading away in many directions, routes to other lost civilizations, joining here at this point, a place where different cultures could meet and exchange their knowledge of the world. Once more, Anya despaired of all that had been lost in The Fall.

"How will we find what we're looking for?" said Amman. "Over a thousand people must have lived here." His voice was hushed, awed by the thought.

Anya had been wondering the same thing. She studied the ruined town below, looking for anything that might call to her, but to no avail. She admitted to herself that she had been hoping to hear a voice inside her head, as she had so often of late, telling her where she should go, but there was no sign of it. Tentatively she went in search of that inner guide, sure somehow that it could help.

Not knowing what to do, feeling slightly foolish, Anya called out in her mind. Although there was no reply, something within her hushed, as though waiting, for what, she was not sure.

"I need your help," she thought.

She paused, considering what it was her intuition was leading her to. On many occasions, a voice inside had warned her of danger, helped to calm her, even offering encouragement when she doubted herself. Each time, it had felt so natural, but part of her knew it was not.

Almost forcefully, a recollection flashed into her mind of the vivid dream she had experienced after her first encounter with the Rahksharu. In it, she had granted permission for… what? She could not remember, even in her dream, she had barely understood. There had been a figure, who looked like her mother, but was not. She had placed something inside her, could it be the voice? Deep within her, something stirred in anticipation. Who are you? she thought. Anya waited, and the voice came. *I think you know.* All that had happened, everything her life had become centred on one thing. The tower.

"Yes," said the voice.

"Help me," Anya silently replied.

Anya turned to Amman, and found he had been watching her, a curious expression on his face. "I know where to go. Follow me." She set off at once, and perplexed, but unquestioning, he trailed in her wake.

The city had no pattern, or design that Anya could discern, as though it had not so much been built as grown. The roads she had noticed from their viewpoint met in the centre, the buildings sprouting up around them, clustered tightly together with smaller paths leading between. With so many people in one place, their knowledge must have been great, perhaps they had a library where their lore was made freely available to the people. She wondered absently if it might still be found.

She frowned. This was not why they were here, this was not a safe place to be. Memories of their last stay within a town burned as a warning in her mind, and she picked up her pace, forcing her leg to endure the pain as she limped as fast as she could, following the guidance of the tower. Anya turned off the main road, down a narrow alley between two high walls of stone. It was darker here in the shadow of the houses, and the path twisted and turned, a rocky maze formed from the buildings around them, as if the very route had been designed to throw off pursuit. Their steps echoed in the deathly quiet of the abandoned city, too loud to Anya's ears, she was afraid they might wake the dead.

Eventually they reached a set of steps, leading down beneath the level of the street. At the bottom, a broken door hung on a single hinge, a fractured portal to an unlit interior.

"Wait, I should go first," said Amman, hefting the metal bar in his hands to emphasise his point.

At first, Anya was inclined to argue. This was her responsibility, not his, but she knew that Amman was only being protective, that he was motivated by love. Pushing aside her retort, she nodded, letting him lead the way.

Inside was a cramped space. There were no windows to admit any light at all, the only source of illumination through the shattered door behind them. A wooden counter divided the room, shielding another doorway in the opposite wall. Amman rounded the counter and peered into the darkness beyond. Anya followed, her feet crunching on something unseen in the gloom.

"We need a light," said Amman, rummaging inside a bag and retrieving a piece of wood, suitable for a torch. Anya focussed her mind, opening a connection to the plane of fire, and the end of the torch erupted into flame.

"I could have lit it, you know, normally," he said.

"There's no time, we have to hurry." Anya could not say how she knew this, merely that she did.

There were no doors leading from the room, it was bare except for a tangle of broken furniture and a table. Amman glanced at her as if to indicate she may have made a mistake. Anya closed her eyes, the path before her not seen, but felt internally. She moved directly to the table and pushed it to one side, before grabbing at a scrap of cloth and brushing the floor where it had been. As she worked, an outline in the wooden boards became visible, a trapdoor leading down beneath them.

Anya found a ring attached to it and pulled, but it broke off in her hand, the wood brittle with age. She brought forth Theelk's knife and traced the edges of the hatch, freeing them from the fine sand that coated everything. She wedged the blade in a gap and pushed down hard on the pommel, leveraging it open. With a creak of protest, it shifted, and Amman straddled the panel, jamming his fingers into the gap, lifting the hatch away.

From the darkness, an unpleasant, stale metallic smell issued forth, and Anya wrinkled her nose in distaste, turning her head away. Amman waved his torch around, but with the glare of the flame in their own eyes, it was difficult to see what lay within, except for the hand and footholds, built into the wall of the shaft like a ladder. He looked seriously at her, before handing her the torch and climbing down into the gloom.

"Alright, you can drop the torch," he called. Anya held it steady, before letting it fall into the hole. Amman caught it, and she could see him looking up at her, its flickering illumination lending his form an uneasy sense of movement. She hurried down to join him, finding at the bottom a roughly hewn space with a cramped downward sloping passage leading off to who knew where.

Amman again insisted on leading the way, and Anya found herself growing irritated by his assertiveness. Hadn't she proved that she was not some kind of helpless girl who needed protection? She sighed and followed behind him, crouching in the low tunnel and coughing as the soot from the torch's flame hugged the roof of the passageway, getting in her throat and stinging her eyes.

At last the tunnel opened up into a rounded room. Far from being natural, it had been carved out of the rock deliberately, concealed from notice beneath the city and inaccessible except via the single route they had taken. In the centre was a stone table, the top of which was carved in the likeness of a snake eating its own tail, the circular form twisted once in the middle to form an endless crossed loop. This symbol was visible in many places around the room, carved as decoration into the floor and entrance.

The walls were painted throughout, and Anya gasped at the horrific scenes displayed, which had been captured with a passionate zeal, showing vivid scenes of murder and depravity, unspeakable acts committed against children and animals. Amongst other themes, she could see an army of the dead, clawing their way up through the earth, and in some cases, breaking through, adding to the mayhem. Above, was a layer depicting the world as it had been before The Fall, people going about their lives in happiness and contentment. Anya could see their expressions, which were suggestive of self-satisfaction and complacency. She walked around the broadly circular room, finding that in the centre, above the plinth, a final image looked down from the apex of the ceiling, a hideous, winged demon, with tentacles spreading from its open mouth, insinuating themselves in the theme of debauchery and death below.

Anya shuddered and looked away.

Amman, still gazing around in distaste, said, "We're supposed to find something here that might save the world?" His disbelief was obvious.

Looking up, Anya saw a recess in the wall at the rear of the room, a small space etched out of the rock to form a seat and table. Lying undisturbed was a book, bound with what looked like a thick velum, stained dark in places, the serpent symbol burned into its cover. Beside it lay an empty ink pot and a quill, which she reached out for, but it crumbled instantly at her touch, becoming nothing more than dust. Realising the age of the objects, Anya gingerly opened the tome. She read aloud.

> At last, he is here, the appointed one, most holy apprentice to Vajnata himself. No more shall we hide, no more conceal ourselves from those ignorant of his power and his glory. Our time is come. Mordenar will perform the final ritual, granting us dominion over all, eternal life, through death.

There it was, the name 'Mordenar', as mentioned in the Acharya's journal. Nowhere else in the monks' texts was the name mentioned, it had been excised from their records. She carefully flicked forward, reading once again.

> His powers are great, nowhere have I seen the like. From his mouth, he may issue forth a swarm of insects, which erupt with fury between his pointed teeth, and with them, devour a corpse in moments. His very presence is like honey to men, who are transfixed in his presence, entrusting their very souls to his care. A mistake, for he cares not for ought. For reasons unknown, only I am free from his charms - he knows this, and plays cruelly with me. Many has he killed, but none have returned to life as promised.

A creeping unease prickled Anya's skin, and she turned over another page.

> The ceremony's effects continue to spread. The dead roam the streets and all whom they touch are consumed by Vajnata's gift. This is the very culmination of our prayers, so he led us to believe, the time of our final triumph over death. I see no triumph, no true life in the death all around. It continues to spread, not even the grass beneath our feet is spared the plague of death unleashed.
>
> We have been duped by a God who cares nothing for his servants. Except one, Mordenar, and he himself has tasked me to record all this, not for posterity, for no-one will ever read of it, except one. I remain hidden in our temple, huddled and afeared as my body fails, knowing I will not live to see another day. I have not the remaining faculties to understand his purpose, but you, my reader, are wanted by Vajnata. Flee!

Anya jerked up from the text, bashing her head on the stone above her in the alcove, the flashes of light exploding in her head did not ease the shooting alarm spreading from her heart with an icy chill.

"Anya!" called Amman, pointing at the exit.

She leapt out of the recess, and saw the dead shuffling into the temple, their heads turned towards her, empty eye sockets fixed on her location. There was no way out, as they continued to flow in from their only possible escape route. Anya's heart raced, pumping in fear, her hands slick with sweat. She backed off, until she pressed against the wall behind her, wishing more than anything to sink into it, to escape her fate. Why had the books led her to this place? There was nothing here, no means to halt the curse, no cure for The Fall. Theelk was gone, there was no one to save them, much less the world.

Amman stepped forward wordlessly, holding the metal bar up, making ready to meet the horde.

"It's hopeless," said Anya, the tears in her eyes pouring forth into her words.

"No, it isn't. We still have you." He glanced behind him. "You're special, and not just to me."

A series of muted clicks caused Amman to turn again to face the undead. Anya peered around him to see the skeletons clambering over one another as though engaged in a fleshless orgy. She was transfixed by the macabre display, unable to tear her eyes away, until the movement ceased.

"Special." A mocking voice issued from the weird shape, which moved as it spoke. With shock, Anya saw each skeleton had combined to form a giant face, made entirely of their bodies' bones. Where the eyes would be, a fiery red glow emerged, and she recoiled from its piercing glare.

"This pitiful wretch, cowering before me, special?" It laughed. "Cast out of her tribe, unwanted by her family. Even her betrothed valued her not." The voice was cold, scathing. "You are but a girl, meddling in that which is beyond you, obediently eating the fruit of your 'Gods' and using the misplaced infatuation of your friend to protect you. They will not suffice."

Amman hefted the bar in his hand threateningly. Again, it laughed. "Pathetic. He has seen you at your lowest, unclothed, waiting to be violated. He dreams of it. Dreams of lust!" The voice was urgent, its sibilance grotesquely suggestive. Anya could see Amman's ears colouring.

"Your own mother is ashamed of you. You are weak, and aberrant."

Anya was jolted by the word, used by Matreyi on their way to the temple so long ago. The thought of her aunt brought her back to reality. She stepped forward, facing the monstrosity before them.

"It means, 'departing from accepted standards'. Aberrant." Anya fought to control her fear, to calm herself, ready for what she knew must come. "But who sets those standards? You?" she said, scornfully.

"At last, some fight." There was no real expression to read in the face before her. "Perhaps you will be of some use to my servant, as he rips your magic from you. But for now, he must content himself with the souls of your family, your mother, your brother. Your aunt. At this very moment, he enslaves your entire clan. Watch!"

The air shimmered in front of the face of Vajnata. They saw, lit almost from below by a blood-red sun, scenes of horror. On the site of the Gods' sacrifice, in sight of the doors to the tower, a fire burned, its flames leaping to the sky. Looking into the blaze, Anya saw the unmistakable shape of human remains, consumed and contributing to the conflagration. She briefly closed her eyes, seeking to shut out the truth. Gathered around were the entire clan, watching with muted faces, their eyes sunk deep within their sockets, many shivering with the cold. Anya was shocked by their appearance, they looked half-starved to her, not a people nurtured by the Gods and sustained by the herd.

A muscular figure, tall and haughty with pride stood before the throng. It had to be Mordenar. He pointed to a figure in the crowd and beckoned. From the rest of the clan, a lone boy walked forwards, Anya saw it was Paras. Something was said, and Mordenar pointed to the fire. A weird expression of hope contorted the boy's features, and he stumbled towards the flame, pausing only to smile broadly before he ran and leapt into the inferno, to be devoured by the blaze. Mordenar turned to face them directly. He knew they were watching. He smiled at them, displaying his jagged teeth and gestured to the side, where Anya could see her family.

"No!" shrieked Anya. The vision disappeared.

"He tortures and kills them while you run away, abandoning them to my servant, seeking false hope."

"At least I look for hope," she sobbed. All reticence was forgotten now, her terror for the fate of her loved ones now fuelled the heat that rose within. "You used your own followers' twisted desires against them."

"I gave hope to those who worshipped me." The voice was mocking. "And *my* hope was delivered. All the world is mine, except that which your Elk and the others protect. But the Elk is dead and very soon your tower will provide Mordenar with power enough to destroy them all."

"No!" Anya shouted. A pattern formed in her mind. She began a trace in the air with her hands.

"Good! Draw on your power, return to your clan. Fulfil your purpose!"

She screamed in rage, her spell amplifying the sound, turning its resonance into a weapon. As the deranged thing laughed, skeletons leapt from its open mouth, running at them. Her voice exploded through them and into the face of Vajnata, obliterating all with the force of her anger, leaving nothing but flying shards of bone.

Place of Sacrifice

Amman clutched at his ears as the spell reverberated around them, the metal bar dropping from his hands with a clanging crash to the floor.

Anya stormed from the shrine, stepping on broken bones as she stalked the low tunnel. Her scream had travelled the passage before her, clearing it of the undead. It was dark, and she held out her hand, causing flames to roar above it, answering her anger but too hot in the enclosed space. Through force of will, she channelled the violence of her temper, and the flame reduced in size, becoming concentrated, casting a whiter light, revealing the exit shaft ahead.

Climbing swiftly, she gained the room above, and seeing yet more walking dead advancing from the street outside, shaped her intense flame into a blade, and sent it spinning out from her hand. The skeletons in its path were cut in half, and such was the intensity of the whirling fire, even the wooden counter and the wall of the building were sliced through with its ferocity.

"Anya, wait. Where are you going?" Amman's voice echoed up from below her.

She wheeled around, shouting into the hole. "This was all just a waste of time. None of it meant anything!" She glared down at him. "We walked out into this..." Her words ran dry, and she kicked at a stone petulantly. "Vajnata was right about one thing, we came with false hope. The books were wrong, I was wrong to believe in them and Theelk died needlessly because of me. There is nothing here to reverse The Fall, nothing."

Her view of Amman was obscured by the glare of the torch flickering below. "Anya, the man we knew as Theelk wasn't just a man. He was the Elk." Though their discovery was many days old, she still detected awe in her friend's tone. "He must have had good reason to send us here."

"Maybe he was wrong too." The weight of her disappointment was crushing and only the heat of her fury kept it at bay. She realised how naïve she had been, to think that books were always good and true, that almost by their nature they embodied the noblest achievement of civilization. Some books lied.

"What are you going to do?" He threw the torch up to Anya and she caught it.

"I'm going to find a way back to the clan, and I'm going to end this."

"But how?"

"I don't know, but I'm going to stop Mordenar, I swear it."

Amman reached the top of the ladder, looking at Anya with concern. "That's not what I meant, how are we going to get back? It'll take us weeks to retrace our steps."

She scowled in concentration. "We could fly," she said. "I could try to give us wings like birds, though I've never thought about modifying something before, I'm not sure what sort of pattern that would require." Feeling her temper cooling, Anya said, "No, that won't work, there must be another way." She paced, thinking furiously.

"If we were as light as feathers, maybe we could use the wind to blow us there? Hmm, I'd need to change our weight and control the wind, and I don't know how to do either!" She stamped her foot, almost screaming in frustration.

"It's alright, you'll think of something," said Amman, a note of reassurance in his voice.

"That's easy for you to say, but what if I don't?" She rounded on him. "Right now, Mordenar is torturing and murdering our clan. He was the one we saw as we left, he's been there ever since!"

"Anya," Amman said cautiously, looking down at the floor. "If it's really him, and he really did trigger The Fall, if the temple books were right, and he was one of the warlocks who tried to enslave the Gods..." He left the thought unfinished, and brought his eyes up to gaze into Anya's. "What chance do we have?"

Without answering, she spun on her heel and marched out into the alleyway. Another wandering dead blocked her path and without breaking stride, she dispatched it with a burst of force that threw it back against a building. It fell to the ground in pieces. Footsteps from behind told her that Amman was following.

"Anya."

She stopped, turning to face him. "I don't know, Amman, alright? I don't have all the answers. The Acharya's book said we might find something to undo The Fall, but all we found was a trap set by Mordenar. We might not stand any chance at all, but what can I do? This is our clan, I can't just abandon them."

"I know. I just mean that we need to think about this. If we get back, we need to have a plan."

Anya laughed, the sound bouncing harshly off the walls of the narrow street. "We don't know the first thing about him, and if we don't find a way back, it's hardly going to matter whether we have a plan."

"But—"

"I didn't ask for this, Amman. It's not fair for you, Theelk or anyone else to expect me to save our people. I never expected to learn magic, it wasn't me who built the tower."

"Who did build it?" asked Amman.

Anya realised that she had always pushed the question away, never wanting to confront it. "I don't know," she said quietly.

She knew the voice of the tower was waiting within, and directed her question to it. "How come you're here?"

"I'm here because of you," came the reply.

"You mean, you're here to help me?"

"No, it's more than that. I'm part of you, I exist because of you, because of your passion to question the world around you and *because you have the intelligence to understand it.*"

"But that doesn't make any sense, towers don't just spring up because someone wants answers."

"Don't they?"

Anya rubbed her face, as though by doing so, she could make sense of what it was telling her. "So, if you're part of me, tell me how I can get back to the clan."

"You could walk."

"That's no help." Anya directed her irritation at the voice inside her. "How can I do it quickly, is there some magic that would help?"

For a time, no answer was forthcoming. Amman watched her carefully, as though he knew not to interrupt her thoughts. "Perhaps. But it is intended for when you gain a greater mastery of magic. You aren't ready, and in light of what awaits you, it would be unwise of you to make use of it."

"Theelk asked me what I would use my potential for. What else should I use it for if not to protect my own people?"

"The Elk and I have different priorities."

"Different priorities?" Anya almost laughed. "If you hadn't arrived, maybe none of this would have happened. You appeared to me, not to anyone else, not to Amman, not to Mordenar. Me. I need your help."

"Are you alright?" asked Amman.

Anya nodded curtly. She could almost feel the indecision of that part of her that was the tower.

"Very well," it said.

Night had fallen. The city square was illuminated by a vista of stars. All around them the outlines of buildings provided jagged silhouettes against the sky, while on one side, the orange glow of sunset crested the skyline in a cold imitation of fire.

Anya shivered, not just from the rapidly plummeting temperatures, but from the exposure she felt to the lurking inhabitants of this place. She scanned the many doorways and alleys constantly, fearful for any signs of movement. As she turned, she almost stumbled, cursing her injured leg. It hurt less now, but in place of the pain, there was now a spreading area void of all sensation, a total numbness that made her clumsy when she was not careful. A memory of Tanu rose unbidden and unwanted in her mind and she pushed it away, not needing a reminder of what awaited her. Absently, she wondered why she had lasted so long against the encroaching disease. What did it matter? She must soon face Mordenar.

The voice of the tower spoke within her. "You must concentrate." Anya nodded to Amman, who responded to her signal with grimly set lips, doubly watchful now for any sign of the undead. "Picture the inside of the tower and the area of seating. Nearby, the wall there is decorated with the outline of a doorway."

"Yes, I remember thinking how odd it was, as though whoever built it had changed their mind about the door," she thought.

"It is a doorway, one that can open almost anywhere you would like. It can open here." Anya frowned in confusion. "Forget what you think you know, and for now accept that it is true. It would take much study for you to come to understand its nature. Imagine the door is before you now, except that you are not facing it as you have seen it before, but from the other side."

"I can see some movement." Amman pointed, but Anya's eyes were closed in concentration.

"From outside the tower?" questioned Anya.

"No. From here. The doorway faces into the tower, but also out from the tower, to anywhere. You must see it from where you are, hold that in your mind, make it as real as you can. Believe that you merely have to pass through the door to return."

Anya imagined standing before the doorway, as she had before, the tower hub behind her. She pictured herself walking around it, until, passing through the wall of the tower, she stood in Patann, as she did now, facing a portal of stone, a ghostly image of the tower interior visible through its arch.

"Anya." Amman's voice was urgent, but she did not dare open her eyes, unwilling as she was to risk the failure of her endeavours.

"That's good, Anya. Now imagine that, though you are standing in the city square, your hand is opening the door from the inside."

"But how?" She could hear a sound of scuffling feet, grunts and snaps of broken bones.

"How does not matter. You must open the door to yourself."

She pictured her hand seizing a handle, turning it to open, but nothing happened, it did not feel right. Instead she imagined a ghost image of herself pushing at the portal. Again, nothing. This was not a door with a handle, it would be a thing of magic, but if she truly was not ready to open it, how could it be opened? The tower should be able to, but it would not. Why?

The sounds around her grew, she could hear Amman grunting with effort and forced down a rising panic. She could not help Amman, except by opening this door. Perhaps the tower could not do it without her? But she was not inside the tower, she was here in Patann. Anya's eyes opened, so amazed was she at a new idea in her mind. The tower was part of her, the voice in her head the most obvious indication, but if it truly was part of her, might it not follow that she was part of it? If a part of her was in the tower, it could open it from the inside.

Facing her, a glowing outline grew, shimmering in the darkness, forming the shape of the doorway. As if underwater, Anya could see through it to the tower's interior, undulating gently as though blown by the wind.

A sudden shove, jostled her from her reverie and she looked about her, seeing Amman, desperately swinging his metal bar, losing ground to several skeletons, both human and animal. Sweat poured from him, his hair slick with it and she could hear his rapid gasps for air.

"Amman, come on," she cried, and together they turned and ran at the gleaming portal, falling through it onto the strangely warm flagstones of the tower floor.

Gasping with exhaustion, Amman panted, "Anya… the doorway." He pointed, and following his outstretched finger, she saw the undead beginning to emerge as they had, into the tower.

"Close."

Immediately the glow of the portal vanished, accompanied by the sound of falling bones, and they were left in silent semi-darkness, facing a blank wall within the arch of stone.

Anya got to her feet wearily and examined the skeletons for any sign of movement. They were still, and she saw they had been sheared in two, caught halfway between this place and Patann when the gateway closed.

"Come on," she said.

"No, you're exhausted. You need to rest and eat."

"I can't rest," she said. "He'll kill them all if we wait too long. You know he will."

"Then at least eat something." Amman was firm. "You can use that stone to see what's going on, if you want."

Amman watched Anya as she moved over to the seating area, his eyes soft. Looking away, his gaze passed the portal, and rested on the wall to the right of it. He frowned. Where before it had been smooth stone, now he saw a relief carving in the wall, which depicted a face of bone spitting skeletons at the viewer. He shuddered and turned his head. Towards the entrance to the tower, he saw the statue of the ogre was gone, and in its place instead was what Amman assumed was a Rahksharu, based on Anya's descriptions. He walked over and circled the new sculpture, stopping abruptly, his face blanched.

"It is Bibhu, isn't it?" Anya's voice called sadly from behind him. Amman nodded.

For a while, Amman remained motionless, standing silently, staring at the horrific likeness of their former elder. He breathed deeply and turned, finding Anya watching him quietly.

"Anya," he began. "What I said to you before – "

"I know. You thought we were going to die."

"No, I mean, yes, I did, but… I meant it, Anya, I've never meant anything more, and…" He paused, swallowing. "I was alright with dying, as long as I'd told you. And now, well, given what we're up against— "

"I'm sorry, Amman, I can't give you what you want." Amman's eyes dropped. "What I mean is… when we faced the Rahksharu, I thought you must have died under the snow as it fell. I couldn't bear the thought." He looked up to see tears welling in her eyes. "I can't do this. I've been pushing it away, not thinking about it because I'm scared. If losing you hurt me so much before, what would it be like if…" Her breath was unsteady, her voice tremulous. "Besides, how could I make myself face Mordenar if we were… you know."

Amman nodded, the distance between them stretched thin and taut. "I understand," he said.

Anya got to her feet, and rummaged in a bag for some food, pulling out yet more dried fish and gaganwa fruit. She walked over to Amman, holding some out for him.

He blew briefly through his nose in a short burst of weary irony. "At least we won't have to eat any more of these, whatever happens," he said.

Wordlessly, Anya led him back to the seat. They sat and ate in silence, and when she had finished, she held Amman's arm, resting her head on his shoulder.

"Thank you," she said.

"What for?"

"You chose to come with me, you didn't have to."

He did not answer immediately. "You'd have done the same."

"Would I?" she said. "I'm not so sure. Maybe you're right, but you did it anyway."

"Besides, I seem to remember you dragging me away, so I guess I didn't have much of a choice." He looked sideways at Anya, smirking.

Anya was quiet, thinking of the charm exerted by Mordenar on his arrival, how she had been so desperate to trust him. She bit her lip and leaned forward, holding her hands over the stone orb resting on the table. Taking a deep breath, she allowed the tension to leave her as she exhaled and touched the stone.

Immediately, the room around her vanished, and she looked out into darkness, lit by the sinister light of the pyre. It illuminated the scene in tones of red and orange, lending it an eerie movement with the flickering flames. As she had seen in Vajnata's vision, their fellow clansfolk were gathered about the holy site. They flanked her view, as though forming an honour guard, ready for her appearance from the tower.

From the direction of the fire, a figure strode into sight, his chest exposed and gleaming wetly, as if he had been engaged in strenuous exercise. On his head, the skull and rack of an impressive elk, acting as both helmet and stolen crown. Mordenar walked forwards, looking straight at Anya, and she shrank back instinctively, only just managing to keep her hold on the orb.

"Come," he said. "Why do you wait? There is nothing to be afraid of, Anya."

He knew her name, and welcomed her like a lost child. She struggled to think why she had been so frightened, why she had come prepared for conflict. Once again, hope welled within her, she was home where she belonged, unsure why she had ever left.

"Come." He was more insistent now. "Re-join the tribe, be restored to the bosom of your family."

Why had she left? The council had banished her, but surely it could be smoothed over, Bibhu would happily reinstate her.

Bibhu. Something itched in her mind, she had seen him, attached to a monstrous body of bones, pleading for her to kill him. With a jolt, Anya let go of the orb, as though holding it was suddenly painful, bringing her instantly back to the interior of the tower. Her breath came rapidly, and she found she was trembling.

Amman put his hand on her shoulder, and looked into her eyes, his face screwed up with concern. "What's wrong, what did you see?"

"Mordenar." She barely managed to utter the word. "His charm, it's so powerful." Anya looked her friend in the eye. "I want you to stay here."

Amman's expression darkened. "I won't stay here while you risk your life."

She wanted to argue, but seeing that he would not change his mind, and heavy with the burden of responsibility, her words were like lead on her tongue. "Then it's time to go."

Together they trudged to the exit. Anya imagined what it must be like for a Defender, the first time they fought a Rahksharu, and sighed. That Defender would be surrounded by his fellows, veterans of many engagements, buoyed by the gratitude of his clan. She would be among those who wanted her dead, the man who had commuted her sentence, dead himself and violated, transformed into a twisted parody of life, and sent to kill her.

Something stirred within her. Hope? Whatever had been thrown at her, she had prevailed. She had her magic to call upon, ready to defend her. And she had Amman.

"Remember Bibhu, remember Theelk, Amman. That was Mordenar." She looked intensely at him, and he nodded.

Finally, they stood before the double-doors. Breathing deeply, Anya opened them and stepped out.

As she had seen in the orb, Mordenar stood facing them, the ranks of her clan arrayed on either side, their eyes unfocussed.

"Welcome, Anya," said Mordenar, his voice booming majestically, warming her, warming them all with its beneficence.

No. That was not who he was, he was no friend of theirs. She clutched at the memory of Bibhu, and the feelings of trust and safety melted away, leaving her drained, tired and fearful. To be free of his charm tasted bitter in her mouth. Alongside her, Amman stepped forwards, and Anya grabbed his arm, holding him back. He turned to look at her, his eyebrows raised in confusion.

"Remember Bibhu," she repeated, desperately.

"It's just a statue, Anya." Amman scowled at her. "Why do you always have to make things so difficult? We're safe now, he'll protect us." She clung to him briefly, before he tugged his arm free and walked calmly over to her enemy, joining their clansfolk at his side.

Mordenar was watching her, shrewdly. "Yes, I am your Protector, long have I watched over your tribe." She listened, stunned by his words. Could it be that this minion of Vajnata had been acting as their sacred Protector for all these years, waiting with patience born of inhuman devotion for the opportunity to finish what he had started? "Anya, you can be proud of what you have accomplished. Now it is time to rest." He held out his arms as though to embrace her.

Swallowing hard, she fought the tears, unable to think of suitably defiant words, not sure she could trust her voice to utter them without breaking. Her lip quivered, but she stood her ground, looking up at him from lowered head, blinking away the moisture in her eyes.

Something in the atmosphere changed. All her clan turned their baleful gaze to her as one, and Mordenar spoke. "I would never have believed it, were you not standing here before me. To think that your spirits of nature would choose one such as you, a pathetic wretch of a female, to oppose me?" His voice was sneering. "I have waited long for this moment, the culmination of my God's work on this world. I had expected more. Stand aside, and I will kill you swiftly."

Anya frowned in irritation. She had defeated Rahksharu, how many men could boast such a thing? Always they sought to use her sex to belittle her. Her spirit rose with the heat of her internal fire igniting. She thought fast.

"I… I'm sorry," she stammered, and stepped sideways, behind the open door, leaving the way into the tower unobstructed.

Mordenar's eyes widened with greed, and he strode forwards, hungry to enter.

"I'm sorry," Anya said once again, as Mordenar approached. "But you can't have it." She pushed the door with both hands, sending it crashing closed, the reverberating boom echoed around them.

For a moment, Mordenar stood gaping, Anya's hands were already moving, tracing a pattern of force in the air. He turned to her, furious, to be met with an impact that lifted him off his feet to sail into the night air, his bulky frame soaring over the edge of the cliff.

Hope swelled within Anya and she moved forwards a step in anticipation, when, lightning fast, she was struck by a chained barb of energy. A sharp, icy pain shot through her side where it pierced her skin, and she looked down to see her clothes, appearing ghostly through the chain, whole and unbroken. A weariness threatened to overcome her, as though she had cast a particularly difficult spell. He was using her own magic, stealing it from her!

Falling to her hands and knees, she blinked in confusion. Magic, her magic did not just sit inside her, waiting to be drained. It did not work that way, she had an understanding of how forces were triggered and controlled, rules that they obeyed, how could he steal that from her, there was no force he could use, what was he doing to her?

She looked up to see an arm appear, grasping from beyond the precipice, and another, as Mordenar hauled himself back to the holy site, using the chain he had cast at her as a kind of rope. Again, Anya recalled a phrase she had read, 'the simplest forms of use are those where magical force is merely channelled or shaped'. Whatever he had taken from her, he had used as a mere tool, a cord to cling to and save himself from the drop. She saw his face was thunderous.

The sight of him brought her renewed energy, a jolt of fear she could use to overcome the drowsiness, and she staggered to her feet. He would not find her some weak and helpless girl, she would fight. Anya looked down again at the chain still attached to her and tried to see how she could remove it, but it looked strong and without flaw to exploit.

"Foolish girl." Mordenar had regained his feet, his voice powerful and full of menace. "Open the door."

Anya ignored him, continuing to examine the force that held her to him. Suddenly, she was yanked forwards, excruciating pain radiating from the barb in her side. She looked up to see Mordenar using the chain like a whip, sending loops of it over her head, encircling her in a tight embrace. Anya struggled, managing to free her arms, but the links constricted her breathing, crushing her, and she staggered to her knees.

"I said, open the door."

"No." Unable to shout her defiance, Anya spoke with a calmness she did not feel, looking her attacker in the eye. For a moment, he was silent. Nodding slightly, he turned and beckoned somewhere beyond her sight.

From within the massed clansfolk, a small cluster of people shuffled into view. Anya's parents, her brother and his family, all with glazed eyes, and also Matreyi. Though the others walked freely, her aunt's hands were bound behind her back and she was gagged. Rahul dragged her by a cord, and it was clear by the look of hatred she directed at Mordenar, that Matreyi was free of his charm.

Despite the grimness of her situation, the sight of her beloved aunt brought tears of joy to Anya's eyes. It could have been an age since they had said their farewells to each other, so much had happened. To see her once again, showing defiance, understanding what others could not, was somehow a wonder, a guiding light and example she was determined to follow.

She made to regain her feet, but Mordenar called, "Stay where you are, girl, I like you better on your knees. You should know your place." He walked among her family now, in his free hand a blade of force, which he ran over them in ways both threatening and obscene, watching Anya all the while, his face a calculating mask of cruelty. Ceasing her attempt to stand, she settled on her knees, fixing him in return with an icy gaze that matched the cold settling in the pit of her stomach.

As Mordenar came to Matreyi, he played idly with the knife. "I will kill them all," he said, his tone neutral, as though what he spoke of was of no greater importance than the weather. "And you will watch, and know it to be your fault." He gestured at the tower. "I will have the power contained within or you will see your entire clan slaughtered before your eyes."

Anya caught her aunt's eyes and Matreyi looked at her with such love, that for a moment they could have been the only two people in the world. Bound together by shared experience, by their eyes, opened to the reality of their situation, and most importantly, by love. Their capacity for empathy and compassion meant nothing to this creature, beyond a means to extract obedience and submission to his will. Such things were more important than Mordenar would ever know, and Anya knew what she must do.

"Open," she said. Behind her, both doors to the tower swung wide, and Mordenar licked his lips, his attention fixed on the darkness within.

He drew himself up to his full height, and said, "For your disobedience." Casually, with dreadful efficiency, he reached out with his arm and sliced across Matreyi's neck with the impossibly sharp blade in his hand. She fell limply to the ground, her blood pooling crimson on shadowed white.

Anya's world imploded. All that she had suffered and endured came rushing in on her, squeezing the breath from her more surely than Mordenar's chains. Her victories, the trials she had weathered, her purpose, all meant nothing. The weight of injustice was crushing. Anya's whole life was nothing more than a mere mote in the air, drifting subject to the random blows of fate and cruel whim. A single tear fell from her bowed head, catching the light of the fire like a liquid drop of flame.

Before it landed, all the wasted, meaningless experiences of her life, crammed together in that fleeting instant, exploded, the heat of their pain her only remaining emotion. Anya spoke a word of power and the chains about her shattered outwards, freeing her from his unwanted bonds. Mordenar, surprised, paused in mid-stride, directing an incredulous look towards her.

"No," he said.

Anya reached within for a new pattern, and weaved her arms precisely, drawing the correct path for her magic. As she chanted, the snow beneath his feet boiled, shooting super-hot steam upwards to engulf Mordenar in a column of broiling gas. He staggered, curling protectively, covering his face with his hands. Instantly, the steam dissipated as the available snow was exhausted, and without pause, Anya cast a bolt of magic, felling him with the force of its impact.

She marched purposefully towards his prone form, which was shrouded in rising water vapour, fashioning in her hand a long blade of energy with which to finish him. As she approached, she could see angry red blistering on his arms and chest, which glistened alongside swelling beads of blood. His hands still covered his face as she raised her arm ready to strike.

As she prepared to bring her arm down, Mordenar lowered his hands, revealing a fierce smile of sharpened teeth amid a cracked and bleeding face. He opened his eyes, and she saw they were ruined, blanched white and leaking fluid. Anya hesitated in shock, the point of her weapon wavering over his heart. As she watched, his eyes began to swell, the fissures knitting back together, colour returning, until he looked at her with unblemished orbs of black.

Desperately, she struck, bringing the tip of her blade down, striking at his heart. An instant before it reached him, he caught the blade in his hands, stopping it immediately, before it somehow transformed into a chain under his command. He whipped it around Anya's legs, yanking it and her off her feet. She struggled, thrashing her legs, but could not break its hold. Instead she began chanting, but a blow to her face caused stars to appear in her vision, disturbing her concentration. She blinked, seeing a second chain spinning around Mordenar's free hand.

He frowned, turning his head as though hearing something for the first time, and crouched by her feet. Nonchalantly, he slapped her, before covering her mouth with his hand. With his other, he ripped the clothes covering her injured ankle, looking at her still bleeding wound with sadistic interest.

"You have already been touched by my God," he said. "It will spread, blessing you with eternal life through death, to serve him for all time." He looked at her with amusement.

"The transition can be long and painful, I would spare you such slow agony."

He clasped his hand about her injury and closed his eyes. Anya's whole body jerked reflexively, momentarily freeing her mouth from Mordenar's suffocating press, and she screamed in aguish as fresh pain seared her leg. Her ankle had transformed from numb, unresponsive flesh to a searing mass of torment, as though she was being eaten alive from the inside.

"Gods, no!" she cried, and desperately surveyed the mass of her clan surrounding her, knowing they were his servants, that no help would be forthcoming. Once again, Mordenar gagged her with his hand.

Anya's head swam, but she fought against the pain and the temptation to swoon with all the fury in her soul. She looked at Mordenar, seeking any slim chance or opportunity to escape and was surprised to see a look of angry frustration on his face. He pressed his lips together in a tight line, and the torment redoubled, ripping a fresh scream from her, muted by his grasp.

"Stop it! What are you doing? You aren't our Protector!" It was Amman, rushing over to them. "Anya, I'm sorry, please forgive—"

A panic rose inside Anya as Mordenar removed his hand from her mouth, standing and swinging back his arm, a fresh barbed chain in his hand. He cast his arm, throwing the razor-sharp spike straight at Amman's heart, deadly, and unstoppable. Amman gaped as it flew, until an instant before it struck, a shimmering ball of force formed around him, causing the weapon to bounce off, harmlessly.

Swinging around once again to face Anya, Mordenar growled, exposing his teeth, but she was casting yet another spell. Suddenly wary, he drew back from her, expecting a new assault, his eyes betraying confusion when nothing happened. He smiled, and swung his chain once before Amman's protective sphere crashed into him from behind, sending him sprawling to the floor. Snarling, he ignored the ball as it continued to roll, and jerked at the chain still wrapped about Anya's legs, dragging her closer. She smiled viciously as the protective sphere containing a waving Amman disappeared through the doors of the tower, which at a gesture from Anya swung shut once more, the finality of their closure a defiant message to her attacker.

Both knew she would not open the doors again. He struck her a blow across the face, causing the world to spin in her vision. Despite having rolled her head to reduce the impact, his strength was incredible. She would stand little chance at close quarters if she could not escape soon.

"You will pay for your insolence, little girl." He lunged at her, reaching for her neck, but found yet another barrier of force in his way.

Anya squirmed her legs free from his chains, and searched desperately for inspiration, wracking her brains for all that she knew about Mordenar, looking for anything she might use against him. If he was the leader of the original warlocks, he would have to be hundreds of years old, how could that be? No creature lives that long, unless... perhaps the dead do not age. She traced the pattern she had used before against the Rahksharu and other undead, forming a connection with the realm containing the positive energy of life, sending a bolt of it to strike at her enemy.

He screamed, writhing spasmodically, in obvious agony, but she could see no sign of damage. In fact, the blisters which had covered his chest were healing, leaving an unblemished expanse of rippling muscle. Mordenar laughed, turning his head to regard her.

"Foolish child. You misunderstand my nature." He rose to his feet, a vision of energetic health, his eyes no longer a uniform black, but returned to their previous more natural hue. "I have died, transformed by my God, given life eternal by the fusion of life with death. Such magic is useless against me. I am immortal."

Anya staggered back, retreating from the unbeatable being before her. "No," she cried, frantically flinging a magic spike at him.

With a flick of his wrist, Mordenar's chain intercepted her spell, dissolving its energy, causing its links to emit a glowing pulse. Again, she cast a spell, only for him to absorb it once more, the whirling chain becoming thicker and more substantial each time. He advanced rapidly towards her, and instead of throwing his barbed chain to bounce off her shield, he pressed against it, holding the blade of force in his hand like a dagger, twisting and turning it as though searching for a point of entry, its edge shining brightly as he worked.

Abruptly, the shield vanished, the energy which maintained it broken and drawn in by the warlock. Anya stood, trembling in dreadful anticipation, tears flowing down her cheeks not just at what was to come, but at the futility of all that had happened. Her banishment, Bibhu, Theelk.

Matreyi. This monster had killed her as though the act meant nothing, as though to do so was only marginally more effort than to let her live. In that moment Anya knew true love and hatred, both. In memory of her aunt, she summoned that hatred, using it to power her will, to defy Mordenar. She began to weave her arms, closing her eyes to better see the connections she forged.

A sudden pain in her chest disrupted her concentration, and she looked down to see his barbed hook embedded in her sternum. She stumbled, barely keeping her feet and shook her head against the wave of fatigue that threatened to overcome her. Again, she tried to summon a pattern, but it slipped away from her, its nature vague and indistinct. It was impossible, this was not magic, just her knowledge of how magic worked. What could he be taking from her?

"He is draining away your life." The voice of the tower sounded distant inside her head. "Only your bond with me has kept you from succumbing before now. The weaker your connection to life, the less you are able to shape the forces you command." The tower's detached information was somehow puzzling to Anya. Her legs gave way, and she fell to the ground.

Mordenar stood over her, grasping the pulsing chain in both hands. He laughed in triumph, and hissed, "Yes!" as his magic grew stronger.

Through blurred eyes, Anya saw him look down at her, astonishment clearly displayed on his face, before turning to face the tower.

"Anya, he knows that I'm keeping you alive, that he now draws on my power. He cannot be allowed to have it, he will use it to destroy your Gods and turn the world into a weapon for Vajnata." She frowned, unable to process what the tower had told her.

Mordenar's eyes widened and he slung his other chain directly into the earth beneath his feet. Where it struck, a crack appeared, a foul stench erupting from beneath the ground. "It is a new Fall, one that will encompass the whole of Sansara. The gaganwa trees will not be able to withstand it."

"Help me," she pleaded silently.

For a moment, there was no reply, and Anya had the disconcerting sensation that the tower had left her. When it again spoke, its tone sounded changed to her. "It is possible for me to take you to another world, but only you and the boy trapped inside." Briefly, hope rose within her, until the dancing light of the fire caught her eye and she turned to regard her people. Because of her, people had died, people she cared about. Bibhu had saved her from the judgement of the council and been killed, transformed into an undead and sent to destroy her. Matreyi... she shied away from thoughts of her aunt, the pain was too great. Theelk had thrown away his life to help her seek a weapon to use against Mordenar, a weapon that did not exist. Their sacrifice a wasted gesture –

if she left, it would all be rendered futile, yet, if she stayed she would die, and accomplish nothing.

"What will become of the tribe?" she asked. "Of my world?"

"They will have to contend with Mordenar, aided only by your weakened deities. They draw from the power of life, which on Sansara is too diminished to give them adequate strength. They will fail."

The last of her hope extinguished. Inside, she was empty, devoid of her usual self-belief and pride in her abilities. She had been wrong, no special quality lived within her waiting for the right moment to reveal itself, to prove herself and change the ways of her people. There was nothing she could do to save them, but the thought of running away, leaving them to their fate was more than she could take.

"I won't do it. Save yourself, and take Amman with you." Despite her resolution, Anya quailed, she was too young to die. The unfairness of her brief life was bitter in her mouth, she had not asked for any of this, the tower, magic, power. At least Amman would be spared.

Her thoughts lingered for a moment on Matreyi, who had sacrificed a life in the temple to save her family's honour, and ultimately to be with Anya. Despite the heartache, Anya was filled with love for her aunt. She looked around, a final lament for her clan, her tribe, her world. All would die, ultimately, even the Gods' sacrifice had not been enough. "Anya, it is time."

Something stirred in her mind, a fleeting wisp of intuition. She spoke to the tower in her thoughts. "Wait, you said Mordenar draws on your power through me?"

"That is true."

"How much can he handle?" she asked, her thoughts coming more freely now. "All the books I've read talk about the warlocks using or transforming the energy they steal, using it to strengthen their own. How quickly can they do it?"

"Time is short, Anya. What is the purpose of your question?"

"What if instead of shutting it down, we gave him all your power at once?"

The voice inside did not respond immediately. "I see what you mean, but Anya, you will still die. You will not be able to handle that much power running through you."

"I think I can live with that," she said, smiling sadly at her morbid humour. "Do it."

Immediately, a searing fire roared through Anya, coursing through her entire body to erupt from her chest. Instantly, the fog of weariness vanished from her mind, and she was aware of the tiniest details of her body, illuminated in an ecstasy of exquisite pain. She gasped and held her breath, as the world around her became crystal clear, each individual of the mass of her clan, the snow, the mountains. Mordenar.

He was surprised, elated at the power made available to him. Anya could feel his triumph, his arrogant pride and his hunger. He would drain all life from the world, gifting it to his God, granting him great power. His eyes widened in sudden alarm. The power was coming too fast, too much to use. He tried to dislodge the barb in Anya's chest, but it was fused in place by the flow of magic, and neither could he dispel it. Uncertainly engulfed him, a sensation not felt for centuries. He began to panic.

A crash sounded behind her, and Anya knew that tiles were falling from the tower roof, to smash against the lower level. She closed her eyes, not wishing to see it and for a moment amid her sapping pain, thought she caught a glimpse of Theelk behind her eyelids. With a sharp report, one of the windows cracked, and the ground beneath her shook. The door to the tower jolted, sagging open on broken hinges, revealing Amman, his balled and bleeding fists raised, poised to strike again. Mordenar began to thrash around, seeking to dislodge the chain, welded to his hand. As his writhing became more desperate, so his skin began to glow, darkly red in the shadow of the leaping flames. From his mouth erupted a cloud of insects, seeking escape from the warring energies boiling inside him.

A stench of putrid meat rolled off Mordenar, and chunks of flesh began to fall away, leaving gaping holes of bone and gore. As it fell, his eyes again turned black, his link to the undead realm the last part of him to give way. His clothes, rotting along with his body, fell with the last of his skin, and devoid now of any trace of humanity, he stood, swaying on twisted skeletal limbs, his dark heart exposed behind blackened ribs. The crown of antlers toppled from his head, and he lifted his arms to the sky.

"Help me!" he cried, before the sickly beating heart exploded in his chest, bursting his ribcage from within, his broken remains falling on the holy site, showering down on Anya's still form in a rain of flies.

For the briefest instant, no sound could be heard except the crackling of the fire. Many of the clan collapsed, others shaking their heads in confusion. Amman clambered over the broken door, and scrambled across the compacted snow to where Anya lay, covered in dead insects and fragments of bone, kneeling beside her and lifting her head into his lap.

"Anya!" he cried, looking down at her pale features. He put his ear close to her mouth, and placed his trembling hand to her neck, tears running down his face.

A wailing sob escaped his mouth, and he gathered her close, clasping her in a tight embrace, unwilling to accept the truth.

Anya was dead.

Aftermath

Amman rocked, as if calming a baby, his face buried in Anya's shoulder. Tears streamed down his cheeks, and his mouth was open in a soundless scream of grief and loss. Around him, the assembled clan began to stir, but their growing murmur could not pierce his misery, until a hoarse cry finally broke his spell.

He looked up, vacantly. Neeta was running to where he clutched Anya's body, her eyes wide with fear of what she might see.

"Anya!" she cried, looking to Amman for a sign, but the anguish on his face was all the answer he could give.

Neeta fell to her knees beside her daughter, arms held out as though to reach for her, but holding back, as if unwilling to make contact, perhaps afraid that her touch would make it real. At last she clasped a dangling arm by its limp hand, kissing it and holding it to her cheek, crying for loss, for guilt and for shame.

"I'm sorry," she whispered amid her tears. "I was wrong."

Gradually, they were surrounded by her family and sympathetic members of the clan, until finally, Amman registered their presence, blinking in slow recognition of the world beyond his misery.

"Go away," he said. Rahul moved to console him, but Amman shrugged him off.

"She was special." He raised his voice, making it carry to the whole clan. "If not for you, she might still be alive! Leave us alone."

"Amman, we all loved her," said Rahul.

"Really? Was it love that made you disown her?"

Neeta closed her eyes in humiliation, not challenging Amman's accusation, but a figure nearby interjected, "Learn some respect, boy. It is not your place to speak that way to your elders." It was Soren, his features more gaunt than usual, his tone dripping with disapproval.

"Elders should earn that respect."

"Like your unfortunate friend there, you have much to learn about our traditions."

"Our traditions are what sent Anya away in the first place. Away from the tower and all that she could have learned from it."

"It is an abomination on holy ground. The girl did not deny using magic—"

"Magic is what just saved us all, you stupid old man!" Amman's was the only voice to be heard, every member of the clan was looking his way, and he saw from behind the elder, the sullen face of Hiranjan. "Anya even saved your bastard shit of a grandson, despite what he tried to do to her. The tradition you cling to is worth less even than him."

"It seems you have learned nothing since you left with that bhakta slut," Soren said, stiffly, his face flushed with indignation.

As one, Rahul and Sabir moved towards him, but Rahul was the quicker. He punched him, striking him on the chin with forceful precision. Soren folded, crumpling with a grunt onto the compacted snow. Sabir, one step behind, kicked him in the ribs, before lowering himself and grasping the prone man by the front of his coat.

"Do not ever presume to insult my family, ever again, or, tradition be damned, I will kill you." Letting go, and rising once again to his feet, he wiped his hands on his clothes and turned away to re-join his mourning family.

For a while, no-one spoke, except for Shanoli, who attempted to quiet her son, unable to explain to him why his favourite aunt would not wake up. At last, in a voice husky with emotion, Sabir said, "I think we should leave her here. It is a fitting place for sky burial."

There were some murmurs of assent, before Amman cut through their discussion. "I think she should be placed in her tower." Not waiting for their agreement, he gathered Anya's legs and staggered upright, the strain of carrying her bringing a flush to his face. Neeta rose with him, still holding onto her daughter's hand, and, the rest of her family in tow, they stumbled towards the double doors.

On reaching the front of the tower, the broken door still obstructed the entrance, and it was clear that Amman would not be able to negotiate it, burdened as he was. Rahul gently lifted his sister from his arms, and carefully manoeuvred himself through the doorway, into the peace of the interior. Once inside, Amman directed him to the long seat in front of the fireplace, first brushing it clean of the dust and fallen grit that powdered it, where Rahul laid Anya's body, covering it with his coat. Neeta sat on the floor alongside, and silently laid her head on her daughter's chest.

Amman stood awkwardly, his eyes fixed on his wringing hands, before looking up at the gathered family, his eyes wet with fresh tears, and said, "I suppose you're right, she should be laid outside in the place of sacrifice, but..." He swallowed, rubbing at his eyes with his arm. "I'd like to stay with her here, just for tonight."

When no-one voiced their objection, he collapsed into a seat, and wept anew, his face buried in his hands.

Amman dreamt. Visions of childhood summers spent playing or climbing with Anya, and stolen glances, unseen by her, warming his heart. In his dream, she knew, but did not speak of it, consenting to spend her time with him, time he relished, knowing somehow that it would end all too soon.

They were sat on an immense, high rocky outcrop, swinging their feet, overlooking the end of the world. Beneath them, the wall of gaganwa trees decayed, crumbling before an onslaught of the dead as they erupted from the sandy ridge beyond. They watched, Amman whistling cheerfully, holding Anya's hand.

He turned to look at her, and found Theelk instead, looking back at him and smiling.

She drifted, floating in a formless white void, like an endless blank page awaiting words that now would never be. She supposed it had always been so, and was content.

Something unexpected disturbed her warm serenity. A noise, she thought, though she could not recall ever having heard any before. Again, the sound came, and she focussed on it, noticing a change to the uniform white of her existence. In the distance, she saw something different - colours were breaking out, splitting the white into shimmering rainbows, surrounding an image of paradise. She was drawn in as she watched, looking around her at a glorious mountain scene, glowing with life under a bright azure sky. Animals roamed lush meadows, grazing tall grass amid a riot of wildflowers. Birds circled above, soaring before a backdrop of snow-capped peaks.

Yet again, the call came, and she saw a figure, walking towards her, one hand trailing through the blooms, the other held out for her.

"Anya," it repeated. It was Matreyi.

At once, she was whole, her restored memories giving form to her awareness, and she leapt forwards, wrapping herself in Matreyi's embrace, holding tight to her beloved aunt, who enfolded her with equal love in return.

"Oh, Auntie, I thought I'd lost you," said Anya, clinging to her with a kind of desperate relief.

The moment stretched beyond the limits of Anya's understanding. She could not tell if it lasted a year or the length of a single breath. At length, she realised that Matreyi had been silent, not offering any response, and she released her, searching her face for unspoken thoughts.

Matreyi's gaze flicked over her niece, and still she said nothing. To Anya it seemed that she was examining her thoroughly, as though seeking to hold every detail in her heart against the possibility that they should part once again. At last, her eyes settled with sadness on Anya's.

"Wonderful child." For a time, she said no more. Anya was about to speak, when Matreyi said, "I have to go, little one." She smiled warmly at Anya's instinctive reaction to her term of endearment. "This is not my destination, in fact, I don't think this is a place at all, more a kind of reflection of what brings me peace."

"I'll come with you," said Anya earnestly.

Matreyi shook her head. "No," she said. "Look at you. You are not fully with me. Something holds you still in Sansara."

Anya looked down at her body, and saw for the first time that it wavered, insubstantial, becoming almost transparent as she watched.

"But I want to be with you!" Anya wailed. "I won't let you leave. I won't!"

"I'm sorry, I cannot stay, I have to move on." She smiled, and Anya realised that the lines of sorrow and heartache had vanished from Matreyi's face, leaving her beautiful, and full of peace.

"Be strong, Anya. I will always love you." With that, Matreyi kissed her one final time on her forehead, filling Anya with a glow of contentment, before the entire vision retreated, flashing away from Anya like a shooting star, vanishing in the distance as though it had never been.

A ray of sunlight disturbed the sleeping form, penetrating closed eyelids and piercing rest. They blinked, and glanced around the space where they lay, seeing two others sleeping near. Mixed emotions washed through them, and avoiding one, the wakened form padded softly over to the other.

"Amman, wake up," said Anya.

Something about her boyhood friend had changed. No longer simply a dependable presence, offering reassurance, always willing to listen to her litany of gripes with the world. His dedication and willingness to place himself in the way of danger to protect her had loosened something within her, and she looked at him as though for the first time.

He stretched in his seat, before opening bleary eyes, that regarded Anya uncomprehendingly for a stunned moment. Not wanting yet to disturb Neeta's sleep, Anya leaned forwards and kissed Amman, gently, firmly, and continuously until she was sure of his silence. His eyes opened wide in joyous amazement, before closing tight, as if making the most of a lingering dream. He encircled her with his arms, holding her tight, lest she take advantage of his closed eyes and vanish.

Joy washed through Anya. Though she knew issues still confronted her, confronted them all, this moment was theirs and theirs alone. They had survived, and at the revelation, her spirit soared on wings of freedom. She held the laughter the bubbled inside her, and pulled back as her smile stretched her lips away from Amman's. Placing a finger to his mouth, her eyes twinkled with mirth at his astonishment, and she beckoned him to quietly follow her.

As they walked, hand in hand, Amma's eyes were fixed on her, but Anya looked around at the interior, searching for signs of damage, but found none. All was as it had been before her confrontation with Mordenar, and she smiled broadly, taking it all in. When they entered the room leading from the tower hub, Amman could hold back the questions no longer.

"How… how is this possible, Anya? I don't understand," he began, tripping over the words with his urgency.

Anya was startled by his animation, the fervour in his voice, and a chill ran down her spine. "What do you mean?"

"When Mordenar exploded, I… you…" He trailed off, his throat constricted with emotion, unable to speak. He looked into her eyes as though searching there for answers. At last he said, "His enchantment broke, and your family, your mother… she was devastated, unable to speak. They all checked too. You were dead."

"What?" was all she could manage, the colour drained from her cheeks.

Amman cleared his throat. "We carried you in here, I couldn't bear for you to be given the sky burial, not yet. And now… Anya, this is wonderful." His voice caught in his throat and he pulled her into a lasting embrace. At length, he said, "What did you do?"

"Nothing," she said. He pulled back, watching her closely, but her thoughts were elsewhere. She considered speaking with the tower, but hesitated, feeling the solution was something she could unravel herself. She recalled the image of Theelk, perhaps the last thing she remembered before waking up, and felt a rising excitement.

"Amman," she said, piercing him with her eyes. "I want you to gather the clan. "It's time they were told a few truths." He stood for a moment, basking in her presence, before nodding and walking swiftly from the room, pausing only for one last wondering glance at Anya.

She looked around her, taking in the familiar room, the books she was now free to study, appreciating the brief peace and solitude. She found the carved wooden box, standing on the table as expected, and pursed her lips. Striding over, Anya flipped open the lid and reached inside, lifting up the perfect round seed and turning it over in her hand.

Smiling to herself, she left the room, walking into the centre of the circle of earth at the hub of the tower. She knelt, and pressed the seed down into the loose soil, covering it with her hand. Bowing her head, she concentrated for a while, seeking a new pattern, and waved her hands, replicating its simple, undulating shape in the air. At the completion of the ritual she cupped her hands, which filled to overflowing with clear, fresh water. She tilted her hands and it ran from them, pouring softly over the planted seed.

Satisfied with her work, she stood in silent prayer to the Gods, her eyes closed with devotion, until a peculiar sound disturbed her meditation. Opening her eyes, she looked down to see a strong shooting sapling, branching and growing as she watched. Anya stepped back, entranced by the unfolding miracle, her eyes bright with tears of joy.

It grew until it filled the available space, and she gazed at it in wonder. It was the most beautiful tree Anya had ever seen, its bark shone a magnificent natural gold, and there was a sparkling silver sheen to its leaves as they unfolded. Through the cover of the foliage, Anya thought she saw movement, and she rounded the tree, walking on the circular path until the tree no longer concealed the object of her curiosity.

Neeta stood, her mouth agape, watching her daughter with a look of fear-mingled, desperate hope. She brought her hand up, trembling, to cover her open mouth, and tears began to flow unchecked down her face. Briefly, a tension lingered between them, tight and brittle, until, faltering at first, Neeta stepped once, twice, towards Anya. She broke into a run, crashing into Anya, arms flung about her lost child restored to her, sobbing uncontrollably with the flood of her emotions.

Anya held Neeta automatically, but her shock at her mother's uncharacteristic behaviour made her distinctly uncomfortable, and for a moment she was unable to respond.

"I thought I'd lost you," said Neeta, her voice heavy with feeling. "That my last words to you would be words of anger. I'm so sorry, I was wrong."

She loosened her embrace, holding Anya by her arms, her eyes flicking over the face of her daughter. "I... I love you, Anya," she said. "Forgive me."

At last, Anya's shock melted, and she threw herself at Neeta, burying her face in her shoulder, clasping her mother to her, just as she felt Neeta do in return. They remained enfolded in each other's love for a long time, and the world faded into irrelevance about them.

A sound behind her caused Anya to break the embrace. She turned and saw a rugged man, smiling broadly through his beard.

"Anya, my wonderful child," he said. It was Theelk.

Anya dashed over, laughing with delight, and threw her arms around him, squeezing as tightly as she could manage.

"I hoped... but I wasn't completely sure." Glancing at Neeta to reassure her, she said, "Mother, this is Theelk." She let go of the bearded man. "He... well, he helped me after I left." Anya looked up at him with a secret smile, and he winked.

Grabbing his arm, Anya assailed him with questions. "It was *you*, wasn't it?" she said. "Amman told me that I was, well, that I died last night." She swallowed. "I thought I saw you, just before I passed out. It was, wasn't it?"

"For one such as myself, the loss of a body can be tiresome, a disruption, but not a fatal one." He looked fondly at Anya. "When you chose to sacrifice yourself, I was distressed, and ashamed of my actions in placing you in such a position. As the tower's magic flowed through you, overloading Mordenar, I used its connection to you, to send you the other way."

"Send me?"

"Your essence, that which is you. You would call it your soul. Already a part of you was in the tower. With its permission, I merely moved the rest to join it."

"But how am I back in my body?"

"We kept the connection open and worked all night to return you safely." He smiled.

"Thank you." Anya squeezed his arm gratefully, though something still puzzled her. "What I want to know though, is, why did you escort us out into that place? Why encourage me to go to Patann in the first place, when there was nothing there?"

"Wasn't there?" he said, his tone idly teasing.

"It was just a trap, set for whoever read the book left there. Set for me, in the end."

"Well, it clearly wasn't a very good trap, because here you are." Despite his ageless appearance, Anya saw crinkled lines of amusement radiating from his eyes.

A spark of irritation flared in her, and she let go of his arm, a stern look on her face. "That's easy for you to say, you didn't have to escape. The Acharya's book said we would find 'the key to unravelling this great evil', but we didn't find anything."

Theelk was beaming now, his shoulders bouncing softly with suppressed mirth.

"What are you laughing about?" Anya said, crossly, consciously fighting against his infectious amusement.

Theelk's continued chuckling was infuriating her further, when Neeta took hold of her daughter's hand. "Anya dear, *you* defeated that warlock, *you* saved us all."

Realisation hit her hard. For a moment, Anya reeled with vertigo, and Neeta put her arm around her to steady her. It could not be that, she thought. "No," she said, unwilling to accept the truth.

"Yes, Anya. You are the key to unravelling this evil." Theelk regarded her warmly. "Only with your help was Mordenar defeated, only with your help will we now be able to push back The Fall and heal our world." He gestured at the tree. "Only with your help, by planting the seed, could I return so soon."

"But... that can't be right, that book was hundreds of years old! How could they leave that for me?"

"If not you, then someone else. But it *was* you, Anya. When Mordenar began The Fall, Vajnata knew that we would oppose him, that we had the power to thwart his plans, but he planted a seed of his own, a lure for someone with sufficient power to break the stalemate he foresaw." Theelk began to move away, into the library where oblique shafts of light pierced the quiet shadows of the bookshelves.

"The arrival of this tower for us represented both a danger and an opportunity. If Mordenar controlled it, or you, he could steal the magic to fuel his powers, denied to him by our historic sacrifice, and destroy the world, finish what he started. But, any who learned from it might be able to defeat him using its magic, different from our own, which is useless against Mordenar. That someone was you."

"And the tree?" she said, knowing some of the answer.

"It will provide fresh seeds to grow gaganwa trees." He stopped and nodded at her. "But it's more than that, as I think you suspected. It is a twin to an earlier tree that all the

Gods created and into which we poured our power. With our sacrifice, we destroyed that tree and so limited our own power. Now it is restored, so are we, at least partially."

"What?" Neeta was looking between this stranger and her daughter, who were calmly discussing distant legends and the divine, as though it pertained directly to them. "What are you saying?"

"Mother, it's alright," said Anya. "I think he'll want to speak with the clan, make plain a few things for them, and for you." She linked her arm with Neeta's and led the way to the tower entrance. When they arrived, she was not surprised to see the doors whole and undamaged. Taking a deep breath, Anya opened them, pushing them both wide, blinking in the bright light of morning.

Amman had gathered the clan, and was still helping or cajoling stragglers, weary from the climb. Those assembled gasped when they saw her, flanked by her mother and by Theelk, and stood up, shouting at each other in amazement or fear. Among and outweighing the joy of her family, she heard mutterings from many, taking her appearance as a sign of dark magic.

Anya spoke to them. "Um," she began, inauspiciously. "Please don't be afraid. You know who I am."

"We know what you are too," came a voice from the crowd. It was Soren.

Annoyed by his continued malign influence, Anya said, "Yes, you do. I am a girl, born to this tribe and to this clan. I have grown up among you, subject to the same laws and tradition as everyone here, but not equal under those laws."

"You're a witch!" Soren spat, disdainfully. Anya noticed Hiranjan, lurking in his shadow, tugging at his grandfather's sleeve in an apparent effort to pull him away, his eyes full of fear.

"I am," she said, "I don't deny it." The murmur of the clan increased, and Anya raised her voice. "Our laws tell us that magic is evil, that it was banned by the Gods, yet ours and every other clan has used magic to defend themselves against the Rahksharu." This raised gasps and angry mutterings. "Our Reflector is an item of magic, it protects the Guide from being turned to stone by the monsters. It's true, ask the Guide. Ask Soren.

"Is it wrong to defend our people this way? We need to open our eyes. Our isolation has made us insular and closed our minds to infinite possibilities. Magic saved us from the man who called himself our Protector, who cast his spell over you, who mistreated you. It's time to change our laws, to look closely at our traditions. We need to change."

"We don't need to listen to you," called Soren. "You are no longer one of us. We will keep our laws." He turned his back on her, swatting Hirajan on the head in irritation.

"You morons," shouted Amman. "Anya saved us all using magic." He walked briskly over to her. "She wants to help you."

"Soren is right, you don't have to listen to me. You can continue as you have done for centuries. But you will dwindle and fade into irrelevance. I am offering you hope for a better world." She looked around her at the faces in the crowd. "Any who wish to learn a different way, to study the wonders of the world without judgement are welcome to join me in the tower. We will look to use its knowledge to rebuild our world, and we will do it with equal respect for all, no matter who they are, or what."

Anya looked around her. Though some had stepped forwards, she was saddened by the dark glances of many. "If you aren't convinced by me, perhaps you will listen to another." Theelk stepped forward.

"And who is this? We don't know you. Save your words, we don't want them," Soren spat at the ground between them.

At a cry from above, Anya looked up and saw a lone vulture circling, watching the gathering below. When she glanced around, she spotted the outlines of fox, leopard and bear, silhouetted against the morning sun, arrayed along a mountain ridge in the distance.

In reply, Theelk said, "But I know you, Soren, son of Fanindra." His voice carried easily over them all. "You have ever been a source of pain to those whom you persecute for your own ends and that of your family. From this day forth, you are denied the position of elder, only being fit to gather the dung of the herd."

Soren laughed in disdain. "And who are you to make such a pronouncement?"

In front of the whole clan, Theelk transformed. He sprang forwards onto all fours, throwing back his head, from which sprouted growing antlers. His clothes morphed into a thick pelt of fur, while his beard spread, becoming a mane of darker hair. His whole body swelled, until a glorious beast stood before them all.

"I am The Elk."

Epilogue

Anya walked hand in hand with Amman in the tower, exchanging curiously shy glances and smiling. The clan were moving on, preparing once again to follow the herd, their long sojourn finally broken, returning to the familiar rhythm of normal clan life. Although migration was itself a part of their tradition, Anya knew other changes would come, and her spirits soared with hope and optimism for the future.

A thought occurred to her, and she asked the tower, "You said that you could move to another world, can you also move within this one?"

"Yes," came the reply.

Anya considered this. "What about the tree of the Gods, will that move with you?"

"No, it will remain here, it is quite literally rooted to this site. It is a very powerful location, perhaps the most powerful on Sansara."

They continued until they rounded the tree, entering the room through the door with no lock or handle, that led off from the central circle. Anya let go of Amman's hand and closed her eyes in concentration. She knew the door opposite was locked, but had never found the key. She knew now, it had none. She began a short chant, which, combined with a series of mechanical gestures, caused the lock to click.

Grasping the handle, Anya opened it, moving through to the space beyond, where she found yet more shelves, containing blue bound tomes. She reached up, lifting one from its place and opened it, seeing formulae for new spells written inside. One she saw was titled, 'Valmar's Latent Library'. The name meant nothing to her, and she placed the book back on its shelf. She looked around and found steps leading up to a higher level, presumably to the tower's central column. She glanced at Amman, reaching out for his hand.

Anxious to discover what wonders might await her in the rest of the tower, Anya grinned and skipped up the steps, Amman following behind.

Please leave a review if you enjoyed this book. It will help me generate more sales. Thank you.

Want to learn more about Sansara?

Please visit my webpage and sign up to the mailing list at

www.robertechristopher.com

to receive updates on my latest work in progress and bonus content.

Acknowledgements

I owe a big thank you to too many people to add here, but I would primarily like to thank Simon Williams. He created the game within which this story grew and without his encouragement I would never have started, never mind finished this novel. Chris for his generous, largely uncredited artwork and phenomenal expertise. My eldest daughter, Daisy, though she never suspected, provided me with a great deal of material as well as the motivation to search for those hardships that I hope she will never suffer as a young woman. Finally, my wife Lisa, who accepted my frequent and prolonged absences while I closeted myself away in an attempt to write something meaningful.

Printed in Great Britain
by Amazon